spark

Bruna

Keep your spark

Alice Broadway

Also by Alice Broadway:

ink
Alice Broadway

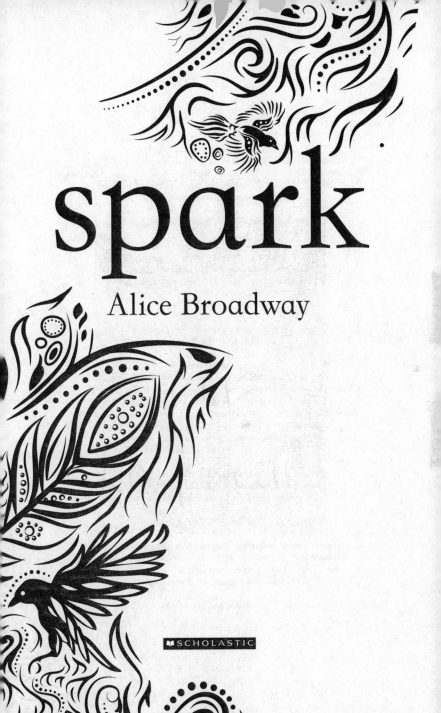

spark

Alice Broadway

■SCHOLASTIC

Scholastic Children's Books
An imprint of Scholastic Ltd
Euston House, 24 Eversholt Street, London, NW1 1DB, UK
Registered office: Westfield Road, Southam, Warwickshire, CV47 0RA
SCHOLASTIC and associated logos are trademarks and/or
registered trademarks of Scholastic Inc.

First published in the UK by Scholastic Ltd, 2018

Text copyright © Alice Broadway, 2018

The right of Alice Broadway to be identified as the
author of this work has been asserted by her.

ISBN 978 1407 17285 9

Printed by CPI Group (UK) Ltd, Croydon, CR0 4YY
Papers used by Scholastic Children's Books are made
from wood grown in sustainable forests.

1 3 5 7 9 10 8 6 4 2

www.scholastic.co.uk

To Rachael Lucas, Keris Stainton and
Hayley Webster. Thanks for the laughs, wisdom,
unswerving love and, of course, all the wolves.

Chapter One

A walk through the woods is never just a walk through the woods.

Not in the stories, at least. A brother and sister are abandoned. A child wearing red takes a wrong turn and meets a wolf. A beautiful girl finds a castle and a beast. The forest is where the magic or the tragic happens. I wonder which one my tale will be.

All I know is that the forest is cold and smells damp. Every step I take, I hear creatures scuttling away, and I feel a constant fear that someone is creeping up behind me. This isn't where I want to be, but it's where I have to go.

What will be waiting for me at the end of my journey? A wolf? A witch? A beast? I can't turn back, because no matter how much I fear what is ahead, nothing is as terrible as the threat I'm running from. There is only one place for me to go: Featherstone.

The mist of the woodland reminds me of the smoke at Dad's weighing. I tread through it, my feet slipping on mud, my soft boots gathering leaves and clods, my feet colder with every step. I can smell the smoke like my lungs hold memories, and I wish I could go back and put out the fire. I thought I could change the world, but I made everything worse.

Obel said the route would be clear, that I would easily find my way. He was wrong. With every step, my feet say, *lost, lost, lost, lost.*

The song of my soul and bones and skin.

Chapter Two

The wording in the letter was polite: *an opportunity to discuss recent events*. But really, I had been summoned.

While I waited outside his office, I took a moment to calm myself. I rested my hand on my chest, where my mentor, Obel, had inked the magnificent crow. I became a person with power that night, when I revealed my mark and spoke the names of the forgotten – and I knew that was why they wanted to see me. I was a threat: exactly what I wanted to be.

Not for the first time, I had no idea what would happen next.

Mayor Longsight stood when I entered the room, which was large and warm and hemmed in by full bookcases. He walked round his desk with his hand held out, and after a moment I shook it. To the side of the desk sat Mel, our town's storyteller. She didn't stand or speak, but her smile, in that unguarded second before it faded, said everything:

she was pleased I was here. I wondered if she'd missed me. I shook my head to clear these thoughts – I needed to remember her betrayal, to be on guard.

Mayor Longsight gestured for me to sit, and it was a relief to have the big wooden desk between us – as ever, his marks were all on display, and I had never felt comfortable seeing all that skin. There was burgundy leather on the desk's surface, which was empty except for a gold fountain pen, an inkwell and a pile of thick, plain paper.

He spoke first.

"I'm glad you agreed to meet with me, Miss Flint." *Like I had the choice.* "I think we ought to talk about your little stunt at the speaking of the names ceremony, don't you?"

Little stunt. As if I was a disobedient child. I felt the heat flare in my cheeks. Longsight settled back in his chair, watching and waiting for my reply. I closed my eyes and recalled the power I'd felt that night. Obel had reassured me: "You've done nothing wrong, girl. You've got them scared, that's all."

"We have discussed your actions at length, Leora," Mayor Longsight said, the hint of a sigh in his voice. "Mel has spoken for you in the strongest terms. She believes there is a great deal of good in you still." His eyes met mine and I dropped my gaze. His eyes: it always felt like they saw too deeply. "She told me she thought you had perhaps been pushed too far." I looked at Mel, wanting to hear her voice, but she just kept her eyes fixed on the ground, deferential in his presence.

I willed her to look at me, to connect with me again. I had felt so honoured to be mentored by her; it had seemed as though she'd really seen me. And I had let myself open up.

I found my voice.

"You used me." I was speaking to both of them, but looking at Longsight. "You manipulated me: fed me only enough information for me to be your puppet." I saw it again: the hall of judgement, the rows of friends and family, the shadows flickering on the walls, and me just standing there, watching Jack Minnow fling Dad's book into the flames. How cleverly they let me do their work for them. Denouncing my own flesh and blood. Turning my back on the man who raised me. I only realized when it was too late.

"Is that really how you see it?" He leaned forward, elbows on the desk. "I saw it another way. I saw a girl of blank heritage, who had no idea where she came from. It was our duty to tell you of your true parentage, especially as the woman who called herself your mother would not. And not only did we let you discover your full history, but we offered you a place in our society – a chance to serve our community, which would protect you from the judgement of other, less open-minded, citizens. Because we knew that not everyone would be so accepting of your … blankness."

My *blankness*. There, he'd said it. It had been hidden from me for so long that it still felt new and ill-fitting, like a boot I needed to break in. The woman I believed was my mother is not. My birth mother was a blank, and I have her blood in my veins; she exists in my cells and makes me *not quite*. I'm marked, yes, but my heart is half blank. I'm blank but I'm covered in ink. I'm not quite either, not quite anything. And in Saintstone there is little that could be more dangerous.

And Longsight was right. No one had been willing to tell me the truth – not Mum, not Obel, not Verity's parents, Julia and Simon. Even Oscar, the boy I thought I had fallen for, knew more about my life than I did. I haven't seen him to speak to since he gave me the remnant of my father's skin – the piece he saved from being burned in the fire. We hurt each other, lost one another's trust. He's not in my life, but he's rarely out of my thoughts.

Longsight alone had given me knowledge. And now I didn't know what to do with it.

He interrupted my thoughts. "I can only imagine what was going through your mind – the things that made you feel you should mark yourself in such a way." His eyes flicked to my neck, where the top of the crow Obel inked on me flutters out. "It seems to me that we expected too much of you."

He didn't know. He didn't know that my body gave me the crow before any ink was spilled. That the dreams I had of the crow gradually began to take shape on my flesh. That purple and pink marks had swirled from my chest like magic, until I was sure of their message. That I had gone myself to Obel and asked him to consecrate that message in ink.

I would not let them make me afraid.

"We made mistakes, Leora, when it came to you. I know that now." He stared at his hands. "Mel is passionate, and so is Jack Minnow. But with that passion comes … well, let's just say that sometimes passion can blind us." Mel shifted in her seat, and I sensed her discomfort. Why did she say nothing? Mel *is* her voice – she has authority because of the stories she tells, which are the key to everything we believe and do in Saintstone, and yet here she was, meek and silent. I didn't like it. I didn't trust it. "They deeply regret that they might have hurt you." I flinched; it was such an obvious lie. I couldn't imagine Minnow ever regretting pain he had inflicted.

"We're not *baddies*, Leora." He gave me a wry smile.

"This isn't a fairy tale. They – *we* – believed that you could help bring even greater peace and stability to our community. Who else is like you? At once both blank and marked: one of us – one of the faithful, in spite of your rebel blood." I shake my head, and Longsight leans forward. "Oh, Leora, don't waste this. The thought of a marked man lying with a blank—" He shuddered. "And yet, from that distorted union something good has come. You represent possibility, hope – a blank who has turned to the true path. Now, I know what Mel would say: she would have you as some kind of emblem for peace – a uniting of Moriah and her sister, the White Witch. I am not so naïve." He looked at Mel, whose face was impassive. "There is no middle way. I find myself in a disagreeable position. The resettlement bill worked well, for a time. We two communities lived separately; peaceably. An uneasy truce, I grant you, but a truce nonetheless. But those blanks have pushed and pushed my patience, overstepping and disregarding the generous terms of our agreement. I cannot stand back and allow my people to be burned and robbed and humiliated by the blanks. There is no value in a treaty that is only respected by one side. They won't listen to reason. The blanks must and will be destroyed; I know that now. Your people need you."

I felt it then: the horrible weight of all I had done. I

had turned my back on my community, on my chance to work and grow and be happy, the way I always thought I would. All I ever wanted to do was to be an inker, to learn and study.

"I had no choice," I tried to explain, and I wondered whether that was true. "Or, at least, my options were limited. Either I worked for you, or I was an outcast, forgotten." I lifted my chin. "And if that was my choice, then I would be an outcast."

"That was never your only option." Longsight smiled sadly, as though I was an errant child.

But, a little voice whispered, *if I'm just a silly child, then why do they still care so much?*

I shook my scruffy hair out of my face and looked at him dead on. "Are the blanks really such a threat?" I asked.

There was a pause, and despite the heat of the room, I felt my arms prickle with goosebumps. "A greater threat than you know, Leora," he said softly at last.

I swallowed.

"What is it you actually want?"

He sighed. "What I *want*, Leora, is for this community to be at peace and for the people I lead and love to be certain of their safety." *Does* he love us? I wondered. Or does he just love what he can make us do? "One girl's small spark of rebellion can soon become a blaze: because

9

of your impulsive act, a whole community is left doubting what they have always known to be true. You are a blank who could be marked. Your father was forgotten – and yet you forced us to remember. You have sown seeds of mistrust. What I want is for you to mend this rift, not deepen it. And for that we need you. Oh yes—" He saw me open my mouth to speak and raised his voice. "It *has* to be you. People are watching to see your next move. I want you to stand by your community and help your friends and family by showing loyalty to your leaders, by repenting of your rebellious and individualistic act and allowing us to be one again as we stand for our values and our unity. And I know exactly how you can show your repentance."

Guilt came so much more easily than anger. Despite myself, I felt the weight on my shoulders. The shock waves I had sent through my little world, my friends and family.

Studying my face, Mayor Longsight continued:

"I want you to go to Featherstone."

His words made no sense.

"To Featherstone." My voice sounded strange to myself. "Wh-why would I go there?"

"You would go there because my patience is at an end. Because my long-suffering tolerance of the blanks – in the face of violence and disruption – is worn thin. And now I will destroy them, and for that I need you." He smiled a slow smile. "You will live amongst the blanks. You will see for yourself what they really are. You will tell me what they are planning. And when the time comes, and they truly accept you as their own, you will turn against them. We know some things about the blanks, and we suspect many others. What I fear is that they are more dangerous than we realized. That Jack Minnow is right, and that by allowing them to live, we have left ourselves open to a terrible attack. That we may have to fight them sooner rather than later. The people here do not want that war; they have grown used to peace." His smile was magnanimous, but there was steel behind it. "What I need is evidence – something that will rally our people, a cause we can be united in fighting. Believe me, Leora – I *have* been patient; if Jack Minnow had his way we would have already smoked them out, like the vermin they are."

My voice, when it came, was little more than a croak. "Do I have a choice?" I whispered. "You are asking me to destroy them."

To my surprise, it was Mel who spoke.

"You do have a choice, my dear." She took a breath, and it was as though she reclaimed her space, her beautifully expansive frame fully filling her form. "And, as your leaders, so do we." Longsight sat back and sighed, but allowed her to continue with a wave of his hand.

Her voice was like cello music – sorrow and hope swimming together. "Leora, you know by now that you are special." My face was set in a frown – I knew nothing of the sort – but she kept on smiling, and as before, I saw love in that smile. Faith. "Not just because of your unique position as both blank and marked, but because of your courage." Her tiny nod as she spoke reminded me of how her words gave me life when she was my mentor. I must shield my heart. "You have zeal and spirit like no one else I have ever met. That is why your misstep hurt so much – we scared you, we pushed too hard, and I take full responsibility for your act of blasphemy at the speaking of the names."

I closed my eyes. Was it victory, not apostasy? In calling out the names of the forgotten and including them with the worthy, I took on the role of judge. I spoke for our ancestors, for our leaders, for our community.

"There are ways of undoing the past." Her voice was low and shadowy. She must have known that her words were as heretical as my actions, and yet she dared to say them in front of Longsight. "As things stand, you have committed crime enough for us to denounce you, for the community to call for your judgement. You know the price for that." I shuddered as I remembered Connor Drew, Oscar's dad, inked with the mark of a crow in front of a crowd in the square. Marked as forgotten. My whole universe shifted that day.

"But there is more mercy in Saintstone than you seem to realize." She looked up at Longsight, who raised an eyebrow, and she stood. "There is a way to make all of this right. And *you* are the only person who can do it. You, our new Moriah."

I gasped; I couldn't help myself. Even if Longsight didn't, was it possible she knew my marks came from within, just like Moriah's – the beautiful sister in the stories? She stepped closer so I could see the ink that wrapped her body. She is our holy book; her voice and her skin tell our community's stories: our history. She lives and breathes our beliefs.

"For this rift to be healed, we need a bridge." She was close enough for me to smell the perfumed oil she is given to keep her skin soft and beautiful. "The blanks hold many secrets and we need to know them. We know they steal from us. We know that lately they have done worse. We know they are trying to weaken us and are biding their time, waiting to attack. But we don't know when." Her eyes were soft with compassion. "We don't yet know how to bring about peace."

At this, I lifted my eyes up first to Mel's face and then towards Longsight, whose mouth twitched at the mention of peace. He looked impatient – ravenous, I thought.

Mel continued.

"I dream of a time when blank and marked can once again become one. To do that, we must have compassion, Leora." I stared at her. I didn't know where this was going. I heard Longsight sigh. "They have stolen our stories. They take them and bastardize each one, turning them to poison, addling the minds of all who hear them. The blanks, as we call them, are not evil, not all. For the most part they are deceived. They need to return to the path of righteousness. They need to hear the truth."

I saw then that Mel was all faith. She believed in the truth and she believed that it could save us all.

I looked to Mayor Longsight, who looked deeply uncomfortable. If Mel wasn't so important to our community and our way of life, I suspected he would have shut her down by now. I wondered: what motivates him? Behind that mask of compassion, he is driven by strategy. Does he care about our stories, or does he want to crush the blanks once and for all?

Am I a bridge, or a weapon?

"There is an old, *old* story." Mel's tone was mellifluous, hard to resist. "A story you won't have seen on my skin. The story says that one day the two sisters will reunite and bring about peace." She paused, letting this new idea settle into my soul. "There are only two ways this can happen, my dear. Through love, or through violence, the blanks must repent." I noticed Mayor Longsight swallow, and it was as though this dream of destruction was something delicious. What he hungered for. Mel glanced at him too, and I thought for a moment that she shivered. "Leora," she said, her voice low. "I would very much hope that we could bring them back to the path of truth with love and not violence."

"You think that, if we persuade them of the truth, they will come back – and be marked?"

"I can only hope, Leora. I can only pray." She sat down again. "You can't believe that we glory in their ignorance: they may be walking in darkness, but their lost souls are souls all the same." Those were risky words, and Mayor Longsight stood then, clearing his throat, interrupting Mel's flow.

He moved in front of Mel, breaking our eye contact, bringing my focus back to his elegantly marked body and his earnest face.

"We believe that if you go seeking refuge, they will accept you. No one else could do this. This is the only way for us to discover their secrets and protect our people."

His voice was caramel smooth.

"We've never seen war, you and I." Longsight stalked round the room. "We are lucky. We read about these things – death and destruction – as though they are stories. We become immune to the horror because we see it only in the pages of a book. We are so used to peace that we can't imagine anything shaking our way of life. But mark my words: conflict is coming. If we leave things as they are – leave the blanks as they are – we are inviting our own destruction. Leora, we protect the people of Saintstone from the worst of it. We don't want them to live in fear. How many of our children must go missing, how many of our livestock killed or crops razed to the ground, before we take a stand against them? They love the sport of killing and they grow bolder."

The cautionary tales of my childhood come to life.

"We know – of course we do – that there are some in our midst who are offering them help and support. We have an idea of who some of those people might be." I looked away, thinking of Dad, of Connor Drew, of Obel. Of Oscar.

"They are misguided, but" – he glanced at Mel – "some of us believe they are not past redemption. They do not have to be punished, not if you can help us."

"What if I want to stay here?" I asked.

"Staying here is not an option right now, Leora." Mayor Longsight straightened the paper on his desk and shifted his pen a millimetre to make it perfectly in line. "You turned your back on us that night. Don't look so

16

shocked – what else were you doing, that night at the naming ceremony? Well – how about you do something that will actually help those you claim to love? Go to Featherstone and wait until my messenger contacts you. Tell them all that you know. It's a simple task."

"You are sending me away from everything I know. I don't even know where Featherstone is." My voice cracked like a child about to cry, and I swallowed. "I have sacrificed so much."

"Ah." His gaze was compassionate as he looked at me. "But not yet everything."

Making my way through the forest, I almost expect to see the little cottage – the one from the story of the sisters. They lived there so happily – until their kind father died. Of course *our* sister – the good one, Moriah – went on to become a princess. Beautiful marks grew on her skin, proving the purity of her soul. It was the other sister, the blank – the White Witch – who was banished to the forest.

I can feel eyes following my footsteps, but when I turn, no one is there.

I found Obel in his studio after the meeting with Longsight.

"So, you made it out alive," he said lightly, and his eyes

raked over me. Those grey-blue eyes that can terrify an apprentice, and yet look at a customer with such kindness. He ran a hand over his brown hair, which he had allowed to grow a little since I first met him. "And unmarked. Did you have to prostrate yourself?"

I didn't know what to tell him.

"Mel was there. They said I should try and … *embrace* what I am."

"Right." Those eyes on mine gave nothing away. "And?"

"And that I should try and work with them."

"Work with them to do what?"

I looked away. "He thinks I should go to Featherstone."

"Ah," Obel said. "And what would you do there?" When I said nothing, he sighed. "Leora. You're not the person I saw this morning who was *angry*, and so sure she wouldn't let them win."

I just shrugged.

"You don't have to listen to me. You owe me nothing. But believe one thing. I have spent my whole life listening to different versions of the same story. I have spent my whole life, like you, being told what to believe. And I know this. These people are *good* at telling a story. Did you tell them yours? Did you tell them that your marks appeared by themselves?" He watched as I slowly shook my head. "If they don't know, then they suspect. I think they know

18

how powerful you are and they want to keep you weak. People in power don't get there by being frighteningly bad, they get there by being frighteningly good – good at convincing everyone, good at twisting words and making people agree with them even if they disagree."

"All right!" I cried, and the snap in my voice surprised us both. "What would you like me to do? I can't stay here…" My voice trailed off into a tired sob. "What do you suggest?"

There was a pause, and then Obel pushed his chair back.

"Tea," he said quietly. "Tea is what I suggest."

I rubbed my forehead tiredly as he made tea. He put a steaming cup in front of me and took a sip from his own. "Then don't stay," he said finally. "Longsight is right; someone needs to go to Featherstone."

I laughed. This has to be funny, because if it isn't funny then it's desperate. "*You* think I should go to Featherstone?"

"Yes, I do." He stopped and looked at me, really looked at me. "I don't believe Longsight can make you do anything you don't want to do. You're no spy, girl. But I think you need to see where you came from. You've told me how you wonder about your birth mother." I looked away. I think about her every day. Obel went on. "I think you need to see that, despite everything you've grown up believing – and for all their flaws, the blanks are not the monsters of legend. They are your people, and you need them – and they need you now. Someone has to warn them of the threat from Saintstone. And by appearing to do what Longsight asks, you will be safe – for now. There is a war coming, and you will be vital in it. It is very important that you are kept safe."

His tone – the assumption that I want this role, that I will sacrifice myself for a cause I do not understand – made my hackles rise. "They're *your* people, not mine. You grew up there: you go." My jaw was tight and my words sounded clipped. He sighed.

"The blanks are as stubborn and slow to change as the people of Saintstone. They will not listen to me."

Obel has never told me why he left his home. I was opening my mouth to ask when there was a sound in the alley outside.

Obel looked up. "Strange – there are no appointments this afternoon." We both stood, and that's when we heard the crack on the door, loud enough to make us both jump.

He put a finger to his lips.

"Who is it?" Obel called calmly.

"Whitworth! It's your lucky day." Our eyes met, Obel's wide with surprise and – was that fear? We knew that voice.

Jack Minnow.

"Go, Leora," Obel whispered. "The store cupboard –

quick. Whatever happens, stay in there, OK? *Whatever happens.*"

I closed the storeroom door behind me and sat on the floor, my knees to my chest.

Jack Minnow. I remembered inking an owl on his shoulder. I remembered his marks screaming at me. I remembered the fear like it was all I would ever feel. I could drown in this feeling; suffocate under its crushing, pouring weight.

The sound of my breath was like thunder in my ears. I calmed myself.

I heard Obel undoing the locks, and the creak of the door, and then Minnow's booted feet crossing the floor.

"Jack Minnow." Obel's tone was clipped. "Did we have an appointment?"

"No, we did not, Whitworth." Minnow's voice was bland, friendly. "But I came to see your apprentice, Leora. I know she had a meeting with the mayor this morning and I wanted a little follow-up chat. I have no need for a mark at the moment. The work Leora did on me is excellent, of course. But then, she had a great teacher."

"You're too generous," Obel said quietly. "I'm afraid I don't know when Leora will be back."

"You're quite the expert at birds, aren't you, Mr Whitworth?"

There was silence.

I *felt* his footsteps more than heard them. I held my breath. He was next to the door, on the other side. I could feel him.

The door resonated with sound, then. Not a knock or a rap, but the jagged flick of a knuckle and the slow scrape of a fingernail across the width of the wooden door. A scratch, a slice, an eerie warning.

He couldn't know I was here, could he? But I got the clear sense that he did. He wanted me to know he knew; he wanted me to hear and to listen.

"You inked a young, impressionable girl with an incendiary mark. What would be the punishment for that, do you think?"

"It wasn't an official mark," Obel interrupted. "That would be on the scalp. There are no rules about choosing a crow for anywhere else on the body."

"Ah, the letter of the law. I didn't have you down as such a pedant, Obel. Of course, it was her choice to make, I suppose."

A pause.

"She *did* choose it, didn't she?" Minnow continued. "She wasn't … persuaded? She looks up to you, Whitworth. Maybe even idolizes you. She would take your lead on something like this…"

I wanted to burst through the door and tell him it was my decision, my body's choice, but I didn't. I did as Obel told me, and crouched shivering on the floor. All my senses heightened, like a small creature hiding from a predator.

"You can blame me if you like," Obel said softly. "I'm training her. I do have influence, you're right. But it was her idea – entirely her free will."

I heard ceramic crashing on the floor and the splash of liquid – one of our mugs.

"Leave it." Minnow spoke with a creeping snarl that chilled me.

"It's a funny thing, Obel. I look at your ink and it tells me how noble you are, how good. Ink never lies. But I know that, with you, it does. I know there is truth under your skin, and I am going to find out what it is."

"Read me then, Minnow." Obel's voice dripped with sarcasm. "Search me, examine my heart. See if there is anything impure in me." He gave a bitter laugh. "I have nothing to hide."

There was a crunch as Minnow stepped on the pieces of mug, shards grinding against the slate, stone on stone.

"Another time, perhaps." He paused. "Well, I should be going, Whitworth. It doesn't look like Leora is coming back today." I was sure his voice was louder now, aimed at the cupboard and me. "Perhaps you could pass along a message, though?"

"Of course."

"Persuasive as our mayor is, I wonder if he is sometimes a little naïve." I leaned closer to the door, surprised that he would speak this way about Longsight. "The Mayor believes in his own power – he thinks that obedience to his rule is something that comes automatically. But I know that rebels require something … *more* to compel them to submit to his command. Tell Leora that she must show allegiance, and we cannot wait any longer. I – *we* expect fealty." His tone was steely. "Tell her – and tell her clearly – that if you are not for us, you are against us. She will go to Featherstone, and she will do what she is told, or her friends here will suffer. Her contact will be in touch once she is there." He paused. "Finished your drink?" Minnow asked softly, and I heard the smooth sound of a mug being picked up, Obel's mug. And then.

A dull thud. A snap. And a cry of pain – no, *agony* – from Obel.

And then quiet, broken only by a low groan. "Pass on the message, Whitworth. For your own good."

Footsteps crossed the room. The door opened easily and slammed shut.

A minute's hush, and then Obel called out.

"He's gone."

I emerged from the store cupboard, dizzy and shaking. It was worse than my imagination had created. Obel was clutching his right hand in his left. A deep purple bruise had already formed around a bleeding laceration; his fingers were limp and seemed to fall at strange and awkward angles.

"He broke it," Obel said, his voice bewildered and, for the first time, afraid. "My hand. It's broken." I reached out to touch it. He tried to move his fingers, and I felt the shards grinding against each other. Bone on bone.

An inker is nothing without his hand.

Sweat, or tears, dripped from Obel's face as he looked dead at me.

"It's time, Leora."

Chapter Three

My feet are cold and wet, my socks sodden. I have walked for two days, and this is the third. All I have is my bag, my steps, the wood and the mist.

I left home at dusk: Mum was charged with telling Longsight I'd accepted his offer and Obel gave me a letter of introduction, plus verbal instructions for how to find my way – "up to a point", he said. He tucked the key to the studio into my hand and enveloped me in an unexpected hug. "You will know the right thing to do when the moment comes," he told me. "I promise." He held me briefly at arm's length. "Good luck in Featherstone, Leora. They are a good people, but better at looking inward than out at the world." He gave a sad sigh. "Maybe that's why they need you."

I don't want to remember Mum's tears. Her frightened, white face. She wanted me to go though; she even packed my bag. "Just do what you have to do to stay safe," she whispered into my hair.

The forest has been dark since I arrived, a brighter gloom when the sun rises, though still all shade and shadow. But now the mist is turning to murk and I know that night is coming again: and with it deep, cold darkness. This realization chills my heart and I scramble on. *I can't be here a third night*, I think, panic rising in my chest. Last night was dreadful, worse than the first; I was exhausted, yet spent it sitting upright, hugging my knees and jumping at every sound. I am so starved of sleep that I feel like I could be dreaming right now.

Stopping in a small clearing, I look around for anything that might tell me the way. I've crossed the river – the symbol of entering blank territory. No marked should come here; if they did, the truce would be broken. I can only hope Obel's letter of introduction is enough to keep me safe. There is an odd comfort in being lost; if I stop here I can avoid it all – what's behind me and what's ahead.

I listen and listen. The leaves, the ground, the mud, the wind. The beating of my heart and the rough sound of my breath in the air.

And there is another sound. A bird. My forehead furrows and I shake my head to dislodge the cry, but the noise continues: it's nearby, and I lower my body into a crouch, scanning the forest around me.

There it is again, and this time I am sure it is real. I hear a fluttering in a tangled bush of branches and thorns, and step quietly towards the sound. I tread carefully on the edge of the path, where large, moss-covered stones keep wanderers away from a drop and a slippery-looking verge.

The bird squawks: a panicked sound and I see the bead of an eye as the animal twists frantically in the undergrowth. It's stuck and scared.

"I know how you feel, little bird," I whisper. It got into the undergrowth but it can't get out. In the dulling light, I try to see the best way to release it from its woody cage. I reach out, and the bird must hear or sense me, because it flaps wildly. I whisper, "It's OK. I'm going to set you free."

And as I grasp the briars in my hands, wincing against the thorns that scrape my fingers and arms, the bird stills. I worry that I've scared it to death, but when I tear the branches apart and clear a way to offer it a route to freedom, the magpie – for now I see that's what it is – peers up, eyes me knowingly and bursts out with a thrum of wings that shocks and frightens me. I step back, stumble; there isn't time to reach for a branch or to ease my fall, and I land on my back, wind forced out of me. The magpie flaps heavily above, trying to gain as much height and distance as possible.

I lie there, too tired to move. Down from the leaves of the tree above me, something falls: a white-and-black feather drifts slowly down on to my chest, and I catch it and call up, like a fool, "Wait! Don't leave this behind." The magpie lands on a branch above me and inclines its head.

I laugh. I am too tired and miserable to do anything else. "I'm lost. Shall I just follow you?" I ask.

The bird flies off again, but not far; I hear it clack and scraw from a tree a little way off. I climb to my feet, wearily, and walk after it. Each time I get close, the bird inclines its head, shakes its feathers and flies on to the next tree. I don't know how long I walk, how far, but I know that if it wasn't for the white plumage of the magpie, I would have lost it in the darkness ages ago.

Sometimes I see more big stones, incongruous in their size, as though some giant dropped them here many years ago. Some crumble into the path, some are stacked, creating a low hurdle that I must clamber over from time to time. Keeping up with the bird becomes more of a trial, but each time I catch a glimmer of white in the trees ahead I stumble on, sure that the magpie is calling to me as much as I call to it. I hold the feather in my hand and imagine handing it back to the magpie, who will rustle it under its wing and bow with thanks. I think I hear water, I think the mist gets thicker, and the smell of smoke haunts me like guilt. I walk on, following my black-and-white guide. Longing for the comfort of a nest and a feather bed.

The dizziness making my head spin causes me to stumble from time to time. But I have a guide in the darkness. A bird that was in a cage and now is free.

And then it stops. It lands a little ahead of me on a collection of huge stones – it looks as though an enormous ancient building once stood here. The bird flaps and hops, just feet away. I am dreamily tired; my head feels as though it is swirling quite apart from my brain and body. Is it the same bird? Have I been following twelve, twenty different birds, only to be lost in the middle of the forest? Have they drawn me here? I blink away the sting in my eyes and try to see through the fog. Doing my best to be quiet, I hobble near, and as I reach out to touch the bird it screeches and fights, pecking my hands and beating its way through the branches and briars. I stumble after it, my momentum taking me, pushing me, falling me through the branches, and I see my bird fly away.

And I see.

Chapter Four

All eyes are on me. And there are so many eyes. They glint with the flames of the fire that they sit around, and I blink away tears from the acrid smoke. The only sounds are my panting breath and the fierce roar and crackle of the flames. The air smells of burned coffee and varnished wood and the ghosts of skin books.

I am tethered in place by a magnetic field of uncertainty. Pushing me away is the fear, the insistent, intuitive certainty that I am in danger, that I shouldn't be here. Drawing me in is the smooth caress of warmth coming from the fire and the people around it. It feels strangely familiar. I feel cords that tug and draw my heart closer, chords that sing of home.

In the end, I don't have to choose. Two people – one woman, one man, I think – grab me under the arms, dragging me towards the fire. Their hands, their arms, their faces. Empty. They are not gentle; their rough hands hold me firmly. I fall to the ground and am dumped close enough to the flames to feel their kiss, far enough to feel the icy glare of the people. I raise myself unsteadily on my hands: my hair is in my face and my shawl has come off and my pendant swings in full sight. And in the light of the fire I see them fully. A whole throng. And they are all blank.

I look around wildly, searching for a mark, a sign, anything. Blankness looks back at me.

A small child a few metres away looks intently at me and starts to cry. Its wail is joined by other children murmuring and worrying. I hear whispers of "cursed one" and see one woman cover her child's eyes with her hand.

"What is she, Ma?" I hear one of them cry.

"Is she a witch?" another voice hisses.

Their emptiness, their absence, slaps my face – it's like they are cloaked, hiding something terrible. Fear makes me dizzy and I sit back. I have never felt so obscenely loud, so uncovered, so bare. And *terrified* – my drumming heart reminds me – I've never felt so terrified.

Beneath the sound of wailing children and whispered comfort from parents comes a deep voice.

"Where did you get that?" The voice comes from behind me, from a man lit by the fire. He has greying brown hair, light-coloured eyes and a beard flecked with white, but there is nothing else – no marks or ink for me to read him by. I feel bile rise. I try to move to stand, but giddiness overtakes me.

He steps closer, leans down, and a leathery hand reaches to grasp my neck. I freeze – I always thought I would fight in a situation like this, but it turns out I am a startled mouse in the clutches of a bird of prey.

But his hand goes to my pendant. He pulls it closer to his face, looks at it, and then he takes it from me – gently, wonderingly. He looks into my eyes as he lifts it over my head, then turns away with my father's pendant still in his hand. He steps close to the fire and holds it out. That's when my courage rises and overpowers my fear. I scramble towards him, still on my hands and knees.

"That is mine and you will give it back." The man turns, an eyebrow raised – the rest of his face remains impassive. He looks at me and frowns ever so slightly and then passes my pendant to the person nearest him.

The fight goes out of me then and I sit without speaking, watching as my pendant, my one remaining memento of my father, is passed around. Each person touches it, looks intently, glances at me.

There are many people here – maybe two hundred. Every age is represented but there are only a few children.

An elderly woman is helped to touch the pendant, words whispered to her about what is happening. A small baby grabs the cord and tries to put the pendant in its mouth.

The final person stands and hands it to the bearded man, who nods and consults the woman next to him. I hear her say his name: "Solomon." He takes a step towards me, and with the deep voice of a god, which seems to shake earth and fire, he says, "Flint?"

How does he know me? The man, Solomon, reaches down and draws me to my feet. He lifts the pendant for all to see and hangs it gently, ceremonially, around my neck once again.

All eyes are on me. A roar goes up in the crowd – of welcome or war, I don't know – and then the tiredness, the unsteady wooziness, the heat, the fear overcomes me and I fall.

Chapter Five

In my dream, it is night, and I dive into a lake shining silver and black under the moon. My pale arms reach out as I swim to the bottom. There are no rocks or weeds, and I touch the lake bed, cold and slippery under my fingers. Eventually, running out of air, I let myself rise, hands aloft, face up to gather breath. But the surface is not where I think it is and the waters do not open.

And then I'm looking down on myself, trapped in a bottle of ink. My limbs creak against the glass that encases me and I open my mouth to scream. But my lungs fill with ink and my tears merge with the blackness and I sink down.

I am in the ink and the ink is in me. We are one and I am gone.

Someone is nudging me awake, and before I open my eyes I can smell that I'm not at home. There's a forest-damp scent, mixed with smoke, and it brings the events of last night back so close that I put my hand to my neck to make sure I've still got my pendant.

"You need to get up," a small voice says. "They want to meet with you." I turn my head, and see a tall, pale girl is standing there, looking at me plaintively. Her white-blonde hair is tightly cropped at the sides and wild at the top, trailing a way down the back of her neck. She is all angles; there seems to be nothing soft about her form. Blank, of course. She tugs at the blankets that cover me and, dazed, I sit and slide my legs out, feeling the cold wooden floorboards beneath my bare feet. I blink. I'm wearing a nightshirt and my legs feel chilly.

Standing, I feel a swoop of dizziness and remember falling last night. My head throbs; I hold on to the bedpost and the giddy feeling passes.

"Who are *they*?" I murmur, trying to get a good look at the girl who has woken me.

"Just get yourself dressed and come into the kitchen," she says sullenly, then leaves the room.

I open a curtain a couple of inches to let some light in and look around the room for my bag. I don't see it. A change of clothes that I brought with me is laid out on a chair, and I cringe at the realization that someone must have got me undressed last night. I don't want to think about them touching me, seeing my body, examining my ink. Covering myself in a sheet, I open the curtains fully and see trees through the condensation on the window. No people – no one watching me. There is black mould growing at the edges of the pane and the glass is wobbly and grubby. A fresh wave of panic sweeps over me now that my drowsiness has worn off. What am I doing here? Am I doing what Obel wants and finding my roots, or what Longsight wants and turning spy? I lean my forehead against the dirty glass. Outside, a dog gives me a long look before turning and loping down the street.

I am not among friends.

I don't know what they mean to do with me. I don't know whether I'll make it out of here alive. If a blank appeared in Saintstone they would be lynched before they even made it to the courthouse. Is that what awaits me here?

I shake my aching head and slowly get myself dressed. My boots are nowhere to be seen; I carry my socks in my hand. Their very familiarity in this strange place makes them feel foreign. Mum knitted these. I look at the stitches, at the way the heel was turned and the ribbed cuff, and feel the cavernous sadness at the realization that I know nobody here. I slump on to the bed and blink back tears that sting my tired eyes. I try to think of the people who care about me. Obel's deep voice, reassuring me. Oscar, close to me in the darkness of the museum, his hand in mine. Mum's face, her fingers playing with my hair. Verity's bright eyes and mischievous smile.

They feel very far away.

We ended up getting tattoos together, Verity and I.

We had always planned to, and had even made the appointment, back when we were still friends.

I had gone to the studio on the appointed day, one week after I'd done my deed at the reading of the names. I was doubtful that she would come, but when I turned the corner, there she was. I drank that moment in, as though I knew it might be one of the last times I saw her, and if I close my eyes, I can picture her now: thick glossy black hair in a braid over her shoulder, brown skin that seemed to gleam even in the shade of the buildings. Beautiful silk dress, but the ratty old scarf that she'd had since she was small around her neck. It was her comforter; she was nervous.

"I didn't think you would come," I murmured when she saw me.

She looked at me, half contemptuous and half amused.

"I said I would, didn't I?" she said. "Well, here I am."

That was Verity all over. She made a promise and she could never go against her word.

Obel let me ink Verity, and then he did me. They're not matching, our marks, but they tell the same story and they're both on the top of our feet – so we can see them when we look down. Mine is a small blue egg; Verity's is a seed pod. We both wanted something that felt like a beginning for our chosen marks: hers, the start of the vine that she would ink up her body, and mine the place the birds grew from – the birds my body had claimed as its theme.

Verity had gone first, Obel watching while I made the mark. He didn't say anything, didn't correct or advise. Verity sat like she was being caressed – a small smile on her face, eyes closed. It was her first chosen mark; I'd waited years to mark my best friend, and here I was, inking a seed: placing all that potential at her feet. I prayed to my ancestors as I did it: *Please let me be part of her vine.* I haven't prayed much since Dad died. I still don't know if it makes any difference. But it felt like the right thing to do.

Obel let Verity stay while he did my mark. The pain felt hot and cold all at once. Fire and ice.

At last, the egg was done. I sat up and took a look at the mark. It was black and grey, with tiny specks and flashes of white. Whole. Perfect.

"Are we finished?" I asked. He hesitated, frowning.

"One more thing, girl." And I remained upright, watching the last addition be made.

And then I saw it appear. A tiny crack in the perfect shell.

He looked up and grinned. "I had to, Leora. It's what your soul was asking for." And I remember the spiritual, almost magical, connection between inker and inked, and the way some tattoos are so much more than skin and ink, and I bowed my head and whispered, "Thank you."

When my mark was covered and Obel was breaking down his workstation, I put my foot next to Verity's. I tried to make my voice happy.

"Matching marks. Just like we always said."

She smiled, but her eyes looked heavy and sad.

That crack in the shell. Light was getting in and life was getting out. The crack felt like a lightning bolt, like a fork in the road forcing our journeys in different directions.

Things would never be the same again.

Even if I went back to Saintstone right now, my Verity wouldn't be there. She isn't mine any more, and I don't know how I would ever get her back.

Now, in this dark little room in an unfamiliar town, surrounded by those I have always known as my enemy, I look down at the egg on my foot and feel the need to hide it, to protect the broken shell. So I put on my socks and pad out of the room.

Chapter Six

The front door is open, letting in cold air: an escape route. I could run now and be gone before they miss me. But where would I go? And if I don't stay, the ones I love will suffer.

While I'm dreaming, someone comes in and slams the door behind them. A broad-shouldered boy with mud-brown hair – older than me, I think – stands staring at me. He's between me and the door, and any plans for freedom I had. I see him swallow and size me up, pushing his hair out of his face, blue eyes colder than the draught was. His face is all hard lines and cheekbones, like the girl who woke me; he might be nice-looking if he wasn't frowning so hard at me.

"Kitchen's that way." He nods to the room to his left and watches me, unmoving, until I walk across the hall to where the sound of clinking crockery and the smell of toast beckon me. A comforting smell, as frightened as I am.

The kitchen is bright but bare. All the warmth comes

from the stove, and for a moment I am able to just observe, before the girl who woke me looks up from her breakfast, meets my eyes and gets out of her chair.

I step forward and realize the boy has been standing behind me. I try to move aside but I end up getting in the way and he steps past with an angry sigh, his eyes flaming at the girl.

"I thought you were keeping an eye on her, Gull." He speaks as though I'm invisible, or at least, as though he wishes I was. She reddens and glares at him.

"I *have* been – I'm not going to watch her get dressed, though, am I?" She shunts a chipped mug towards me, and I sit at the worn wooden table.

"It's lucky I came back when I did." His voice is shards of ice. "She was going to make a run for it." I open my mouth to protest but he carries on talking. "I'm going out to get some work done." He picks up a slice of toast from the girl's plate. "Mum and Dad are relying on you. Don't mess this up, Gull," he calls as he leaves, and I think he deserves the look she gives his back as she watches him go.

I clear my throat. "Thank you for letting me stay," I say tentatively. I don't know what I should fear, and so I fear everything.

The girl – Gull – doesn't hide an expression of curious disdain when she looks at my face. Her gaze takes in my neck tattoo, my marked arms, my crumpled clothes and my socked feet.

"I'm meant to make sure you have some food before your meeting," she says, getting up and scooping something out of a pot on the stove into a small bowl. "And he's right – Fenn." She tips her head towards the door. "I'm supposed to make sure you don't escape." Her brow furrows at the memory of her brother's words.

"I wouldn't have gone anywhere." I'm almost sure I mean it. I consider for a second. "I don't have my boots, anyway." She doesn't return my smile. "Am I a prisoner, then?" Saying it out loud makes me feel foolish – like a kid playing at being bandits. But Gull doesn't say anything and my words fall into an uneasy silence. I drop my gaze and examine the bowl of soupy porridge in front of me. No toast for me – a small but clear message.

"Not a prisoner." She gives the merest smile. "But … don't try to leave." The inference is clear. She drains her mug and washes it up at the sink. "My parents are not popular for taking you in." She points to the door. "My brother's a real charmer." She raises a sardonic eyebrow. "You met my dad, Solomon, last night at the fireside." I remember the tall, bearded figure with the calloused hands. "You'll meet my mum when you get to the elderhouse; she's called Tanya. Eat something, at least."

I stir the porridge, hoping that it might become less lumpy, more appetizing. The tea Gull gave me is weak and tasteless and there's no milk. I close my eyes and take a spoonful of the food. Swallowing a hot sip of tea to wash the mouthful down, I shiver and wish I'd brought more layers – the stove doesn't stop the chill I feel. I glance around. In some ways, it's nicer than I'd expected here – ordinary, like any kitchen.

Gull leaves the room, returning a moment later, dropping my boots on the floor next to me and resting a blanket on the back of a chair.

"It's cold outside."

I take a quick final sip of tea and hurriedly lace my boots, noticing that most of the mud has been cleaned off them. The front door sticks as Gull tries to pull it open and she sighs, frustrated. She wrenches the door towards her, and it creaks and clatters against the wall with a bang.

"Come on." She wears a draping rust-brown coat with a hood that hangs low over her eyes. Wrapping the blanket around my head and shoulders, I follow.

It's like when you dream about a familiar place. You're in a setting you know, only *something* is off.

Featherstone feels like that – so *almost* like home. There are things that remind me of Saintstone but the distances between things are smaller – it takes us only a few minutes of walking through scruffy streets before we get to what must be the centre of town. All the houses are small and dilapidated, but they are cared for: pretty curtains frame misted windows, chipped front doors are neatly painted. But everything looks old, faded, and the streets are grimy with sandy ground, pale stones and rained-on mud. The misty morning doesn't help make it feel any less dreamlike, or any more lovely; there's no paving or cobbles on the ground, just earth. As though the village hasn't been finished: money or resources, or hope, ran out.

The centre of the village is busier; there are flimsy stalls with food and clothes, and then some larger, barn-like buildings. There is one brick building ("the elderhouse", Gull tells me). The old house, the outbuildings and the sandy ground make it feel more like a farm than a town centre. Dogs are everywhere – each close to an owner, but there is the odd bark and growling face-off. I can smell manure; there must be stables nearby.

I walk past people whose eyes skitter away from me. The sensation of not being known makes me feel untethered. Conversations stop abruptly as we walk past, and I have that breathless, squeezed feeling of knowing everyone is watching me.

These are the people who have been terrorizing us, all this time. *Be a good girl, or the blanks will come for you*, I was told as a kid. Every time a child went missing we would fear that the blanks had got them. Poisoning our livestock, our water, our people.

Seeing so much blank skin is nightmarish. My head throbs and my feet feel like they're on a delay – as though everyone's eyes are making the air thicker and harder to walk through.

"You should know something before you go in." Gull's voice is quiet, her head just barely tilted my way. We must be nearly at the elderhouse. "Don't let them frighten you. All they expect is honesty."

I want to laugh. If only it was that simple. I've got a pocketful of truths and I don't know which to choose.

My thoughts are broken by the clatter of hooves, and a crowd gathers around a group of riders on the far side of the square. There are about six riders on horseback, and just emerging is a cart drawn by two horses – there are more people on the wagon, and a long-haired man with grubby skin flings a sack on to the back and climbs up.

"What's happening?" I whisper to Gull, but she's absorbed by the action and doesn't notice me.

"Good luck!" shouts a voice, and it is followed by others offering well wishes and cheers. Some of the people on the cart wave and call out goodbyes, but before they move off, a woman on a chestnut mare shifts the horse into the crowd, making a space in which she is the centre. Her eyes meet mine.

"That's Sana," Gull tells me in a voice so soft it almost misses me. She and I take a step back and I drop my gaze. Sana urges her horse closer and I find my face level with her boot, able to smell the musty warmth of the horse and hear its breathing.

I look up, and the blanket covering my head slips. People either side of Gull and me move away, and disapproving murmurs pulse through the group.

The woman, Sana, holds out her crop and raises my chin with it. We stare at each other silently. She has dark curls which skim her jaw and bright eyes that give her a playful, impish look. She must be about the same age as Mum – and my birth mother too, I suppose. I try to stand my ground and not look away, but when she speaks my courage fails.

"We riders leave today on another raiding mission," she calls out for all to hear. "We will be gone just a little while – don't worry, we will return with the things you need. Saintstone has so much, they don't notice when a little goes missing." There are a few cheers, but most are looking at the two of us – at this woman, and at me to see how I react to the news that this group are heading to Saintstone on what I now realize is a looter's errand. Her gaze is thoughtful as it rests on me. "A shame to leave now, when we have a guest."

For a moment, I feel hot anger in my chest. This is how they survive, then – by robbing us. Longsight was absolutely right.

Glaring at the woman, I let my anger and disdain show. I will not be easily cowed. Urging her horse closer still, she leans down and, looking around to make sure she is far enough away from the crowd to go unheard, she speaks softly.

"You are so like your mother." She sizes me up with secret warmth in her eyes. "We will talk on my return. Welcome, Leora."

As I open my mouth in dazed astonishment, she abruptly calls out to summon the others, and the riders depart. I stare after her and then realize Gull is tugging on my sleeve.

"Come on," she says. "We'll be late for the meeting."

The elderhouse is a taller building than the others, made of grey stone and clad in strips of weather-beaten timber. The tall, thin windows reflect the dark sky back at me, and it seems ghostly still apart from a woman standing at the top of the steps waiting, her hair blowing back in the cold breeze. She gives an exasperated grimace when she sees Gull.

"Oh, Gull, can't you take that hood off for once?" Gull pulls her hood down and makes the exact same face I pull when my mum tells me what to do.

"Mum." She bows her head and mumbles, "I've brought her."

"I see that." The woman smiles briefly. She has highlights of silver in her long mousey hair, freckles on her cheeks and a mouth that looks much quicker to smile than scold. "Now, leave us – see if Fenn wants a hand, but don't go too far. I'll need you again when the meeting's over." Gull nods and walks away, and as she goes I see her bend and pick something up from the ground and put it in the pouch around her waist. As she stands, our eyes meet. Mutual curiosity ebbs between us; I wonder what she thinks when she sees me.

I follow Gull's mother into a gloomy hallway – it's a bit like an ordinary house inside, nothing ornate or special-seeming, a far cry from the aged dignity and opulence of our government building. This place has the same tired look and institutional smell as school or the truth-teller's room. There are doors off the wide hall and a staircase which is blocked off by a waist-height door: more of a suggestion of privacy than a real attempt to prevent anyone getting past. The tiled floor must have once been lovely with its faded yellow-and-red pattern, but now the tiles are cracked and uneven, some missing. The front door shuts, leaving us with even less light. Gull's mother ushers me in to the first room on my right and I steel myself for the inquisition.

There is a low, circular table of raw wood with cushions around it. The room is large, and the soft-looking bolsters that surround the table are beautiful but clearly not new. They are embroidered with cross-stitch and I wish I could pick them up and examine them one by one – my inker's mind would love to play with the motifs, turning them into marks and ink. From where I stand I can't tell whether they depict scenes, text or just simple patterns. Obel would have me sketching them in an instant. To me they're exquisite, but they're ordinary here; the colours are faded and the images blurred and worn.

Four people, including Gull's father, Solomon, are already sitting around the table, cups of coffee in front of them, and they move further apart for Gull's mother, who guides me gently to a stool by the window and gestures for me to sit. Everyone is quiet and reserved. Cold air slices through the loose glass and I wrap the blanket around myself more tightly.

I wait and watch. Somehow whatever I had expected of the blanks, the most shocking thing is sitting here watching them drink coffee and murmur quietly to each other. I even catch a suppressed giggle and a cough. Blanks aren't meant to be like this. They're not meant to laugh and chat and drink coffee. They're not … *normal*. I close my eyes and see that blank man kept behind glass in the tank at the museum, and I remember the throat-clutch of fear that place always brought me: the lists of the dead, the tales of the feral violence and evil done by the blanks. A gesture from one of the elders – an older woman – and everyone bows their heads and closes their eyes. Some sort of prayer, perhaps.

At home, it would be obvious who was who: I would only have to look at their skin and I'd know what their roles were, who was most worthy of respect: their marks would tell me. But here, without ink, they all look the same to me.

Something about the silence and the fog outside and probably my exhaustion lulls me into a kind of trance. I let myself ease into the silence. My eyes close and I smell the coffee, the wood; even the walls seem to have a certain fragrance. In the darkness behind my eyelids, I see little flashes – my brain trying to create some picture. I tune in to the sound of everyone breathing. One person's breath whistles slightly in their chest. I begin to relax and someone coughs, and I open my eyes to find everyone staring at me.

"The meeting will begin."

The voice comes from the elderly woman who has been sitting, straight-backed. Her grey curls spiral down to her shoulders and her brown eyes are kind. Her shoulders are soft and she looks like she is not afraid to take up space and take command. Her brown skin, with its wrinkles and lines, makes me think of a shaken blanket or furrowed earth.

"Last night's community fireside time took an unusual turn." She lowers her eyes and I see a small smile. "We were joined by a newcomer."

"Don't sugarcoat it, Ruth. She is a marked runaway at best. More likely a spy," one sour-faced man spits. His brown eyes narrow as he looks across at me, and he tucks his greasy, jaw-length hair behind his ears. His face makes me think of a deflated ball – slightly saggy and sad.

Ruth assents with a small nod. "A marked girl, Justus. Wearing one of our feathers. Feathers that only the elders can bestow – and are only given to those who have done a brave act."

He scowls.

Ruth nods to Solomon.

"Her bag, please." I feel panic in my chest. Of course, *they* took my bag. My mind traces back to try to work out what was in it – what they could have found. Solomon lifts my canvas sack and carefully empties its contents on to the table.

From where I stand I try to take inventory. A notebook, half-full of sketches, the rest of my clothes, the dull metal key for the studio, some food and an empty flask. Obel's letter.

They pass this last between them, poring over the words.

Eventually Ruth turns to me. "You have come from the marked. And as such you have no doubt been told many things about our community. Terrible things. It must be strange to see that we are just … us." I drop my eyes and she laughs. "Don't be embarrassed. We all believe what we are taught, until we can learn to teach ourselves. I hope that this will be an education for you if nothing else. Perhaps it's an education that can work both ways.

"Now. This" – she opens her arms – "is our government. You've met Tanya." I nod at Gull and Fenn's mother and smile shyly. "And this is her husband, Solomon." He looks my way without changing his expression. In the light of day, he seems younger and less frightening, although still solemn. He has very blue eyes and lines around them that suggest he smiles often. Just not now, not at me. "This is Justus Spellar." The greasy-haired man holds my gaze coldly. "And this is Kasia Main." A broad woman with blonde hair and a kind and soft face nods at me. "And I am Ruth Becket. Our group of elders changes each year – some stay, some go, but our values never change. We must work together, grow together, agree together. There is no class or difference in status. We are all citizens and therefore all equal. I tell you this for many reasons, but mainly so that you know there is no one you need to impress – all views count here. This meeting today is to decide what to do with you."

I can't help looking at Ruth's skin, and feel a longing to mark it. She both intrigues and repels me. Her skin looks soft and loose and would be beautiful with flowing shades making it look like bark or moss or spilled wine. I want to know how ink would play in her wrinkles and how the needles would feel against her flesh. But she is empty, and with her skin's silence there is a disquieting peace. I want to mark her, so I can place her. I want to mark them all and own them and pin them down with needles and ink.

A violence shudders through my hands. They must not see how conflicted I am: that I don't know whether I am here to light the fuse or extinguish the spark.

"The thing is, my child" – and Ruth smiles at me with her eyes – "we don't know you and you don't know us. Your marks tell us some things. We have not yet forgotten their meanings or their prominence. I am the last of our community who remembers Saintstone—" She sees my mouth open, and seems to anticipate all my questions and simply raises a hand as if to say *wait*. "But we believe that marks are not the whole truth and, indeed, that often they shade the truth. Distort it. We want to talk about why you're here and why you're not *there*. We need to know about your pendant. And I would like to hear about that crow that sits on your chest."

I am being scrutinized, and I stand taller, letting my shoulders straighten and my crow tattoo peep out at them.

"Let's begin at the beginning." Ruth's voice is warm, encouraging. "Will you tell us your name?"

"Leora. Leora Flint."

"Your age?"

"I'm sixteen. I think." I feel my cheeks flush.

"You think?" Justus, the sour-faced man, who has been noting down my answers, jumps on that.

"I'm not completely sure of the true date of my birth. But I'm either sixteen or I've recently turned seventeen." I take a deep breath. "In fact, you may have more idea than I do. I'm here to find out about my roots – about my birth mother, Miranda Flint."

A gasp at that. A collective drawing in of breath. They glance at each other. Justus is frowning as he writes, his cheeks a shade ruddier.

"Miranda Flint," says Ruth, her expression unreadable. "Well, well. Let us come to that. You travelled from Saintstone?"

I nod.

"And you were given directions by Obel Whitworth?"

I nod again and see Tanya close her eyes suddenly, as though in pain.

"So that's where your boy ended up, Tanya," Justus says, but he is silenced by a glare from Solomon. Ruth continues.

"And why have you left?"

I am here to warn you that Mayor Longsight will see you all wiped from the earth, and soon.

I am here to spy on you and take information to the Mayor, so that he can better destroy you.

I am here to tell you to renounce your stories, to take up ours instead, and to make peace with us.

I—

"I left because I wasn't welcome in Saintstone any longer. I'm considered a traitor and a half-breed. It appears that my father lived here, in Featherstone, and that my mother – my real mother – was part of your community. From what I have been told, I think I must have been born here, amongst the—"

"*Blanks* – that's what you call us, isn't it?"

I nod. I wonder what they call themselves.

"And that is how you know Obel Whitworth?" Ruth's tone is soothing and encouraging – I find myself lured by it. "Because he is living in the town of Saintstone?" I nod; she's piecing it together.

"And so, exiled from Saintstone, you have come here – to discover your blank history?" I nod again. "I see." She folds her hands decisively. "Well, Leora – we have much to discuss. You should know that this is not an easy decision for us. There is more to consider besides your marks. Your father was a hero, Leora – that is why he wore that feather. But he was also a traitor. He betrayed us—"

"—as all marked have and as all marked will," interrupts Justus, his voice thick with rage. Ruth pauses, waiting for his words to fade into tense silence.

"My proposal," Ruth says to the group, "is that we

spend these next days and weeks testing this girl and teaching her. We will decide whether we can trust her – not in a few hours, but over time." There is agreement from all but Justus. "We can learn much from each other, I hope."

"A few weeks with a traitor in our midst could be our death sentence," says Justus coldly. "We must allow the community to decide. You cannot make this decision – this *dangerous* decision – alone."

There is a pause, and then Ruth says: "Of course, you are right. This is for us all to agree – not just the elders. We will make that decision tonight at the fireside. And Leora, you should know this: if you are to remain with us for any length of time – be it days or years – you must live by our rules. No marks, no secrets, no lies. Honesty is our watchword here." She passes me Obel's letter and I am dismissed.

No marks, no secrets, no lies. Honesty.

I have a sick feeling in my stomach. Honesty is the one thing that I cannot give them.

Chapter Seven

Gull is waiting for me when I leave the building.

"They're going to talk about it some more tonight, at … at the fireside, they said. Looks like you're stuck with me for now at least."

There is a pause, and when she doesn't say anything, I say, stupidly, "I'm sorry."

"It's not a problem. You'll be bored, though," she says with a shrug. "Shall I show you around?" I nod, yes.

Gull is tall, and she walks quietly, with her eyes on the ground and her shoulders slightly hunched. There's something about her that makes me think of someone trying to avoid a fight, but ready for it all the same.

As I walk next to her, for want of any conversation, I unfold the paper in my hands to read the letter of introduction from Obel.

He was always a man of few words.

This is Leora.

She is who she says she is. The feather was Flint's.
I trust her.
Obel.

I feel the warmth in those words: *I trust her.* Words for me as much as the blanks. I fold the note and slip it into my shirt. But the warm glow fades, for I'm not to be trusted; I am here to spy on these people and ruin them. Then I think of Mel and her belief that these people just need bringing back to the right path. I try to imagine my birth mother, one of these blanks, and my father. They came together once. Perhaps – and I wonder whether this is Longsight's voice in my head or my own – I could be the one to unite these two communities. To repair what has been broken for so long.

"How long ago did Obel leave?" I ask Gull. "He's your brother, isn't he?"

"I was too small. I don't remember."

I bite my lip in frustration. We continue in silence again.

As we walk slowly through the town, I'm struck again by the similarities to Saintstone, but everything here is smaller, shabbier than back home. It's like Saintstone but washed out and tired. The similarity confuses me more than difference would have. I had imagined a place completely alien from the town I'd left – a place where there would be no reminders of the past.

And I can't help thinking that this isn't a town equipped for war. That these tired-looking, grey-faced people are not the terrifying figures of my nightmares. What is Longsight so frightened of? I think of the riders who left this morning. Some threat.

"I'd never really imagined you people having pets," I say, smiling at a dog at the heels of a woman who hurries past us, avoiding eye contact.

Gull stops walking. "*You people?* You do realize we're not a different species?"

My heart sinks. "Oh … that's not what I meant." I'm blushing. "I'm sorry."

Gull shrugs. "We're just the same, only in Featherstone we're free from all that … mess." She gestures at my marks and I pull my shawl closer.

I raise an eyebrow. "Mess? Is that really how you see my marks?" It's Gull's turn to blush, but she doesn't look away.

"Honestly?" She takes her hood down.

I nod. "Yeah: honestly."

"Well, your marks are pollution. Tattooing yourself

like that, it's a rejection of the natural order of things."

There is so much I want to say. That my marks *are* me. That they are good and holy. That it is *her*, with her screaming blank skin, that is deeply, hugely, *wrong*. But then I pause for a moment and imagine going back through the mirror. What it would be like if I was walking with Gull through the centre of Saintstone. Stares would be the least of our worries.

"No wonder everyone's looking at me," is all I say, eventually.

I try to change the subject.

"Have you got a dog?"

Gull grins. "Yes, she goes out with Fenn during the daytime. She's gorgeous."

Smiling, I ask, "What's her name?"

"Lago. You'll see her later."

"Where's Fenn now?"

"Doing whatever they ask him to do today. He's often working in the fields. But nothing much has been growing."

I look around. "And they sell what they've grown on that market stall?" I point to where people mill around a table with various bits of fruit and vegetables on display.

"We don't sell our wares — we share. If it weren't for the riders we wouldn't survive."

"The riders?" I ask. "The same ones we saw leaving this morning?"

"Yes." Her eyes meet mine. "They get supplies for us."

I feel a renewed stab of annoyance and can't stop myself from voicing it. "*Stealing*, you mean?" The people of Saintstone, Morton and Riverton work hard to farm and provide, only for the blank riders to just take it.

"You make it sound like we're lazy – as though we have any choice." I raise an eyebrow – that's exactly what I think. And yet… I look across and take in the sunken cheeks and skinny arms of the woman working at the stall. They're all like this. Thin, worn and hungry-looking.

"If the marked hadn't taken our land we wouldn't need to."

Gull's voice is harsh, angry. "We were evicted, sent to live in a land where nothing grows. Where one bad harvest means starvation. Without our riders and the sympathizers in your towns – the crows – we wouldn't survive." So, this is what they call the ragged band of rebels that Dad, Obel, Oscar and Connor were … *are* part of. The brave or foolish few who try to help the blanks. I smile at the thought of them, but Gull interprets this as mockery. "Do you think we like it?" She glares at me.

I hesitate – this doesn't tally with the version of events I know: the resettlement agreement, with the blanks striking out alone to form their own colony. But just then, a grubby-brown dog dashes up to Gull. She crouches and buries her face in its curly fur. She's laughing. This must be Lago. At a distance, I see Fenn leaving a small group, walking slowly towards us, unwilling to close the gap. I reach to touch the dog, to let her smell my hands and get to know me, and I see Fenn's face grow stony and full of ire.

I look right at him – I won't be the one to drop my gaze, I won't let him intimidate me. I find I'm glad that he's not hiding what he thinks – there is no politeness to decipher. He's the closest thing to a marked I'm going to get here in Featherstone: his emotions are almost as easy to read as ink.

"Leave that dog alone." His eyes are fixed on my face. I let my hand fall to my side.

"Dad's serving lunch," Fenn says, finally looking away from me. "Are you coming, Gull?" He is the kind of blank I had prepared for: cold, hard, vicious. Gull, on the other hand … she's quiet, and when she looks my way, she gives a half smile, reassuring me, I think.

"We'll come in a bit. Don't wait," she says.

"Wasn't intending to," Fenn says gruffly and walks away, whistling for Lago to follow.

He's like that man, Justus, I think – he hates me so much he cannot look at me.

But then he is right not to trust me.

Lunch isn't that different to breakfast – some kind of watery soup, and flatbread shared among us. But the kitchen is warm and the food is filling. I feel a constant sensation of nervousness as I sit and eat with Gull, Fenn, Solomon and Tanya. I can't know what their mealtimes would normally be like, but I sense everyone is on edge. Fenn stirs his soup and picks his bread into crumbs. Finally, Solomon clears his throat and speaks.

"Why did he vouch for you?" His eyes slowly lift to my face.

I put down my spoon.

"What do you mean?"

"Obel." His eyes are curious. "Why did he vouch for you?"

He glances at his children's puzzled faces and explains. "Leora brought a letter of introduction with her. From Obel."

Gull squeaks out a surprised gasp and Fenn lets his bread drop on the table.

"He – he was my teacher," I begin, nervously. I have no idea what they know about Obel's life now. "He was helping me get better at what I do."

"And what is that?"

I swallow, looking at them all – Gull, wide-eyed;

Fenn, his mouth hard; Tanya apprehensive; Solomon, his expression not unkind.

"Well, I'm an inker. At least, I was."

"Obel is an inker?" The quiet incredulity in Solomon's voice tells me they know nothing about their son.

"Yes, one of the best. He's famous for it."

Fenn stands, his chair dragging against the floor. His expression is somehow both sour and sad.

"I'm going to back to work." He clicks his fingers, and Lago, who has been dozing near the stove, pricks up her ears and scrambles to follow him, her claws clicking gently on the floor. Solomon calls after him without any real urgency.

Wordlessly, Tanya picks up Fenn's bowl and tips the contents back in the pot. She piles the bowl on top of her own and carries them to the sink. Gull's face is expressionless as she signals to me to come.

"Let's go, Leora," she says quietly.

Back in Gull's room, she sits on the chair at her desk and gestures that I can sit on the bed. I close my eyes, briefly; a memory of me and Verity studying in her room before the exams flashes into my mind – her with her hair in a messy bun, me crying and telling her about seeing Oscar's dad marked in the town square. It feels like someone else's life.

Gull removes the leather pouch from her belt and empties it on to the desk. White pebbles scatter and, in silence, she sorts them into rows and piles. I watch from the corner of my eye, intrigued but not willing to push my luck and ask questions. I'm a terrible spy.

I take my notebook out of my bag. I wish I was good with words, that I could write out everything in my head; but, when I try, it's pictures that come more naturally than words. My sketches are the closest I can get to poetry.

Whenever I let my thoughts wander, they always seem to wonder about Oscar, so I draw his face: bright eyes hidden behind glasses, his hair wild and unruly, the way the ink sat so perfectly on his smooth, dark brown skin. I draw his hands, strong and gentle, and the exposed bit of his wrist. His mouth, a corner always half-lifted, always ready to smile.

I stop myself from filling the book just with Oscar and draw someone else: someone with furrowed eyebrows, jaw set. I remember him as he was before Minnow got to him and I let my pencil show him in his most perfect element: putting ink on skin. Obel.

And it surprises me, but next I'm drawing a bare torso and shading the deep, dark skin. I draw him at his best too

– with eyes that were concerned – kind, I had thought. Eyes that shine with compassion.

Longsight.

And Mel. The pencil sways and dances as I let her emerge on the page. I can't reproduce the red of her hair, but I can show how it trails down her back like a waterfall. I try to show the gold of her traditional dress, the beauty of her ink that tells every one of our town's stories. But she is too full of colour. Graphite will never capture her. I could kick myself for still caring about Mel. Mel who wants unity. She wants the blanks to surrender their stories and turn to ours. To turn to the truth. Now that I'm here, it seems impossible. It would take a miracle. Or a massacre.

My pencil moves, and almost gives away the secrets of my thoughts before I stop it. I can't even fully think it, let alone draw it. It flickers like a flame, like wings: a whisper. *What if there isn't just* our *truth – what if Featherstone's truth counts too?*

Heresy, the whisper bites. *Blasphemy*, the word kisses my ear.

Chapter Eight

"I told you we were late," Tanya whispers as she ushers us ahead of her towards the fire and the people congregating around it.

It's early evening and we are joining the fireside the elders spoke of. This is when the community decides if I can stay, for now at least. My judgement.

I have to convince them to let me stay. Longsight will send word for me soon, to meet my contact, and I need to have something to tell them. Remembering Obel's crushed hand, I shiver in the warmth from the fire.

"We meet every evening," Gull explains as we draw closer. "We eat together around the fire, share stories, make decisions, deepen our faith."

Flames and judgement, I think. I am no stranger to either.

There is a space for us all around the fire; mostly the community sits in family groups. Fenn is with us, and as I cross my legs, trying to get comfortable on the dusty ground, my knee brushes his. He jerks away as though burned.

Once we are settled, Solomon stands and, in a warm, resonant voice, calls out.

"We are one. One family. One people. One heart. One soul. We all share the warmth of the same fire; we all feed it, we all feed from it. Just as these flames require our love and service, so we require the fire's service. We are one. We have nothing to hide." He smiles, looking around at the people lit by the golden flames. I see happy, peaceful faces looking back at him, and it reminds me of the way Dad used to be at birth days – always insisting on making a speech, always so openly joyful and proud.

Sonorous voices join Solomon's as the entire community respond to his words: "We feed the fire. The fire feeds us. We feed one another. We are one. We have nothing to hide." There is familiarity here – not just in the words that everyone (except for me) knows, but in the ease and the obvious pleasure they gain from being together like this.

The warmth from the flames feels comforting for the first minute, and then the heat becomes oppressive. It's too hot on my face and I edge my body round a bit. Gull sits, relaxed. She's picking up little scraps from the ground. Using a tiny dried twig to scrape lines in the dust, stabbing a hole in a leaf and letting it stay on the twig like a sail. I can imagine my mum tapping the back of my hand and telling me off for fiddling, but there is no such formality here. The atmosphere exudes freedom: at least, for those who belong. I wrap my shawl around me more tightly, hiding my marks from view. I imagine what it must be like to be blank, and for your secrets to stay hidden. For the first time that feels appealing, rather than frightening.

Solomon raises his hands and gazes around the people.

"As your elder for this season it is my honour and my duty to remind you of our past and to allow the past to bless our future. On this beautiful evening, I am called to tell you a tale. But first we have a decision to make. A decision regarding our visitor."

I hear Fenn mutter, "Visitor? Intruder, more like." Gull nudges him, but looking around the circle, I see concerned faces – he's certainly not alone in his mistrust.

"This morning the elders met, and we want to ask you to consider a proposition. Our newcomer is Leora Flint, a marked girl who has come from Saintstone." Solomon waits for the whispers to subside. "And yes, she is the daughter of Joel Flint – who was both a hero and a turncoat. You all know who her mother was." Solomon's voice continues, strong in spite of the rising murmur. "Leora arrived with a letter. A letter from Obel Whitworth." He drops his head and I see his shoulders rise as he sighs. "He vouches for her." Justus spits on the ground in front of him.

Ruth stands, using a stick to help her keep steady.

"Leora told us that she has been exiled from the marked community of Saintstone for allying herself with the forgotten. Some of the forgotten are crows: those who help us in secret. She comes here with nothing but the clothes on her back. She asks us for mercy. She wants to find out about her roots, about her mother." Again, the low murmuring. Maybe it's my imagination, but it sounds softer now. "I am willing to at least give this girl a chance. To take this opportunity to teach her about our way of life, and to share our stories." She looks at Justus, whose face is stony. "If there is any hint that she is here for any other reason – to undermine our community, to work against us – I won't hesitate to banish her. But for now, let's embody our values: peace and tolerance and trust. I put it to our community: Leora should be allowed to stay until such a time as she shows herself unworthy. Please raise your hand if you wish to disagree."

There are many hands raised, including Fenn's, and what happens next seems to go on for ever.

"She means us harm."

"She is marked and not to be trusted."

"Our land is already speaking out against us – this will only cause more hardship."

"Our stories will be lost."

"She will steal our children. She will teach against us."

Each person speaks and everyone listens, even the little kids, dozing against their parents' shoulders.

As each person voices their fears, a member of the eldership goes and sits with them and holds their hands. They talk quietly, face to face. Solomon speaks to the elders and calls everyone to order; he has rallied and takes control once again.

"These concerns are valid. I say only one thing." He looks around the circle. "Let us not shut out someone in need because of fear. That is not our way. More and more we have been looking inward, and now I ask of you all – what has it gained us?"

There is a pause, and Solomon looks at me.

"Child," he says quietly. "Have you anything to add?"

Everyone is staring at me. I swallow. I sense that this is a crucial moment, and I cast around for the right words.

"You're right not to trust me," I say, finally, and a prickle of interest sweeps the circle. "You don't know me. All you know is where I am from – from a community who hate the sight of you and would destroy you if they could." I catch Solomon's grimace; I am not helping myself much, he's thinking. "But I am here because I want to know where I'm from. That's the only reason." *Lies, Leora,* I think. "If you let me stay," I finish, "I will work alongside you. I will respect your beliefs and your stories. I won't force my own on you. That is all I ask – to stay and to listen. I just want to know who I am." My voice cracks on the last words and I stop.

How much of that was true? I don't even know any more. All I know is that I'm fighting to stay here, to save my friends. And that perhaps I'm a more convincing liar than I thought, because I almost believe myself.

Solomon nods gravely, then looks to the circle. "A recount, please. Anyone who is against our visitor remaining, please raise your hand."

This time only two hands are raised, and I'm not surprised that one of them is Justus's and the other is Fenn's.

"Thank you for your courage in speaking your hearts," he says to Fenn and Justus. "Do we all consent that this vote has been fair and that Leora will remain, for now?" I see Fenn's jaw clench but he nods, and after a moment so does Justus. "I believe Ruth has expressed willingness to tutor Leora; to teach her our ways." Ruth smiles in assent and calls out the same words she spoke at the meeting earlier.

"Remember, Leora. No marks, no secrets, no lies."

The whole community repeats her words, and they resound like a spell.

No marks, no secrets, no lies.

When the group is quiet once again, Solomon smiles. "Good," he says quietly. "And now – let us return to the past."

Everyone begins to drum their fingers on the ground, and it sounds like rain or snakes. An oddly comforting sound.

Solomon raises a hand and, like a tap shutting off, the drumming stops. Instead, a hum begins. A hum that goes around the circle, passed from person to person. Low, and from chest-deep, it is passed like a chalice, beginning slowly, then getting faster until the circle is practically vibrating with it. I join in, somehow knowing just when to hum and when to stop. I feel it in my chest, as though we are instruments being played by a passing spirit.

Just when I think the hum can't get faster or louder, it stops. I don't know who gave a cue but we all stop at the same moment – even me, as though the vibration in my throat just left me. The silence leads my ears to pick out new sounds, noises I hadn't noticed before. I hear Gull's breath, in time with my own. I hear the crackle of wood splitting in the fire. I hear the leaves on the trees that surround us whispering and conspiring with us. It is in this attuned unity that I feel my difference more than ever.

I will watch, I think. *I will wait. And then*—

And then I will do what I have to do. To survive. To save my friends.

"And so…" Solomon's voice is like gentle footsteps. "A story."

Chapter Nine

The Sisters

In a wood, near a village, there was a woodcutter's house. The house was small, but it looked friendly enough. Neatly planted flowers grew in rows beneath the tiny shuttered windows. An axe rested against the wall; a well-stocked woodpile beneath a canopy. Even on the hottest day, you would see cheerful wafts of woodsmoke puffing from the chimney, and you might just smell the coffee brewing or the cakes cooling or the bread baking or the meat roasting. For the quietest of visitors, the reward was great: a song sung by a voice so pure and light that you would look to the sky to search for birds or angels.

And if you were lucky, you might see the door ajar. And if you were brave, you might walk up the path. And if you were good, you might be invited in, and if you were poor, you might be fed, and if you were tired, you might find a chair, soft with cushions. And if you were looking for an adventure, here one might be found. For the woodcutter who lived at the house told stories that took you to wonderful worlds you had never known existed. Moreover, the woodcutter had twin daughters – one as bright as day, with a voice like an angel; the other as shadowy as dusk and quiet as midnight.

Lovely as the house, the stories and the daughters seemed, when there were no visitors to bear witness, the woodcutter was a cruel man. Each day the daughters were forced to work till their fingers bled, cooking, cleaning and gardening. When their father came home he would berate them, calling them lazy and wicked. But any visitor who called saw only a mask. The man had spun his own life into a tale. A story that read beautifully to the untrained eye.

Just as, if you moved the wood in the woodpile, you would see insects and worms and spiders, so too, if you looked closely at their storybook life, the worms and bugs and eight-legged things would soon creep out. But no one looked deeply once they had been bewitched by the stories, songs and the girls' beauty.

"Sing!" he would hiss at the brilliantly bright twin, Moriah.

"Write!" he would hiss at the shimmering shadow twin, Belia.

For the woodcutter was sure that his stories would one day bring his fortune. Each story was meticulously recorded by the sister, Belia. One day, the woodcutter was certain, a king would pass their way and hear Moriah's song and be so enthralled by his stories that they would beg him to be their court storyteller. He would refuse, of course – claiming humility. The woodcutter saw no reason to disrupt his very pleasant life in order to perform like a monkey at court. And, of course, he knew his cruelty would no longer have a place to hide if he moved away from the cottage and the life he had built himself.

Instead, he would tell the king that these stories were all written down in a book. A book filled with every story he had ever told. "I'm not sure I could sell it. Name my price? Why, I can't imagine…" he would say. The king would offer him gold upon gold and the woodcutter would live the rest of his life a rich man.

And so, each day, the daughter Belia would sit next to her father, pen and ink at the ready, to take down each word he spoke. He would test her, believing that she would attempt to change his story or that she was too stupid to keep up, but each time she read the words back perfectly. He congratulated himself on sending this one to school. At least one of them could read and write; they could make themselves useful. Moriah was beautiful and she had no need of learning. She was the lure and that was enough.

In his dreams and schemes the woodcutter had never accounted for the possibility of death, which, of course, is the very best way to beckon death to your door. One night he dreamed he had been cursed and, on waking, he believed with absolute surety that the dream was a warning. He grew ever more merciless.

He was convinced that his daughters were poisoning him and so he stopped eating. He was sure he heard voices in the trees and became too afraid to cut them down. He grew crueller and his stories became more and more frightening, until at last, the visitors dwindled to nothing.

"Wasting away, I am," he moaned. "I have nothing — no food to taste, no work to satisfy me, no one to hear my stories."

His daughters tried to coax him. "Just eat a little, Father," they begged. "We cannot bear to see you starve." But he just glared at them and bared his teeth. "After everything I have done for you miserable children. All you have brought me is trouble, and here I am, dying" — ("but, Father, eat and you will not die") — "dying and you taunt me."

For he was dying. And that night, a terrible storm blew up and roused a devilish wraith. And as the woodcutter spoke his bitter last words, they were heard by the spectre, and the woodcutter's final utterance became a binding curse:

"I will be a millstone around your necks. I will be a rat biting your toes. My stories will follow you, my children. They will haunt you, and taunt you, and you will never ever escape them. You will be smothered by stories until you see the burden I had to bear, and you, like I, will die in misery."

And, to spite them, he died then and there.

The tears the twins cried were sorrowful but dutiful. They couldn't help secretly wonder if this meant freedom.

Less than a year after the woodcutter's death, his fantasy came true and a prince came riding by. The prince was, indeed, so delighted by Moriah's beauty and song that he begged her to come with him to the palace right away. Moriah, carefree as she now was, agreed immediately and hushed her sister, who reminded her to be watchful and whispered about their father's curse.

"All will be well, sister," Moriah consoled Belia. "See how life has only got better since Father died? That ridiculous curse went with him."

As much as Belia admired her sister's sunny character, she could not agree, and wept as she waved goodbye to her sweet sister.

But she couldn't rest. She worried for her sister. One night she had a terrifying dream that her sister was drowning in a lake of blackest ink. She woke deeply troubled and resolved to set out and find her twin, Moriah.

Belia travelled for days before she reached the kingdom where her sister lived. And there she was struck with fear. For the people she saw in the streets were strange and frightening and their faces were painted. When at last she reached the castle and saw her sister, she dropped to her knees, crying out in horror.

For she realized the truth. While Belia's skin had remained clear, her sister had been marked with the curse, like a terrible disease. Stories had destroyed her. They covered her skin in pictures that oozed their secrets to the world. Belia noticed that in the hidden places were the most tragic and truthful stories of all – their father's cruelty, their mother's death. And more and more secrets showed themselves. Looking at her sister's face, she saw a snarl.

"The curse," Belia whispered. "Sister, I can help you."

"I don't need your help," Moriah spat. "And you had better not speak a word of the curse. Why would anyone here call me cursed? When these marks appeared they all thought me beautifully exotic. All in this kingdom wish to mimic me and become marked with their tales. I am the talk of the nations: people bring us all their wealth just to glimpse my skin."

Belia looked at Moriah, her skin covered in pestilence, and she wept. It was only a matter of time before the same fate befell her. She begged Moriah to come with her, and together they would find a way to break the curse, but her sister only became more and more angry.

"I will have you executed," Moriah screamed.

And, followed by dogs and wild boar and men with knives, Belia was driven from the kingdom. She was chased into the bleakest, barest part of the forest and, hearing the barking of dogs still in pursuit, she ran deeper and deeper still.

When she was completely lost, she sat on a fallen tree and cried. She was hungry and thirsty and frightened.

As she sat and wept, something fell on her with a sharp crack. Rubbing her poor head, she cast around to see what had hit her, *and she saw a tiny white stone. Peering into the branches of the tree above, she saw a crow. It flew on, every few metres picking up a stone from the ground, flying a little way and dropping it for Belia to find. She picked up each stone and followed the black tail and the white trail. Soon she had a pocket full of white pebbles and she found herself on the edge of a lake so placid it looked like glass.*

The crow landed next to her, picked up one last stone and flew over the lake, dropping it from its beak, where it landed with a splash in the centre of the pool. Belia paused then, for a moment. It would be madness to walk into the lake to her death. But the crow beat its wings, pressing her on, away from the shore. She waded in, the water soaking her clothes and pulling her under; the stones in her pocket weighing her down until she was pulled beneath the surface. She tugged at the pocket, tearing it from her dress, and watched as stone by stone cascaded and sank to the bottom of the lake.

When she finally resurfaced she dragged herself out of the water, away from those white stones that had so nearly anchored her to her death.

And as she stepped on to dry land, she knew in her heart that any curse that had once held her had been broken. The journey, the crow, the stones cast off under the waves. Deep magic that was beyond her understanding had occurred. And she was free.

Belia created a home in the woods, and soon she was joined by more who resisted the prince and princess's rule. Those who did not wish to be marked, to be defiled, to have their secrets ripped from them and painted on their faces. Belia taught them and read to them from her father's book and every year, the people would cast white stones into the lake and remember that the curse had been lifted and would never return.

Chapter Ten

I listen. At first I am excited – *I know this one* – but soon my excitement turns to a confused kind of fury. How dare they talk about Moriah, our beautiful queen, as though she was a kind of leper? Is that what they think of me, sitting here, covered in "pestilence"? The heat from the fire makes me feel sick and I long to leave. But I just sit there. I keep my mouth shut and my head down. This is why Mel wants me here, I realize. To witness this distorted mirror image of the truth and do my utmost to destroy it.

There is a silence after Solomon has finished, a contented one. After a while, Solomon raises his hands again and everyone stands, relaxed chatter between them. I feel eyes on me and see Justus looking at me, a smirk at the corner of his mouth.

I watch as a member of each household wraps waxed cloth around a stick of wood. As one they step close to the fire and plunge the ends of their sticks into the blaze, waiting for each to catch. The light bearers then lead their family group back to their homes: we follow Fenn, who holds the torch high. Like moths, we follow the flame.

I'm shivering by the time we get back to the house – the night seems extra dark and cold away from the fire. Fenn puts the blazing stick on to the grate, where embers glow in wait. His face in the firelight is dark – dark brows, dark shadows under his grey-blue eyes. The light catches his cheekbones, flushed from the fireside.

"We all share the fire," Gull whispers to me when she sees me watching. "We bring fire back home each night and return it each evening at the fireside gathering. It is always burning, somewhere."

"It's beautiful," I murmur, blinking away thoughts of the eternal flames of the fire in the hall of judgement. Another distorted version of something I hold dear.

Gull exhales audibly, not quite a sigh, and I see a sweet radiance in her face. "It *is* beautiful," she says quietly. "But it's more than just beautiful: it's life. It's everything."

We walk back to her room in silence.

That night I dream.

I dream about water again. This time I feel its cool kiss as I dive in; see my hands outstretched through the clear water. I swim with ease; it feels like flight – as though I was made for this. The sun's rays call to me through the still lake and I am drawn upwards. I step easily from the water, the warmth of the sunshine like an embrace. I look down and see that I am naked. More than naked: one half of my body has been stripped bare; my ink is gone. The right half is still full and talkative while the left is a yawn; an empty chasm.

I look down at my hands – one marked, one blank – and slowly I bring them together. My fingers shake and my palms grow clammy, and the moment before my hands touch, in that split second of breath between them before they clasp, I see it. Lightning quick, star bright.

A spark.

Chapter Eleven

Gull takes me to see Ruth the next morning, at the elderhouse. I have been summoned for my first lesson.

I notice that the pouch Gull always wears, full of little white stones, slaps against her thigh as she walks. I am curious about it but I don't dare ask her just yet. She is like a wild animal whose trust I must gain.

Mel would want to know too. This is what she hoped for when she sent me here; she needs me to understand their stories. See how far they've taken this twisting of the original tales. And then maybe there will be a way to bring them back to the right path.

On the way to the elderhouse, I notice that among the people carrying bales of hay, watering horses and sweeping the streets are a few little kids. "Don't they go to school or anything?" I ask Gull when I almost trip over a ragged child who has run past, chasing their dog.

"Not at the moment." She shrugs. "We used to have a

small school, when times were better. But now everyone is needed: we all have to pull together."

I imagine a world where I grew up digging potatoes instead of learning to be an inker, and I shudder the thought away. Inking is all I've ever wanted to do.

I wonder when Longsight's contact will send for me and what I will tell them when they do. I'll tell them about the riders, perhaps – but it's not much, not for a spy.

Once inside the elderhouse I'm led, by Gull, into a different room this time; bowing shelves hold wooden boxes and a small number of books. Each box has a small handwritten label.

"What's inside those?" I whisper to Gull, but her eyes widen and she shakes her head. Ruth is seated at a rectangular table, a jug of water and two glasses in front of her. She smiles up at me and shifts out a seat, inviting me to join her. I glance up at the nearest shelf as I pass close to it – written on the labels are names. Some I can read – *Peter and Merry Newton, Ted Yorke* – but others are in ink that has faded to brown and I can't make out the words without getting closer. I want to touch them, and I remember the story of the beautiful girl who was given a locked box which she was forbidden from opening.

Gull mumbles a goodbye and shuts the door as she leaves. The curtains remain closed and there are candles around the room, each at different stages of burning. The light makes Ruth's lovely wrinkles look deeper and more carefully sculpted, and her eyes are almost lost when she smiles at me.

"Welcome, Leora." She pats my hand and unexpected tears spring to my eyes. I realize it's been a while since anyone touched me, or even looked at me without suspicion. "I am very glad that the group agreed that you could stay for now. We have much to talk about." She raises an elegant hand to indicate the boxes. "This is the memory room."

"Thank you," I say, feeling shy yet unutterably curious. "I'm keen to learn more. Where do we begin?"

Ruth pours us both some water, her hands showing hints of a tremor, and she takes a long drink.

"That is a question I've been asking myself." She smiles, and looks just beyond me, as though trying to see something just out of view. "Where do I begin?" Her smile drifts, and she looks pensive and sad. "I suppose last night's story was a good start. What did you think of it?"

Again, this is where I wish I could read her; to know how to pitch my answer and know exactly how honest it is safe to be.

"It was … interesting. A good tale." I hesitate, seeing if she will say more, but Ruth just chuckles and nods for me to carry on. "We have a story a little like it. But … the differences are greater than the similarities."

Ruth nods, knowingly.

"Many years ago I was told the tale you know. I wonder if you could tell me it now? To remind me?" she says.

I swallow, but she smiles encouragingly.

"Well…" And I tell her about the sisters – *our* sisters. I tell her the truth: that the one who remained blank was cursed, and our Moriah, the beautiful sister whose skin blossomed with marks, was the one to show us the way – the path to righteousness; eternity. And Moriah built a wall to keep the blanks out and to preserve the purity of her new marked kingdom.

When I finish, feeling dazed by my own words, I look up and see that Ruth is smiling at me.

"Yes, I have heard your version of our story, Leora. And when I did, I felt such … such *horror*. Perhaps you felt the same last night at the fireside?" She inclines her head at my reaction to this. "Oh, I could have killed – whoever it was that had stolen our story and broken its bones so horribly."

"But ours came first," I blurt. "We existed before you – before the blanks. Our story *is* history."

Ruth tops up her water.

"It's time for you to listen."

And I know my lesson has begun.

"I believe you call it the Blank Resettlement Bill." Ruth speaks as though the words are bitter in her mouth. "Is that what they tell you in school?" I nod. "We have a better, more truthful name for it: the Eradication." She lets silence give her words weight, and I hesitate. "You will have heard that it was a mutual decision made for the purpose of peace: that it was decided that two groups with such divergent ideologies could not live well together and so, we went our separate ways. It sounds nice that way: reasonable, fair – for the best. But it was a decision our people were not party to – we had no say and we had no choice." She swallows, her voice a little hoarse, and takes a drink.

"I was just a child, younger than you are now; my memory of it is cloudy. But some things stick. Saintstone was our home; we had no intention of leaving. Blank and marked could live together in peace, we thought. When the edict came – only then did we fight. But those who fought had no idea that the marked were prepared for such an eventuality." Ruth raises a shaking hand and points at the boxes. "Any opposition was brutally crushed. I saw my neighbour stand up to them and be beaten – I watched his skull crack. I didn't even wait until he hit the ground. I did not fight for him or myself. I ran."

She's lying, I think. *She's lying.* The blanks wanted to leave. They wanted their own community. *They* fought and rebelled; they hurt *us* – that's what it says in the museum.

"Those who didn't move fast enough that day were killed. Men, women, children. They let a few of us escape, to come here. For years, I wondered why. Why not pursue us and slaughter us there and then?" She pauses for a beat and looks fixedly into my eyes. "And then one day I understood. They're clever. They let us live because they need us." The slightest smile lifts her lips, but there is no humour in it. "They let us live so they could have something to hate."

Chapter Twelve

"And that was how the second wave of blanks came to Featherstone."

She gestures around at the boxes. "These are the things we could salvage, the small tokens we could take with us to remember those who were killed. These are the memories we have left. They are *all* we have left." I look around at box after box and wonder at how many people are represented here. Some of the candles have burned themselves out. I don't dare speak. What would I say, anyway? How do you respond when someone tells you something so terrible? *Lies*, I think fiercely. Clever lies. They must be.

"Featherstone itself was founded by Belia, as you know from the stories, yours and ours. A small community of blanks, safe from the brutality of your Queen Moriah. With the Eradication – well, the village tripled in size in a day. No one was turned away. And with more people came need and heartbreak like the citizens of Featherstone had never seen. We arrived with our lives ripped apart – and lives don't heal quickly. The numbers brought great pressure to the village – there were so many more to feed and home, and the land had to make way for new houses. There was less space to grow food or pasture animals. We came for refuge, and we brought with us nothing but hunger."

I sense that our time together is almost over, but there is so much more I want to discover.

"Our stories are true, my dear," Ruth says as she pats my hand, squeezing my fingers for a moment. "As true as yours." And she heaves herself out of the chair, picks up her stick, which has been resting against the table, and hobbles away.

"Ruth," I call out, and she stops. "Will you tell me about my mother? You knew her, didn't you?"

She stops, her back still to me, and for a moment I think her shoulders tense. Then she keeps on walking.

My lesson is over for today.

Chapter Thirteen

The clouds whisper threats of a storm and the air is muggy and close. I tie my shawl around my waist. My arms are bare and I feel people's eyes on me. I begin to see myself the way they do. I've never thought I was beautiful, but here I feel monstrous. They can't read me, not like I could be read at home, but I still feel exposed. I had never considered that my ink might give my secrets away to outsiders; that all the wrong people might know all the right things about me.

Ruth has instructed me to do simple tasks to integrate, and I am briefly hopeful that I will learn something that will be useful to Longsight. Instead the week passes in dull, menial work. I shadow Gull and do whatever she does. We go where we're needed. We build and whitewash a fence. We spend an hour digging in the vegetable garden one morning, unearthing a few small potatoes that we take to the central storehouse, where all resources are kept in different sections. We bake flatbreads and I see how low the levels are in the sack as I scoop up a cupful of flour.

"We'll need more soon," I tell Gull, but she just looks at me.

Every day people line up at the vegetable stall to collect their food allowance. We are allotted fewer vegetables and no fruit and the bits we are given are past their best.

"Something's wrong," the woman at the stall says. "A blight on the earth can only mean blight in someone's heart. We are being judged. Or cursed." She looks pointedly at me. Gull takes me gently by the arm and leads me away.

I'm listening all the time, desperate to find out something – anything that might be enough for Longsight. And really, I want a reason to keep on distrusting these people, something that justifies all those years of fear, information that will make what I am going to do feel less like betrayal. I am a citizen of Saintstone; I shouldn't be easily swayed.

Another day we assist Tanya at the village surgery. I am struck by the paucity of the supplies – so primitive compared to home. No vaccinations, or drugs, or proper sterilization equipment. It's run by willing volunteers but I don't think any are formally trained. A small boy is brought in coughing, his cheeks red and eyes fever-bright, and I see the healer's worried face and the fear in his father's eyes. *It's just a cough*, I want to say. But then I realize. A virus could spell death in Featherstone.

No wonder Gull isn't thinking about dream jobs and her ambitions. They're all just trying to survive.

A few days later there is nothing for breakfast at all.

One morning, still half asleep, my stomach aching with hunger, I shove my feet into my boots and yelp when I feel something stabbing the sole of my foot. I pull the boot off and reach inside and there's a small, jagged white stone. I shake the boot to get out any other dirt and a slip of paper flutters out. I palm it before anyone can see.

"Are you all right?" Gull asks, swigging back the last of her drink and joining me at the door.

"Yeah, just a stone in my shoe." I smile, feeling the crackle of paper between my fingers. I pocket the note, waiting for a moment alone so I can read what it says. And I realize: someone in Featherstone must have slipped that note into my shoe. Someone must know why I'm here.

> *Monday. Wait until full dark.*
> *A lantern will be left by the blue barn.*
> *Follow the stones.*

Monday. That means I have two days. Two days to find

something out. Two days to find enough evidence to prove myself to Longsight and save my loved ones.

Two days until I betray the blanks.

"When will you tell me about my mother?" Ruth has me collecting water from the well today. (Monday. *The day* and still nothing has happened.) It's hard and heavy work, but it's one resource the people can count on. The well is just a little walk away from the main settlement. They call it Belia's Well.

As I release the bucket and hear a distant splash, I wonder if this is the same well where Saint met the White Witch. In the story – our story – Saint crosses a boundary, leaving the safety of the inked community he knew. He meets the witch and he hopes to save the blank people he meets. He's so kind in that story, and the witch … oh, she's so cruel. Full of falsehood she flayed him. But even that couldn't stop him. Our Saint.

I'm tired, hungry and frustrated. It's Sunday night, and I know nothing more that I can give to Longsight – no information to feed his hunger.

Ruth is sitting on a big square stone, eyes closed, freckled face turned up towards the sunshine. I keep meaning to ask about these stones — I saw them when I was walking to Featherstone. We stand by a large cluster of them, pale rock showing though lichen and moss, like the ruins of an old building — but I'm not going to ask today. Today I want to find out about Mum.

"I'll tell you when the time is right." Ruth's voice is rasping, as though she is fighting a cold.

"I could just ask someone else." I heave on the rope until I feel the bucket rise, and I pull hand over hand, my palms burning. "I'll ask Tanya." My patience has never been a strong point, but with the sun on my head and my aching shoulders and my empty belly and Ruth just sitting there, I feel irritated. Tonight I am meeting my contact, whoever it will be, and I have nothing of use to give them. I don't apologize when Ruth is splashed by water when I lift the bucket over the edge of the well.

"You'll wait," is all she says as she wipes her arm dry. And she's right, I'll wait — even if I don't like it. Because it seems as though Ruth has more to tell than most.

I carry the buckets back to the village centre, not waiting when Ruth stops to cough and wheeze.

I'm stacking the empty buckets in the storage barn when

I hear footsteps and the door opens. I retreat further into the shadows behind a broken cart. I can't face yet more unfriendly Featherstone locals.

"I can't go on like this," a gruff voice says quietly, and I realize it's Fenn. "Waiting, like rats in a trap. They're starving us out. I ... I just wish I could *do* something."

"Our time will come." I see the dim light from the window shine on Justus's face. "We have to be patient—"

"I'm sick of being patient!" Fenn tosses the metal spade he's carrying to the ground, where it clangs horribly.

He sighs and sits on a wooden box. Justus draws up a stool and joins him.

"I know you're tired of waiting, but we can't rush this," Justus says. His head inclines and he gives a brief smile. "The riders are working – hard. They want what we want. Our time will come."

"You've been saying that for months – for years." Fenn leans his forehead against clenched fists. "Some days I wish I could take a torch from the fire and go to Saintstone and burn it to the ground."

I swallow, and it seems so loud I almost expect them both to turn and see me.

"I know, my boy," Justus says. "In fact ...well, let's just say you are not alone. Sana and her riders are less than patient also – this visit of theirs might prove very interesting for the good people of Saintstone."

"What do you mean?" Fenn's dark brows furrow. "I thought they were just going to get resources – and hopefully get into the hospital..."

Justus nods knowingly.

"The hospital?" I can hear the excitement in Fenn's voice. "Would they attack it?"

"I can't say," says Justus maddeningly. "You know I can't. But the riders had explosives on them. Now, no more. We have to tread carefully. But a new beginning is coming, you can be sure of that."

"This changes everything," Fenn says, and I catch the excitement in his voice. I don't hear the rest of their words over the noise of tools being put away, but a cold shiver makes me certain I don't need to know any more. A planned attack on Saintstone – on the hospital of all places.

Fenn's right. This changes everything.

There is no danger of me missing my meeting with Longsight's contact that night; I couldn't sleep if I wanted to. I keep thinking of Sana, the rider with the curling hair and dancing eyes, and a satchel full of explosives. What if she hurts the people I love? I toss and turn in the semi-darkness until it's time. Gull does not stir as I slip from the room.

I catch up a coat from the hooks by the door and keep a careful look out for Lago as I tread past the kitchen. The front door closes soundlessly and I pull the coat on, allowing the great hood to cover most of my face. I breathe in the scent of the fabric as it enfolds me and take in a lungful of Fenn. I hadn't noticed it before, but this is definitely *him*: it smells like ice and smoke, dry mud and wet bark and like the air after lightning. I do up the top button and smile grimly to myself. It feels apt that I am wearing his coat as I reveal all he has told me tonight.

The lantern is where the note said – a place cleverly chosen because no one would see it from their houses or any of the footpaths. I lift it.

Follow the stones.

I hold the lantern out and squint my eyes, looking into the darkness. Nothing.

Except. I see a little gleam as the light bounces off something bright on the ground ahead. Treading forward, my soft boots making scruffling sounds on the gritty ground, I see it – a stone – a white stone like the one that was left in my boot. A white stone like the ones Gull picks up – and another, just a few more metres away. I don't know how long I walk for – an hour maybe. The light of the lantern casts evil-seeming shadows that make me gasp and jump.

My heavy footsteps scare the animals, and more than once I jump as a fox or a rabbit leaps out of my way. It occurs to me that this might all be a blank trick, one of Ruth's clever tests: they suspect me of spying and are luring me out into the woods to my doom.

I look behind me to make sure that the stones are still there – I would never find my way back without them.

A sudden cackle makes me drop the lamp in fright, and the flame is dashed out. A flutter of black and white, a caw and the beating of wings are all I can sense of the magpie as it flies away and I am left in absolute darkness. I reach out to find the lantern and burn my fingers when I scrabble hold of it. I can't see the stones; I don't know which way is forward and which way is back. Trees and clouds refuse to give way to moonlight, and as cold mud seeps through the knees of my trousers, tears well in my eyes, making me blinder than ever.

"Effortlessly elegant there, Leora."

The voice is quiet – so quiet I think I must be imagining it, because it is a voice I have missed so much, my soul hurts. Verity.

"Come here, and I'll light your lamp." The warmth of

her voice is like a hot bath, like a deep breath, like a belly laugh, like a friend.

A dim torch flickers on and I see her.

Verity. My Verity.

I'm crying – and I'm laughing too – as I run and sink my face into her hair, clinging on and relishing the Verity-ness of her. She seems taken aback by my embrace, but after a moment's pause brings her hands up to hug me back.

"How did you get here?" I'm incredulous, greedily gazing at her face, trying to soak it up.

"I was brought with a couple of Longsight's men – they had me riding a horse, Lor – can you believe it? You know how much they scare me." Verity takes my hand but drops it a second later, as if remembering how things are between us. She leads me to a little clearing where a small pile of twigs and branches is waiting to be lit. With nimble fingers Verity lights a match and gets the fire started. I take a burning twig and relight my lantern. "We rode all day."

"Where are they now?" I look around, anxious at who might be listening in.

"They're back at the camp – they'll come back in an hour or so." She rubs my knee. "Don't worry. They seemed frightened of this place. I don't think they would be able to stay even if they wanted to. We're alone."

"How are you?" My question seems so small, but it holds everything: Is she safe? Is she afraid? Are her family OK? What about everyone else? Mum, Obel, Oscar … *Oscar.*

"I'm fine." She closes up. "Anyway, I had no idea I had been chosen for this great mission" – I can hear the eye roll in her voice – "until this morning. Jack Minnow came to the house at dawn to tell me." She warms her hands by the fire and I think about the night we went into the woods near school for the party. We'd just got our results and had our trades confirmed. We sat around a fire then, and she drank beer and almost sprained an ankle with those ridiculous shoes.

Too much has changed since then.

A cold wind blows through the trees and leaves me blinking smoke from my eyes. When I wipe away tears and soot it's like the whole atmosphere has changed.

"You didn't tell me you were leaving." Verity's voice is quiet and she's gazing at the flames. "I'm always the last to know your plans these days."

If I had known I was going to be seeing Verity, I could have prepared for this, but the words I blurt out are messy.

"There wasn't time – I just had to … go." I rub my knees where my trousers are drying; the damp patches have become scaldingly hot, the mud beginning to dry in crusty patches. "The more people who knew ... well, I just couldn't risk it." I want to tell her everything but I don't know if she'd believe me.

"I'm sorry I am a risk to you," Verity says in clipped tones. "I suppose I thought I might have mattered enough."

"I'm sorry," I murmur. I'm tired of those words, but I'm only going to have to say them more and more often. "It was Longsight's decision."

Verity is silent for a while, and the crackle of burning twigs has drowned out the sounds of the forest. Eventually she sighs.

"I realize that now." She throws a leaf at the fire but it flutters to the floor before it reaches the flames. "Anyway, I've been told to take back a message. Information on the blanks. So, Leora the spy, what have you got for me?" She is efficient, businesslike now.

"It's not at all like we were told, Vetty," I whisper, scared of all the truths I have to tell. "They've – some of the blanks – have been kind to me." Verity's lip curls in disgust, and I know it will take more than my words to convince her. "They aren't the savages we imagined. There are no crops, they have barely enough food to feed themselves, yet they share it with me."

Verity shrugs impatiently. "I don't think this is the kind

of thing Longsight was hoping for," she says derisively.

"But there is something." I steel myself to tell her the news. "The riders are at Saintstone right now."

"*Riders?*" Verity asks.

"They're the ones who go to Saintstone and collect resources – food, medicine…"

Verity shakes her head. "Stealing from us, you mean."

I interrupt her.

"I think they're planning something bigger than just taking food this time. I overheard something about an attack on the hospital." I swallow. "I think one of the riders has explosives."

Verity's eyes flit to mine. She's thinking of her parents, Simon and Julia.

"Mum's working nights this week." Verity's eyes are wide. "When?" She leans forward. "Do you know when?"

"All I know is what I've just told you."

Verity stands and begins to stamp out the fire.

"I'm sure they wouldn't attack the maternity ward…" My voice trails off.

"Can you hear yourself?" Her voice breaks. "If they're willing to target a *hospital*, there are no limits, are there? What, do you think they'll bomb the fracture clinic but leave the babies? Anyway. I have to go." She gives me a brief, contemptuous look. "Longsight will be pleased with you."

"Just wait, Verity," I plead. "Just wait a bit longer. You don't know what all of this has been like – you have no idea how hard this is."

"*No idea?*" Verity's voice is a harsh whisper. "Are you under the impression that things have been easy for me? I am the one left behind. I am the one who had to fight for her job while you get special treatment again and again from Mayor Longsight. I am the one who is just a messenger – just a pawn. I am the one who has to stay and keep my head down and do Jack Minnow's bidding, while you take centre stage."

"You think I want all this?" I cry. "You don't know half of it – how bad it's been for me. And, what – you're jealous because I'm getting all the attention for once?" I see her face close in anger, but I can't stop myself. "And you didn't fight for your job!" I retort. "Your parents went and talked to your boss and everything was fine – you couldn't begin to imagine what it's like not having parents in high places making it all so easy for you. We all know your dad is doing his hush-hush specialist skin research because Longsight specifically appointed him – your family can get anything they ask for. You're used to being the star turn, I know that – Verity, so beautiful, so talented, so perfect, not like boring old Leora. Well, if this is the worst things get for you then you're lucky!"

I'm shocked at my own spite and clap my hand across my mouth. But it is too late. Verity's eyes are shining and she looks at me as though I am a stranger. An enemy.

She takes a step back and has almost faded behind the smoke of the extinguished fire when she appears again, tears leaving trails through the ash on her cheeks. Without a word she holds out a note. By the time I've registered the heavy paper envelope and Longsight's own wax seal, she is gone and it is just me, the smoke and the lantern.

Your friend is one more who will suffer if you let me down.
I will send for you again. Be ready.

Once safely back in bed, I stare at Mayor Longsight's letter until Gull wakes. I feel nauseous with tiredness and racking hunger.

"Where's my coat?"

Fenn's voice calls out and I sit up with a jolt, slipping the note beneath my pillow.

Gull rolls her eyes and leaves the room, shouting out, "On your peg."

A pause, and then, "It's on yours. Did you borrow it?"

"Why would I wear your coat? Why do *you* wear that coat? It's horrible."

I dress quickly, noting that my socks from last night have dried off and my trousers aren't too caked with mud.

When I enter the kitchen the chill makes me shiver, but worse is the look Fenn is giving Gull.

"Just look at it." He holds up his coat and pats it down, doing little to get rid of the obvious mud patch on its back.

Gull turns her back, putting the kettle on the stove.

"Maybe Dad mistook it for Lago's blanket." Gull's voice is light, but it just seems to fuel Fenn's fire. He drops the coat over the back of a chair and storms over to Gull, pulling her to face him.

"Get off me, Fenn. Don't be so touchy." But he is looming over her, eyes flashing with ire and seeming so big and broad in comparison to Gull. She is brave though – braver than I expected. "What's your real problem – has Justus told you to stop stalking him?" But he just ignores her words.

"You went out last night, didn't you? Where did you go, Gull?" He speaks quietly, but I think I see worry in his face.

Gull frowns in confusion and turns away.

"I don't know what you mean," she mumbles.

"I don't believe you." He looks at me, eyes narrowed. "I knew that marked would influence you. Justus told me she would. That's it, isn't it? You've been sneaking out at night. Just wait until I tell the elders." Gull turns back to him, her face pale and anxious.

"No! Don't be ridiculous. Leora's just a girl, like me. And we've not been going anywhere."

I can see Fenn draw himself up, ready to retaliate or run to the elderhouse right now. I can't let this go – I can't have him find out and I won't allow Gull to be blamed for my actions. I clear my throat.

"Actually, Fenn, um – I'm really sorry, that might have been me." I reach for his coat and brush at the mud. He turns, his anger pointed at me now. "I couldn't sleep, and I … thought I heard Lago whining and so I took her out for a bit and I borrowed your coat. The wall I sat on must have been dirty." Fenn's brows dip and he glances at Gull.

"I didn't hear Lago," he says quietly. He looks at me through narrowed eyes, obviously not believing a word I've told him. Will he tell Ruth and the elders his suspicions?

"Maybe you're a heavy sleeper..." I keep my tone bright and pick up the coat from the floor. "I'm sorry though, I'll clean it." And I hang his coat on the peg.

"The pair of you." He almost spits it. "I am watching

you, Ink – and you, Gull. Freaks." And he storms out, taking his coat with him.

When we hear the door slam, Gull sighs and gives me a tentative smile.

"Tea?" she asks.

Tea is all we have this morning and there is so little to do that Solomon tells us we can relax today. After last night I am ready to go back to bed, to sleep and to work through my thoughts. But Gull has other plans and she whispers conspiratorially, "Come with me."

"Where?" I ask, and she gives me a brief smile.

"You'll see."

I'm exhausted but I recognize that she is trying to be friendly, and that's too precious to pass up right now. I follow her into the forest – a different route to the one I took last night, but it has the same smell – the fragrance of growing buds and rotting leaves brewed in the same pot. I think I see a flash of white in the trees, and I think of the bird that brought me here, and the one that scared me last night – but then it's gone.

"You mustn't come here alone. Only with me. It's not safe." Gull's voice is low. She turns to me and grins. "Come on, I'll look after you." We walk to the trees. As we go, Gull spots a white stone on the ground and picks it up, putting it in the pouch at her waist, and I hear it clink against the other stones. As we enter deeper into the gloom of the forest, Gull eases her shoulders back and seems to grow. She bends and unties her shoes, taking them off and tying the laces together so she can hang them around her neck.

"Your feet are going to be bloody freezing." I smirk.

"So are yours, then." She smiles – a mischievous glint showing in her eyes. "Take your boots off. If we're going to sneak away and still be safe, you need to learn how to walk through the forest and not be heard. If that bird hadn't given you away on that first night, *I* would have still heard you – you were crashing around like a woodcutter."

I open my mouth to start to defend myself, but instead I just laugh. I feel like a different human from the one who burst into the fireside that night. I snort, remembering my ungainly entrance. "I must have looked like a wild thing."

"You still do, with all that ink." I look sharply at Gull and see that she's giggling. Her laugh is almost completely silent – but interspersed with gulps and sighs and squeaks. It is the funniest laugh I've ever heard and I can only laugh too; the relief at finally having a reason to laugh seems to make everything funnier, and soon I'm holding my aching stomach. The release of laughter is so intense

– I don't know how I lived without it. I feel like I'm breathing for the first time since I got here.

"You're all right," Gull manages to gasp, eventually. "You know, for a savage." Something has changed between us, I can feel it.

"You watch out, blank!" I snigger. "If you weren't so tall, I'd have taken you down by now." Gull only laughs again, which sets me off. Silently she tugs at my sleeve, and still squeaking her stifled giggles, she pulls me to follow her.

We emerge in a clearing, where the sky is open and bright again. I wrap my shawl around myself more tightly and Gull puts her hood up. We are at a lake.

At the far shore, I can see some gentle ripples, but where we have stopped there is nothing but glassy, torpid stillness. The water looks clean and clear at the shore where we stand but soon gives way to blackness. It must be deep, and the thought of that still water going down and down into the darkness makes my bones shudder.

This is the lake in my dream.

"This is Jackdaw Lake." Gull turns towards me a little, as if gauging my reaction. I try to smile and look impressed. But truly, I want to run. There's something about the water. I want to step towards it, as though drawn there by an invisible tide.

"Are you scared of water?" Gull asks. "Is it a marked thing – are you all like this about open water?"

I shake my head and try to smile, but I can't. It's like this lake is made of nothing but tears. I can feel the sadness coming off it, like a steady pulse.

"It's not the open water. It's just this lake feels … a bit scary," I say hesitantly. "Sad."

"It's not scary or sad!" Gull is aghast. "Oh no! Don't say that. It's beautiful. It's the lake where Belia was freed from her curse – you remember the story. It's where we come to receive absolution. You'll see on Fenn's birth day – it's all about peace and hope." I notice that she's not letting the lapping water anywhere near her toes.

I can't think of what to say, so I reach down and pick up one of the flat, white stones. I am pulling back my arm ready to swing and skim it across the still water, but Gull catches my hand, a look of horrified fear in her eyes. "Don't!" she cries. "You mustn't." She holds my wrist and shakes it sharply until I loosen my grip on the stone and it clacks on to the ground.

"Maybe I brought you here too soon." She breathes deeply, as though she's just stopped a terrible accident. Her eyes look around the ground until she sees the stone I dropped. She reaches down for it and slips it into her leather pouch and murmurs, but not quite to me: "Sorry. My fault. All my fault."

We walk slowly away from the lake towards the wood. I want to say sorry and I want to ask what I did and I want to tell her it's OK, but I don't know what just happened.

I walk a few paces behind Gull, both of us silent, our cheerful mood all dispersed. I watch the way she walks, managing to place her bare feet firmly and gracefully, never making a sound or breaking a twig. She's not having to concentrate on her feet or make an effort like I am. It's just perfect, instinctive. She's looking up at the trees and glimpses of sky.

We're further into the forest now. It's unnervingly the same wherever I look, and I wonder how Gull can find her way.

She stops, letting me catch up, her eyes still up in the crowns of the trees. She glances at me as I reach her side and says, "Can you climb?"

Chapter Fourteen

Something has happened to trees since I last climbed them. I used to be able to scramble up and down without a care, but this time I'm aware of the bark making my hands dry and sore. I never used to think about falling then.

Gull is calling out suggestions – she's been sitting comfortably on a branch for a while now. I can hear her trying not to laugh as she asks, "You're sure you want to keep on?" But I don't have enough breath to answer. I keep climbing, bough by bough, until I'm level with Gull's toes, which seem to be clinging on, ape-like. One final push and I'm up with her and she's gesturing to a wide branch.

"Saved the best seat for you." She grins at me.

I shake my head. "I can't believe you made me do that," I say breathlessly as I ease myself on to the bough. "You do realize I'm going to have to live here now – there's no way I'll make it down again."

Gull only raises her eyebrows and smirks a little. She's

looking at my red-raw hands and she reaches out to hold them in hers. Whether it's just the relief of being accepted enough to be touched so kindly or whether it's some blank magic that Gull knows, I don't have a clue. I only know that the burning soreness eases and tears come to my eyes.

If she knew what I had done last night, she would push me away and let me fall. And I would deserve it.

"Thank you," I manage, gulping, feeling shame heat my cheeks. I take my hands from hers and hold tightly to the branch I am sitting on, trusting that she can't read my thoughts.

"So, this is where you hang out?" I try to make my voice sound light and easy.

"I'm not a monkey." Gull smiles. "But, yeah, it's the best place. Strictly speaking, the forest is out of bounds – don't tell anyone we've come."

"Why?"

"It's too dangerous. The marked won't come into Featherstone; we're well hidden. Besides, if Longsight's men crossed the river, that would be a declaration of war – they know the rules. But a few years ago, some kids went missing in the woods, and the rumour was that the marked took them." She turns her face up to the branches. "I don't feel like anyone can find me here though."

"That doesn't surprise me – I have no idea where we are." I laugh and Gull smiles. She looks around dreamily.

"When we're eighteen we get to choose our life-tree. It's the tree we're buried under when we die. And this will be mine. You need to promise you won't tell anyone about this place, OK?" She looks stern. "I'm not meant to have chosen yet."

I snort. "Even if anyone in town was speaking to me, I wouldn't. Why do you have to choose a *tree*, though?"

"It's our way of giving back to the forest, to nature. The earth gives us so much, and when we die our bodies can give back some of that life and energy." I nod slowly, taking all this new stuff in. I want to point out that the earth hasn't been giving them anything much recently, but I don't want her to push me off this branch. "Anyway, you'll soon get your bearings," Gull says. "If you stay long enough."

"That's still down to the community and the elders," I tell her.

Gull is quiet for a while. I can tell there's something she wants to say.

"Do you know Obel well, then?" Gull says eventually.

I smile at the memory of Obel's surly kindness and wonder what he was like when he was Gull's age. "He's training me to be an inker. Well, he *was*," I correct myself. "Maybe my career is over. There doesn't seem to be much demand for marks round here." I smile at my own joke but Gull is looking serious.

"He might still be here if there was," she whispers.

I didn't speak to Obel much about why he left Featherstone. Sure, he told me about wanting to be an inker, but what motivates someone to leave their family – to break away from everything their loved ones value? And then I realize I've done exactly that.

"He's a really good man," I offer. That much I do know.

I close my eyes and picture him. His cropped hair – showing the merest hint of curl now that it is longer – his beautiful, unreadable tattoos. I see him pacing around the studio in his grey uniform, his forearms flexing as he holds the machine and eases the skin gently with his left hand. He couldn't keep a low profile if he tried. I miss him.

"He didn't talk much about home," I tell her. "But when he did, his voice would go quiet and his face would look all dreamy. I'm sure he misses you."

"He never told you about his family, though," she retorts. "And he never tries to send messages. I think he's forgotten us. Not that he ever knew me – Fenn remembers him."

I think of my home, and the smell of baking and coffee. I think of Mum's hot chocolate. Her strong hands stroking my hair. A lump fills my throat. "Sometimes I think it just hurts less not to remember."

We drift into thoughtful silence and watch the leaves flicker in the breeze.

"You know what's strange?" Gull says slowly. "I've known you a couple of weeks – less than that, even – and I've already brought you to my secret hiding place and talked to you more about Obel than I have in all the years he's been gone. You had better *not* be a spy." She laughs at the idea.

"I would be the most useless spy!" I hope she can't see my face redden. "I can't even lie – all my secrets are here." I show her my arms and feel such relief that there are some things I can keep hidden. *I had no choice*, I tell myself.

"I don't know what half your marks mean. Do they all mean something?"

"Pretty much. I'll explain them all to you one day." I raise my foot and point my toes. "But this one – this is one I got at the same time as my … as my best friend."

Gull stares, fascinated, at the little egg. Slowly, she stretches out a finger to touch it, then pulls it back abruptly as though the ink could infect her.

"I'm sorry you've ended up having to be with me." She doesn't make eye contact. "Fenn's right – I'm the freak. I think they let me be your guide out of sympathy." She laughs wryly. "You know it's bad when your parents are happy for you to spend time with a marked traitor just so you have a friend."

"I'd have chosen you out of everyone. You're not a freak– well, no more than I am."

Gull's eyebrows rise, and she giggles. "There's no hope for either of us." And before I can reach out to stop her, she's thrown herself backwards from the branch. I yelp, sure she'll fall, but she's hanging upside down, legs hooked over the branch where she had been sitting, swinging with her arms outstretched.

"Gull! You nearly gave me a heart attack!" My heart is racing and I want to shout, but her laugh is hard to resist. She curls up and pulls herself back to sit on the branch, grinning so brightly that all I can do is shake my head.

"Freak," I say, smirking.

"Why *thank you*," Gull says, and we crack up laughing again.

"But why though?" I say after a companionable silence. "Why aren't the others your friends?"

"It's not a short story — you're sure you're warm enough?" I nod, and Gull looks up at the chinks of sky showing through the leaves. "Well, sometimes a person is just born at the wrong time, I suppose." She runs her hand along the trunk as she talks. "We have a tradition that if a baby is born during a fireside meeting then that child will bring a blessing or a curse to the community. Anyway, that was me. People were excited at first – only since I've certainly not brought any blessings with me, most people assumed it meant I was the other thing…"

"They think you're *cursed*?" I'm incredulous.

Gull shrugs. "I don't believe anyone would actually say it out loud, but I scare them. You've heard what they say; we're being judged; nature has stopped nurturing us. People like having someone to blame, I guess."

"Is that how you think of nature? Like it's some kind of supreme being ready to punish or protect you?"

"People describe it in different ways: god, mother, nature, power or a kind of creative spirit; but yes, we have a responsibility to maintain a balance, and when we don't…"

"You starve? You don't deserve this, Gull. No one does."

"Your feet are *blue*." Gull gives my tattoo another tentative prod. "You should have told me you were cold. I forgot you're a wimp in need of toughening up." She wiggles her toes and arranges my boots round her neck on top of her shoes so they're well balanced and I don't have to deal with them. "We should get back anyway. Want to go first or second? It's just like coming up, only backwards and you can't see where you're going. Easy."

By the time we reach the bottom of the tree it has

started to rain; I can hear it on the leaves above. I go to put my boots back on but Gull reaches out a hand.

"While we're still in the forest, we don't wear shoes. It's a mark of respect."

"Is it one of your community rules?"

"Nope, just a Gull rule. But it's a good one. I am a creature here, so I should walk like a deer or a rabbit or a bird – this is their home, and I don't crash through my home leaving footprints and broken pieces. Plus, it means it's harder for anyone to find us."

"What are these stones from?" I ask Gull as we pass more of the giant, squared-off stones I've been seeing. She turns to me with an amused frown.

"From the wall," she says brightly, as though it should be obvious.

"What? The wall that Moriah built?" My voice is dubious, but Gull nods quickly and bounds ahead. And I'm left stepping gingerly over the forest floor, wondering what wall she means – it couldn't really be the wall from the stories; the wall that was built to keep the blanks in their place? In my heart, I had always imagined that was more of a symbol in the story than an historical record. Again I am left to wonder about truth and reality, but no answers come.

The forest is dense enough for most of the rain to

miss us, and the sound is soothing and glorious but it also makes me think of fingers tapping on glass. The air is chillier than ever and smells green and mulchy.

I try to catch up and walk closer to Gull, attempting to match her stride and her poise. She's right; she's a different creature in these woods. I slip and whimper when I step on a twig or a sharp stone. Every step is reluctant and cagey. Gull doesn't turn to check on me or slow. This is my training. Or my test.

When we reach the edge of the wood I scrape debris off my feet using a tree root and put my socks and boots back on. It feels both warm and restrictive. We hurry through the rain, Gull's body already dipped forward, her head and half her face hidden by her hood.

"You and that hood!" I tease.

"You and that shawl!" she replies. "What are you, eighty?"

"Rude! I'll have you know this is the height of fashion."

"For the almost dead." I snort at this and follow as she picks up pace, jogging and dodging puddles filled with clay-stained rainwater.

We are giggling, our empty stomachs forgotten. And just for a brief moment I forget something else too.

What I am here for, and what I have done.

Chapter Fifteen

"Where have you been?" Tanya is waiting by the door when we rush in from the rain, smiling and panting. Her expression is anxious.

All the ease Gull and I had when we were alone is lost.

"Where were you, Gull? I couldn't find you anywhere," she asks again, and she draws her daughter towards herself protectively, her eyes on me.

I sigh. I forgot for a moment, out there, that I was a creature to be feared and hated. I was just spending time with my friend. *Is* Gull a friend? I'm so used to it just being me and Verity.

Unless … would I call Oscar a friend? His face flashes into my mind – brown skin, that quirk of mischief in his eyes, a mouth that laughed so easily. No, not just a friend. There were times when I wanted it to be more, but the events of the last half a year have changed things. I find I don't care so much about milestones like first kisses, or first love, or first anything. I suppose wanting those things are the signs of someone who doesn't have any other cares. Those things can wait, I tell myself.

"They will come," Justus assures the people, pushing his lank hair away from his face – his annoyance clear to see. "The riders will come."

"They've never been gone this long," a man named Ted calls out; he's the one whose son was sick when I was helping at the surgery. "How do we know they're safe? How do we know they haven't been taken?"

There is a murmur of agreement.

"What if they've been taken?" asks a woman, the strain showing in her voice.

"They haven't been taken!" cries Justus over the noise. "They are being careful—"

"Then *when* are they coming, Justus?" a man called Blake asks. He's kind, I think; I remember him catching me as I stumbled on a rutted bit of track on one of my first days here. "Penny's pregnant, she can't carry on without some proper food." As though a gate has opened, a rumble of assent builds, some calling out in support. But others, quieter voices are hushing the dissonant ones and saying, "Let the elders speak. Let's hear what they have to say."

Justus looks around at his fellow elders – his exasperated face flushed. He raises his hands as though to say he gives up, and Ruth gestures to another elder, Kasia, who stands a little shyly and takes over. Ruth hunches over coughing, and I feel bad that I was churlish and grumpy the last time we were together. I'm due to see her tomorrow for my next lesson. I'll make it up to her. Justus walks away from the fire and watches us broodingly while Kasia speaks in his place.

"You know I see your pain. Blake – I see your beautiful family; I see Penny's need," Kasia says. "We have tried, you know we have – we have made lists of those in the greatest need and given you more, as much as we can spare." There are grudging murmurs of assent here. "But there is not enough food for us all. And there will be more mouths to feed." She nods towards Blake, but I feel eyes on me: on my marked face. Have I taken someone's share? Is someone hungry because of me?

"I believe we are being tested," Kasia continues – her gentleness wins the people over and they are quiet, letting her soft voice be heard by all. "We know that we are promised plenty – we know that paradise is ours for the taking. It is our own failings that deny us this bounty." I frown; this is just like Gull's talk earlier.

"When we are faithful – when we purge the sin in our hearts and our town, then creation blesses us. Our hunger is a warning: there is transgression in our midst and, if we root it out, confess and atone – then the land will give us her reward."

"We all know where the transgression lies," a voice cries. "The traitor has brought pestilence with her – she is cursed, like all the inked, and now, so are we."

It's like my first night all over again – all eyes on me. Fenn and Justus nod, finally having heard something they agree with. But Ruth pulls herself up, assisted by Tanya and her stick. The group falls silent again.

"We were hungry long before Leora came." Ruth's voice sounds weaker than usual. "See how she joins us in our suffering."

An angry woman raises her voice in derision.

"And see how she eats our food. We are wasting rations on her. She should be banished." Justus and Fenn lead the cheers at this, and I stare at the ground.

"We are fools if we blame our visitor for this, and we are no better than those devils in Saintstone if we cannot offer kindness to a stranger." Ruth coughs again, and Tanya holds her while she wheezes and regains her breath. "There may be sin in our community – but we must trust the old ways. If we obey, if we continue to faithfully mark our sin with white stones and if we atone at our birth day, then we have hope – we will not be punished for ever." Ruth turns and catches Justus, Fenn and a couple of their friends whispering behind her.

"Your birth day is soon, is it not, Fenn Whitworth?" she calls. Fenn stops his whispering and his face pales.

"Yes, Ruth," he mutters.

"Well, then. That is a new opportunity for redemption for us all. Let us see what happens after that. Atonement – a fresh start – it's exactly what we need. Don't let us down."

Her eyes flicker to me just for a second, and I feel like she is speaking to me as well as to Fenn. Fenn bows his head and the meeting is over.

Gull and I are alone in her room, candlelight flickering and Gull humming while she reads. I draw in my sketchbook.

I'm trying to draw this evening's fireside meeting and I close my eyes to bring back the image of the people's faces. For all their disagreement, one thing united them: the deep and unyielding fear that was in their eyes. A fear and a hunger that frightened me.

But now I'm drawing I feel calm start to rise. Sketching

goes a tiny way to satisfy my longing to be inking again – it feeds something in my soul that needs ink and beauty and the joy of creating something where there was nothing.

"What did Ruth mean about the white stones, Gull?" I ask suddenly. "And what's so important about Fenn's birth day?" For a long while I think she won't reply, or that she hasn't heard me, but after a minute or two she puts down the book she was reading and pushes her covers aside. Leaning precariously out of her bed, she picks up the leather pouch that is on the floor. Loosening the ties, she opens it up and tips all the stones out on her blankets, as though they are coins ready to be counted.

"You've seen me collecting these, I suppose?"

I nod.

"And you remember Belia's story, about how she stepped into the water laden with stones. And then the stones fell from her and the curse was lifted." She picks up a smooth white stone and holds it gently between thumb and finger, scrutinizing it as though it might be about to speak. "Each stone represents a sin, a failing, a mistake, a trespass or an act of negligence: the things that would leave us open to the curse." Her lips are tight as she drops the stone back on the pile.

"But … Gull. There are so many. These aren't all yours?"

Gull looks up at me, brows raised in surprise. "Of course they're all mine. I've been collecting for almost a year now. I was given this pouch on my last birth day to fill, and when my next one comes, I will be allowed to carry out the ritual – like Fenn is next week."

"I'm lost," I tell her, shaking my head. "You're going to have to spell this out for me."

"Right…" Gull closes her eyes and screws up her face while she thinks. "OK, you have your marks, don't you?"

"I do…" I reply with a smile.

"And they are a way of recording your crimes or misdemeanours, right?" I nod. "Well, this is how we count ours. Those in our community aged between fourteen and twenty-five collect stones for our sins over the course of a year, and when it's our birth day we take them to Jackdaw Lake with the stones bound to us, and we let them go – they sink underwater and all the bad stuff is gone, washed clean. Like Belia, you know? It's our duty – we don't just pay for our own sins, we are there for the whole village – we represent everyone."

I'm frowning, trying to understand.

"Right, but why only the young people? It's not like adults are perfect." Gull smiles at this and I'm relieved; the whole conversation feels taut and strange.

"It's just how it goes – everyone does their bit: all the

adults here have served the community in this way." She begins to take fistfuls of stones and drop them back into her little bag. The noise is jaunty, almost musical – it doesn't sound like the sound of sin. She suddenly giggles and then puts her hand over her mouth to stifle it. "Fenn once said that Obel told him it was just because the adults liked to see us shiver."

"That sounds exactly like the Obel I know." I grin and reach out to help Gull put the stones away, and wonder at the echoes in my and Belia's stories: a trail of stones, a feathered guide. And yet Belia is not part of my world and I'm not part of hers. I don't think.

Chapter Sixteen

Gull's a heavy sleeper. I know this because I'm *not* sleeping and Gull's deep, steady breath at night feels like a taunt. Insomnia isn't new to me: sleep has been hard to grasp since Dad got ill. It always felt that if I went to sleep I might be allowing something bad to happen.

You don't get used to not sleeping. You almost get used to the half-drugged feeling of walking through days unrested and you almost get used to not looking forward to bedtime and you almost get used to people looking at your face and telling you to have an early night. But the middle of the night hurts no matter how many times you've seen it. Time travels slower in the dark, I'm sure of it. And it's at night when the questions come.

I think of Mayor Longsight's speeches about the blanks and their terrifying army, and how close we are to war with them.

How they kill our children and our livestock.

How they are biding their time until they overthrow us and all we stand for.

How we must look over our shoulder, and if we feared anything, fear them.

And, lying there in the dark, I allow myself to consider another version. That maybe, maybe – it was all lies. That these ragged people I have come to know, weak from lack of food, tired and desperate and barely living – they are no threat and maybe they never have been.

Don't forget what they're planning to do to the hospital. And yet, in spite of my endeavours to keep on believing in the evil of the blanks and the tales I've always been told of their terror, for the first time, I wonder. Whose stories are real? Which do I listen to?

"Come on, Undead One." Gull shakes the bed to stir me the next morning. I must have dropped off at some point. "We've got to get up. You've got a meeting with Ruth this morning, remember?"

I haul myself into a sitting position and rub sleep out of my eyes. "You really don't suit bedhead." She laughs at me. "And you're going to need to open both eyes." I scowl at her through the one eye I have tentatively opened and run my hands through my tangled hair. It's almost at the length where I could tie it back, which would be so much easier, but for now I just try to tuck my fringe to one side and hope I can get the knots out with a comb later.

I dress quickly without washing – the idea of putting cold water anywhere near my body this morning is too grim to consider.

Gull's stomach gives a groan and mine rumbles in reply. We both laugh, but then I remember that there is no food and I complain, "I am so hungry."

Gull chucks her nightie at me and it lands next to me on the bed. "Tea?" she asks.

I nod and heave myself from the bed.

"Solves everything. I know," I sigh. And I walk with her to the kitchen.

Ruth is waiting for me in the memory room. There is a book on the table near her. Now that I know I'm surrounded by the remnants of those who were lost, there is a terrible but sacred air. It's like the memento mori room in the museum in Saintstone, I think. Are we really that different after all?

"Come in, Leora, sit down. We don't have much time."

Ruth's face crinkles as she smiles, and I remember how sad she looked at the fireside last night. "Today I get to tell you a story. But first, I need to ask you to open your heart. I want you to listen without judgement. Without thinking of ways round what I am telling you. I want you to allow the words to prick your soul – let down any walls you have built up to protect yourself from our ways and see the world with new eyes." She grins at my expression. "Can you do that for me?"

"I don't know," I say truthfully.

"Well." She sits down opposite me. "Let's give it a shot at least."

She holds my hand, as she did last time, and I breathe deeply, trying to do as she asks.

Chapter Seventeen

The Guest

After the princess Moriah cast out her sister, she became frightened that Belia would return and tell the people about their father's curse. She knew in her heart that her marked skin was an affliction, brought on by the dark magic of her villainous father. But she enjoyed her easy life and relished the power her royal position gave her. She couldn't have Belia spoil all that. She had earned this life. So, she declared that a wall would be built.

The citizens obeyed and built a high wall around the land Belia had been banished to and where she now had her own realm. The wall was higher than many of the trees and impossible to scale. Upon the top of the wall were shards of glass and blades, and there was no way in or out.

Except one. The builders had created a secret door – a door to which only the princess Moriah had a key. She made sure that all those who had known the door's whereabouts met untimely ends – she knew how people loved to tell secrets.

Belia and her people fought – they ruined the foundations and groundworks when the building began. And so Moriah brought in soldiers and many of Belia's people died. They had to allow the wall to be completed. Just before the final bricks were laid, some of Moriah's citizens secretly slipped through to join Belia – they saw that this was their one chance to escape Moriah and her marks.

Belia's people were poor and hungry; the land they had been contained in was not good for farming and they had few livestock. They could not break out, and there was little they could do to help themselves. Belia promised she had a way to help them; she assured them all would be well, and at least they were safe. Or so they thought.

Moriah had hoped that the wall would be a surgeon's saw – a blade to cut those terrible blanks off. A nice clean amputation to get rid of the poison and save the rest of the body. She knew that soon the people inside would starve to death. But Moriah had underestimated the extent of her sister's power. Moriah sent spies with ladders, telling them to look over the wall, observe and see whether the people had perished yet. But every emissary came back, head hanging low, to tell her that the people lived; indeed they flourished.

"What magic is this?" the princess howled. "What sorcery?"

She envied her sister and wished to steal whatever power Belia held that allowed her people to survive.

And so she sent another spy. And this time, she gave him a key.

This man was, by far, the most shrewd and skilful of all her agents. At home, they called him "Saint", but for this mission he went by the name of "Nate". He was a master of disguise; Nate could curl his spine until he looked like an old man; he could make his face handsome or grotesque. He could shudder with weakness or shoulder the greatest weights.

As he walked towards the hidden door in the wall, he came up with a plan. He felt with his fingers through the bracken and thorns, and his hands found the brick and the lock. The key fitted and turned as though it had been used every day.

He pushed the door, crept through the briars – allowing them to rip his clothing and scratch his skin – and he shut the door behind him, locking it carefully and rearranging the plants he had disturbed to ensure none but he would know of the door's existence. He took time to shred his clothes some more, and, using the razor in his pack and his own closed fist, he inflicted wounds which made him appear to have climbed rough stone, to have crossed over blades and glass and to have fallen from a height on to the hard ground. Close to fainting from the pain, he crawled and lurched and made his way towards the settlement, towards the place where woodsmoke puffed. Closer and closer he got. Weaker and weaker he became. He heard their chatter, their laughter and their love, and he smiled a cruel smile. He would soon bring silence and death to this oasis.

A girl came past and screamed at the sight of this bloody and *bruised man cowering beneath a tree. But the girl was kind, and although he was marked, and although he was not one of their people, she called for help. And help came. Nate's wounds were cleaned and bound, his clothes were mended, and he was given food, water and shelter. The good people of Featherstone showed him love and care. He told them he had rebelled against Moriah, and her soldiers had flung him over the wall. He told them he had wanted to join them before the wall closed but had been prevented. He was a wanted man: a freedom fighter. An ally covered in ink. And because his story was like many before him, and because his face looked kind beneath the swelling, the people welcomed him, and soon, Nate was home.*

As Nate regained his strength he offered to work. "Can I hunt or farm or cook?" he asked, keen to discover the secret to their plenty. The people smiled and shook their heads. "We will provide," they told him. And they gave him the job of teaching the children. He did it well. He taught them to draw and write and read, and what the stars meant and how to read the weather. Each day the children went to him, and he taught them. Each evening the children would return, full to the brim with new knowledge and joy. It was a happy time and the people were thankful for whatever good fortune had sent Nate to them.

Still Nate offered his help. "Can I gather, can I sow, can I help with the harvest?" he asked. The people smiled and shook their heads. This was one secret they weren't ready to share.

One night, Nate stayed awake and stole away from the village, hiding just at the edge of the woods where he could wait and watch. Just as dawn was coming and he was about to doze he heard a quiet rumble of thunder. He looked to the sky but saw no clouds. He kept his eyes up and, all of a sudden, a murder of crows soared overhead. He noticed the way the birds kept away from the village; no wonder he had never heard them. The crows flew near the lake and Nate crept towards the clearing. He saw the birds drop bundles, and when they had flown away he checked them. One had bread, another had meat, another was full of fruit and still another had cheese and vegetables. Whether this was blank magic or treachery from the marked, Nate neither knew nor cared. Chuckling to himself, Nate crept back to the camp and slept. A plan formed in his dreaming mind and, from that moment, evil crouched at the heels of Belia's people, ready to pounce when the time was right.

Nate continued to teach. He took the children and taught them songs and stories and rhymes and rules. They loved their teacher and trusted him as they trusted their own parents. For this was the place where no one had anything to hide. They were one.

They were wrong.

Nate had one other secret. Every day he would write his stories on his skin, as Moriah had commanded him to. And one day, he was caught; a friend stumbled across him carving marks into his flesh in the forest. The man ran back to the village and screamed for help, and Nate took his chance to hide.

"He is a spy! He has been marking his body with our secrets. We must hurry, we must be quick!"

The people gathered and parents told their children to stay indoors while they searched for the man.

"He can't be far," one voice said. "There is the wall to contain him, after all."

When every one of the adults went to the forest to find him, Nate stood in the centre of town and whistled. He whistled a song that the children knew. One that they loved, one that he had been whistling each time he lured them with his marked magic. And, as if in a dream, the children came. They held hands and followed him. They followed him through the forest, past the lake and all the way up to the wall. Nate reached for the key and put it in the lock, whistling all the time. He pulled the door open and led the children out, each of them beguiled by the sweet tune. Then, just before the last child had passed through, a yell came from the forest. Nate's whistle abruptly stopped and he pulled the door to, slamming it shut and locking it behind him.

Just one child was left weeping and afraid, wishing he hadn't been so slow as to have been left behind.

And the parents wailed. They screamed so loud they thought the walls might fall down. But there was no way out. He had stolen their secrets, and worst of all, he had stolen their children.

The next day when no food came, the people heard screeching which sounded like their babies crying. Instead they found crows, tied to the tops of the highest trees, wings beating but unable to fly.

Their life was over. All because of the marked man.

Chapter Eighteen

Ruth's eyes are closed and a tear shines on her cheek. The Leora who first came to Featherstone would want to point out the problems with the story – show Ruth the inconsistencies. She would say, they've got it wrong, again – the blanks have blamed the wrong man. The old Leora would want to show her that it doesn't make sense.

But the old Leora isn't here.

She knows, I think. *She knows all about me.*

"That was Featherstone?" is all I say, and Ruth opens her eyes and nods.

"Our people have been here since Belia first settled. There will always be new souls wanting to escape the inked tyranny. But" – she gestures to my skin – "not all those who seek refuge are blank."

"That story … that's why people are wary of me?" Ruth inclines her head. "But…" I try to smile. "I'm not Nate – I'm not here to hurt anyone." Even as I say it, my heart lurches. For I am more like the Saint than I ever knew.

"I believe you, my dear." Ruth reaches out a shaky hand and strokes my cheek. "Most of us can see how sweet your soul is and that you are here to heal, not to harm." I gulp back tears; she doesn't know what's in my heart. "It's not *you* that people resent. It's your history." Ruth stops and studies me, trying to weigh her words, trying to predict how they will be heard. "You know about your father – that he left us?" I nod. "But I wonder if you know everything."

"That's the main reason I'm here. I want to know the full story." My heart beats harder at the hope.

"Are you sure of that, Leora?" Ruth is serious and rubs her forehead. She looks so tired – small beads of sweat glitter on her brow. She should be resting. "Sometimes the stories we tell ourselves are the safest ones. Are you ready to know the man your father was, even if that changes the man you knew?"

"I'd rather know the whole messy truth than have a neat lie," I tell Ruth, drying my tears. I feel like the girl in a red cloak alone in the forest – ready to start on a new path. I cannot know whether I will meet a wolf or a woodcutter; an enemy or a friend.

Ruth breathes deeply and passes me the book, letting me read in silence.

It is my mother's – my birth mother's – diary.

Chapter Nineteen

Monday 1ˢᵗ

Khalid reappeared tonight. Stumbled into the circle at fireside, his face filthy and weary. All those weeks of being lost in Riverton: I was sure he was dead at the hand of the marked.

Everyone flocked to him, their voices raised as he struggled to answer their questions. As we had guessed, he had been found and arrested after the most recent trip to Riverton to gather food. But, unlike the others, he had escaped.

"But how?" came the cry. And Khalid held his hands up for silence.

The man who had saved him was a marked man.

In the deathly hush that fell, Khalid called in a low voice into the shadows behind him, and out stepped a man. I've never seen anything like it. His head was bowed, but his eyes — they were on us all. He looked like a wild dog, waiting for us to drop our guard or attack. Actually, he wasn't far wrong.

And he was marked. Marked all over. My eyes swam at the sight of him. I wanted to cover my eyes and shut out all that confusion, all that dirt and sin.

Khalid told us of his rescue — "This man is a hero!" he said. "He overcame the executioner and cut me down from the hangman's noose. He hid me in a safe house where I was well taken care of until we came here."

I can't imagine any marked doing that; it doesn't make sense. They hate us, want us dead. But it's Khalid's story. "This man, Joseph Elliot, was arrested for what he did. He was taken and inked with an accursed mark. We left together: he is in exile, and I assure you, he is as much a citizen of Riverton as I am. He is my brother now. I have promised him safety and a home here."

Tuesday 2nd

The elders have been in meetings all day, and Khalid and the stranger have been kept hidden in the elderhouse. But this has, at least, left the rest of us free to talk. And there is much talk. Some say we should kill the stranger before he kills us.

I don't know what I think.

The fireside was short tonight. They will talk more tomorrow, Ruth and Greta said.

Wednesday 3rd

The outsider can stay. It was decided tonight, at a fireside that seemed to go on until the birds were calling. We drew lots to see who would house him and Justus won – or lost. So the marked man is in our house, my own cousin's home, sleeping in the room next to me. If I put my hand on the wall, I can almost feel his marks spreading their decay. And I am so afraid because I don't seem to mind.

Friday 5th

They did a ceremony tonight, the same one they did for those who came in the eradication. He has a new name – a new life here – and he has been honoured for his courageous rescue of Khalid. They gave the freedom to choose his own tree and, more than that, he will wear the feather.

He promised before us all to honour the elders and be one with the group. His voice did not shake as he made the oath. No marks, no secrets, no lies. Honesty.

His name will be Joel. Joel Flint. A new name, a new start, a new life.

He is everywhere – in the street, at the dinner table, squeezing past me in the hallway. Passing me on the stairs. I avert my eyes from his marks. I look away, look anywhere that he isn't. He

may be one of us, but he seems anything but safe. Justus warned
me to keep my distance.

But at night I see him even when I close my eyes.

Thursday 18th

There are not enough stones for what I have done. He kissed me.
I kissed him. Maybe it's true that their marks can hypnotize. You
can drown in them. But I go under willingly.

Wednesday 24th

He has marks that only I know.

The diary stops abruptly, just at the point where I feel
I'm seeing the real person my birth mother was. I turn
blank pages frustratedly. And then, close to the back of
the notebook, without any date, I see a frantic scrawl.

I can't write in this book. Words don't work. He wants to go back
to where he's from. He sees our suffering and he wants to help
us and bring us aid. He sees our poverty; he sees the injustice.
He says there is no reason for us to live this way. That he can
persuade others to think the same. That blank and marked could
live alongside each other. He is a good man.

He wants me to go with him, but I know the people will see leaving Featherstone as treachery. And if I follow, I will have betrayed them all. I know many still see him as a marked man and nothing more.

The child in my belly moves.

This baby will be a blessing; not just for Joel and me but for our land. We both feel it: this is the change we have longed for, a way to bring peace between warring communities. I know every mother believes her baby is special, but this is different. I have dreams every night of Belia and Moriah walking hand in hand.

The pouches around my waist grow heavier every day. I would carry the earth if it meant I could be his.

The book finishes there, with so much still to be said. I close it and think about the book I already own, written in the same hand. It tells the next piece of the story.

Ruth fills in the gaps.

"When Justus discovered that your mother was expecting a child, he had Joel put out of the settlement." She takes the book from my hands. "Your father was welcome when he was simply someone who had risked his own life for one of our own, but it was clear that the prejudice still held when he and your mother fell in love. To many, it felt like a pollution. Justus meant well, Leora – believe me. He thought he was protecting your mother from a predator, and many assumed the same. But I know now that we misjudged your father. He would not leave. He hid in the forest and left your mother letters. In each one he told her he would never forsake her; that he would be back for her and their child. Only a few of us knew the full story; most of the town were happy to believe that he was just another marked – another ink-stained snake who had run away with our secrets. He would have been killed on sight had he dared to enter the village."

Heat builds in my chest and my teeth clench. Justus. I hold the outrage I feel tightly to me. I won't forget this. Didn't he care about my mother? Didn't any of the blanks see her pain?

"When you were born your mother cried." I feel those words like a stab, and Ruth reaches out to me. "No, not for you." She speaks tenderly. "Oh, my heart, no: for you she only had kisses and sweet, sweet words." I feel tears run and Ruth lets me cry. This person who loved me, who screamed me into the world; I never knew her. She touched my naked skin, and I can't even picture her face. I think my heart might break, and my head pounds. Sobs shudder through me and for the first time I ache for her – I miss my mum, the one I never knew existed, the one who loved me from before my world began. I wipe my tears away with a ragged cuff and slam my hand on the

Waterstones

Refunds & exchanges

We will happily refund or exchange goods within 30 days or at the manager's discretion. Please bring them back with this receipt and in resalable condition. There are some exclusions such as Book Tokens and specially ordered items, so please ask a bookseller for details.

This does not affect your statutory rights.

Waterstones Booksellers,
203/206 Piccadilly, London, W1J 9HD.

Get in touch with us:
customerservice@waterstones.com
or 0808 118 8787.

table. I have a sudden, absolute certainty and my howling anger needs to be allowed to speak.

"She never needed to die, did she?" I sniff back tears, but the anger – the rage – rips my throat and I want to destroy this whole room. Every bit of their history that they kept. But my mum is not here. She is forgotten and I want to say her name. I want to bring her back.

"Justus – he did this. He killed her." I am certain of it. "Tell me, Ruth. Tell me the truth."

"They saw the mark on you; it showed as soon as you were born. I was there – I was your mother's midwife." Ruth rests her hand on the book and closes her eyes. She shudders at the memory. "Justus saw. He ran to the fireside where the town was meeting and he roared that you were an aberration. A curse."

My lips form a snarl.

Justus. My mother's own cousin spoke against her? I want to shudder at the thought that I could be related to *him*. My mum was barely fledged; she could have soared. I want nothing more than to repay the harm he did our family.

"He blamed your mother. He said it was punishment for her behaviour, that she had given birth to a new Moriah." She swallows. "His eyes. He has always been zealous, but for a moment that night I thought he might have killed you both had Sana not acted."

"Sana?" I frown.

Ruth nods.

"She leads our riders – they left on a mission the day after you arrived." And, in my mind's eye, I see the spritely, strong woman on horseback whispering before she left, *You are so like your mother.* "I believe it was she who told your mother to run. You were bundled up, and although she was still weak and bleeding, Miranda left – you were the only thing she took, her prized possession, her only treasure. She kept on repeating the word 'blessing'; she truly felt you were no ordinary child."

I remember what Gull told me about a baby born during the fireside meeting – the tradition that said that child would either be a blessing or a curse. My mother did not see me the way Justus did. She had hope – I gave her hope. I want to please her – I want to believe like she did and to be the one who brings peace. I want to claim Featherstone as my home; I can help them, I am sure of it.

"Those of us who loved her began the search the next day. We found her body at dusk." She swallows. "She was too weak, and she had the beginning of an infection. She stood no chance. We thought you were dead too – taken by one of the scavenging creatures in the wood. We had no idea. It was only when you arrived that I realized what

156

must have happened. *He* found you – your father. He was too late for Miranda but he took you."

"He just left her body in the woods?"

"If she was dead, then you surely were starving. If he had tried to create a grave for her body, he would have forfeited your life. Let the dead bury their dead, I think they say. He saved you, Leora. And I am so grateful that he did. The guilt I felt the day we buried your mother beneath her tree has weighed me down all these years.

"Do not judge us too harshly, my dear. Justus saw something he did not understand. Fear is a terrible thing. I think it has taken us all these years to put ourselves back together again. And then, just when I thought we had" – she gives a little smile – "you arrived. Coming out of the darkness into the fireside, the very image of your mother, with your brown hair that doesn't know whether it wants to be wavy or straight, your pale skin and that worried, amazed look in your big eyes." Ruth smiles tenderly. "You even walk like she did." She sits back and lets the story settle.

In my mind, I take each piece of the tale and lay it out, right side up. I put it together and try to see the picture from their point of view. And, for the first time, I think I understand it.

No wonder the blanks are reluctant to trust me. My

own father confirmed every fear they had. He was the stranger Nate from the story, made flesh. A marked man can only steal and destroy. My father stole one of their women; he destroyed her, he destroyed a family.

But he wasn't that man. He was not the villain they have always believed him to be. He fought for their rights back in Saintstone till the day he died.

They think I'm like him.

I'm not like him, not nearly as good or courageous. But I want to be.

And they truly believed I was someone special, Mum and Dad. They thought I, this tiny baby born to a blank, yet born marked, could bring peace – just like Mel said. And at last, I know what I want. I want to honour them, to please them and prove them right. I don't feel as though I'm a blessing, but at least I can choose not to be a curse.

I sit before Ruth and, through tears, I promise. That I am not Nate, come again to destroy them. I want to be the child my parents believed I would be.

And in my heart I promise myself this is it – I will not do Longsight's bidding any more. I can't save my loved ones, but I can at least not betray the blanks. I will stay and I will not lead others astray. The salt stings my face and I embrace the pain.

"I will pass on your assurances to the elders. You are

brave, little light." And I gasp at hearing the name my
parents called me. "I saw you when you were just born."
Her eyes twinkle her affection. "It was an honour to be
your mother's midwife – I was the first to see your mark. I
knew your name before your parents did." And she holds
me so close I can hear her heart beating and feel her breath
on my skin. "I think your mother would be glad you have
come back," Ruth whispers. "You're home now, Leora."

Chapter Twenty

When Ruth stands at the fireside that night and tells the people she is pleased with the progress I am making and proud of the way I am assimilating, I can't contain my smile.

"She is learning quickly and proving herself faithful and, as such, we will allow Leora to remain with us, on the condition that she continues to keep our secrets and follow our ways. Remember, Leora: no lies and no marks. This return of our lost child is a blessing – a sign of good things to come. We should embrace Leora – it is no less than her mother would have asked of us."

There is silence when I stand. I can only hope they see how much I mean what I say.

"I have heard your tale of Nate and his evil. I know that you see my father as no more than another marked traitor. You have been treated badly, and the presence of a marked citizen in your village has only ever meant division and pain. But I promise to be different. I vow to be faithful to Featherstone and to protect, love and honour you as my own." I raise a hand. "No marks. No secrets. No lies."

They put it to a vote and the majority agree with the elders: I have the freedom to remain with them. I feel the weight of their trust – their expectation – and I try to believe I have the strength to shoulder it.

The Whitworths let Fenn tend to the fire when we return to their house and then call us to sit at the kitchen table before we go to bed.

"Solomon and I are so glad that the community made their decision today," says Tanya. "We want to thank you, Leora. You have been a willing worker and a cheerful addition to our home, in spite of the hardships you have had to share." Gull is smiling widely while Tanya talks. "We want to invite you to call our house your home for as long as you are in Featherstone; we want you to receive our acceptance into our household and into our family."

I look around the table, into eyes that smile and faces full of love. Except Fenn's, of course; his eyes are dark and bitter as they meet mine across the table.

And that's when something in me that has been hard and brittle starts to crack. Like the boxes in the memory room, I put them away: Verity, Obel, Mum and Oscar. I let them go – figures from a different tale, one that has come to its end.

"Th-thank you," I stutter. "I would be honoured to be part of your home." Gull jigs in her chair and claps her hands, and Solomon laughs.

"We need you to be ready early tomorrow, then." Tanya grins. "It's Fenn's birth day and the whole family must attend the ritual." Fenn slides his chair out and leaves the kitchen to go to his room, Lago at his heel. It's obvious that if Fenn had a say, I would be nowhere near him, his family or his birth day ritual. But Tanya's eyes are warm and shining across the candlelight.

I want to settle into this moment – into this family and community. I want to be a blessing, a protector, the one who finds a path to peace, but even as I feel this hope, guilt sings softly in my ear. It's a familiar tune: everyone I love, I betray. I am a curse. I am.

Chapter Twenty-One

It's Fenn's birth day. We leave the house just before dawn and follow the people ahead of us as we walk to the lake.

"So, this is a really big day for you all?" Gull and I are holding our extra layers tightly round ourselves, already shivering in the misty air as we walk towards the lake. At home, on our birth days, we get a new mark, some cake and some singing.

Gull is full of energy, almost breaking into a jog. "This is the one day a year a person gets to really feel free. For the person whose birth day it is, it's a fresh start – it's like you're as pure as the day you were born, again. And it's a great day for the community."

Her excitement is infectious, and I can't stop my smile as she holds my hand and we continue towards the lake. My heart fizzes in anticipation. There is already a small cluster of people congregating on the lakeside. They make room for us to join them, but I can't quite see past the tall woman in front of me. A few minutes later, we are motioned to sit, and I see Fenn standing between Tanya and Solomon, who both look solemn – anxious, even, I think. Fenn's head is bowed and he is dressed head to foot in white linen.

A simple long tunic, a little crumpled, reaches just past his knees. His feet are bare – the only one of us with no shoes on – and his ankles look vulnerable poking out from plain trousers. He looks exposed – I've never seen Fenn like this. When he shifts his feet, the hem of the tunic swings oddly in the breeze. Fenn seems nervous – shy even – and when he sees me his deep eyes hold mine for a moment. It's the first time he has allowed me to look right at him without it feeling like a fight – the first time I've met his gaze and his eyes aren't full of fire. Instead I feel like he's telling me something. *Watch this*, he's saying. *Watch this*.

I try to imagine what it feels like to have to be the centre of attention on a day like this. In Saintstone the only public events are the markings. I shiver suddenly and feel a flash of fear for Obel, for Oscar. I hope they're safe. They will be. I can't let my heart be led astray by thoughts of Saintstone. This is home now.

"It's starting," Gull whispers, interrupting my thoughts. "Listen." Both Solomon and Tanya hold Fenn's hands proudly, protectively, as Solomon speaks.

"Our own founder, Belia, showed us that we must throw off our old ways and enter into a new life, leaving the mistakes of the past behind, looking only to the future. Just as she plunged into these waters, so Fenn will step into the lake. In the same way as the waters passed over Belia's head, they will wash Fenn clean. And just as Belia cast those weighty stones into the lake, Fenn, laden with sin though he is, will, when under the lake, cast off these cumbersome robes and leave each transgression beneath the waters. And he will return to us, free, as he fixes his eyes on the shore, and we will bless him. He will have won for us all the freedom and blessing we so long for."

Sin, sin and more sin. I think of Gull's anxious face as she loads her bag with stones. I push my unease away. I am here to understand, not to criticize. I wonder what Mel would make of this – would she understand them? They love their stories, just like she does.

Tanya and Solomon place their hands on Fenn's bowed head.

"Have you collected your sins, dear son?" Tanya asks Fenn.

"I have."

"Have you carried them – your own burden to bear?"

"I have."

"Have you embedded them in your robes as a symbol of the sin embedded in your soul?"

"I have."

"Do you intend to tell and embody a good and true story for as long as you live?"

"I do."

The community draw nearer, and those who are close enough place their hands on Fenn.

"As we share our sin, we share in your atonement. As we share in our sin, we share in our glory."

And they take their hands off him and he turns to the water.

"Let us be witnesses this day of Fenn's rebirth. Let us watch as he faces the waters alone – just as we will one day face judgement alone. Let us pray that he succeeds and is set free. Let us celebrate our community's redemption."

No one moves. Only the lake waters make a sound as they lap and suck at the stones on the water's edge. I see Fenn clench his fists and I shiver.

He steps into the water, not seeming to notice the cold – not flinching or making a noise. The hem of his tunic darkens in the water and he walks on. Step by step, getting deeper and deeper. He is almost ten metres into the lake when the water reaches his shoulders. He is walking away.

I wish I could see his face. He pauses; his shoulders rise as he takes a breath and dives under.

We wait.

We wait until the ripples hit the shore and we wait until the breath I've been holding is released. We wait until I'm sure we can wait no more and I cling to Gull's hand. But she stands calm, and just when I am going to cry out that we must save him, Fenn breaches the surface.

I feel a rush of pure relief that seems to be echoed in every soul around me. The congregation gasps air with him, our tears warm on our cheeks. He swims towards us and then stands, eyes locked on the shore, and with each step I see a ripple of his skin, a wave, a trickle, a flood, and he steps out of the water bare-chested, tunic gone.

I glance up at Gull and she's looking at her brother, unedited joy written over her face. I look back down at the ground. I see a white stone and I realize.

The stones.

The tunic and the way the hem moved. They sew the stones into their tunics and step into the lake, on their birth day. And if they are truly good then they cast off their heavy sins and rise light. A re-enactment of Belia's own curse being broken.

Fenn is being wrapped in colourful sheets of cloth

and blankets, and I have a sudden memory of Dad being wrapped in blue after he died – but I blink and he's gone.

Fenn's skin is beginning to glow as he warms up, but I can see his teeth chatter. Fenn is passed the lit torch and he leads the way back to the village. Triumphant, enrobed and pure. At one with himself, the people and their world.

A feeling I hadn't anticipated begins to bubble within me. This passion and happiness at such an act is infectious. Fenn looks remade.

It's lies and nonsense, Longsight would say. *Not the true way. Not real.* But I look at Fenn, at the happiness in his face, and I wonder: Who is to say what isn't real?

Later on, shivering as I get undressed in the chilly bedroom, I look at my marks and wonder if perhaps I am no different. I carry my sin with me now – and not enough of it is on my skin. I would give anything now to free my soul.

I think of Fenn's face – the freedom as he stepped out of the lake, his body light. And I have only ever felt that way once. The day I walked out into the snow with my crow around my neck, I felt drunk with peace. But it was really the start of the war.

I don't know what I believe any more; I only know that today has shaken me. Because right now I have nowhere for my sin to go. It's neither being inked on my skin nor placed in a pouch, heavy round my waist. It is in my soul, and all of a sudden I feel it, clutching at my heart, burying its roots in my lungs, sending its trail of evil and wickedness around my body.

Chapter Twenty-Two

The fireside tonight is all about Fenn and his birth day. The party has already begun; people clap rhythmically and whoop and cheer when Fenn appears. I can't help but grin. For just a moment my empty stomach isn't the first thing on my mind. When everyone has gathered, Solomon stands and the clapping continues, different family groups tapping out different rhythms which together sound like a heartbeat, like a dance, and I can't help but move.

I watch Gull, taking in her beat, and I join in. She smiles at me, but our eyes are fixed on Fenn, who is passed around the group as though he is a gift. He smiles and talks to people as they dance together, and then he moves to the next. I've never seen him like this – so open, so part of the crowd. When he turns to face the fire, golden in its light, and roars in primal delight, everyone whoops with overwhelming joy.

I am lost in the celebration too, clapping and dancing,

letting the warmth of the fire kiss my eyes and lips and cheeks. I watch the fire crackle and listen to the wood burn and suddenly, for a horrible moment, I am back in the hall of judgement watching Jack Minnow throw my father's skin book into the flames.

I shake myself, reminding my anxious mind that it wasn't really Dad's book I burned, in the end. I don't even know where his is. If they were telling the truth, Mel and Mayor Longsight, then it's out there somewhere still. There is hope for him. I shiver despite the flames. In turning my back on Saintstone, have I ruined Dad's only chance to be remembered? Does any of that even matter now?

Someone is pushing their way through the dancing crowd – Kasia, her eyes wide. She sees Tanya and grabs her by the arm.

"Come quickly," she cries. "It's Ruth."

We huddle, anxiously, outside the house. Everyone is here, I realize, flaming torches raised in the dark, people huddled into small groups, waiting to see if she's OK.

Justus comes out of the house, followed by Tanya. Justus raises his hands.

"In life, we are one. In death, we are one. Ruth has begun her walk to her blessed home and we will accompany her on the final journey tonight."

I look around. It can't be true – not Ruth.

Tanya puts her arm around me, her eyes bright with tears.

"She was old, Leora, and she was getting tired of life. She had become very sick. Every day was a struggle for her."

She was my ally here, I realize. And she was the only person who would tell me about my mother. She taught me so much in such a short time.

That I was loved. That I belonged. That stories are just stories and what they mean depends on the teller.

Those standing close to me bow their heads while raising one hand, and I see that the others in the square have done the same. I tentatively copy them and then, smothering the silence, the wails begin.

Chapter Twenty-Three

All the next day I feel an ache in my throat that won't go away. I feel like a fraud. Who am I to mourn Ruth when I barely knew her? And yet she knew me – from the first cry. And I wonder whether I am mourning for Ruth, or for what might have been. A hole where something like family might have blossomed.

But I don't deserve to mourn, I think. I look at the reddened eyes of those who knew her, worked alongside her all their lives, and I feel guilty. She was so good to me and I repaid her with betrayal. I'm glad I've vowed not to respond to Longsight's next call, but it doesn't change the fact that by meeting with Verity that one time, I've already done the very thing Ruth taught me that Featherstone most feared. So I keep my head down, keep my mouth shut and get on with my chores. Mum would be proud, I think, with a rueful smile.

They hold the death ceremony without delay, at the following fireside. I am not squeamish about death, about the body. And I wish I could have marked Ruth's skin, wishing my dad was here to flay her, wishing we could tan her, bind her and remember her. I am sick at the thought of her works imprinted on her soul. They say she is journeying to her final destination. But what if it's not enough? What if she is not righteous? Can they really trust in stones and water and face death unafraid? My legs shake, for once not from hunger but from fear. I don't know what I believe any more, but ink is in my blood and it's hard to shake the belief that it's the ink that saves.

What if her soul is not ready? I'm not ready.

We reach the fire and everyone is standing. I don't take my usual place next to Gull. I want to stand at the back so I can hide. But the circle opens out for each new person and we are not standing in groups as we normally do, but as individuals. The circle is so wide that I can't see the other side clearly. Faces wobble in the heat and I feel laid bare. I feel like an intruder.

Tears come to my eyes and I let them fall.

Music blooms from behind us and I look over my shoulder. It's the funeral procession. Ruth didn't have any family left, but her neighbours come up the hill, carrying a mat between them. Ruth is wrapped in white linen, the same as Fenn wore as he went into the water. Gull told me that her body will be buried tomorrow beneath the tree that Ruth called her own. The procession hums a low melody, and as they come closer the circle opens to let them in and the community joins in the tune. The bass tones make my chest feel like a bird is inside trying to beat its way out. The circle closes again and we surround the pallbearers as they place Ruth's body on the ground.

I see tears shining on their faces. The humming continues though, through their tears. No breaking voices – in fact, the tears seem to fuel the music. Our communal mourning resonating in our chests, in our throats and heads and hearts.

Tanya steps forward, and those who carried Ruth join the circle. Tanya's nervousness is apparent and there is heavy-hearted sorrow in her small smile. She raises her hands and the humming softens – never stopping, but quieter now, allowing her to speak over the lull.

"My friends." She pauses and gulps back tears. "Oh, my friends. We have all been blessed to have Ruth, our eldest, with us for every day of our lives. Tomorrow will be the first sunrise we see without sharing it with Ruth, and we will have to trust that the world can keep turning without her."

She stops, overcome. The song rises to give her space,

and her shoulders shake. A long moment passes and she looks up at us again, nodding thanks. "Ruth lived a long life and, we can all agree, a good life. Her story is one full of joy and blessing and laughter and above all, kindness. She brought many of us into this world." I swallow, thinking of my mother and the night I was born. She must have felt so frightened, so alone. I listen to Tanya. "So many of us will testify to the way she would come alongside us when our babies were small, and she soothed them and soothed us, telling us it was always this way for new babies and new parents, and she would hold our infants and hold us when we needed her to. I remember the day she brought me chocolate." Tanya's eyes widen and she grins at the smiles that change the sound of the hums to something clearer. "I had never eaten it before and I've never had it since. But I can assure you that if I came into possession of chocolate again I wouldn't choose to share it." She shrugs and a small flutter of laughter ripples through the congregation. "But for Ruth, joy wasn't complete if it wasn't shared. In giving she lacked nothing, and she will remain always in my story. Always the best and the most wise and good. A princess in wrinkled skin."

I fight back tears again. She fought for me to stay. She was the only one here who believed there was good in me. And now she is gone.

The hum rises again and hands are raised too. Hands with palms open to Ruth. Receiving, sending. Giving but not lacking.

"Kasia, please bring her pouch." She crouches and takes something from on top of the body and passes it to Tanya, who weighs it in her hands before lifting it up for all of us to see. It is empty, of course – as all adults' are – but I can't imagine her ever needing to collect stones for sins, even as a youth.

"Ruth was good. Her story was so beautiful and pure, and we send her on into the light unburdened by any sin that may have bitten at her heels and clung to her in her last days." She unties the strings on the pouch and tips it to show its emptiness. The bag is passed one to another, each person clutching it close, some pressing it to their lips.

"In our community it is custom to acknowledge new life, even when we face death. For this reason, and with the blessing of the elders…" She holds my gaze and walks towards me.

"This is for you, Leora. We know that Ruth counted you as her newest sister." She puts Ruth's pouch in my open hands. "We pass on to you Ruth's hope and we assure you of the same love and friendship as we felt for her. She would have wanted this."

I don't know what to say. I see that it's a blessing – an

honour. In this act of inclusion and remembrance, I know that I have been accepted: even more fully than two nights ago. I am not only allowed to stay in their midst, I can share in their beliefs and practices. I, a marked soul – *an enemy* – am being allowed redemption.

Even so, it seems like the pouch is full already: full of expectation that I will assent to their beliefs and submit to their rituals and rules. They have handed me captivity with this gift and, until I fill this pouch with stones to pay my ransom, I will be enslaved.

I hold it in my hand as though it is a living thing.

Tanya takes her place and calls out.

"Ruth, our mother, our sister, our friend. We send you on to the next world. We release you with our blessing and with our certainty that your next dwelling place will be where the grass is green, the water is clear and the sun shines on your face." As Tanya speaks everyone in the circle has raised their palms to the sky, and with each word we lift them a little higher until we stand together in silence, our arms outstretched and our hearts broken.

It is just then, at the moment that life and death mingle into one, that peace is shattered.

The riders are back.

Chapter Twenty-Four

It feels like a miracle; as though Ruth has brought us some parting gift.

Food.

We sit down right there and eat. There are tears in my eyes and I don't know if they are still from sorrow or simply the utter relief at the knowledge that my hunger will end. Someone calls out, "Here's to Ruth!" and we sit around in our family groups and eat. Some sit close to Ruth, kneeling near her body, cups raised as wine is poured into them.

I have bread in my hands. And cheese. *Cheese.* I raise the bread to my lips and bite the sharp crust, letting the fragrant wafts enter my lungs as I breathe in. The bread below the crust is soft and sweet and salty and sprung with bubbles of air. I see Sana, the leader of the riders, shaking her hair loose from a hat. Tanya is talking to her quietly, telling her what has happened, I suppose. I try to remember that old anger I felt at the thought of them robbing our town, and I wonder vaguely, as if in a dream, whether they attacked the hospital – but none of that matters to me at this moment. All I feel is intense gratitude that they have risked their lives for me to eat.

Sana's eye catches mine for a moment in the firelight, and she nods. My mother's best friend, I think. Like me and Verity, only she never betrayed Miranda.

It is only when everyone is eating, chattering and laughing that the full party advance to the fire. The horses have been tied up and wares unpacked. One man comes forward with another bottle of wine, holding it out, pouring it into cups. All the faces gaze upwards, smiling. I see their mouths move: "Thank you."

My sleep is patchy as always, a quilt of fractured dreams and images.

The jar in my hands is cold, and although I shake and shake the oil and ink will not mix.

I shake again and the jar slips from my hands. Among the shards of glass the oil and ink dash apart, tiny globules chasing one another away. I try to clear up the glass but it slices my finger. Blood drips on to the floor and I watch the ink and oil and blood swirl into one another as though they were made to be together.

Gull shakes me awake the next morning, her words eventually making sense as I come to.

"Dad says you have to go to the elderhouse; you've been sent for. There'll be breakfast when you get back."

Breakfast. The word is so good it's indecent. I dress hurriedly and head to the town, wiping sleep from my eyes and wondering why exactly the elders want me, and why it had to be *so* early. The door of the elderhouse is ajar, and I knock quietly before letting myself in.

The hot, tangy smell of freshly made coffee almost hurts my eyes – flavour and fragrance and all those sensory pleasures disappear when food is gone and you're just surviving. I could almost get drunk off the scent of the roasted beans and, in my weary state, I feel light-headed.

When I walk into the meeting room, my eyes focus not on the people waiting expectantly, but on the plate of cookies and pastries on the circular table. They are squashed and greasy – beyond their best. But I would recognize them anywhere – these are from the bakery where Seb, Verity's brother, works. And suddenly I'm right back in Verity's kitchen with Seb smiling at me and helping me with my shawl, telling me to take a cookie with me when I go home. The smell is my walk to the studio, passing the bakery and peering in to see whether I can spot Seb. This feels sacred. I don't want them to have this – this is *my* memory and it doesn't feel like it fits here in Featherstone.

A mug of coffee is handed to me and I sit. The plate is passed round the group and I swallow back tears, watching as people take their first bites of the sugary, buttery perfection; hearing them groaning their delight. This is just silly, I tell myself. But it's not – it's sorrow. Suddenly I miss home.

The coffee makes my insides ache – it's all a bit much after having so little for so long, and so I place the mug down on the table and look around at the people gathered. Most of the elders are here; Tanya smiles at me and Solomon nods. Sana and two of the other riders are here as well. Justus introduces them as Rory and Helina; out of all the elders, he seems to know the riders the best. I stoke the fire in my heart – one day, I will make him sorry that he ever hurt my mother. When he goes to introduce Sana, she interrupts him with the flick of a hand.

"We've met." Her smile makes her eyes crinkle and she takes my hand. She is slight, I realize, and yet she gives the impression of height; I feel small next to her. She shakes her head to get the deep brown curls out of her eyes and in doing so her chin rises, giving her a queenly authority – in a place where all are supposed to be equal, it feels electric to have someone's charisma so obviously outdo everyone else in the room. She gives an impish flash of her eyebrows and speaks.

"Leora Flint." She gazes at me, that small smile still on her face, her hand still clasping mine. "I've been looking forward to coming home and getting to know you." Her teeth shine with her smile, making me think more of a woodland creature than a woman.

I free my hand from hers, feeling embarrassed and on show. All I care about right now is news from Saintstone – I wonder if Verity was in time to stop their attack on the hospital.

Sana takes charge of the meeting. She stands and speaks to the elders who sit at her feet like children at story time in my school.

"I'm uneasy," she begins. "Our eyes and ears in Saintstone are worried; they seem to think we need to be ever more careful. And I have ample reason to agree – time and again on this mission our plans were thwarted."

No one speaks, but the carefree atmosphere has changed. The mood is sombre now. "For the few in

Saintstone who support us, the crows, things are riskier than ever. Those who used to turn a blind eye to bits and pieces going missing are becoming paranoid. Everyone is frightened. The rumours have stepped up – that we are not just stealing, but burning their crops. Killing their livestock." That sounds like the Longsight I know. "And there are rumours of Longsight imprisoning crows; anyone he believes is a rebel is unsafe. Anyone." As she gazes around the room our eyes meet.

Who, I think, panic rising in my chest. *Who is unsafe?* I am protecting my friends by coming here; Longsight promised.

"But you managed nonetheless. You have brought supplies – and such bounty!" Kasia says kindly, and we all nod and murmur in agreement at the memory of last night's meal.

"Look closer, Kasia." Sana's voice is gentle but firm, steel running through it. "We have never been this hungry before, not for many years. We may not have much but this is the first time we have gone without meal to make bread. Our usual paths to Saintstone were filled with traps and we lost one of our horses when she broke a leg. Other mayors have hated us and kept their distance and made sure we did not have much. But Longsight is different. He came to power preaching against us. We thought that was just talk; a means to an end. But he has people preaching against us, people like Jack Minnow. He listens to them. And now his purpose is clear: he is starving us – you – out."

There is a pause, and then Kasia says, "It is a punishment. The natural order of things—"

"No," Sana's voice is so crisp it makes me jump. "We are not being *punished*. Nature has not turned against us. We have done nothing wrong except try to live. We have food now, but soon we will feel the hunger, and even more keenly. You know the rest: every problem the marked have, they blame on us. They paint a picture of us as the greatest threat to their way of life so that they can convince the people to fight – to wipe us out. We may not have a wall any more, like in the stories; but a war, I can imagine."

What she says rings true. Missing livestock, a poor harvest; it all gave fuel to Longsight's fire, especially recently – everything was the fault of the blanks, it seemed. But I see now that in Saintstone we were safe – we never lacked. We never really went without. I think of Longsight's message – of a fearsome community of blanks ready to rise up and destroy our way of life – and look around at the ragged group of people in the room, their faces gaunt with hunger, and I want to laugh. The very idea of this community of people rising up to fight. They can hardly lift their own children on some days. I am frightened, suddenly, for these people. This is my home now, and it is being attacked.

"What do you think, Leora?" Solomon asks, and I'm surprised to hear my name. "What is your view of this?"

I clear my throat and remain seated.

"You're not far wrong," I admit, weighing my words. "Mayor Longsight does speak about Featherstone as though it were a threat – as though you're waiting to wage war." I look down at the table, nervous about meeting anyone's eye.

"But surely he can't believe that's true?" Tanya asks, and I shrug.

"I think he wants people to believe you are a threat to our ... *their* way of life," I say.

"Which is a polite way of saying that Longsight would like nothing better than seeing all blanks destroyed," Sana says. "The time for peaceful coexistence is over. Who did it serve anyway? We stayed meek and what did it get us?" Her voice is rising. "For them, the resettlement" – she says it as though it's a joke – "the resettlement isn't enough. It's not enough that they're *out*. They want us *gone*." Her eyes are bright as she stares around at us all. "Do you think we will survive another winter like this?"

"What about the hospital?" Justus raises his voice above the hubbub. "Did you manage your mission?"

The hospital bombing. I swallow. The room is silent at that – did they all know? Was this the plan of all of their hearts?

"I don't know what to tell you." Sana's light dims and my hope is fanned into flame. "It was – it was as though they knew we were coming. We barely escaped with our lives."

"How could they possibly know?" Tanya asks, and out of the corner of my eye, I see Justus stiffen. He's looking at me now, I can feel it. I stare straight ahead.

"There must be a traitor in the crows," Solomon breathes.

"No … no, I don't think so…" Sana is thoughtful. "The crows didn't know about this particular mission. And even if they had…" Her voice trails off. "How could they have begrudged us that?" She shakes her head. "I'm so sorry we failed you. If we had managed it, and made it back sooner, we could have saved Ruth…"

I stare at her, bewildered. Nothing is making any sense.

"No, Sana – don't think like that." Kasia rushes to reassure her.

"We brought you nothing," Sana whispers. "No medicine, no antibiotics or bandages or instruments." She sighs. "We couldn't even get you painkillers. There were guards at every point."

It's as though I'm at the end of a long night and dawn comes. There was no attack planned on the hospital, no bomb; they were just going to get medical supplies. Relief courses through me, swiftly followed by guilt.

Tanya stands and goes to Sana and takes her hands.

"It's not your fault. You tried. Longsight is making it impossible." She rubs her temples, tiredly. "Maybe you're right, Sana. Longsight's mercy is at an end."

"That's not all." Sana pulls her hands away, face still grim. "Tell them what we saw, Helina." Sana gestures to the tall black woman, who is still dressed in her rider's gear. She stands, looking uneasy, as though she would much prefer to be back on a horse than here in the small room.

"We were followed on the way back." The outcry is immediate. She holds up her hand for silence. "We lost them, but not before they crossed the river. They are getting close – *closer*. They've never tried to find our exact location before. It won't be long before they find Featherstone. And when they do – we have nothing to defend ourselves with."

How could they, I wonder; how could anyone penetrate the forest, know the intricate set of signs and clues that unlock the secret path to Featherstone. And then, with a plunging horror, I remember the stones, laid out for me that night I went to meet with Verity. I didn't think to collect them as I returned to the village. My vision dims; did I lead them right to Featherstone? But there is another traitor in our midst, I remember; a true blank who is doing Longsight's bidding. Whoever put that note in my boot is surely even guiltier than I am? Who could it be?

There is a long silence, and then Solomon speaks. "You're correct, Sana; this … changes things. The one assurance we had at the eradication was that the marked would leave us to our own devices. The river has always been our border. This – it is an act of aggression." The elders murmur their agreement, and Solomon turns to Sana.

"This is something our people will have to know – but not at tonight's fireside. This will cause panic. We need time to talk and think." He looks around at his elders and asks, "Do you agree, friends?" And, for all their talk of complete transparency, they all agree to keeping this news secret from the people. But who am I to question? I've never had to lead people through a threat like this.

Justus speaks up then, his voice cutting clear through the low, anxious murmur.

"What about Leora?" His eyes are on me. "Are you all

so willing to ignore the obvious? Is it a coincidence that this marked outsider joins us at exactly the same time as Longsight decides to starve us out? At the same time that he begins his campaign of hatred against us? The exact moment that security in Saintstone increases – that they know our every movement – and our riders are pursued?"

There is a silence, but I can't tell whether it is protective or whether they are weighing his words.

I realize that no one will speak for me. I will have to speak for myself.

"I had nothing to do with any of that." My voice sounds small.

"Of course she didn't," Solomon says warmly. "Leora is an exile from Saintstone. Why would she collude with them?"

"Ask her." Justus is looking at me, and a nasty smile is beginning. "Ask her where she went on Monday night."

The night I met with Verity in the forest. I feel sick. I don't know how he knows, but he does. He must have known this for days, and he's been saving it up to destroy me with.

"She was at home with us, fast asleep," Tanya says indignantly.

"Was she?" says Justus. "I don't think so. Oh no, I think Leora was passing messages to someone from Saintstone.

A contact who she met in the woods. Telling them our plans. Telling them how hungry we are and how broken. Telling them how to steal through our forest."

"If this is just conjecture—" Tanya says coldly.

"No conjecture," Justus says, and his voice is exultant. "She was *seen*. She was seen leaving your house."

Fenn. It must have been.

"I…" Tanya begins, her brow clouding with confusion, but she is interrupted by a louder voice. Sana.

"And was she *seen* leaving the town? Was she seen meeting this imagined contact?"

For the first time a shadow of doubt crosses Justus's face.

"I— No. But what else could she possibly have been doing at that time? Why leave the Whitworths' furtively under cover of darkness if she wasn't spying on us?"

"Perhaps," Sana says, "Leora could tell us that herself."

I look at her. Her expression is unreadable.

"I…" I swallow. "I couldn't sleep for hunger. I haven't been sleeping well anyway." I'm stalling and I'm sure they know it. "I took the dog out and … and that was it." I shrug. "I took her for a walk around the town and had some fresh air, and then I went home."

To my surprise, my voice sounds utterly genuine – nervous, but honest. There is a pause.

Justus is looking around at everyone. "You believe this?" he asks incredulously.

"There is no reason for the child to lie," Solomon says gently. "Ruth believed in her. Ruth, our eldest and wisest, believed that she was here to do good, not evil. I trust Ruth."

Justus gave a short bark of laughter. "So, you are happy for this ... this *aberration*" – I flinch – "to walk around, hearing our secrets, and carrying them back to her own kind? You seem determined to walk into a trap of Longsight's making!"

"We trust no one mindlessly," Solomon says firmly. "Leora has been accepted into our community, with the caveat that she should learn from us, and that we continue to test her honesty. Ruth believed that was right, and we shall continue her work." He looks around. "Who will guide the child?"

I see Tanya open her mouth, but before she can speak I hear Sana's voice.

"It would be my honour," Sana says, "if you would allow me to be Leora's mentor." Her eyes meet mine, and they are unreadable. "I would consider it a great privilege."

Chapter Twenty-Five

"It's your birthday soon," I say later that morning while Gull and I are stripping the beds ready for the laundry. "Are you excited?"

Gull sinks back into a pile of dirty sheets and blankets, her stones clinking as she stretches back. Sighing, she talks to me with closed eyes.

"My tunic is nearly ready." She runs her hand across her pouch. "And then I have to sew these into the hem."

"Well, I think you'll have enough." I throw the pillowcase at her. "In fact, you've got enough to build an entire white house."

"Oh, don't." Gull sounds defeated.

"Am I allowed to help you sew them into your tunic?" I ask.

Gull is quiet for a while. "I don't know," she says thoughtfully. "It would save me a load of time."

"Well, then, if there aren't rules saying I can't..." I raise my eyebrows and grin at Gull, and she gives me a hesitant smile.

"You are one weird girl, Leora." She heaves herself up to stand. "But maybe that's why I like you."

Lessons with Sana begin right away. She and I stroll around the village while we talk. People are sorting through the supplies the riders have brought, and there's a contented, hopeful buzz in the air. They don't yet know there is more at stake than their next meal. Sana is good-humoured and I notice the way she smiles at and chats with people as we pass. She's popular, and a little awe-inspiring.

"This must all be quite a shock," she murmurs to me as we watch a small child chasing after a puppy and giggling. "Coming here, finding out we're not quite as barbaric as you expected."

Her tone is challenging but not unfriendly. I give a wry smile. "I'm beginning to see that nothing is ever quite what I expect."

Sana chuckles and looks at me. I keep my face forward, hoping she can't see how nervous I feel. "You look so very like Miranda," she says softly, and I jerk my head to look at her face. I remember Obel saying the same. But then he thought I looked like the White Witch too. I should get used to calling her Belia. "You've got such delicate features – lovely cheekbones. Your mum always wore her hair long, and it was a shade lighter than yours but hers had the same tendency to tangle. Maybe it's your pale skin and blue eyes – always looking curiously at the world. But there's no question who you belong to. You're just like her."

"You said that on my first day, remember – as you were leaving," I say quietly.

"Miranda and I… We were best friends. I've never really come to terms with losing her – and when I saw you that night when you appeared at the fireside, stumbling from the forest…" She stops and catches hold of my hand. "I thought I was seeing her ghost." Sana's eyes are shining and she's softer than before.

"I didn't know…" I try to sift my thoughts. "No one would tell me anything about her. Only Ruth." A sigh heaves through my body. "I just want to feel close to her. To understand what I am."

Wordlessly, Sana opens her arms, and I fall greedily into her hug. She strokes my hair and I feel like she is trying to soothe herself as much as me. When I break away, she looks at me steadily.

"I'm sorry. I never thought I would have this moment; I never thought I would see you again after Miranda left."

She gives a shaky laugh. "And now I am to mentor you and instruct you in our ways. Humour me, let me do my duty: there's so much I've missed. I owe it to Miranda to look out for you."

We feast together at the fireside that night, sitting in small groups eating blood-red tomatoes and sticky, oozing cheese, and we are even given a piece of dense madeira cake. I could cry at its sweetness.

The elders look anxious when Sana gets up to speak. Anxious because they wonder what she'll say, or because they know already? I think about Solomon asking them to stay quiet about Longsight's troupe getting closer to the village.

"We give thanks for this food," she says quietly. "But, my friends – I have to tell you this. I do not know when there will be more." An uneasy, almost angry hum starts up. People are relaxing for the first time in weeks, and she is telling them they can't enjoy themselves.

"I know this isn't what you want to hear. But I believe the threats from Saintstone are real. The tide is rising. The propaganda from Longsight is relentless – they all believe that *we* are preparing to attack." She gives a bleak laugh at this. "The opposite is true, but Longsight wants an easy victory. He wants you broken. And indeed, I believe that he has succeeded. I have never seen you so weak, so in need, so starved of hope." Whispers now, uneasy shifting.

"I want you to hear me clearly: they killed Ruth." There is a surge of confused chatter at this. "Oh yes, they did. They starved her. She was sick; she needed food and medicine, and they denied her. They have never wanted us to thrive but now they want us gone. Don't you see?" She looks around at us, our faces fixed on hers. "They are *killing* you, slaughtering you slowly, so slowly they're hoping you won't notice. Yes, they killed her. And this is just a beginning!" There is a call of agreement, a shout of "She is right! We're treated worse than cattle." I look around but can't tell who spoke.

"They want you beaten and broken and frightened," Sana whispers. "And I do not want them to succeed in making you afraid, for fear will freeze into your bones. It will make you weak." She casts a look at the elders, who shift uncomfortably. "And now that we are frightened and weary, they will strike. They will annihilate us with one stroke. Why do you think Longsight is impeding our gathering of food and medicine now, after all these years of the leaders of Saintstone turning a blind eye? Why is he suddenly discovering our ways through the forest? Because he intends to attack, at any moment. We need action, and fast." She lets the words rest and settle once again. "The marked tell their people that we are like a hungry beast, growing bigger and stronger. Longsight has painted himself as the fairy-tale hero. They long to slay the monster and free the kingdom. They will only feel safe again when we are gone. And if any of their own preach tolerance, then they are marked as forgotten." I lift my eyes. *She is right*, I think. "Little do they know – *they* are the monster."

Fenn stands then, and others join him. Soon many in the group are standing, all stamping their feet.

"Of course, I am only the messenger," Sana says. "It is not for me to tell you what your next move should be. But know this. Longsight expects to destroy us with ease. He is expecting a massacre." She lifts up her eyes and her voice. "Let's give him a war."

The next morning, fumbling with my boots, with the angry fireside cries still ringing in my ears, I find another note. Neat, cramped writing, summoning me to my next meeting with Longsight's contact. Verity.

Who is writing these notes?

I breathe deeply and throw it on to the smouldering fire – watching it all burn to ash.

Chapter Twenty-Six

The first person to be taken is the boy I saw at the surgery, the day after I arrived. A small boy with huge eyes and tousled hair.

He hasn't been well for some time. His fever didn't break, and so he was taken from his home and looked after by the healers. But he got worse and worse. He couldn't stop vomiting. And now he is gone.

And he is only the first. That week more and more start to fall ill with cramps and vomiting. Tanya comes home at odd hours, exhausted from caring for the sick day and night.

It is only after the third death that grief turns to suspicion.

The fireside that night is silent. Penny, who is pregnant,

leans against Blake, who strokes her hair. She is very pale. Fenn doesn't sit with us as usual; instead, I notice him prowling the edge of the circle, his fists clenched. And then, when Solomon calls for silence and the nightly tale, Fenn interrupts.

"Their symptoms are all the same." He looks round at us all. "Do you not understand? This is no ordinary sickness. We are being poisoned."

I thought I had seen fear before, but this suggestion breeds instant panic.

Sana stands, worry and confusion on her face. "It's not fair to scare people like this, Fenn," she says. "We need to be strong, not to panic. What grounds have you to speak of poison? We have had sickness before—"

But Fenn is undeterred. He lifts his chin and meets her eyes squarely.

"This is no ordinary sickness," he calls. "I suggest that we visit the well at first light."

The fireside time explodes into angry arguments and accusations. As I watch, it is like ice breaking – families draw together, apart from the group. Fractures. Cracks.

It won't take much for this community to break.

At dawn, Fenn is at the head of the group as we set out to walk to the well. He has rope over his shoulder and Lago at his heels and a look of determination that makes me unsure whether to hope or fear for the outcome of his search. Sana watches as more join him.

"He is wasting your time," she calls out, and a few people hesitate. "Go home, do your work. We have sick people to care for. Longsight wants you frightened, paranoid – can you not see that?" A few do fall behind, but I hurry after Fenn. I need to see this for myself.

The walk to the well is a short one. Our breath mists on the early morning air and our faces are grim.

When we reach the well, Fenn and another boy lift the cover, and then a rope is tied around his waist. I hold my breath as he goes over the edge and out of sight. The rope is well tied and is being held by strong arms too, but it feels like when he went under at the lake. We hear his echoing progress and his grunts of effort as he eases himself slowly down. Once he cries out and must slip on the slick wall of the well, but the rope holds fast and he continues down.

And then the sounds stop. No one speaks – they hardly seem to breathe. Each of us waits for a sign that Fenn is OK. All I can hear is my own heartbeat and a buzz in my ears that seems to get louder the longer we wait.

And then, one solitary fly rises groggily from the opening of the well.

The buzzing grows oppressive – it isn't in my head; it is coming from the well. A blur of flies, like a plague, like a cloud of evil, bursts out from the hole and we scatter, crying out at the terrible swarm. A helpless cry erupts and Fenn's friends rush back to the rope. They strain and yell as they drag the rope up, inch by inch. The rope still holds Fenn – but his cries have stopped. I can't look away. Gull screams as a diabolical shape, dark as nightfall, rises up from the mouth of the well, carried aloft by Fenn.

A crow.

A huge crow – we can almost still see past its decay and rot, but it is mostly feathers and bone, beak and claws. And insects. Blowflies, wasps, beetles and larvae ripple over the carcass. The stench is how all your worst memories would smell if they met you at night. I will never get it out of my nose.

Fenn is pulled up and out of the well by the brave souls who can bear to go near. He drops to the ground and retches.

"Who did this?" he gasps. The people are silent – in shock at his terrible trophy and the rage in his eyes. "You know. You all know. Now say it. *Who did this?*"

First it is just a voice or two, but before long the chant goes up.

"Marked! Marked! Marked!"

I don't wait to see what they will do next. I run.

"It could have been an accident," Kasia says that night at fireside, ever the voice of peace. "A terrible mistake. Perhaps someone forgot to replace the cover..." But the majority drown her out and she sits, a look of desperate sadness on her face. When I see Justus glaring at me I stare back, wishing I could shout aloud that I know he as good as killed my mother.

It is only when Sana stands that quiet returns.

"An act so brazen in its cruelty could only come from a singularly devious heart. One who is willing to target the very weakest of our people – a person who wants nothing less than war." Cheers like battle cries rise up and seem to make the fire wilder and more bright. I shiver as I catch my name in the outcry. Sana holds up her hands for silence again. "But that person is not Leora Flint."

Sana waits for the jeers to pass, looking absolutely at ease. "On our return from Saintstone, we feared we were followed." The air is electric with terror. "I thought we had shaken them off. Clearly, I was wrong." She begins pacing then, walking around the clusters of people, their faces upturned, waiting on her every word. I wonder at the elders allowing this – letting her take charge of the meeting again. "This is but a taste of their depravity, and our dead just the first fruits of the terrible harvest they long to reap. It is only a matter of time, now that they know where we are. We must act now."

Someone cries out at this.

"Oh, I know – we are not ready yet." Sana's voice is rich and clear. "But we will be." She raises her hands to calm the frenzied cheers. "Do not blame one innocent child." Her gaze falls on me. "Save your anger for the guilty men who would see our people wiped out. Have patience – you will not be asked to relent for long."

Gull holds my hand as we walk back to the house. It is just us – Fenn has stayed behind, and Tanya and Solomon are nowhere to be seen. The night is cold and dark, and I am grateful for her warm hand in mine, but all I can think is how I have betrayed her.

Traitor, traitor, traitor.

There are no more deaths.

We carry on as best we can, but there is a feeling like we are at the top of the pendulum swing – that moment when it feels almost like a pause, before it hurtles back with ever-increasing power. These are people waiting to fight, they are brave – but I am sick at heart. They don't know their enemy – not really – and although they may be brave and resilient, they can never win.

Fenn, Gull and I are at the storehouse, sorting through the supplies. The riders don't just bring back food: there are shoes and boots of various sizes – all worn-looking. There are a few tools in various states of decay. There is a hacksaw without the blade, which strikes me as a deeply useless thing. Piles of blankets and sheets – there are people sitting to examine them and mend the inevitable holes. I swallow back a rush of guilt that reminds me how these would be considered in Saintstone: rags, fit only for the dog's bed or for mopping up leaks. Now I see these things differently: an extra blanket will be such a blessing for Blake and Penny's new baby. Despising my ignorance a little more today, I willingly crouch down next to Gull and Fenn, and lend my hands to the work.

"You must have had a good laugh when you saw your rubbish leaving the town," Gull says bitterly. "I can just imagine you sending it out to the dump, dirty charity for the rats across the river." She's sorting clothing into sizes and doesn't look up, but she sounds sad – sad and embarrassed.

"Gull, I didn't know. None of us did."

"You know we would look after our own needs if we could." Fenn's voice is cold. I am so used to him ignoring me that I jump, startled. He glares at the pile in front of him, dropping a half-folded pair of trousers on to his lap. "Do you think we like relying on your scraps? But what do we have? We've got this useless land that hardly grows anything. You have the mill and lights and school and food. Perfect land for growing, for grazing. You keep us low, you keep us tired and weak. Sana is right about you." His cheeks are flushed with anger.

"Not me."

Fenn stands and kicks away a sheet with a frustrated sigh.

"You expect us to trust you, as though you haven't come from the enemy?" he snaps, his eyes hard. "If you're one of us then you'd better start proving it."

With that he's off, hands thrust into pockets. Gull and I look after him. I put a hand on her arm. It feels so thin underneath mine. So fragile.

"Blame me if you need to," I say quietly. "Saintstone has treated you terribly. But I am not your enemy. I'm part of Featherstone now."

And I mean it with all of my heart.

On the way back to the house I see a small, alabaster-pale stone and I hesitate briefly before picking it up. I slip it into the pouch that was once Ruth's.

The next day Gull comes home with a tunic, the selvedge ends ready for stones to fill the hem. Gull passes me a needle and we cut thread. I start on the sleeves, trying to create deep pocket hems to fill with stones. And with each stone I add, the weight of it sinks deeper into my lap and I wonder how anyone can believe they have sinned this much.

Sana's next lesson takes place in the stable; she hands me a curry comb and tells me we're grooming the horses. I have no idea what I'm doing; the horses are huge and I flinch when one whinnies at me.

She speaks first. "I understand that Ruth had been telling you our stories, yes?"

"Yes." I concentrate on working a knot out of the horse's mane. "Some of them are very similar to ours... I mean, the ones they have in Saintstone."

"Ah." Sana laughs and the horse she's grooming swings its head close to her. "Well, we'll get on to that, I'm sure. But for now, I'll pick up where Ruth left off. I believe the last tale she told you was about Nate? I know that you call him the Saint." I nod, and Sana looks at me appraisingly, as if trying to work out what will be the right match for me to hear next. "Well, I have a different story for you. One that not everyone knows. Let this be a secret – between you and me."

I nod again, feeling a flare of warmth that I am trusted by someone.

She pats the horse firmly on its flank and begins, her voice low and lulling as she speaks the sacred words.

Chapter Twenty-Seven

The Lovers

What do you do when you're ruled by power-hungry, narcissistic maniacs?

What do you do when one of them is your brother?

Of course, with your brother, Metheus, being told every day by your mother that he was the sun — that he was the source of light and life for all those around him — well, eventually that had to go to his head. After all, the world revolves around the sun — it was only natural that Metheus wanted the world to revolve around him. And when he met Luna, it got even worse. He called her the moon. The moon only shines because of the sun's light. She didn't seem to mind, though.

And that left you and the people. You, together, were only the earth: at the whim of the sun's rays.

The sun and the moon set themselves up as the only truth, the only voices to be heard and obeyed. They needed everyone to love them, worship them, obey them and serve them. And they ruled with all the cruelty of the sun's fire and all the remote apathy of the cool lunar rays.

And the people accepted their rule. Things weren't so bad. Although their minds felt empty, at least their stomachs were full. But you longed for another way. Maybe, if he was the sun and she the moon, then you were the wind. Yes – you were the wind. You could whisper in people's ears without being seen. You could propel them into the path of the truth, bluster around them until the detritus was blown away and they could see as they should. And so, wind that you were, soon you had a group of faithful brothers and sisters. People who had seen the light and knew it didn't shine out of Metheus's backside.

Metheus threw a banquet one day – he was always throwing banquets. Some of your friends came.

As the wine flowed, more boastful and arrogant did Metheus become. He taunted his guests, including your friends. The desire for justice burned in your heart.

A beautiful chest had been brought to the banquet – mysteriously, no one knew who the giver was. It was filled with bottle after bottle of the most delicious wine. As the casket grew emptier and Metheus grew drunker his voice carried across the banqueting hall.

"I am so favoured by the ancestors, they will not allow me to see decay!" he declared. "See how they gave you a ruler so splendid and wise."

"Wise indeed," you murmured, hating him.

He banged the chest on the table.

"In fact," he boomed, "I am sure I am the only man in this room who is flexible and strong enough to fit in this chest."

You couldn't help but roll your eyes. He was not subtle.

But his wife, Luna, only smiled indulgently.

"You are the delight of all the world, my love," she assured him. "What you say is surely true."

"Immortal, too?" you asked quietly. "Able to survive anything? Even … a day in that chest?"

"Three days!" cried your brother. "In fact, put me in this chest, bear me on to the waters and let me die. And three days later, I will be restored to you – I will return, alive for ever."

You looked at your friends and each nodded their heads. He was begging to be killed, and who were you to disobey your lord and master?

Metheus lay down in the chest, keeping one bottle of wine ("for my final journey," he winked) and you each drove a nail into the lid, watched all the time by a strangely serene, smiling Luna. It took many of you to carry the chest and your feet slipped on the muddy banks of the river as you heaved on ropes and pushed him into the rapid waters. You watched as he bobbed a little way downstream before one end began to sink lower and lower, and with a gasp of bubbles the chest was submerged as it was swept along with the furious waters.

You prayed: the whole of creation had seen him boast; seen it

211

was his own wish. You held your hands up for the ancestors to see, you washed them in the river. His blood was not on you. His fool's destiny was his alone.

And so, when you saw him on the third day of mourning, you thought you were seeing a ghost. Pale and thinner, he looked spectral. But you could see from the smile on his face and the laugh in his eyes that all his devious soul was still within him. Luna presented him to the people as a hero returning from battle. For he had fought death and won. He had received the favour of his ancestors and now he held immortality in his veins. You had never loved him, but today, for the first time, you truly feared him.

One night, as you walked past the throne room, you heard voices. You stopped to listen, as you often did.

"Oh, it is good to be divine, my dear." You heard your brother's gloating voice dripping through the cracks in the door. You had to strain to catch the queen's placid reply.

"You didn't hit your head while you were in that box, did you, darling? Divine, indeed! You do remember how the plan played out?"

"Tell me again, my moon. I like to hear the story." You could have sworn you heard her sigh.

"It's no great tale, Metheus, my angel, my light," she said, indulgently. Something in her voice reminded you of your mother. "We planned every nail in that coffin of yours, remember?

Your poor brother's face…" And they both howled with derisive laughter. Soon she spoke again. "My love, glorious you may be, but divine you are not. You were under the water for no time at all. When you sank out of sight, your faithful servant down the river pulled on the ropes and drew you out of the depths. You were no more drowned than I am."

"Ah, but I sank and then by magic I was revived. I remember it, I drank nectar."

"No, dear," said Luna calmly. "I used a hammer and broke you out and you had a cup of tea – remember? You had better not start believing in your own legend."

"I didn't think I would get so tired when I became immortal," you heard him murmur. "But I find I am slipping away again. I must sleep."

"You must, dear one," you heard her say without emotion, and you crept away.

And so you planned another banquet. Your brother would be the guest of honour. His wife was not invited. And you told the truth of what you had heard in the throne room to a few of your friends. Let us feed him wine, you said. And then, when he is drunk, we will force him to admit the truth, in front of everyone. That he is not divine, not immortal, but just a trickster.

Again, there was wine, again there were your friends – those you entrusted with the secret. And again, your brother began to talk.

Metheus spoke of many things. How he hated the poor and the sick – a drain on the kingdom's resources. There would be no more hospitals, no more free schools. Only those as strong and brave as he would be allowed in the kingdom.

"We will determine their strength with a test," he murmured, his eyes bright. "And those who fail … well. They have no place in this life."

You lifted your eyes to the heavens and prayed that the ancestors could see his cruelty and your own innocence.

"Immortality is so very fatiguing," Metheus said, yawning. "You wouldn't believe the stress that is involved in living for ever. I choose clothes every morning and then I wonder why I bother wearing things that will wear out. My own skin is more resilient than any silk or velvet."

"Remove them, then," you snapped, patience worn out. "Let your own body be unfettered."

And he did. He began removing his clothes, a little more drunken madness slipping out with each piece of naked skin. "Why adorn myself with gaudy cloth when my own body is this beautiful? I am invincible; why clothe myself in the rags of mortality?" And Metheus began leaping about the banqueting hall, his faithful people hastening after him to protect his modesty. Your own friends clutched their sides and laughed, and you were delighted. He was proving himself as crazed as you had hoped.

"Why do we eat this animal?" He gestured to the shoulder

of lamb on the table. "Why consume this lowly creature when I am the never-ending one? I can feed you. I can be your meat, my people, and your drink."

"Go on then!" you cried, through your laughter. "Show us how."

And he began carving away his own skin.

You screamed. You struggled to wrest the knife from him, but he seemed possessed of a terrible strength.

So caught up in his own madness was he that he seemed to feel no pain and see no blood. He kept on talking. "Come and taste, come and eat. You will never be hungry again. For my body will not see destruction, it will be restored and you will know that I am the favoured one."

You reached for the knife in his hands, slick and sticky with blood. You wrenched it from him at last. You had only wanted them to hear him boast, to see how crazed and wild he had become. You had never intended for his grandeur to lead to such destruction. He continued to rave and to fight you for the knife until his words began to slip away with his blood, with his soul. And you sat on the ground, clutching his body in your hands, eyes on the sheets of skin that surrounded you; and you could only see the blood on your hands.

When Luna woke and wandered down to breakfast the next morning she saw red footprints wherever she looked. She followed the ruby-red carpet to the banqueting hall and when she saw you still holding your brother, still trying to wrap Metheus in his skin, still praying that the ancestors would show mercy, she screamed.

She confessed to the people that they had been duped, that Metheus's supposed death and resurrection were no more than a trick. That he was no more immortal than they were. She took off her crown and it was buried with their fallen ruler. She left the land, never to be seen again.

And so you came to rule, and rule you did, with wisdom and caution. You warned the people that from that day on no man should ever seek immortality. No man should be the sun; no woman should be the moon. No one should ever think they were better than another. And from that day on, no man would lord it over them; no one would claim to be a king or queen. They would be one, and their skin, intact and beautiful, would be the sign that they belonged to the earth and would never again seek to become the sun, moon or stars. And every year, on the eve of his death, you fell to your knees and mourned the tragic loss of your skinless brother and his poor deluded soul.

Chapter Twenty-Eight

The tale stings like a flaying as I listen. *But that's my dad's funeral story*, I want to say. Only told all wrong. It should be a love story – it should be beautiful. It should show how our skin can be broken and love can last and how our own souls will live on for ever. Not a tale of horror, greed, lust for power.

The difference between our stories is like the light refracted through a diamond. The same prism, but the light thrown and scattered in different directions. And each takes us down a different path and each takes us further and further from each other.

This is the stuff Mel wanted to know – how the blanks and their stories shape their lives and lead them further away from the truth. She seemed to think that if only she could understand them – these blanks and their tales – she would be able to save them. Her faith in the stories is so deep; I wonder if she thinks she could change their minds. Her magic words. Maybe she wishes she could break the spell that has been cast over these people – the one that keeps their eyes closed to the truth.

Sana's face is unreadable as she gauges my reaction. I'm not ready to answer her.

Which one is true, which is the lie? Their story or ours? Or perhaps both are a little true and a little false all at once?

I break the silence. "It's the same as a story my father used to tell me. But not quite."

"Your father told us his version," she tells me, still not looking my way. "But the elders ordered him to stop. It's not worth hearing lies when you know the truth." I look at her quickly; her words remind me of something, or someone. Her mouth is grim.

I want to delve deeper but I don't know where to begin. I tuck my thoughts away, like a stone in my pouch – I'll look at them more closely later. Instead, I coax Sana to tell me more. "Did you like him?" I ask, as we put the brushes away. "My dad?"

Sana pats the horse and brushes hair and dust from her clothes. "Come for a walk." Her smile is back, but strained. I get up and follow her towards the hill where the fire is burning. For a while I don't think she means to answer me. But then she says, "Did I like him? I don't know. He loved my best friend – almost as much as I did." Her eyes are bright as she shares her memory. "He switched something on in her – lit a spark I'd never seen. She was even more beautiful when she was with him. Her laugh, her joy – it was infectious." She smiles and walks more slowly now we are nearer to the fire. "I lost a bit of her when she gave her heart to Joel. I suppose that's how it goes." She swallows and we stop, standing close to the fire, both gazing at the flames. It looks so different in the light. The fire's mystery and power seems muted in the daylight. Even the smell of the wood and the smoke isn't as good.

"And then you lost her completely," I say, my voice quiet against the crackle of burning logs.

"Losing my best friend hurt like nothing I've ever experienced," Sana says.

I want to tell her then – want to say that I know what it's like to lose your best friend. Verity may be living, but she's out of reach. Just like Mum and Oscar and everyone else. Love is the one thing that lures me back to Saintstone. The tantalizing joy of being with people who hold shares in your heart and soul. And now I only have more people to love – more people to hurt and miss and mourn – here in Featherstone.

Love is a bloody business; I don't know why we do it. Except… The look on Sana's face: love's agony is the pain of ink on a needle buried into skin, the necessary sting, and something beautiful blossoming under its touch.

Chapter Twenty-Nine

"Do you even remember what all of these are for?" I ask the next afternoon, a couple of weeks before her birth day, while Gull and I sew stone after stone on to her tunic. I'm teasing her, but she only gives me a brief, distracted smile.

"Oh … lies I've told, things I've done and said that I shouldn't – things I haven't done and said that I should have," she replies, her voice vaguely sing-songy, as though she's repeating words she's been told. "But I try not to remember all the reasons. That's the point. When I gather stones, I can put them in my bag and forget. They are each a moment of penance and purification all at once."

"You sound so serious," I tell her.

"It's serious stuff, though, isn't it?"

"I don't know, Gull. I don't know what I believe any more."

She frowns. "But you're collecting stones? You have a pouch?"

I nod – on the outside I look like I'm as devout as Gull, walking round with this bag round my waist. But I've still only put that one stone into it: a concession for Ruth's sake, I suppose. I don't know how to explain. I can't turn my back on everything I ever believed overnight.

I look up and see Gull's eyes on mine.

"I don't always know what I'm meant to collect stones for," I try to explain. "I feel like I'm looking for things to feel guilty about, and I'm not a bad person, I don't think."

"But you're not perfect." Gull's voice is quiet.

I laugh and try to joke. "How can you say that?"

She frowns earnestly.

"It matters, Leora. Please. You mustn't treat this lightly. You must be pure."

"But at home, that's what all *this* is about." I gesture to my marks.

"You're home now. Home is here."

"I'm sorry." I put down my needle and reach out to hold her hand. "This is hard for me too. I've believed for all of my life that you blanks are the sinners and that we are the righteous. I've been told every day that if I am like you I will forfeit my soul. But then I come here and you've got all the same stories. Only they're not the same. And I don't know who has got it right. And what if neither of us have?"

And, of course, there's no way to answer that. We each have a truth that is impossible to prove. Can both stories be true? Can my marks be beautiful and Longsight's words ugly? Can I believe in some, but not all?

Chapter Thirty

"OK, I admit it." Sana is digging in the garden as I fork compost into a wheelbarrow, and I wonder what I would be doing now if I was in Saintstone – not handling rotten vegetables, that's for sure.

"Admit what?" I ask her, and Sana grins.

"I *admit* that I was jealous of your father when he came to Featherstone. From that first moment it was obvious that your mum had fallen in love – or probably at that point it was just lust. And in spite of all the ink, you could see why."

"Yeah, I don't need to know that bit," I tell her, and Sana laughs, her face creasing with her smile.

"For all that they were deeply wrong, they were still the perfect couple, Leora. I had never believed in soulmates until those two." She lifts her head and I see the tears in her eyes. Hurriedly, she wipes them away. She smiles, a little embarrassed, a little amused. "When I first saw you – I held you." She stops, takes a shuddering breath. "When you were first born, I held you, and I whispered a promise that I would always protect you, that I would never leave you…" She drifts into silence.

"But that it wasn't safe for me to stay?" She looks at me in surprise. "Ruth told me that he – Justus – would have killed us both, and you helped Mum escape?"

Her eyebrows shoot up, as if surprised I know this part. "Yes. I wanted to help – but I failed you both, and for that I will never forgive myself. I only hope that I can help you now, as penance. And that Miranda will somehow know that. For as long as you are with me, you will be safe, and maybe in a strange way she will be too." She grips my hand.

A rider, Helina, runs up to us, feet skidding on the gritty ground as she tries to stop.

"Sana, come now. Quick!"

Fear slaps me then – before I've even seen, before I've moved to follow Sana as she runs to the square. It is as if my soul knows something is terribly, desperately wrong.

Lago's teeth are bared and she is wolfish and snarling, a primal beast rather than a domestic dog. Other dogs bark and scrap, trying to release their owners' hold. White teeth gleam like daggers and their throats resound with hunger for blood. They are all trained on the centre of the town square.

Because there Fenn stands, his arm tight around a boy's neck, his hand twisting an arm firmly. A boy with glasses bent and askew, skin purpled with bruises, blood over teeth making him look like a nightmare. He is the dream I know too well.

"Oscar!" I scream, and run to him, ignoring Sana's hand as she tries to hold me back. Fenn loosens his hold for a moment – shocked, perhaps, at my reaction – and Oscar falls to his knees. I am there just in time, and, as though sensing that her master has lost his grip, Lago's teeth close on my shoulder as I cocoon and shield him.

Oscar.

I barely feel the pain or hear the screams as Lago is pulled off me by someone. I barely register the hands that try to drag me away. All I feel is him. Him against my chest. Him beneath my arms and under my cheek and between my fingers.

Chapter Thirty-One

Somehow, we are back at the Whitworths' house. I have a vague memory of Solomon swooping in and carrying us off. Oscar is lying on the sofa and I still can't let him go. I don't know where Fenn went, but he's not here and neither is Lago.

Gull brings freshly boiled water and clean linen scraps and I wash his wounds. Oscar is unconscious but breathing steadily. Tanya said it was shock and exhaustion and that I shouldn't worry. I worry anyway.

"What did he do to you?" I whisper like a prayer, as though my ancestors or nature or whatever it is I'm meant to believe in now might answer. And just then I think of Mum, and her tending to Dad's head wound when I was small, that terrible injury that threatened to expose everything.

I feel gentle hands on my wrists, and someone – Tanya – takes the linen from my shaking hands.

"Let me, Leora. Please." And she starts to clean his injuries more deftly than I ever could. I rock back on my heels and let Gull stroke my hair and bind the deep bite on my shoulder.

Gull wakes me with tea and toast – I am in her bed again, like my first night here. She reaches out to pass me the mug but I slide out of bed and scramble in bare feet to the room where Oscar lay.

He is gone, and I let out a low, animal moan.

"Leora."

I know that voice, but I am afraid to turn towards it in case this is just a dream.

"Leora," he says again, and he's closer this time, breath on my neck, heat from his body already making my arms turn to goosebumps. A tiny touch – his fingertips on mine – and I know he's real. I twist and hug him and we both squeeze so tightly that we each cry out in pain. He holds me at arm's length, so that I can look into those brown eyes, and he just shakes his head.

"I can't believe it. Leora."

Our reunion is brought to an end by Tanya tutting as she walks in. "You, go and have breakfast," she says to me.

"And you…" Her face is mock-stern. "I've not finished with your bandages; come back to the kitchen, please."

"Mum thinks your injuries are probably more severe than his," Gull says, thrusting food at me once again. "But his just looked worse, you know, because of the blood?" She drinks from her own mug and frowns. "I still can't believe Lago. She has never done anything like that."

I smile weakly, trying not to remember the fear I felt. "She was protecting Fenn." I touch my shoulder gingerly. "She was very good at it," I say as I wince. A realization runs through me then. "You missed the fireside last night?"

Gull nods. "Yes. Mum and Dad did too. But don't worry – I think Kasia did a good job of explaining things – as far as any of us understand what happened yesterday."

"How do you know all this?" I ask, feeling tired and confused and horribly sore.

"Fenn came back after the fireside." I flinch at this, feeling a kind of larva of hate bubble within me, but Gull holds up a hand. "He said he didn't hurt your friend, apart from holding him down to stop him running off. Someone else did that. Fenn said he just found him, dazed and wandering on the boundary of the forest."

228

I say nothing but I raise an eyebrow.

"I believe him," Gull says stoutly. "And anyway, we'll be able to talk to … what's his name again?"

"Oscar."

"*Oscar*, soon enough." She looks at me appraisingly. "Now, Verity I knew about, but why didn't you ever mention Oscar?"

"I…"

"No, don't worry." Gull grins. And she giggles her marvellous, squeaking laugh. "I have to go to work. You finish your toast, OK?"

"He's the one who poisoned the well. He is a murderer and must pay the price." An older man speaks out, to much nodding and calls of *hear, hear.*

The fireside that night is tense before we arrive, flanked by Tanya and Solomon. I know that they will not be easy on any of us; they could turn at any moment. And yet I am so simply happy that Oscar is here that I cannot worry too much. I steal a glance at his battered face and my heart surges in my chest again.

"My children are starting to ask about getting *marks*. Tolerating one of Saintstone's exiles is one thing, but this is unprecedented. Do the elders not care about purity?" It's the woman who is in charge of the food stall. Her children look small and nervous in her shadow.

"If one marked can reach us, then so can a second. Isn't it obvious? Our two marked spies should be returned to where they came from, with a message that Longsight can't ignore," Justus calls out, and I spot Fenn behind him – face unreadable.

Eventually, after accusation and hate have been pounded, nail by nail, into Oscar and me, Sana calls for order.

"You know…" Her voice is low – thoughtful. "This is what I've been longing to see from you." Her gaze skims the crowd. "*Anger.*" Her words pulse with ferocious heat. "At last, you are angry. At last, you are ready not just to whine and complain but to *fight*. Only – you do not wish to fight the true enemy. Instead you clamour for the blood of a boy, without reason or sense. Where are your minds, friends? Where is your vision and wisdom? Honesty – remember that word? Truth and openness are what define us. Let us get to the truth of this matter, or we are no better than the marked themselves. If Ruth were alive to see you like this it would kill her all over again."

I see those who spoke shuffle with discomfort.

"So, let's hear it, shall we?" Sana calls. "You—" She gestures to Oscar, and he steps towards her. "Come and tell us the truth. If you lie, I will not be responsible for their actions."

Oscar looks around the crowd, his first time seeing the whole community together. He bites his lip and breathes deeply before addressing them all. And his words, softly spoken as they are, go off like a bomb.

"I came because of Obel." I see Solomon and Tanya stiffen, become more alert. "We are friends. I am one of the ... crows, you call them. Things have been very bad in Saintstone. The night I set out, he was arrested."

This is payback, I realize. I missed my meeting with the contact. Longsight said he would punish me by hurting those I love, and he has acted as swiftly and ruthlessly as I knew he would.

Oscar goes on. "For all his time amongst the marked, Obel has remained blank. No one except me and Leora knows his marks are faked." His voice does not shake, and I marvel at his composure. "There is talk that he is going to be publicly marked. He gave me instructions to find this place in case anything happened. I never imagined I would need to use them. I saw them take him; he asked me to say goodbye."

Solomon's bellow of grief is almost enough to drown out my cry of horror. And, as though underwater, I watch the ripple of Oscar's words reach every member of the fireside.

Goodbye, I think, and it settles into sense. By not taking on real marks, Obel had always left the door to Featherstone open a crack. If they mark him, he will see himself as cut off for ever.

"He left us," Justus cries. "He washed his hands of us and we owe him not one thing." There is a smattering of applause.

I can't bear this. I catch at Sana's arm and whisper:

"Do something. Please. They will listen to you."

She shakes her head. "This is how we decide, Leora. Not one voice, but many. I cannot force them to do anything."

"You don't understand!" I hiss desperately. "This is all my fault."

Sana frowns then, and draws me aside. The commotion is enough that we go unnoticed down the hill towards the barn.

"What do you mean? How can this be your fault?"

I take a look over my shoulder and make certain that no one else can hear.

"I was sent here by Longsight," I confess. "Longsight sent me here to spy – I was to meet with his contact and tell them what I could. He said if I didn't, then he would hurt my friends and family. And I did as he asked – once. That's how they knew about the hospital."

Sana is shaking her head, her eyes wide.

"Please — I know it's the worst possible betrayal. But I've refused to help him any more — I never went to the second meeting. That's why this has happened. Longsight is punishing Obel to get at me; to make me fall back into line. This is all on me."

A friend with the knack of bringing people round to her way of thinking might have been the best gift my mother could have left me. Sana didn't have to say a word for me to understand the look of sadness and betrayal in her eyes, but she stood by me anyway.

Don't tell the others, she said. Not yet.

The community don't know about my betrayal; they think we are going on a rescue mission out of compassion. But I know that this is penance; I must fix this. First thing in the morning we will set out: Sana and two of her carefully chosen riders, me and Oscar. We'll save Obel. We have to.

Oscar and I meet Sana by the fire as we agreed. It is so early the dawn has not yet broken. She is dressed in her rider's gear: soft leather and cotton in the earthy colours that must hide her well in the forest. She's on horseback and has a horse for both Oscar and me. The riders with her help Oscar and me on to the horses, assuring us that all we have to do is stay sitting in the saddle – the horses will follow Sana's lead. When the other riders – the burly man called Rory, and Helina – are sure that we are all set, they mount their horses and we leave. No one waves us off.

Tanya and Solomon said goodbye, of course, and Tanya gave me a message for Obel.

"Tell him he is loved," she begged as she pressed it into my hand. "And that he can always return. Always." They wished us luck on our journey, and I slipped the studio key that Obel gave me into my pocket and tucked my father's pendant under my shirt, and then I left.

We ride in silence till we are well clear of Featherstone. The woods are different from this vantage point – dizzyingly mysterious – but Sana knows them intimately, you can tell. We pass through them like air. She instructs me as we ride, pointing out every secret sign: a fallen tree, an almost invisible brown shoe hanging in the boughs of a tree, a cluster of stones. At night we build a makeshift camp. My shoulder aches where Lago bit me.

I wait until the hasty dinner is eaten and we're sitting round the fire before saying my piece, which I've been mulling over since we left.

"When we get to Saintstone, I'm going alone." They look at me, startled.

"Leora—" Sana begins, but I hold up my hand.

"It's me that Longsight wants. Arresting Obel is his message to me. He wants me to step back in line. I'll go into Saintstone alone, I will meet with the Mayor and I will face the consequences of my actions. If he thinks I have brought blanks with me, he will show no mercy."

I hear Oscar sigh; I wonder if this is what he expected. His bruises aren't so visible in the woods and his face is half in shadow.

There is a pause after I speak and then Sana nods. Her expression in the firelight is rueful as she looks at me. "We will respect your wishes, Leora. And I admire your bravery. But if we hear nothing from you, we will come for you." It's a fair deal, but I daren't say what I truly fear, which is that none of them will hear from me again.

As the fire begins to turn to embers, the others go to their beds but Sana draws me close and, sleepily, I rest my head on her shoulder as she talks.

"My dad was a rider, and when I was a child our envoy from Featherstone would meet the crows halfway – not far from here. It was safer for us." The dying fire cracks, and it feels like I'm dreaming. "It was different then; less fraught, less fear. It would be almost like a party in the forest and Dad would bring me with him – I knew I wanted to be a rider from the moment I sat on a horse. They would sometimes spend days in the forest, drinking and feasting, telling tales around the fire. There was a boy – the son of one of the crows – who was a few years younger than me and we would sneak away when we got bored of the adults' chat. I liked him, for all that he was marked. We would talk about our lives and our families and share stories."

"What happened to him? Why don't you still meet partway?"

"His father was killed on one of their trips. It was blamed on the blanks..." I nod my head which rests against her shoulder. "After that, things were never the same – they helped us, still, but I don't think they trusted us again. And the boy? Well, he left the crows and that was that. He just left me with memories and stories."

I drift into an uneasy sleep, thinking about all that Sana has shared, and am roused what feels like seconds later. The riders go to fill our water bottles, leaving Oscar and me alone, for the first time since he arrived.

"You can't go on your own," he says urgently, without preamble. "I'm not waiting in the woods while you walk into the wolves' den." His face is worried. I wish I could reach out and touch him, tell him it will be all right. But I have to tell the truth.

"I need to do this alone, Oscar. You brought the message and that was enough – you don't have to protect me. You don't owe me anything."

"Is that what you think? That I'm here out of some sense of … duty?" he says, obviously hurt. "I'm here because of Obel. Because it was the right thing to do. And because…" His jaw clenches and he is quiet for a moment. "Because the last time I saw you I said all the wrong things and I couldn't bear for that to be it. I'm here because I needed to see you." He looks down, flushing. His face, his bashed-up glasses, the mouth that moves so carefully when he speaks, as if each word must be moulded to the right shape.

Before I can stop myself, my hand is moving closer, my

fingertips just brushing his lips. His eyes close and I feel his sigh, hot and hesitant. I let my finger trace the outline of his mouth, wondering what it would be like if he just lowered his chin a little closer. Oscar's hand covers mine and draws me nearer. On my palm, I feel the gentlest of kisses.

A horse whinnies and Sana's voice cuts through the calm. "Are you two ready?" I turn and see her watching us with an expression that is half amused and half something else I can't read.

We're not alone again after that. I have to trust that Oscar won't take any risks. I clench my hand into a fist to stop me from thinking about how his lips felt and from wondering what could have been.

We decide that it will be safest for me to enter the town at night, so we time it so we are passing the outskirts of Morton in the late afternoon, making sure to stay unseen. I try to remember how long it is since I've been home.

As we cross a stream on the edge of Morton, I can just see a house in the distance, and I am suddenly struck by a memory so strong I can almost taste it.

I was off school – I must have been sick or on holiday –

and Mum had to work. She took me with her to a reading at a house in the heart of Morton village. I recognize some of the scenery as we walk. It must be about five years since I've been this way, but not much has changed.

I idolized Dad in a way I didn't Mum – I see that now. Mum was just Mum. I never even thought about her work as a reader. But when we got to the house where the appointment was, she changed in my eyes. She stood taller as she opened the metal gate and walked down the path with confidence and grace.

She didn't need to tell me to follow; I knew from her manner that I should keep close and keep quiet. She shook her hair out and rapped on the door. It was opened by an elderly woman whose marks – that each showed a part of an intricate sewing sampler – looked almost dusty on her crinkly skin. She reached out and held Mum's hand for a second longer than felt normal, and I looked into her eyes. A younger man with greased-back dark hair stood behind her, looking agitated. Her son. I remember he kept smoothing down his bushy moustache, and he didn't hide his displeasure at my presence, but when Mum told him, "She'll join us," he didn't argue.

The house belonged to the old woman, but the man made it abundantly clear that Mum was there at his request. He said more than once that *he* would be providing the payment for the reading; he was paying, so he was in charge. Mum said nothing, but if he had known her – if he were her kid – he would have known to watch his mouth. She wasn't impressed.

"Will you show me the book, please?" Mum said crisply when we had all sat down at a small dining table. The woman placed a hand on the man's shoulder when he moved to get it.

"He was my husband. I'll get him," her voice croaked.

I looked up at Mum and her face softened as she nodded to the woman. With shaking legs, she stood on a step and reached up to the bookshelf, selecting a new-looking book, holding it with tenderness. In a flickering moment I read the ink on her shin – a darning needle, which in a flash became a fish hook that winked in the light, and I saw her then as a creature swimming in a river – a creature who had been caught and tamed. One who never quite felt she belonged here. I averted my eyes when she stepped off the footstool and shuffled back to the table.

"How long since he died?" Mum asked gently.

"It's only been a month," the woman said.

"You must miss him very much," Mum said. I looked at her nervously, worried she had upset the client, but it seemed like she knew the right thing to say. The woman talked about him with a smile at her lips and tears in her eyes. The man shifted impatiently as she talked, but my mum kept her attention fixed on the woman. I wondered – could a fish hooked out of water love her captor?

When the woman had finished, my mum drew the book towards her. "Now," she said quietly. "I am here to guide you through your husband's book. There are things I can see as a reader that you may not have known and that you may not see. But I want to remind you" – she reached forward and held the woman's hand – "no one knows him like you did. I can read him, but you *knew* him. Your memories are true and can never be diminished." The old woman nodded.

"My usual method is to read page by page, telling you what I see. But I suspect in this case" – she glanced briefly at the man – "you have some specific questions."

His words fell over themselves in his eagerness to talk. He was sure there was more money than was mentioned in the will. He was sure it was hidden somewhere, and he wanted to know what had happened. The old woman looked stonily ahead, her grey eyes sad.

Mum nodded assent and took a sip of water. She opened the book and gave a commentary as she read. I read along too, allowing my eyes to relax and letting the marks swirl to life, ears ready to listen to any hidden secrets. Mum read clearly and accurately, but when she reached his family tree, she paused just for one second, and then ever so gently put her foot over mine, and I knew it was a message. I read the tree as she described what she saw, and there was one thing that for a moment made me pause. At the base of the tree it looked like a small hole had been dug. But when I blinked again, it had disappeared.

I waited for Mum to tell them this but she turned the page without mentioning it. She eased her foot from mine.

At the end of the reading, the man let out a brief sigh of disappointment and then rose to get our payment. As soon as he was gone, Mum drew the woman aside, speaking quickly and quietly. There *was* money hidden, but it had been hidden for her and her alone. Mum whispered urgently that he had intended them to use it together. And I have an image of this old woman being able to swim freely once again.

"It's an important job, reading," she told me on the way home. "You have to be able to read the living as well as the dead."

I have gone for so long now without reading a soul that I have forgotten how easily it came to me. I have become used to people with nothing to say on their skin. I have become better, perhaps, at reading the other things. But I have a longing now to see Mum – or the woman I will always think of as Mum. To tell her that even though I know now about my birth mum, Miranda, nothing will replace the woman who raised me. To tell her that I understand so much more; that I see now that every time she frustrated me, shut me down, denied me answers, she just wanted me to be safe.

As we cross the bridge in the forest between Morton and Saintstone, I taste the fear again. I stand tall. I walk back a different person. A less certain, more curious person. Longsight doesn't know this Leora.

Sana, who has edged ahead, reins in her horse and waits for me. "You're best waiting a little longer," she says, looking at the slices of sky that wink through the trees. "We'll stop here and eat. Dusk isn't far off."

The season has almost changed – it must be full spring now, and in spite of the dulling light, I notice flowers cluster beneath trees, leaves and buds that have appeared, the yearly miracle that always amazed Mum, whose marks were flowers and plants. She would tell me the names of the flowers and trees and gather little specimens to take home and stick in a jam jar. And I would wonder which would be the next one to grace her skin.

Chapter Thirty-Two

"You won't follow me?" It's more of a command than a question, and Sana smiles at my assertiveness.

"I promised, Leora. You can trust me." She looks concerned, though. "I wish you would let me come, but I understand this is something you must do alone."

As I hug Oscar goodbye, he whispers into my ear:

"I will be looking out for you. Every moment."

I try to speak, to beg him to take no more risks, but Sana tells me to hurry.

Rolling up my sleeves to bare my forearms and wrapping my shawl around my head, I sink back into my marked self. I've spent so long hiding, being discreet, that revealing my marks feels like a call to be noticed. I hope that it's late enough that no one will see me, but if they do, hopefully all they will see is a marked girl walking alone at night – nothing wrong with that.

I will go to the studio first, I think. Obel gave me the

key for a reason; there is something there he wants me to find, I just know it. And then … well, it's me Longsight wants, or the information I can give him, at least. He'll let Obel go if he has me, I am sure of it.

I begin to walk. I've dreamed about this: about being back home; walking through these familiar streets. But, in my dreams, I didn't hide in alleyways or keep to the backstreets. The night is cool, and sporadic spots of rain fall like reluctant tears. My feet are heavy and the distance seems longer than I remembered; every sound feels like a threat, but it's just a cat or someone putting out their rubbish. I imagine just for a moment that this has all been a bad dream. That I could go home, clamber into my own bed and see Mum in the morning.

Close to town someone walks down the street and passes close enough for me to smell their cologne. But he doesn't look twice – I am dull enough to go unnoticed – my ink is just camouflage that lets others know I belong.

I walk down an alleyway and arrive at the door that leads right into the back room. The lights are off, of course, and I wonder how long it's been since anyone came this way. The key fits, just like always, and I think of the story of Nate with the key to the world of the blanks, intruding so easily. I lock the door behind me, letting the key fall back around my neck.

Everything is spotless, as always. I put the kettle on the single burner; it's automatic, like muscle memory or the knowledge that if he were here, it's what Obel would do. If I know Obel, he would have seen his arrest coming – he would leave some message, somehow. But there's nothing. I take down the old *Encyclopaedia of Tales*, unwrapping it from its protective cloth. This book is so precious, so ancient. It is like a paper version of Mel – a record of our tales and stories. And until Obel showed me this copy, I didn't know it still existed. I open the cover, searching for a note or a clue or anything that Obel might have left. The parchment feels heavy with beautiful illustrations and handwritten text. I turn page after page until I reach the one he made me draw all those months ago – the page with the White Witch, the beautiful Belia – the one that looked just like me. I go to flick this page over too, but it slides out at the touch of my fingers. It has been cut, this perfect book purposefully defaced. I hold it up to the light to see if there is a message, but I see nothing but the naked woman.

What does this mean? I whisper. *Am I meant to know what this is about?*

I lift the book, intending to shake it to see if there are any other loose pages, but something makes me stop – a feeling that I am not alone, a feeling of being watched. I roll the paper and put it in my bag and creep away from the store cupboard and into the front of the shop.

The studio space is lit by the street lights outside, and the room is pale and shadowed. The antiseptic smell feels like the embrace of an old friend, instantly bringing back all the memories: my first mark, that day when Karl inked without permission, Obel's silent work as he marked my skin, the cold horror of being forced to ink Jack Minnow. The noise of the kettle rolls like distant thunder. I take another step.

Only when he speaks do I realize I'm not hallucinating.

"I thought I might have to wait a little longer than this, Flint."

Jack Minnow is reclining on the inking chair, hands behind his head, feet crossed, looking relaxed as a well-fed lion.

I stumble backwards, but his languorous voice stops me in my tracks.

"Don't make me chase you, Leora." I turn to face him. He swings his feet to the side and sits, watching me, head cocked. "There really is no point." His smile is humourless and his eyes dead-looking in the gloom.

"Why did you take him?" I ask, trying to make my voice steady. "On what grounds?"

"Obel?" Minnow stands slowly, running strong hands over his waistcoat to smooth away non-existent creases. "Oh, we found a reason. You always can, if you look hard enough." And his smirk is a snarl. "We knew you'd be back for him. We could have arrested the girl, Verity – but how much do you care about her these days?" I swallow down the hurt. "And I couldn't be sure you would come back for your *mother* – not now you have a new family. So … Obel it was. And you came even more quickly than I imagined."

He takes a watch from his pocket. The kettle starts its angry whistle. "We had better be going. We don't want to keep the Mayor waiting, do we? Not at this late hour." I'm frozen to the spot, and it's pathetically easy for him to grasp my wrist and lead me into the back room. Minnow reaches out and switches off the burner, giving a small chuckle. The steam has left the steel backsplash clouded and two words have emerged. The page from the book was not Obel's only message.

LEORA. RUN.

I try to pull away from Minnow while he uses his right hand to lock the door, but his grip is too strong – he only raises an eyebrow. "Stay put, Flint. We wouldn't want that wrist to break. Inkers need their hands, don't they?"

From a distance, we look like lovers, walking hand in hand across the moonlit square.

Chapter Thirty-Three

The government building is sickeningly bright. Jack Minnow leads me down corridors, still gripping on to me tightly. I think I recognize the route, in which case I know where we're heading.

We reach the door to Longsight's office and Minnow gestures me in. Karl is there, my old fellow apprentice, standing tall with his blond hair swept back. He wears black, like all of Longsight's hirelings. He's had more marks since I last saw him; his muscular bare arms make dramatic claims about his achievements. His wrist mark has been added to, I know it – it used to be like mine, showing he was an inker, but now it proclaims him as one of the Mayor's bodyguards. I should have known he would have wormed his way into Longsight's good books. People don't change. Karl stands straight when he sees Minnow, hands clasped behind his back. But when he sees me, his eyes gleam. I glare at him when he steps aside for Minnow and me to go through the door into Mayor Longsight's study.

"Well, isn't this nice?" Longsight is sitting at his desk; he actually looks tired. Usually he radiates good health. "You got my message, then?" His voice is silky and he gestures for me to sit. Minnow releases his hold on me and stands just behind the chair.

"There was no message," I say stupidly.

Longsight laughs because, of course; Obel's arrest *was* the message. And I came scurrying home. "My watchmen tell me you even brought friends with you, Leora. How sweet. I wonder if they're still waiting for you in the forest?" He picks up a piece of thick paper from his desk and starts to fold it neatly.

I stay silent, although my heart is starting to pound. I should be afraid, for the others but also for myself.

Longsight continues.

"In case you were wondering, Obel is fine. Behaving himself, or so my jailers tell me. Perhaps he just needed a little … reinforcement." I think of his broken hand and shiver. Longsight keeps adding creases and folds to the paper in his hands. How long will it take for Obel's painted-on marks to fade and for his secret to be exposed?

"So… You missed the second meeting. Your friend Verity was quite reluctant to come and tell me. I think she was worried about you." He laughs. "I told her that I was sure there was a perfectly reasonable explanation for your failure to show up. I told her that there was no reason to think you had been won over by our enemy. That we just needed to bring you here to straighten it all out." He leans back, paper still in his hand, and with an eyebrow raised he waits and watches me. "So, Leora. What information do you have for me?"

I am silent, thinking fast. He raises his hand and I flinch, but all he does is place the folded paper between us — with surprising deftness, he has folded the paper into a bird. A crow.

I clear my throat. "You told me that if I became your spy in Featherstone, you would keep my friends and family safe; but you forgot that my family includes blanks too." Longsight's jaw tightens. "You always told us that the blanks were our biggest threat; that they wanted war at any cost. You've always told us they would destroy us unless we beat them down. I went expecting an army of savages. What I found" — I swallow — "what I found is a broken little town, its people in tatters. They haven't enough food to feed themselves, let alone fight. And you know this! You keep them this way."

He looks at me then, head tilted to one side and blinking fast.

"You lied to us," I continue quietly. "You built the blanks up to be monsters and yet the only threat is from you."

He laughs at that. "Is that what you believe? Oh, Leora – our one-woman soldier for justice. You *are* a treat, you know? It's so refreshing to see a young person with passion – it's hard to come by these days." He sighs. "I think it's your earnestness I like the most; that naïve certainty that you're on the side of the righteous and that if you just shout loud enough, something will change. It's endearing, it *is*." Behind me Jack Minnow shifts his feet, and I can imagine his creeping smile. "The problem is, it's old – it's been done before, and so we can map your journey ten steps ahead of you. Of course you would go to the blanks to save your family. Of course you would take pity on the blanks and decide to take their side, despite everything I warned you about them. And of course, *of course,* you would come home immediately if you thought you could save your hero, Obel." He traces the outline of the leather on his desk and looks at me from the corner of his eye. "You make it so easy."

I look round at Minnow, who is smiling, eyes fixed on Longsight, as though he were a saint. They are both enjoying this moment so much and I'm worried – because I think they might have got me.

"I will tell them," I say. "I will tell everyone here in Saintstone the truth. That the blanks fear us as much as we fear them. That you keep them starved and weak. That you deceive your own people just to gain control."

"Oh, my child! And what if you do? Do you think our people will believe you when you whine to them that the poor blanks are sad and hungry? Do you expect them to show compassion?" I take a breath. "Or will they trust their leader: whose marks are so exemplary, who always acts for their good and fights their corner?" I shift in the chair. He is right, I know he is.

"I have a much better idea, Leora. Something that I've been planning for some time. The whole reason you were sent to Featherstone, in fact. You were never meant to be my spy; what you are, Leora, is the spark that will ignite a war."

I stare at him.

"What do you mean?" I whisper.

"What will happen is this. I call a town meeting, first thing. The good people of Saintstone know something is brewing." He smiles, and I shiver. "I introduce you as our little informant and tell the people all that you've risked to find out the truth about those vile blanks. And then you will tell them *that* truth. The shocking things you've discovered: blanks champing at the bit, hungry for war, filled with hatred, desperate to destroy our ways. Those children who went missing last year – the blanks got them, didn't they? That poor boy who never came home last month, whose body was found in the quarry – the blanks. Those crops that were burned to the ground – well, I could go on. They've been particularly *active* this month." He actually laughs. "You'll enjoy it. The prodigal returns, our hero; the poster girl for the new campaign to preserve our culture. Of course, you'll have to tell them yourself. So that it has a real ring of truth."

I have no words. Because he's right, he's *right*. His word will always drown out mine. It's not truth that matters; it's power. It's telling people what they want and expect to hear.

"I will never lie for you." But my voice quavers.

"Oh, you will say exactly what you're told to say. And do you know what the best thing is, Leora?" I feel myself shaking my head. "The best thing is that you can't go crying back to the blanks." I grip the sides of the seat so that I don't fall. "Because when they hear the truth – that you were in Featherstone as my spy – well, I don't suppose they will be counting down the days until you return."

My arms are shaking and I don't know if I can hold on. Gull, Tanya, Solomon, Fenn – they will all hear this version of the tale, and it's exactly the storyline they expect. That I am Nate, the Saint, come again to undermine them from within. And, worst of all, it's the truth.

Chapter Thirty-Four

They've erected a little platform, big enough for me and the Mayor to stand on. It's right in the centre of the square, next to the statue of Saint.

I've been given my lines and told in no uncertain terms what will happen if I fudge them. Jack Minnow holds out a waistcoat and Longsight slides into it, brushing his hands over his chest and stomach.

"This morning isn't about me and my marks." He winks at me as he does up the buttons – only his strong arms and his striking face are on show. "We've sent word that you have returned. I don't want to distract from the main event."

We wait in the shadowy foyer of the government building, looking out at the crowd that is gathering. I can see Karl by the podium, rocking back and forth on the balls of his feet. He looks sweaty and anxious; probably keen for this big public meeting to go to plan; to look good in front of the boss. His eyes meet mine, and I look away.

I stand with Jack Minnow horribly close to me and Mayor Longsight a step behind, feeling dread build more and more as the scatter of people swells to a crowd. People are chattering excitedly. Fear and lack of sleep keep me dizzy and sick. I scan the crowd, frantically searching for Mum. I'm torn between being desperate to see her, to see if she's OK, and horror at the idea that she will be present to witness my betrayal. Can I do it? Can I be Longsight's mouthpiece? Or can I, at this very last, be brave and refuse to speak his words?

How many will suffer if I don't?

As I look out at the crowd I see a flash of red and I look closer, hoping that it might be Mum wearing her red shawl – but it's a child wearing a red coat, carried on her father's shoulders. I nearly cry then, because just seeing the kid's face wide open with joy makes me feel all the lost hope that is just beyond reach. Another glimpse of red, and I turn – but it's not her; just someone else.

One of the government heavies who has been out there controlling the crowd as they arrive comes to the doors and nods. Minnow takes the cue and steps forward, opening the doors for Longsight and me to walk through. Jack Minnow leads the way, and we walk right through the crowd.

The message is clear, as it always has been; Longsight isn't untouchable and remote – he's with them, one of the people. The platform is closer with every step, and I can hear people say my name, whispering it through the crowd. *Leora Flint*. The steps leading up to the platform seem like a mountain.

Longsight climbs on to the platform and I put one foot on the steps, but Minnow's hand lands heavily on my shoulder.

"Not yet," he murmurs in my ear. "Let him warm the crowd up for you first." I shudder under his touch.

The chatter dies down and Longsight holds out his hands. His smile is warm, as always, but he lets it fall away and then his face is serious.

"People of Saintstone. My friends." He doesn't need to shout; his voice carries widely. "I brought you here to share urgent news – and it is news that you will find hard to hear." He stops, and any whispers or coughs in the crowd stop too. People's faces are anxious. Fear is always close to the surface here.

"As you know, our policy with the blanks has long been one of peaceful segregation. We have allowed them to live according to their ways and beliefs, on the condition that they do not interfere with ours. It was how my predecessors wished things to continue" – he pauses –

"even when the blanks did not always maintain their side of the bargain. Their nature is violent and, as you know, soon they began to encroach on our way of life. Small things at first. Livestock going missing. A poisoned dog. Our convoys waylaid and food stolen."

I think of the run-down band of blanks back at Featherstone, too weak with hunger to stand.

"My predecessors chose to look the other way. To live and let live." He gives a small, sad smile. The smile of someone who knows better.

"And, my friends, that just made them bolder. More daring. Our children went missing. To swell their numbers, no doubt." A sob breaks from the crowd. "Rumours began to reach my ears of a mass uprising being planned, of an attack that would leave us broken. That they had weapons and strength beyond what we imagined. And so I made the decision to send one of our own into Featherstone." He glances at me. "One of our own, who had strayed but was willing to atone for her sins, not just through marks but through deeds. One who was willing to risk her life to bring us valuable information about the blanks and what they are planning."

He pauses and drops his voice, just a touch, but the crowd draw nearer, a surge, all eyes fixed on him. "Because what they are planning, friends, is terrible indeed. We will need all our bravery and all our nerve to rise up – and quash this attack on our values and our liberty. But I will let you hear that from the woman herself." He turns to me again, and his gaze is full of compassion. "I will let her tell you everything. Friends, please welcome with love in your hearts – Leora Flint."

He holds out his hand to me.

And then two things happen. The first thing is, I see Mum. On the other side of the square I see her. She's not even wearing red; she has a purple shawl and her hair is down.

The crowd draws in tightly; they press in on us as though more people have joined it, and the square seems as full as on that awful day when Connor Drew was marked. But I pay no attention to them – all I see is Mum. She is just metres away, and I watch as she picks her way through the people. She hasn't seen me and I don't shout – my voice would only be lost and for this moment I want to soak up the sight; the sight of my mother coming for me. She loves me, she must still love me.

Then the other thing happens.

There's a weird breath of silence, as though everyone has inhaled at once. And then it's like I am twenty people seeing it all. A figure in black clothes, black cloth wrapped around the face, is on to the platform next to Longsight, and they raise their hand up with something in it – it's shining, but I can't understand what I'm seeing. The person shouts something.

"Our time has come! Watch us arise. We blanks fear you no longer!"

Their voice is hoarse, and for a moment I think I know it. And then I hear a man's voice shout, "The Mayor!"

I see it – I see the blade penetrate the fabric of Longsight's waistcoat, plunging deep into his belly. The blood comes at once. More than I would have thought possible.

Longsight drops to his knees. It's his eyes that scare me more than the blood – surprise, turning to horror.

Minnow hurls himself at our broken Mayor with a howl, covers his bloody torso with his own body. Someone close to me screams and I look around, but the person in black has gone already.

The crowd is pulsing like a murmuration; following each other in every direction as though someone knows where they are going, but they're going everywhere all at once and the figure in black is gone, lost in that crowd. Have they been caught or have they escaped?

And then it's as though someone flicks a switch, because in one breath everyone has the same idea. Everyone runs, but they all go in different directions. Some, perhaps, chasing the person with the knife, some going towards Longsight. And I look at him again. He is lavish with blood; it swims from him as though he has plenty to spare. Minnow's hands are on him, stained and filthy with the carnage, his face a mask of rage.

I back away – stepping down from the platform. *Now is my chance*, I think numbly. But I'm not sure whether to run – or where to run. Where is Mum? Wherever I go people roar towards me, and I'm stretching my body, my head, looking everywhere for her. Where did she go, my mum? Someone clips my shoulder as they pass and I am taken down in the tide. I can't predict the rapids or the rocks, and I feel myself sinking. Hands, feet plunging me down in their desperation to get past. A foot hits my jaw and a foot is on my back, on my ankle, on my hand, on my head, and I feel I know what it must be like to be a grain of sand running through the timer, being pushed down and squeezed from every side. I taste blood, feel it rush from my nose, and I know this is it.

Until I find I am rising again. Strong hands grasp me under my arms and my feet hit the ground, pain sizzling through me. I think that death isn't much better than life and I hear the words, "Stay with me. Stay with me."

I look across the crowd for what seems like miles and she's there, blood trickling from her head, and she sees me. Her eyes widen with shock and her arm reaches out to me, her mouth open in a howling cry.

And I am taken away. Broken from her grasp and from her view. An umbilical wrenching that separates us into two once again and I am being dragged, limping, crying, begging, by Oscar. Oscar, whose face I want to touch and whose eyes make me sad and safe all at once and I follow and I keep up and I run run run with my lungs begging for me to stop time. I'm hardly thinking when we reach the woods.

Chapter Thirty-Five

We're clear of the town and I try to make Oscar stop, but he tells me we can't, not here. Blindly, we make our way deeper into the wood until, stumbling and slipping, we almost fall into a clearing and Sana is there, holding two horses, her eyes wide, a spot of colour in each cheek. She gasps when she sees us.

"What – what happened?" Her voice is like a sob.

Oscar is bent double, catching his breath.

"The Mayor was attacked. Someone with a knife – killed maybe, I don't know."

"I don't understand…" She looks between us. "Who…"

"It wasn't one of ours," Oscar gasps.

"And it wasn't one of us…" Her breath is slowing and evening out. She looks at me, dawning realization in her eyes. "Minnow. This is him. He persuaded Longsight to bring you in, back from the blanks, summon a crowd, and then… I was so *stupid*. I should never have let you come. We've been set up."

"It wasn't you?" I can barely get the word out; my teeth are chattering with shock. "It wasn't you?"

"No! I've been here the whole time." She is almost wailing, and the horror on her face saps the final bit of courage in me. "Why would we attack Longsight? They made it *look* like one of us." She paces furiously. "It will have been one of Minnow's people. For years the rumour has been that Longsight is just his stooge, that Minnow used him to get to power but he's been biding his time, trying to turn the people against us…" She groans. "Longsight is a politician; he used hatred of the blanks to come to power – but he doesn't care about us, not really. Whereas Minnow wants us *gone*. Longsight has served his purpose." She smiles grimly. "And now Minnow will get his wish. He can wage war with impunity. That fool Longsight will be a dead figurehead for war."

"The blood…" I whisper. "There was so much blood."

Sana passes round a canteen of water and we all take greedy glugs.

"How were you there?" I ask Oscar. "How did you know to come and find me?"

"It was Karl," Oscar says as he breathes deeply, trying to calm himself. "He's been working with us – with the crows." He catches my eye and grins. "I know – but we came to believe we could trust him. He's changed since you knew him. Anyway, he listened to your conversation with Longsight, and came for us. Sana sent me ahead to see what was going on and I arrived just as the attack happened."

"We need to go," Sana says abruptly. She gestures at the horses. "I sent Helina and Rory ahead of us, back to Featherstone. Hurry, we can't stay here."

In silence, we begin the journey back to Featherstone, back to the place that felt like home for a moment. Sana sets a brisk pace.

I shiver as I imagine our return. The truth that will have to be told about what I was doing in Featherstone and what horror I have brought to them now. The horror of war. I imagine Fenn's dark, angry face. I imagine Tanya's: the shock and betrayal. I can't even bring myself to think about Gull.

It's too much to bear. And so, while we keep moving, I decide to pretend I'm not here. If I'm not here then I don't have to think; I don't have to feel the pain or the tiredness or the coldness that creeps ever deeper with each new rain shower. I hold tight to the reins, eyes fixed on the path ahead, and imagine I am in the treetops. I imagine I am Gull, sitting in a tree watching all this happen. I imagine

I am a bird, flying over and seeing our destination and singing *not far now not far now.* I imagine I am just the wind and that I can pass through it all, that there is nothing behind me, nothing ahead and I don't have to worry any more.

A bird calls, harsh in my ears, and I see a flash of black and white darting through the trees. I try not to be brought back to earth, but the floating feeling of being above and around everything has gone, and there is nothing to do but to go on.

Chapter Thirty-Six

I've never known it to be so quiet at the fireside. We stumbled in just as it was beginning and now Sana is relaying the awful truth. She starts with my betrayal – she told me there was no other way – and she ends with Longsight's death.

"It must have been their plan all along," she finishes. She is exhausted and her voice sounds at the edge of breaking with each word she says, but she forces herself to reply to the questions that come from the frightened community.

"He's dead?" Ben calls out. "Is Longsight dead?"

"I didn't see," Oscar says. "But there was a lot of blood."

Silence. Then Sana continues, her voice rough. "Oh, it sounds like they orchestrated it very nicely, Minnow and his goons. From what Leora said, it sounds as though they created a perfect storm of panic and confusion in the square and pinned it all on us. Helina says that she and Rory were pursued; Rory has still not returned."

Justus speaks up. "You betrayed us," he says quietly, his eyes on mine. "I knew it all along."

There is a long pause and I close my eyes for a moment.

"I'm so sorry," I say wearily.

I have no choice now but to be honest.

To lay myself bare.

"Yes. I betrayed you. Mayor Longsight sent me to Featherstone in the first place." I look at my hands folded in my lap. I can't look up and see their faces. "He asked me to bring him information."

"And you did?" Solomon's voice is so quiet I could cry.

"I had just one meeting with my ... contact." I risk a glance up and wish I hadn't; they all look so stern and so sad. "I told her the truth," I continue. "I told them you could never muster an army; that you had so little—"

"You *snake!*" cries Justus. "You revealed to them just how little fight we could put up!"

"She also told them about the plan to raid the hospital." Sana speaks slowly, as though each word hurts.

"Ruth's blood is on your hands, traitor!" An angry voice calls out and I sink lower, shame overtaking me.

Justus rounds on Sana. "Did you know about this?"

She refuses to be bullied; she meets his gaze squarely.

"Leora told me. I thought we could get Obel back," she says calmly. "Leora had already refused to tell them anything else. We can trust her, Justus."

"Trust her!" His expression as he looks at me is pitiless. "Trust a traitor?"

"I just want to say one thing." My voice cracks. "It's true that I met with a contact from Saintstone and I told them things I shouldn't – that you were exhausted, starving. I thought that if they knew you were no threat, then they might leave you alone. I see that I was wrong." I look around at them all – Gull, Tanya, Solomon, all these people who gave me a home and trusted me. "But I only went back to Saintstone because I hoped I could save Obel – your son. I would have handed myself over willingly if it meant he would be all right. I would never betray you, not now—" I choke. "Not now. This is the only home I have. Please don't send me away."

There is an uneasy silence as I finish, and I see that Gull's eyes are bright with tears.

"Leora, I think you should go," Solomon says, his voice gruff. "We need to talk about this – as a community."

I stand on shaking legs. A community which I am no longer part of. Head hung low, I leave the fireside and go back to the Whitworths' house. I hide under the covers when Gull comes back; I can't bear her disappointment.

I hear Solomon and Tanya come in, and Oscar's voice. They are giving him a bed too.

I feel like I'll never sleep again. My shoulder aches and my heart is beating too fast. So much has happened, and a jumble of images fills my mind. My mother, screaming for me across the square. Longsight, dropping to the ground, his eyes wide with surprise. Minnow's roar of fury. Sana's shocked face, her breath coming fast.

I roll over, force my breathing to slow, and gradually exhaustion takes over. I drift off with thoughts of my ancestors in my mind. Joel. Miranda. "Fear not," they say, "Fear not. Fear—"

I dream that night that I am in a house. It's a house like gingerbread; pretty and sweet. There is a knock at the door and I hear Mel's voice clearly.

"Come on, Little Light," she calls in sing-song tones.

I open the door and look around but no one is there. There are two small cottages identical to mine on either side. From the house on my right comes the sound of someone crying. I go to see if I can help.

I push the door and inside is a marked woman, just a little older than I am. Her ink is exquisite illustration, the story of her life plain to see.

Her face is buried in her hands as she sits by the table. On the table is raw meat, dripping with blood, and potatoes and pumpkin and a bowl of flour.

The woman looks up at me, her face stricken.

"I have all this bounty, but I cannot eat." She weeps. "Help me, please."

I look out of the window, across to the third house, and I tell the marked woman to wait.

I push the door of the other cottage and I see a blank woman, just a little older than I am. The mirror image of the woman in the other house. Her skin is inkless: bare and pink, beaded with sweat, for the fire in the grate burns brightly.

"I have warmth and flame, but I have nothing to eat." She weeps. "Help me, please."

Mel's voice echoes in my ears: "Come on, Little Light."

I wake, sweating and ravenous.

Chapter Thirty-Seven

It ought to be raining. The sky should be low with storm clouds and that high-pressured tension that comes before thunder, which feels like prophecy.

But instead, the kitchen floor is warm under my feet from where the spring sunshine has shone through the windows. I've ventured out of bed knowing it's late, hoping that no one is around.

I make toast – still amazed at there being food in the kitchen. There is butter and jam, and if I could only go back a few days this would seem like heaven. Tanya comes in while I'm standing eating, waiting for the tea to brew, her slippered feet soft on the tiled floor. We stare at each other for a long moment and then she takes a step towards me. She rubs my shoulder and I start to cry. When she bends down to hug me, great sobs shake my body.

"I am so sorry I lied to you," I gulp. "I thought I was

doing the right thing; I'm sorry, I'm so, so sorry." Tanya wipes away my tears and speaks tenderly to me.

"Oh, Leora. I know your heart is good." She strokes my hair, trying to stop me shaking my head and rejecting her absolution. "It's not your fault, love. What's happening now is the fruit of many years of hatred and division." She holds me at an arm's length and pushes my hair back. "It is no surprise that they would use an innocent child to carry out their evil schemes. Not everything can be fixed in a hurry, no matter how much you want it to. You really are your mother's daughter. She followed her heart just like you do – she wanted to bring change."

Following her heart didn't do her much good, though, I think.

"What happened last night?" I sniff, wiping my eyes with my hand. "What did you all decide about – about everything?"

"Well, we've agreed that you can stay – for now, so long as you remain under my protection," Tanya says. She turns as Oscar comes into the kitchen; it's clear from his face that he's been listening. Her warm gaze takes him in. "Both of you. The people aren't happy; you won't be forgiven for a long time, Leora. But you may stay. And as for Saintstone…" A shadow crosses her face and she shrugs. "There is a meeting of the elders this morning. We have to decide whether to fight now, or later."

"You mean…"

"Solomon and Kasia think we should lie low." Tanya sighs. "Muster what weapons we can so that we're ready for an attack and wait it out. I agree with them. To me it seems like suicide to try to start an uprising; Minnow would like nothing better than an excuse to wipe us all out. And some … well, some say that waiting means starvation and death – a slower, more lingering death. They want to attack now."

I don't have to ask who wants that course of action. It has to be Sana, and Justus of course. And I shudder, thinking of the might of Saintstone. Featherstone has no hope.

Tanya forces a smile on to her face. "We will decide among ourselves, and if it is the will of us all, then it will be the right decision," she says, but her brow is clouded and I know what she's thinking.

Whether they attack or stay hidden, Featherstone is doomed. I look across to Oscar and see it in his face too: fear.

Mid-morning, Tanya walks me across the square towards the elderhouse. She says Sana wants to give me my next lesson. Oscar is with Solomon. I pick up white stones on my way and I'm no less burdened; I just feel more heavily laden with my failure.

Tanya leaves me at the steps and I collide with Sana in the corridor, coming out of the meeting room. I can hear an angry murmur of voices within.

Her shoulders are slumped and she moves without her usual energy.

"Leora." Her words seem like an effort. "I'm glad you're here. Come with me." And I follow her down the corridor towards the memory room.

She lets the door bang closed behind us and throws herself into a chair.

"I think today will be a different kind of lesson." Her voice is weary. She gestures to the stacks of boxes on the shelves. "Pick one," she urges. "It doesn't matter which. Take it down and open it up."

I'm reminded of the shelves of skin books in the museum, the ones of people who have died and have no family left to care for them in their homes. I think of the books on that special, secret floor that were the hides of unnamed, unremembered storytellers. I look around, as though there might be a box that looks or feels different to the others, one that calls out to me to choose it. But they are all alike, and so I reach up and place my hand on whichever one is in reach and I take it down. It's heavier than I expected, so

I catch hold of it with my other hand and hold it against my body as I turn towards the table. I place it down – a little too quickly – and wood smacks on wood.

"Go on. Open it." She nods towards it.

"Are you sure this is OK?" I pause and frown.

"You've waited long enough." Sana shrugs. "You told me that Ruth had shared a little of the eradication with you and it's time you knew the rest. It's time you know the reason why we are what we are. And why we need to fight."

Still, I hold back; it feels like I'm intruding.

"Open the box, Leora." When she sees me hesitate again she reaches out and undoes the clasp. I push the lid open. *It's just a box*, I tell myself.

I'm right; it's just a box. A box of things. I see a bent pair of glasses, a little wooden doll, small leather shoes – hardly worn. There's fabric underneath – clothing? An apron? A shawl? I don't know. And then Sana holds the lid up so I can see a label with an inscription. There are four names.

"Mabel, James, April and Ada Jones," I read out loud. "What is this?"

Sana goes to the shelves and takes box after box after box down. Each time, she reads out the names as she opens a box and lays it on the table. Each box is filled with mementoes. A plait of hair, a necklace, a drawing – the paper grubby and almost worn away. I see tools, needles, a tooth – a fang from a dog, maybe. There are pipes and dice and yarn and pressed flowers and a hat so small it can only have been made for a newborn. With each box, the air is thicker with new scents and less air to breathe. It smells of insects and paper cuts and panic and graves and broken bones and bitten lips and held-back tears.

Her held-back fury is obvious now. "These are just some of the people your marked community *resettled*." I daren't speak.

"I know how it's taught, the story you all heard. Religious differences, best to separate everyone. It was *suggested* the blanks leave and join the ancient blank community of Featherstone." She pulls out a card, looks at it and places it back in the pack. "It would be a homecoming, just what everyone wanted: that was the story, anyway. The pretty story. There would be no compensation for the land we left, no provision made for the half-schooled children. We protested of course. Somehow the leaders of the protest vanished though. And then came the day of the *resettlement*." She fans out the cards in her hand.

"This is what happened half a century ago. Listen to me, because it is the truth. This is the story that has been handed down, and we saw it in their eyes, in their faces, in their scars. Now that Ruth has died all of our eyewitnesses are gone – and so we have even more of a duty to make sure the truth is known." She breathes deeply.

"Before dawn, the mob arrived. Their faces and actions hidden by the night. They were armed and they drove people from their homes, with only the possessions they could hold in their hands. They drove people out of the town, into a field where pigs are kept." Her eyes fix on mine now. "They were kept there for weeks, with only very little food and water. The sick became sicker, and were given no medical help. Disease began to spread. But at last – at last the day of the resettlement arrived. The people gathered by the gates, desperate to get out now, desperate to leave this hell. And the gates opened and – they slaughtered them. Like animals." The cards fall from her hands.

"Only the ones who could run fast enough and could hide well enough were saved. Those who survived would return at night, and night after night they gathered what they could – these memento mori – so that we won't forget them. So we won't forget how they were murdered for the sake of your people's ease. Their families couldn't bury their bodies," she says hoarsely. "But at least we have this."

It's too much. The horror of it – the meticulous execution of their plan. I try to think back and remember who was Mayor then. I think it was Beeston Carlisle – a man whose time in power was lauded when we learned about him in school. But then, what I was told at school was lies. The stones in my pouch rattle as I sink my head in my hands. *Nothing can atone for this.*

She is closing each box now, and she places them back on the shelf one by one.

"Why didn't you tell me? Why did Ruth only tell me some?" I whisper. "If this happened, why not tell me the day I arrived in Featherstone?"

She turns, and her cheeks flush.

"*If* this happened?" She takes a step towards me. "Don't breathe a seed of doubt in this room. *This* is what we ran from." She gestures to the boxes. "This is why we keep running and this is why we need to fight. This is the evidence, right here."

I want to tell her about the room in the museum with all the evidence of the evils of the blanks – the exhibits that talk about the blanks' gruesome habit of cutting off the hands of their victims so that their skin book couldn't be complete, the rebellions, the fear. That all happened, didn't it? I want to tell her it's more complicated than she thinks. But anything I say will sound like defence, will smell like justification and – how could I? In this room, there is a whole world of history that I didn't know – history that was kept from us, untold, reworked, suppressed. And it is a horror story like none I've ever heard.

"Do you see why we need to fight? We are desperate. And we can't lose again." Her voice is fierce.

"There must be a way that doesn't mean war," I venture. "I'm sure if the people in Saintstone *knew...*" But my words are hollow. No one there wants to know, I think. They prefer the easy lie.

We thought we were the victims.

"Whatever happens next, Leora – you need to stand. Why do you think Minnow had Longsight killed now? The people of Saintstone have been whipped into a frenzy of fear and hatred this last few months, and now he needed a catalyst. Years of mistrust have come to a head. He will destroy us without mercy. We have no choice but to strike first." She pounds her fist into her palm. "I love these people, do you hear me? They are all that is good in this world. I love them and I won't see us cut down."

And I can't think of anything else to say.

Sana watches my face. "There will be talks. There will be plans. And we need your allegiance. We need you, a marked, to turn your back on them and to stand with us. Tell me now, Leora. Can I count on you to stand up for Featherstone and to fight for justice?" She holds out her hand.

I look at the boxes and can feel every soul begging me to agree, and I stand. I stand and I take her hand and shake it.

Chapter Thirty-Eight

I can't sleep the night before Gull's birth day ritual, and I don't wake when she leaves. It's Fenn who wakes me, knocking briefly on the door.

Oscar is waiting in the hallway and he gives me a bewildered smile.

"Funny moment for a birth day party," he says, and I roll my eyes. He nods at Fenn's retreating back. "I can't help feeling we won't be welcome."

"Gull has been preparing for this for so long." I know he's right though; Gull is barely speaking to me and I don't want to force myself on her. We follow Fenn at a distance towards the lake and then, as we near it, I make a decision and catch at Oscar's arm. "Come this way – we won't be noticed but we can watch from the trees." And I lead Oscar round to a different path that will take us to the other side of the lake. I remove my boots and walk lightly but Oscar crunches through the forest, and I smile at all I've learned from Gull.

We find an ideal place to watch, almost perfectly opposite the gathering of people on the other shore. I see Gull, pale in her white linen, so tall and serious. My breath catches when I see the crowd of people. The gathering is huge – bigger than at Fenn's. Fear of war revives faith, I guess. We hold on to our beliefs and rituals in a different way when we know they are under threat.

Her tunic falls in jagged pulls; she must have finished the sewing without me. All those stones that have been weighing her down for so long. I shake my head with a sigh – at last, she'll be light and free again. I tell Oscar what is going to happen.

When the time comes for the torches to be raised, I see Gull's mouth move, agreeing to the promises she must make, and when she steps into the water, a bird flies over the lake. I am jealous of Gull, I realize – so close to absolution. I want to wade in and meet her in the water. But of course I don't; I keep my mouth shut and stay hidden, and Oscar and I watch as she gets lower and lower in the water. We see her face as she takes a final breath and, in her eyes, so much closer now, I see a flash of fear, and then she sinks down and is gone.

The ripples from where she sank slowly reach the shore on our side, and in silence we watch the still and calm water. It is so peaceful, and in my giddy tiredness I remember the dream I had my first night here. I can taste the slightly scorched scent of black ink; I hear the sound of my fists beating at the glass, and I feel the inky liquid entering my lungs.

I look across the river at the elders and the community and we wait.

And I wait and I wait.

One of the elders shakes their head.

Solomon rushes forward, but strong hands wrestle him to the ground. I hear Tanya scream. And then I see Fenn shoving himself through the crowd. Justus blocks his path and Fenn pushes him out of the way. I lose sight of him in the fighting crowd.

And they wait.

I hear a song rise to overpower the screams, a song from those on the shore. The wind whips their words to my ears, and I hear them say *lost* and *bound* and *gone*.

I break out from my hidden place. I hear Oscar shout something but I keep running. I wade through the water until it is up to my waist, my chest, my neck. There are shouts from across the lake too, but I won't turn back. I take a deep breath and plunge in, heading for the spot where Gull went under.

The cold shocks me into complete alertness. I keep on, swimming to the centre of the lake. I know people are watching, a shadowy host. I hold my breath and sink under the water, eyes open, hands reaching out. Somewhere in this dark and slow world is my friend, and she doesn't deserve this.

My clothes are heavy; with every movement they slow me down and whisper *be still, be still, stay here, be still*. I will not listen, I keep looking for her – keep hoping that the next surge of water will give me Gull.

I have to rise again and breathe, but I take as few gulps as I can risk. All I feel is the cold. My fingers don't feel like mine and my hair wraps round my face.

I can't stop. I swim on, looking left and right through the murky depths, and I think I see a piece of driftwood but it is drifting too limply to be wood and I reach out and I grab her. The tunic is weighing her down so that even in her stillness she cannot float. I rip at it, cursing the seamstress for making the seams so neat and firm. I find the neck and I tear down the middle where the buttons are, and I feel my nails rip too and see little puffs of red as my bloody fingers keep working and like a final gasp the tunic tears open and she is light and free and I hold her and with all my might I swim up. Up is the only word I know right now. Up is the only way, but what if I've forgotten? What if I think I'm going up and really I'm taking us deeper and whatever I do she must be dead. Up up up.

Hands grab me by the hair and rip my face into the air. I heave a breath and wrench Gull's head out of the water. Whoever is next to me guides me, calls my name and says *this way this way*.

Oscar. He brings us back to shore, far away from the side where the blank community is gathered. Then leaves me and staggers with Gull on to the shingle, drops beside her and begins pressing on her chest. I stumble after him but the heaviness of walking in the real world is too much and I'm on my knees. I fall forward and someone else catches me. It's Fenn.

Together we stare at Oscar, working on Gull. Nothing, nothing – and then. Water pours from her mouth and she vomits. And a breath sees its chance and squeezes its way into her lungs and she snatches it, claims it and another and another, and she's crying too and coughing and crying.

I blink again, and it's just me and Gull and Oscar and Fenn, who has a flaming torch in one hand – he must have run all the way round when he saw me go after Gull. I stand, my whole body juddering with the violent shivers that have taken me over, and I turn to look at the blanks on the other side of the lake.

They were going to leave her to die.

And one by one, they turn and walk away, into the shadow of the trees.

Chapter Thirty-Nine

There is a fire.

My face is resting against rough ground and, when I sit, I sway with wicked vertigo that makes me feel like I might sink; like I might go under again. Fresh tears fall from my eyes and I hate them. I hate the way they remind me of the water, the way they come from within me, and I'm scared they won't stop and I will flood the earth.

But there is a fire.

When I wake up again, the first thing I see is Gull. She's here, next to me and asleep on brightly coloured blankets. The fabric that she should have been wrapped in when she came up from the water, triumphant.

The fire is close enough to warm us, far enough away for us to be safe. My hair smells of smoke, which is better than lake. It's just the two of us here, but I see evidence of Oscar – his satchel on the ground – and of Fenn too. He must have gathered up those robes; brought the torch around to the side of the lake where Oscar and I were watching. Gull stirs a little and I try to lean across to check that she's really OK. She looks paler than ever, and her hair is weed-ragged from the water. I'm dizzy just sitting and my chest feels like someone punched me in the ribs. I doze.

"Are you OK?" Fenn places more wood on the fire, making me jolt upright. His voice is gruff but not unfriendly. Oscar sits next to him, silent and thoughtful.

"I'm fine," I croak. Then: "What are you going to do?"

He stares at the fire, watching it crackle. "We'll have to take her back."

"We can't go back *there*. You saw them – they just left her. How could they leave her?"

"It's not easy to explain. You've not been here long enough to understand." But his voice is heavy with doubt at his own words.

"Well, I understand that you don't just leave someone to die." I'm watching him tend the fire.

"I'm not saying it was right." His teeth are clenched – the fire in his gaze is still there, only I think it's a little less bright than before. "You could never understand. You come and you play at being blank. But you're not one of us."

"Then why are you here?" Somewhere along the line I have stopped being scared of Fenn. "Why didn't you stand there and watch her drown, like the rest of them?"

He is silent, poking the fire.

"That lake would have been her grave. Is that really what your beliefs require?"

There's a pause while Fenn rescues a piece of wood that is about to fall. Then: "Obel never told you why he left, did he?"

"Obel doesn't tell anyone anything," I say honestly.

Fenn laughs bitterly.

"He's an awkward swine."

Fenn sits on the blanket next to me, crossing his long legs. He takes a flask and drinks, then hands it to me. Then he begins to speak, almost dreamily, and for the first time I see the similarity between him and his older brother. The same slow, deliberate voice. That sense of weighing every word.

"Obel always did everything right. But he did everything wrong too. He did his jobs well, he was nice to people, he always worked hard and showed up at the fireside full of attention and zeal. But ... he had to question everything. You know?" I nod. "Always curious, always questioning. I was only four when he left, but I remember that. He would read our stories and argue with the elders about what they meant. And he was always sneaking off from chores to draw." I shift a little in my seat, imagining that grave, curious little boy, with his sketchpad in hand. "He was fascinated, always, by your bloody ink. He couldn't get enough of stories about Saintstone, about the marks, about what they meant. The stories behind them. He was always trying to accompany the riders to Riverton or Saintstone. A stupid, stupid risk. He'd always get caught by Dad."

"I was too small to think of him as anything other than my big brother, but eventually people began to talk. Anyway, on his birth day the same thing happened to him as happened to Gull." He rubs his hand across his forehead. "He went into the water so sure of himself, and..." Fenn shrugs.

"It was Mum and Dad who went in after him. They brought him out. He wasn't down for long – not long at all." He glances at Gull and his brow furrows. "Not as long as Gull. They tried to convince people it was a mistake – that his foot got caught...

"You know the story of the lake. If someone stays

under the water it is a sign that their sin has not been cleared. It shows that they are cursed and must be left to their fate. They thought Mum and Dad had been blinded by their affection – that they had turned their back on their community in saving Obel. And that in so doing, they had cursed us all.

"They tried to keep it from Obel, but he knew what everyone was saying. And one day he went to the elders and told them he didn't believe they were right about the birth day ritual."

The fire crackles and I hear Gull's steady breathing. It sounds just like Obel. He went away, worked it all out, and when he was ready he would have presented his case.

"Obel challenged them," Fenn says with amused pride. "He said the ritual was never meant to be taken literally. His reading was that it was a ritual of remembrance rather than something they must do each year to atone. Well, *remembrance* – you can imagine how much they liked that. It sounded too much like the words of the marked." I incline my head; I can just imagine how incendiary it must have been. Remembrance rather than purification.

Smoke drifts in Fenn's direction and he squints his eyes, fanning it away. The fire smells different out here in the forest – more real somehow.

"Anyway, this all coincided with a terrible year. We'd never had much, but that season all our fruit trees were attacked by insects, our potatoes came out of the ground rotten. There was water – plenty of water, too much perhaps. But everything else was a failure. And there was a reason for it, people said. A curse brought to our land by Obel, the day he was pulled from the water." He shrugged, his eyes troubled. "I don't know whether they were right. Maybe breaking the ritual *did* bring a curse to our land. But I also know that when you're hungry, you'll look for a solution anywhere."

He's right. Hunger does something to your brain and your conscience. I know that now.

"They talked to him for months, the elders. Mum and Dad. Trying to persuade him that they were right and he was wrong. In the end, Obel told them he would break the curse by undertaking the ritual again. And he walked out to the lake one day, wearing his birth day tunic with the stones still in it. A crowd gathered as he went under. When he resurfaced people were cheering – he was barely under a second.

"But he didn't turn around. He swam on and he emerged from the water on the other side of the lake – where you came out with Gull. He stooped to collect a bundle – he must have hidden his things over on that side of the forest – and we never saw him again." He flings the fragments of leaf into the fire and I watch them blacken and burn.

"They say that from the day he left, the land began to yield something. Not much, but something, and it made people hope. They believed the curse had been broken because Obel had been obedient. He had proved Belia's story. His atonement, his absence – it had fixed all that had been broken." He shrugs. "Until now, I guess."

There is a long pause after Fenn has finished speaking. I clear my throat.

"And you never saw him after that?" I ask, and Fenn shakes his head. He raises the flask in a toast. "To Obel. Who messed everything up and walked away. To Obel. Who might have saved us, but didn't stick around to find out."

I take a long look at Fenn, and it's another piece of the puzzle – all his anger, all his devout obedience and earnest faithfulness – he's been trying all this time to not be another Obel, to prove himself, to save himself. Toe the line. Be perfect. It's a heavy burden to have been carrying.

I pull the flask from his hand and hold it up. My voice

shakes when I speak. "No, Fenn. To Obel, who has done all he can to help you since he left Featherstone. To Obel, who has remained faithful to your ways even while living like a marked man."

"You know, from all I've heard about Obel, I think he would *love* this much attention." Gull's voice is scratchy and her words end in a hoarse cough that leaves her gasping for breath.

Fenn goes over to her. "Come on, we're not having a toast without you. Sit up and drink this, it'll help." Gull sits, supported by her brother, and we pass the flask between us.

"And now it's happened again." Gull's voice comes as a whisper; her eyes are full of fear. "Is our family cursed? Or am I?" Her shaking becomes too intense and I pull her close to me. She burrows her head into my shoulder and her sobs frighten me.

"No one can hurt you, Gull," I whisper to her.

"I should have died. I wasn't meant to come back."

I think back to her tunic, sewn so tightly, not one button undone, and I daren't ask whether she tried to save herself. Maybe she did; maybe the buttons in the water were too stiff. Or maybe she was trying to make things right by— And I hold her more tightly and whisper that I love her, that I'm here and I won't leave her.

Oscar, who has been quiet, stands and stretches. "What will you do now?" It's the question none of us want to think about.

"I don't know." Fenn is gazing into the fire. He smiles. "You know, it's time for the fireside, back home. I've never missed one, not even when I was sick as a little boy."

"Me neither," whispers Gull. Then, "Fenn – we've got a fire – why can't we do it here instead? We can make it just like a fireside gathering at home."

"OK." Fenn smiles at her fondly and Gull claps her hands. "How should we begin? A story?" She nods eagerly. There is some colour in her cheeks, although her eyes are still sad.

"Go on, then, Fenn. You tell us one of your stories," Oscar says. Fenn seems a little embarrassed but he looks at Gull, shining with excitement, and steels himself to begin.

"OK, then." Gull tries to look serious but her grin breaks through and Fenn is smiling back and I can't believe he is here, with two marked and an outcast blank, and I've never seen him look so at peace. "Time for a story. I hope you're sitting comfortably – but if not, there's nothing I can do, so deal with it."

"You two might not like this one." He looks at me and Oscar. "It's a story about power and control. It's the story of how we escaped."

Chapter Forty

The Sleeping Princess

Once upon a time, a king ruled his kingdom. He liked to think he ruled well, but his people lived in fear. They obeyed and served because the alternative meant torture and death. The kingdom grew rich as the people slaved for their king, but it was only he and his queen who saw the bounty, and she was as cruel as her husband.

When the queen became pregnant, a small group – a band of brave ones – began to pray. They begged that this child would somehow change things, that this baby would bring the hope and release they so desperately needed. They had prayed before and their appeals had gone unheeded. But this time they persisted.

They prayed so hard and their magic was so strong that the forces of evil began to worry. Surely the king's rule would not be thwarted? And so, one night, just before the baby was due to be born, a demon visited both the king and queen in a dream. The demon warned them that the future looked bleak and that the baby could bring down the kingdom. The demon told them of the brave band of prayerful worshippers and warned them of the magic that had been laid down as a result.

"The day your daughter pricks her finger with a needle is the day your kingdom is destroyed."

The king and queen woke in terror – staring at the shifting mass in the queen's belly as though it were a monstrous thing. The queen's panic brought on labour – the king gave futile orders: he told her to stop, told her to cross her legs and not let the baby come! But, of course, their daughter was born the very next day.

Now the king was adamant that the curse could not be allowed to take hold.

"We must kill her," he said to the queen. "Let's be rid of this albatross and carry on our days in peace. We shall tell the people the baby died at birth."

And so the queen assured the king that a guard would take the baby into the woods and kill it. But although the queen would not dream of letting her kingdom be spoiled by her own daughter, she could not bring herself to kill the baby. And so, instead, she sent her baby to a desolate place – a place where only the cursed blanks lived. The baby would be cared for by a group of women who – she made them promise – would never use needles. Her child would be safe, for these cursed people lived in a land surrounded by a wall – a wall that her grandmother, Moriah, had built. The queen would make sure the blank women caring for her child had what they needed, but the daughter would never be allowed to leave her confines; and of course, she would never be allowed to see a needle.

And for the next sixteen years all was well, if well meant "as things have always been". The king and queen continued in their cruelty, the people suffered, the daughter was kept within the walls, safe but neither happy nor whole. By this time the brave band of the faithful had dwindled to just one woman – for when prayers aren't answered quickly, people's faith has a tendency to die. But this woman kept on praying every day. She had almost given up hope – after all, hadn't the princess died at birth? Would there ever be a chance for change to come?

And yet through her prayers, the magic was kept alive – the tiniest spark was enough – and the princess began to ask questions.

She asked many things, but one of them – one that made her guardians' faces blanch with horror – was how clothes were made. She was sick of dresses. She wished she could make trousers that she could climb in. She examined the pieces and saw tiny holes, thin thread, and wondered at what magic had brought the pieces of material together. The women who cared for her never told her, and the queen sent new pinafores and tunics each year as her daughter grew.

One day, a new pinafore arrived, and on it was a pocket. And in the pocket was a needle. A negligent seamstress, no doubt. But *the princess kept it in her pocket; she would take it out in secret and examine it, wondering at its shininess and tiny, brittle strength.*

And another day, the thread on her pinafore became loose. It had never happened before and, as the princess watched the thread unravel – over under over under – and the seams come free, she began to see what the needle might be for. And in secret, she began to sew.

With the magic growing ever stronger, the king was visited once more in a dream.

"Your wife has tricked you and the girl lives!" the demon-visitor howled. "Just look at how your daughter thrives. Your downfall is near!" The visitor gave the king a vision and he saw the princess behind the wall, sewing busily, and when he woke he knew he must act.

And so the next night he rode through the woods and found the wall. He used ropes to scale it and crept in to where his daughter slept. He would not see her beauty nor her hope. He could only see his fear; and yet, he could not kill her. Something – magic, perhaps – stilled the blade in his hand. And so, while she slept, the king took up a pair of scissors that she used to cut cloth and swiftly, he cut off each of her dainty fingers – snip, snip, snip – and placed them in a velvet bag around his neck. He stole away through the night, back to his palace, and slept well, knowing he had solved the problem once and for all. Now and then he would pat the bag that remained around his neck and smile.

When the daughter woke, bed full of blood and fingerless, she howled. She called out to the ancestors to save her, to pity her, to vindicate her. And her voice entwined with the old woman's prayers and made the magic even stronger.

That night a mysterious sleep came upon the whole kingdom – including the princess and all those within the walls. Everyone slept so deeply, so dreamlessly, so peacefully that even dawn did not wake them. For good magic takes time.

As the king lay in his bed, snorting in his sleep, the little velvet bag twitched. And then the bag shifted and then the neck of the bag began to be eased open – as though something within knew how to get out. And in the quiet of a sleeping kingdom, a single severed finger emerged from the bag. After it came its sisters, and soon there were fingers and thumbs upright on the king's chest, and magic – good magic – moved them.

Up up up crept the fingers, guided as though by invisible strings, one thumb one finger either side of his nose and they drew together, almost close enough to embrace. And the rest of the sisters stood either side of his lips and did not let them part. No matter how he pulled at them or heaved or struggled, the fingers kept to their posts, and soon he was still and the fingers heard their blood calling to them from behind a great wall.

No one knows how, but in the morning the princess woke to

the blank women screaming that the walls had fallen down in the night. They were free! But the princess did not care about the walls; she only saw that her fingers had returned — and, with neat stitches, they had been reattached. The only clue was the needle between her thumb and forefinger, with its point embedded deep in the pad of the index finger of her other hand. She tugged on the needle and sucked her pricked finger and something — maybe it was magic — told her to stay in the broken-walled town and find her own true destiny.

And soon enough, the people lived happily ever after.

Chapter Forty-One

"We have a story like that one," Oscar says. His voice is eager. I want to shake my head at him – we were so comfortable just then, so relaxed. *Let the stories be,* I think. But I am too tired to move.

I had been piecing it together as Fenn spoke. It's the sister story of the one Mel encouraged me to read before Dad's weighing of the soul ceremony. A story about parents hiding the truth from their child in the hope that they might protect her, forgetting all along that she could have saved herself.

This story Fenn has told is angrier, darker: more of a protest song than a fable.

It sounds like a story that's meant to warn the baddies that they can't defeat the forces of good – not for ever. Magic will save them, if they pray hard enough and long enough. A story about those leaders who will not submit to change – who would murder their own children for the sake of their own power. The blanks aren't so different from us. Not really.

"There *are* similarities," I say, "but it's also completely different." I try to get them to see. "It's got the king and queen and the curse that comes with their baby, but in our story they're trying to save her by locking her up. They're trying to protect her."

And then I realize. "They did everything except tell her about the curse so that she could avoid it herself."

"There are other stories that we sort of share – Featherstone and Saintstone," I go on. I expect derision from Fenn, but his expression is thoughtful. "Yours sound like the stories I've grown up with, only they're like a mirror image, or a reflection in water."

"Do you remember arguing with me about whether the stories were true?" Oscar asks, and I roll my eyes.

"You were so smug – telling me they were just stories."

"You believed them then." His eyes meet mine, and my heart turns over, just like it did that day in the museum. "What about now, Leora?"

"Maybe neither of them are true," I say quietly. "And I don't know what to do with that idea."

I know deep down that I want to believe. I want *something* to be real and true. I believed Mel when she told me I would find my way in the stories of the past. But what if they're only stories and nothing more? And what if so much of their truth depends on the teller?

I let my tired eyes rest, facing the fire as the flames lull and entrance me, and then a quiet voice speaks as though from the burning wood.

"Maybe they're *both* true."

Gull's sitting up straighter. Her forehead is furrowed and her breath is clearly still causing her pain. But she carries on. "One doesn't have to cancel out the other." She stops and looks at us pleadingly. "And aren't those two versions just saying the same thing in the end?"

"What do you mean?" asks Fenn.

"Well, both stories have these people who think they know best." She coughs for a long minute and it takes time for her to recover her breath. "The king and queen who make decisions to try to protect what matters most to them." Oscar's nodding slowly. "But then ... sometimes you need to be left to make up your own mind. And that's what they refused to do. But then ... change happened anyway, didn't it?"

"I don't know," Fenn ventures. "One is this happy kingdom and the other is all oppression."

"If you're not one of the people being oppressed, you can be pretty happy," Oscar says drily. "In Saintstone, people believe that our leaders have our best interests at heart. But then if you question it — even just a little bit — life gets much harder. My dad is proof of that, stuck in an underground prison. And if you question the status quo here, you end up like Obel — an outcast." Oscar looks around and picks up a blanket he cast off earlier. "It's like, if we're all under this blanket." He grins, stands, and tries to cover us all with it.

"Watch the fire!" Fenn says, but he's laughing too. All four of us in a line, the blanket on our laps. I feel a bit silly, squashed with Oscar to my left and Gull on my right.

"Right, well — if the blanket is on you, you're happy and warm and you think everything is all right, don't you? But if you're on the edge and the blanket is being hogged by the others, you feel the cold — you're left out in the elements. It's only the people who are struggling who see the problems. Everyone else can carry on believing everything is OK, because for them, it is."

"And that's why you two are here?" Fenn asks. "This is why you've left Saintstone?"

And I think it is. When I was living like Mum told me to — head down, mouth shut — it was easy enough to feel like Saintstone was a good place, fair and happy. It was only when a bit of cold crept in — when I realized about the forgotten and found out about my dad — that I saw things might not be as just after all.

"Oscar's right," I say. "If you're in, you're in, and you can't see the problems. It's only when you look at it from the outside that you see the cracks."

"But just because there are cracks, it doesn't make it broken." Fenn is defensive.

"I know," I say. But I think of Gull, limp as I pulled her from the water.

"We have to go back," Fenn says quietly, and Gull nods.

"What will happen?" I ask. But no one answers me.

Darkness is fully fallen and we settle down ready to sleep, Gull's head against my shoulder.

Our decision has been made: in the morning, we'll return.

Chapter Forty-Two

"I'm still here, then."

Gull's words force me into wakefulness. I sit up and everything aches. It's still dark. I look around and see that Oscar and Fenn are gone.

"They went to get more water," Gull tells me. "I think it's nearly morning." She shuffles nearer to me and we huddle close.

"I dreamed about it last night, about being under the water." Her voice is quiet. "You should have let me stay under. I could have saved us all. Broken the curse, just like Belia."

I try to get a look at Gull's face in the misty glow of the dying fire. I can see her hands gripping the blanket tightly.

"Gull, enough of this. You've sacrificed enough. Now you get to live, OK?" Gull nods again, not looking at me. I wish I could know whether she believes me.

"OK." She is quiet for a while. Then she says, "Can I ask you a question?"

"I guess…" I say, but I'm nervous.

"So…" she ventures. "I want to know about your marks."

"Oh!" I laugh, pleased and relieved. "I can answer that."

"What does it feel like?" she asks. "Does it hurt?"

"OK." I think about how best to describe it. "So the first marks we're given are the age marks. Imagine it's your birth day. You've got to see an official inker at the government building. Your mum has put some cream on your hand – she says it's magic cream and it'll make it hurt less, but actually when you're older, you'll find out that it was just face cream and it did nothing at all." Gull snorts and nods. "They call your name and you go into this room and sit you on a chair. The inker always says the same thing: *just a tiny spot, won't take long.* But you don't want to put your hand down because you know they'll do it then, and so in the end your mum grabs your hand and holds it down on the surface and nods at the inker. And the inker – it's usually a man but I've been trying to change that – switches the machine on – for years you'll think he does it by magic, but it's a foot pad on the floor, and he dips the needle into this tiny inkwell thing and draws in this little spot on your hand. And then you're done."

"Wow." Gull rubs her own hand. "It sounds a bit mean."

"It really only hurts for a bit." I wonder if I'll ever ink someone again, and the thought that I might not makes me feel desperately sad.

"That's an official mark. But then, there are the marks you choose. They feel completely different," I say wistfully. "It's as though your body has been hungry for something, and as soon as the ink hits your skin that longing is sated. Until the next time. It's glorious. It's release; a kind of untethering."

"But you don't get a choice about the age marks?" Gull asks.

I shake my head. "No. Some the government choose for us. Marks which tell our age, or if we've done something wrong. But they are good for us. In the end. All our marks are for our own good."

There is a hollowness to those words, and I feel like the old Leora for a moment. The Leora who could answer all the questions with the right answer, the one who believed because she had been told it was true. Because whatever has happened, I still believe in the marks and all that they stand for. It's just now I know there's space for more than one story in the world.

We sit silently for a while, both thinking, both holding on to each other. We don't know what's coming and I think we both would like to stay here in the wood for ever. We could build a house and live like sisters.

Gull shifts closer.

"What marks would you make on me?" she whispers.

Chapter Forty-Three

Letting go of Gull's hand, I lean forward and reach towards the fire, which has all but burned out. Gull says my name, but I'm concentrating too hard to respond – looking for just the right thing.

I use a stick to dislodge some of the burned wood, and when I find the right piece I drag it out of the embers and let it smoke a little on the bare ground. The wood that has been burning for so many hours has become charcoal. I dribble the last bit of water on to a clean leaf and test how hot the wood is. It's warm, but if I wrap a bit of blanket round my hand, it's fine to touch. I crush the stick into the leaf, letting charcoal splinter and puff into tiny shards and dust. I used to do this with Dad and was always so amazed at how the heavy wood could turn into something so dark and delicate – almost like stale bread, more brittle than chalk.

I close my eyes. How would I mark Gull if I could?

What could possibly reflect her dreamy nature, her kindness, her seriousness, her spark of spirit and mischief? And I think of her at the top of the tree, looking up even higher, beyond the leaves and fine ends of branches. And I see it. I don't want to mark sins on this beautiful skin – she deserves hope.

"Lie down," I tell her, and she does, her head resting on a folded blanket, her eyes shut as though waiting for the pain. I loosen the blankets that cover her and I lift her arm, freeing it from any fabric and clothing. Her pale skin looks golden in the first gasps of dawn, blonde hairs gleaming on her forearms, her hands relaxed, fingers just slightly curled in. It's like she is asleep – like she is dreaming, and I am the dream she is having. I straighten her arm and let it rest on my lap. I test the skin, as though I am going to tattoo – checking the texture, the movement, the spring of it, and when I brush my fingers across her arm it is like the inside of a beech nut pod – so warm and soft, and I want to bring it to my mouth and sense the smoothness with my lips. I brush the ground to find the right implement and there is a tiny, flexible twig that will be perfect. Dipping it into the charcoal dust, I let it cluster on the end and then I mix the charcoal into the water to make a paste. Holding Gull's arm firmly, I begin to mark.

She flinches at my first touch. "Am I hurting you?"

"No. It tickles," she whispers, with a tiny smile.

I spit into the charcoal to make it inkier and then I go again, imprinting her with all that I feel and remember. And the connection is just the same as if I were using needles. Gull's breath is steady and deep and I wonder if she has fallen asleep, but when I move her hand to get to her inner arm more easily, her fingers grip mine and she strokes my thumb. Her touch makes me forget where I am, and for a while it is like I am back at the studio – connecting once again with a client – being able to read them, and flow through their emotions and memories, hearing their soul, and in a kind of dream I continue drawing tiny dots on Gull's arm. Every constellation tells a story and she is the sky, she is space – the universe – and she goes on for ever.

Wild voices and fast, crunching footsteps bring me back and I drop the twig. Gull sits up quickly and wraps her blanket around her as Fenn and Oscar burst out of the dark wood into the clearing.

"Can't you hear that?" Fenn shouts, and we just look at him, confused. But then it drifts on the wind, over the rustle of leaves or the scuttling of insects. It is the sound of screaming.

Chapter Forty-Four

Nothing could have prepared us for the sight that meets us on our return.

Light is just breaking through and sleep-creased faces stare around the village. Children are crying and covering their ears but they will never be able to forget this sound.

Above the elderhouse door is a crow.

A live crow, wings nailed to the door frame.

In its agony and fear the bird's poor body rises and falls as useless wings try to beat against their moorings.

The crow's screams – for that is the only way to describe the sound coming from this poor bird – the screams are like those of terrified children.

I try to see where the nails have entered its perfect wings, try to work out if there is a way to release them without causing more pain and inflicting greater injuries. The gleaming black beak stabs and scrapes and pierces my hand, but it is nothing – nothing compared to its own pain. I shout for help and someone passes me a clawed tool which I wedge against the head of the nail, trying to tell the crow to be still, trying in every way not to hurt it or harm it. I wrench one nail out, bringing with it blood and feathers. I hold the bird with my hand, pushing it as gently and firmly as I can against the door, and I go to work on the next nail. Its free wing tries to move and it screeches raggedly, twisting its head to try to peck at my fingers. I release the second nail and, freed, it tries to flutter and flap in my hands but its wings are too damaged. I let it down on to the ground but it just hops and caws and screams that terrible, haunting shriek, dragging itself around in circles in awful scraping, fluttering misery.

And suddenly, Sana is beside me. She grasps the protesting bird's neck, jerks her hands quickly, and the flapping stops. And there is silence.

That silence that follows is almost worse than the screams. Sana stands tall and looks around.

"They know where we are."

We step through the door of the Whitworths' house, and

it's like Tanya is waiting for us. She falls on Gull, envelops her in a hug, kisses her hands. Lago is leaping around them and Solomon bursts in, falling to his knees and sobbing when he sees Gull.

"Thank you," Solomon mouths over Gull's head, and then he ducks his head, as though ashamed.

I steal away, retreating into Gull's bedroom, and sit heavily on the bed. I reach underneath it and find my notebook. I turn to a new page, find a pencil and begin to draw again. My ragged hands are sore and blood spots the paper.

Thinking of Gull in Tanya's arms, I draw my mum, her kind eyes and generous mouth, her strong jaw. That hurts too much and I turn the page. I draw Sana in the forest, the shape of her small against her horse. I draw the square that day that Longsight was killed, the assassin, a lithe figure all in black, the bloody knife and my mum's eyes. I draw Gull underwater, mermaidish and serene. I draw the fire at the camp and Oscar and Fenn's smiling faces lit by the orange-embered glow.

And I draw stars. I draw every constellation I put on Gull's arm, and every planet and galaxy that I wish I had time for, and I wonder how a person can hold a universe inside them.

Chapter Forty-Five

Sana is in the memory room when I finally find her, putting something in one of the boxes. I need to talk to her and find out where I stand after what has happened at the lake. She may be the only one who can sway the community in my favour.

She looks over her shoulder as I come in and seems surprised but not displeased to see me. She closes the box and puts it high on the corner of the top shelf.

"Well, well, Leora Flint. You really do have a flair for the dramatic, don't you?" Sana sits and rests her feet on the table, an oddly irreverent act. "Interrupting a birth day ceremony is forbidden, you know. Luckily…" She stretches. "Luckily the elders have other things on their mind. Like war."

She sees my furrowed brow and leans forward. "Oh yes – it's war. That stunt with the crow convinced any doubters that the marked know where we are and plan to attack. The question is … whose side will you be on?"

I stare at her. She seems so angry, almost contemptuous. "I don't…"

She stands with a gesture of frustration. "You have all this power, Leora – more than you even know."

"I don't have power!" I laugh.

"Open your eyes, Leora. See yourself for what you are. You know: born blank and yet marked. Both Belia and Moriah."

I remember Mel saying the same – that in some mysterious way I link the two worlds. She spoke of an old story where the sisters united everyone. Somehow I don't think this is what Sana wants.

"I really believe that you have been sent for such a time as this. Show the marked that you reject their ways. Show your allegiance to us, Leora. We need you. These people need you. And now that Longsight is dead…"

"You think he's dead?" I ask.

"I think so," she says quietly. I remember – all that blood.

"I want to help," I tell her. And I do – the crow was just a warning; it wouldn't take much for Saintstone to destroy this village and I can't let that happen. But if I have learned one thing these past few weeks, it's that no one side is right. I can't turn my back on everything I have believed in my whole life – on everything that I still believe. That would be as wrong as what has happened here today.

"Then trust me," Sana whispers, and I close my eyes. "Leora – I have been fighting for these people longer than you've been alive. I have been getting Featherstone ready for this. Sometimes I've had to make difficult choices, take dangerous paths – but it's all so we reach the right destination. I don't like seeing my people starve. I don't like seeing them in need. But sometimes it's only when you're hungry enough that your appetite for justice really grows. Sometimes—"

That's when Justus bursts into the room. His face is pale and for once there is no complacent smile on his lips.

"It's Rory." He swallows. "He's back. You must come, quickly."

Chapter Forty-Six

They took his hand.

They bound it just enough to stem the gushing blood and they let him leave, so he could pass on a message. He gasps it out to us right there in the square, as Tanya calls for hot water and bandages.

"He's dead. Mayor Longsight is dead." He coughs. "Minnow said to tell you … to tell you that the crow was just a warning. *Get ready*, he said."

Sana nods as though satisfied.

I push past her.

"What about the others?" I ask urgently.

He looks at me, his eyes dark with despair.

"I know nothing specific. Except that he has them. He has them all. Minnow. He has them all." And then his eyes close, exhausted, and he slumps back.

"Why don't they just kill us all now?" Justus is asking at the fireside that night. "If that's what they mean to do. Why taunt us with these ... games?" He has been scared by the latest attack, I think. But he is not so afraid that his thirst for blood has been sated.

Oscar is next to me, and he reaches out and clasps my hand. I feel as though he's reconnected me to something I had lost.

"They are warning us," Sana tells us. Her eyes are bright, feverish in the light of the fire. "They want us to see that they could destroy us so easily. They could have killed every one of us – but instead they leave a crow. They could have killed Rory but instead they took his hand and had him relay a message. They are playing with us and at any time they could stop the game – they have the power to end it."

We are eating together again: mostly bread with mould spots on it that I pick away, and some vegetables in a watery stew. There is enough, for now. But hunger is a memory I cannot forget, and I can't be the only one who fears it.

"We have been warned, not just by this crow." Sana looks at Gull. "You saw Gull's ritual. It was a failed absolution, a sign that we are not honest, not whole. We need to destroy the poison that creeps at our borders. We need to cleanse the land that belongs to us and claim it as our own."

Tanya stands. "Those are strong words, Sana. I do not

know what happened at the lake. But look at us: we are weak and tired and few. We have no weapons. We have nothing on our side but passion and belief. If you lead us to war, then I fear you will lead us to destruction." A number of people clap and call out their agreement.

Sana shakes her head. "We are not as isolated as you think. We are not the only enemies of Saintstone." She looks around, taking in the reaction to her statement. "Saintstone creates its own enemies. You've heard of the forgotten?" Some nod. "The forgotten are those marked who have been judged to have committed crimes so heinous that they forfeit their right to salvation. These rebels are marked with a crow." She looks over at me and I feel my heart start to race. "Leora's own father, Joel Flint, was marked in such a way. Many of us can remember him showing us that mark. Punished for saving one of our own." There are murmurs of assent. "But do you see?" She stops and lets the silence swell, looking at each of us in turn. "In marking its own, in driving them away, rejecting them from the community, Saintstone has created its own enemies." She laughs mirthlessly. "Its own people. People who know the ways of the marked but hate them with all their soul."

I look at Oscar, thinking of Connor locked in his cell. He must be angry. But is he angry enough to turn on his own people? I squeeze Oscar's hand more tightly.

Solomon speaks. "What are you saying, Sana?"

"We can work with them," Sana says.

"You want us to ally with Saintstone's worst criminals?" a mocking voice calls out. "You're mad."

"They are only criminals in Saintstone's terms. These people are no different to us. Soldiers of conscience." The crowd is quiet. "I believe that if we rise up to fight, they will join us."

I turn to Oscar in shock and he looks as astonished as me. Some of the forgotten are good people like Connor, victims of Longsight's cruelty, but others have indeed done terrible crimes. Featherstone should think carefully before we ally ourselves with them.

Solomon speaks and his voice is heavy. "You would risk our lives to ally with the worst of Saintstone. Destroy us all in a war we cannot win."

"A war we *can* win," Sana whispers, her face aglow. Justus turns to Fenn then, expecting to see the light of agreement in his eyes, but Fenn shakes his head and edges closer to Gull. "Do not forget our secret weapon, Solomon." And she steps towards me and I know what is coming and I shiver. She takes my hand in hers and pulls me to my feet. "Leora Flint!" She holds my hand and raises it with hers. "Half marked, half blank. She will be with us, and that will be like a knife to Jack Minnow's heart. She will stand with us, as Belia risen, as Moriah, as the child born both marked and blank. Do you not think the superstitious will turn and flee at the sight? The tide is changing," Sana urges, and for the first time this evening the murmurs that rise around her sound excited. "Longsight is dead – Minnow is using that to his advantage. Well, let's use it for ours. Jack Minnow will not be expecting an attack, not now. He knows us only as weak and broken. Now is our chance to prove him wrong. For too long, the marked have underestimated us. For too long we have been grateful for the rotten scraps from their table. For too long we have been kept meek and passive. No more, I swear it. Together, we will fight. And if we stand together, we will win. A victory not just for us, but so that our children and our children's children do not have to know the privation and the indignity that we have suffered. Who is with me?"

They don't even have to vote. There is no doubt that the people are behind Sana. Justus leads the crowd in cheers and applause. She is lifted on to their shoulders and the jubilant cries drown out even the loudest doubt. As I look around I see only a handful of worried faces. Kasia, holding her head in her hands. Fenn, his dark brows drawn together. Solomon and Tanya, who have a son held captive across enemy lines. And Oscar, his eyes thoughtful as his gaze locks with mine.

All around us, the cries of vengeance rise.

And that is how the war begins.

Chapter Forty-Seven

The Box

There was once a woman called Trickster, who spent her time thinking up extravagant cons that she could play on the people of the land. She had intellect and humour, creativity and courage, but she would disguise those qualities using the cover of her beauty. For she had learned that when people saw her beauty, they would never think she might also be cunning. And that was just how she liked it.

One day, Trickster was bored. Humanity had become wise to her tricks. Things were too peaceful – dull, she thought. There was not enough deception and strife in the world for her liking. She yawned.

"I suppose I will have to create a diversion myself."

She walked the land, thinking and thinking, and a plan came to her. Her beautiful mouth spat out a gleeful laugh. It was perfect.

There were four brothers in the land and each was king of his own kingdom. For a long time the brothers and their peoples lived peacefully; but peace is terribly dull. So, Trickster invited the brothers to a ceremony. Each came at the appointed time, each wearing their best cloak and shiniest crown. The brothers were happy to see each other. They embraced and chatted and joked as they reminisced about their happy childhoods. But each went quiet when Trickster entered the room. She wore red robes and her milk-white skin gleamed as she walked slowly towards the men. In her hands she held a box. She placed the box on a table and smiled at the brothers. Each man secretly felt that she was smiling particularly at him. Each brother wondered what it would be like to kiss those lips.

"You brothers have been toiling," Trickster said, her brow knitted in sympathy. "You sacrifice yourselves for your people and what do you get in return? Nothing but complaint and conflict. You have done faithful work, maintaining peace and caring for the land. I want to reward you." Her delicate fingers stroked the box and the men shivered with longing.

"In this box are gifts – prizes, if you will. I will open the box and, oldest to youngest, you will each choose one of my treasures. When you return to your land, that treasure will be constantly bountiful in your kingdom. Choose well, choose wisely – eternal riches are to be found within." And she eased a key into the lock, turned it gently and, with a sigh, the box opened. Beautiful light shone from within.

The eldest brother stepped forward and his eyes were saucers when he looked inside the box. He took a long time choosing, umming and ahhing until the rest of the brothers grew impatient. At long last he reached into the box and pulled out a great diamond. The other brothers grudgingly congratulated him.

After much deliberation, the second brother put his hand into the box and pulled out a perfect gold nugget. The third brother chose for himself the most splendid of pearls.

While all this was happening, the fourth and youngest brother had been watching carefully. He watched as his kind-hearted brothers grew hungry with greed and more selfish with each new treasure. He watched their eyes narrow and their expressions turn sour. He watched as Trickster goaded them and urged them on. And he saw beyond the glamour to the heart of the woman. He saw her glee at their division and he waited his turn.

When he reached the box, he did not look at Trickster, for he knew she had the power to put him under her spell once again. He gazed into the box and saw two treasures left. One was a bottle filled with purple potion; the label on the bottle read "power".

The second treasure was small and hard to see in the dark corner of Trickster's box. It was a wrinkled, speckled seed: the type you would reject from a packet if you were planting a garden. But the youngest brother took the seed, paying no heed to his brother's laughter or Trickster's suggestion that he choose again.

Each brother went home to his kingdom and Trickster's promise came true. The first king's land was a paradise of diamonds; the second king's land produced so much gold that even the merest beggar became rich; the third king found that the beaches around his land had more pearls than grains of sand.

And the youngest king? His land provided plants, trees, and produce of every kind. There was never a bad harvest and there were always flowers on the table and food in the belly.

Trickster watched the brothers and waited. She didn't need to lift a finger – for soon the fights began. The king who had gold longed only for diamonds and the people whose pockets were laden with pearls begged their king for gold. The king refused, hoarding it like a miser. At night, he would send men to steal pearls and diamonds. And from that day those three kingdoms have been fighting, backbiting, envying and stealing, moaning and murdering. All because of Trickster's gift.

But Trickster knew she had been outwitted by the youngest king, whose land quietly prospered; she even came close to respecting him. And so she let him and his people live in bountiful peace, happily ever after.

Gull tells me this story through tears as we lie in our beds that night.

"So you see," she whispers, "there will never be peace. Not while we can never understand each other and never share."

But all I can think of is that seed. Because it sounds like hope.

Chapter Forty-Eight

"We can't lose again," Sana whispers in my ear, her breath hot and quick.

I wake with a start. For a moment I think I have dreamed her. She doesn't look like she's slept or washed. Gull sleeps soundly in the bed beside mine. Everyone around us is preparing to fight. Weapons are being collected. Houses are put in order. Everyone's wits are sharpened too. Food is scarce again, and this time it's like the hunger is salt on an open wound. I have never seen this community so sharp-eyed, so quick to argument. Even now everyone is at the elderhouse, thrashing out plans of attack.

"Every time it is us who lose," she goes on, talking feverishly, as though picking up a conversation we were already having. "We lose homes, land, mothers, fathers, children, limbs. Every time it is us who are hungry, us who are cold and poor and sick. We could never win. And your mother knew it."

I put a hand out to calm her. I take her wrist and ease her to sit on the bed. "This isn't to do with my mum, Sana."

She pulls away from me and her brow furrows, as though she's working out some horrible sum. "But it is. It's why she left us. Betrayed me – us – with that man." She pushes back her chair. "She picked her side when she picked him over us. She claimed you were born marked. Ridiculous, heartless, deceiver." I am not sure Sana even sees me, whether she knows I'm here. "I was sick when I found out about them." Sana spits her words out. "I couldn't eat again for days – just the thought of her and him and you. Disgusting." I want to put my hands over my ears but I don't. Something tells me I need to hear this.

"I would have stopped her leaving, of course. If I had known." I frown my confusion; *didn't Sana help my mother leave?* "She didn't deserve to escape so freely. I would have done to her what your people did to our ancestors. The treachery can't be forgiven. You can see that, Leora?" She is calm now, her voice almost soft as song – a dangerous magic. I take a step towards the door. I need to get Tanya, I think. Get help.

"My people have spent too long under the yoke of the marked. I had to make them angry. Hunger helps."

Her eyes on mine are, I realize, wild.

"What can I do?" I ask her, stalling for time. "I am who I am, the way I was born. I can't change that now."

"Well, that's true. I'm in an awkward position, Leora. You see, in spite of everything, people believe in you." I edge nearer the door, ready to run for help, and suddenly she is beside me, her hand closing around my arm. "They've heard too many fairy tales, perhaps. For them, you are a sign that in the end we win – that the marked can't stand in opposition for ever. If you speak, they will listen to you." She smiles, a very sweet smile. "We need you in battle. You are the spark that will ignite the powder. We need you on our side through the fire." She finally lets go of my arm and turns towards the door.

"Through the fire, Leora."

That night I dream of a box and a knife and a figure dressed in black.

Chapter Forty-Nine

A knife and a box.

I am woken by stifled whimpers but my dream will not fade. There is something, *something* I need to grasp … but my thoughts are silenced when I see Gull. She is in bed but awake and weeping, writhing in pain.

Gull is clawing at her skin, tears dripping off her chin. When she sees me, she looks in my eyes with such complete terror I can hardly bear it.

"I'm being judged," she whispers urgently. "I'm guilty and the punishment is here." I hold her hands still, fighting against her strength, and I look closely. Beneath the scratches are blisters. Burns, in perfect constellation formation. Livid, raised stars.

It's where I marked her, with the ash from the fire.

"But I don't understand," I whisper, staring at the marks in horror.

"I didn't want them to fade," she tells me.

"Gull. What did you do?"

"I couldn't sleep and I kept thinking how if only I could mark myself I might feel … lighter. Like that day in the forest. So I got some stuff from the fire in the sitting room and I mixed it with water and I…"

My heart sinks. *She made lye*, I think. She has poisoned her skin. "Wait here. We need to get help."

Oscar is asleep on a pallet by the fire, Fenn in the rocking chair. I shake Oscar awake.

"Wake up. I need you."

I lead him into the bedroom. He looks at Gull's arm in horror and when he touches it she cries out in pain. Fenn appears in the doorway, rubbing his eyes.

"What is that?"

"She said she took the ashes from the fire…"

"Lye?" Oscar says. I knew it. The tanners use it on skin, to cure it before it's bound into a book. It can be made using ash and water – and it's horribly dangerous.

"What was she doing with lye?" Fenn says, his mouth hard. He lights a lantern and inspects Gull's arm, swollen with blisters and burns. "What were you playing at, little sister?"

Gull is crying and shaking.

"I wanted a mark, like the one Leora did for me in the forest."

Their eyes are all on me now. "I didn't mean any harm," I murmur, but I am heartsick. I let my pleasure in making marks run away with me.

"We need water," Oscar says. "Now."

The treatment is as torturous as the wound – Gull holds her hand over her mouth to stem the sound of the screams when Oscar pours water on her arm. "It will get rid of the lye – I have to. I'm sorry, Gull. Be brave." His voice is gentle. He wraps her arm in clean bandages.

"How could you, Gull?" Fenn says. "Did you want real marks?"

"No. No, that's not it. I thought I was just making it last a bit longer."

"You used ash, not charcoal," I say. "A mistake, that's all."

And Gull is talking quietly, words overlapping. "It's all so awful here now and I didn't want to lose that feeling in the woods – safe and quiet and peaceful."

"Gull!" Fenn takes her by the shoulders, almost shaking her in exasperation. "None of this has anything to do with you."

"I let them down, Fenn. Like Obel. Until I am gone,

the curse will remain." She crumples into a chair and starts sobbing.

"I'm worried," Fenn mutters. "They're looking for any excuse for violence. They're desperate for a scapegoat. They say they won't go into battle until Gull is absolved."

I look at Gull, weeping in the chair. She can't go through all that again. Why should she risk everything for their stupid superstition?

I think of Sana, her breath hot on my neck. *Through the fire, Leora.*

My dream is tapping on my shoulder.

"Come with me," I whisper to them all, drawing my shawl about me, and when they look at me in surprise I just put my finger to my lips and lead them from the house.

We run across the square to the elderhouse, and I am thankful for the blanks and their trusting nature and unlocked doors. Fenn has brought a lantern and it sheds ghoulish light in the memory room.

I know which box I need and I climb on a step, reach up to the top shelf, and grasp it in my hand. Quietly and quickly as I can, I set it on the table before Gull, Fenn and Oscar.

"What's this about?" Fenn asks.

"I have to know the truth," I say, breathless and afraid.

"We all do." And I steel myself to open the box. "I think I know what's inside."

I click open the clasp, loosen the lid and lift it off. Inside is a creased pile of black fabric. I raise my face and nod to Fenn, sliding the box towards him. He lifts the material, weighs it in his hand. "What is it?" he whispers. And slowly he unravels the cotton and something heavy and shining lands on the table with a crack. A black handle, a gleaming blade and the rusty red of dried blood.

The voice comes back to me like a nightmare:

You cannot hide. The blanks will never be defeated!

The tone of it – the passion; why didn't I recognize it sooner?

There is a noise by the door and we turn. Sana is standing in the doorway.

"The box," she says dully. "Your mother's."

"The attack had nothing to do with Minnow. You did it. You killed Longsight." And I know this changes everything and also nothing.

She shrugs.

"How much longer could we go on?" Her voice is tired. "Being beaten down. How many more years would go by with us grateful for handouts? While the marked grow rich off our land… Minnow gave me an opportunity, that's all." I can only stare at her.

"You're working with Minnow?" I whisper, and she nods.

"We have an … understanding. He told me to wait for a sign – that something would call you back to Saintstone: he made it easy for me. We may be enemies, but we are enemies who want the same thing."

"But why now?" Fenn asks softly, and her gaze lands on him, fever-bright. "Because they stopped feeding us? Was that it – they withheld the food and medicine and you decided enough was enough?"

There is a pause, and Sana's eyes meet mine, and then I know.

For too long, the people here have been numb. Now I want them angry.

Hunger helps…

"I thought Longsight looked confused when I told him how weak you were," I say quietly. "He wasn't starving us, was he?" I take a step forward. "He *was* allowing you to collect food and medicine, plenty of it. He was happy with how things were; you keeping to your land, a nice threat to his own people not to step out of line. He had no interest in a war with the blanks. He couldn't understand why the attacks on his own people were happening – that's why he sent me here. There *was* food and medicine; you just made sure it never reached Featherstone. What did you do with it?" I take a step towards her. "Did the other riders know?"

She smiles, as though pleased that I've worked it out.

"I trusted two of them with the secret – Helina and Rory. They understood. They understood it was for the greater good."

"What did you do with the food?"

She shrugs. "We buried it."

"And the well?" I can hardly get the words out.

"We poisoned it." She nods. "That was all me. I knew what I had to do."

I think of all those weeks where we were desperate for food, medicine. The fear that struck us when the well was polluted. Those who died… I think of the little boy with the big eyes, and Ruth, and my stomach turns.

"You did all this?" Fenn whispers. "We trusted you. I thought you were one of our own."

"I *am* one of you," snaps Sana. "I did this *for* you. Foolish boy – do you not see? If I hadn't taken action we could have remained enslaved for years. Picking over scraps, dying before our time? This is our land, and we shall take it back."

"We'll tell everyone what you did," Gull says bravely.

Sana laughs. "Tell them," she says scornfully. "Tell them. It's too late now. War has begun. Besides, they've been baying for Longsight's blood for months – I was the only one brave enough to do it."

She turns away in the face of our silence. At the door she pauses, and looks back at me.

"I really did love your mother, Leora," she says softly. "Miranda was my best friend in all the world. That was why I could never forgive her for what she did. She came to me the night she left – came to me and begged me to help her escape, with the baby. I told her she was on her own if she chose him over us." She shrugs again, a sad small shrug. "And she chose."

In the cold dawn light, the four of us stand looking back at Featherstone. Clouds of breath puff from the two horses' nostrils.

For a moment Gull looks as though her courage is wavering, and I hold her good hand.

"This is the right thing," I tell her encouragingly. "If you stay, you won't be safe. Fenn's right – their superstition has a hold of them; they were ready to throw you back in the lake. And if they see your marks, I don't know if even that would be enough for them. We have to get away from here; the crows will help us – any that haven't been arrested. They have to." I am not as confident as I sound, but Gull has to believe me; she must leave Featherstone. Oscar backs me up, putting a strong hand on my shoulder. "I will fight for the blanks, every day," I say, and I mean it. "Whether I am Moriah or Belia or Leora Flint or no one at all, I will fight, I swear it. I will convince people of the truth – let them know what the blanks are really like: good, and kind and afraid. Just like they are. Minnow can speak his truth but I will speak mine, and they will hear me."

Oscar's arm holds me tightly then, and I lean into his tall, strong body. I wish I could stay here safe in the lee of him.

Gull wipes her tears. "What will you do when they find out we've gone?" she asks Fenn as she hugs him.

"Don't worry about us." Fenn gives her a fond smile. "We'll be here to tell the truth. They need to know what Sana has been doing. I think they'll listen – I hope so."

I have my bag – inside it is a change of clothes, Obel's key and the picture he cut out for me to find. One day I hope I will understand what that message meant.

Oscar hands me a saddlebag. "Packed a few things for you. There's some food and water too." I take it from him, our fingers touching for a second. And another second. And I am desperate to hold on to him – I want to ask him to come with us. I want to beg him. But I know I can't.

"What will you do?" I say softly, and he shrugs.

"Dad would want me to be here. Maybe I can make all his suffering worth it."

And I won't cry. I won't.

Chapter Fifty

I know my own way through the forest now. We go unseen. We barely stop to rest, and as the sun rises on the second day we take our first steps into Saintstone.

I want the beauty of the dawn to be a sign, to be hope. But all I can think of is the red of the blood in the square, the shine of the blade and the horror in Mum's eyes.

"Keep covered," I tell Gull. She nods, exhausted, afraid and awestruck as she looks around at huge buildings, paved roads, gardens, parks and so few trees. We cut through town. I need to make it to Obel's studio; it's the safest place for now.

The town shows all the signs of mourning. There have been flowers laid at the side of roads as we walk through town, and in all the shop windows there are swathes of black fabric. On all the doors are marks of ash – an "x". This is the official, communal mourning of a person of power.

I am returning to a town with no official leader. Longsight is dead.

This knowledge breathes on the spark of hope in my heart – he's dead and things might be different now. This could mean new freedom. Minnow has his version of the truth, but I will shout mine from the rooftops. I will speak with love, not fear.

I have hope.

As we near the square I hear noise. The funeral preparations will have begun; they must have been working through the night. And his body will be lying in state – on display for everyone to view and pay their respects before his skin is taken and his soul is weighed.

The noise becomes a cacophony; no wonder the streets leading to the town centre are so quiet. Every single member of Saintstone must be here. We stand out of sight and watch the enormous queue of people that snakes from the square into the market. I listen out for the songs of lamentation and the wailing of the people, but even as I strain to hear, all I catch is conversation and excited whispers and – can it really be? Laughter.

The people are not dressed in black, but in their brightest colours.

This is not a people in mourning. They are celebrating.

I push through the mass of waiting people, dragging Gull behind me, and we turn the corner into the square.

The crowd is colossal. The music is triumphant and the people are singing, embracing, crying with joy. I edge forward, sharing smiles with some familiar faces as I get closer and closer to the front.

Leora Flint, the whispers begin.

Not far from the front, the crowd breaks, and I walk between them, a parting of the seas. I look to my left and right, trying to understand this magic.

And then I look up, and I fall to my knees.

"Welcome back, Leora." Mayor Longsight smiles down at me. "You look surprised to see me." He seems bigger than ever – more alive than anyone I have ever seen. He is like the sun king from the story.

He raises his hands and the people are silent. His words echo across the square.

"I was dead." He gazes beatifically at his rapt audience. "But now I live. And see! I will rule for ever." His arms stretch out, the mortal wound in his flesh still visible.

And the people bow down and worship.

Acknowledgements

Amazing editors, Jenny Glencross, Genevieve Herr and Lauren Fortune. I needed you so much and I am so very grateful that you are so gracious and bright and patient and brilliant. I wish your names were on the cover.

Jo Unwin, you are absolutely the best agent I could hope for. Thank you for your kindness, wisdom and humour. I love being part of the brilliant team of JULA.

There is so much hard work done unseen and I am very grateful to copy-editors Jessica White and Peter Matthews, and proofreader Emma Jobling. Thank you to the astonishing rights team at Scholastic: you have all worked wonders.

Olivia Horrox, you are amazing. Thank you for guiding me through the first year of publication with such grace. I would have been lost without you.

Every author hopes their cover will be good, but the covers that the in-house team at Scholastic have created are beautiful – works of art that have been THE reason people picked up the book. Jamie Gregory, Andrew Biscomb, you are magicians.

My Scholastic author friends – you inspire me and make me laugh. Being part of the Scholastic team is a constant thrill.

Special thanks to the 2017 beauts – the other newcomers who have been so fun and supportive as we've walked this path together.

The last year has been a dream. Thank you to the booksellers, bloggers and, of course, readers who have been such champions. Thank you to my lovely book group, the Monday group, to the friends who keep my head above water (Shona, Tanya, Steffy, Julia, Jane) and the incredible array of family and friends who have cheered me on. I am lucky to have you in my life.

And, Dave Buckley. You're still my favourite. I love you.

ALICE BROADWAY

Alice's first book, *Ink*, was one of the bestselling YA debuts of 2017 and was shortlisted for many prizes, including the Books Are My Bag YA category and the Waterstones Children's Book Prize Older Fiction category.

Alice drinks more tea than is really necessary and loves writing in her yellow camper van.

About the author

Dianne Lowther first started learning NLP in 1992 after graduating in Psychology. Since then she has delivered or co-delivered almost 1,000 days of NLP training. Dianne qualified as a Master Trainer of NLP in 2009 and is the author of two self-study programmes, 'Leadership through Everyday Conversation' and 'Use Your NLP'.

Applications of NLP in the workplace have always been Dianne's principal focus. Since forming her company Brilliant Minds in 1996 she has become a sought-after consultant and coach, working with organizations in a variety of sectors including technology, finance, engineering and leisure. At the 2009 National Training Awards, Brilliant Minds won a Welsh Training Award for Partnership and Collaboration with Schaeffler (UK) Ltd on an NLP Practitioner programme for the leadership team that enabled significant improvement in business results.

Author's note

It's important to note that there are many frequently used stories, anecdotes and metaphors employed in NLP. Where I know the source I will be sure to reference it, but my apologies to the originators of any material if I have overlooked them here.

Contents

Introduction

What is NLP?

Have you noticed that people are different? Of course you have. Have you ever wondered how those differences are created? I can explain. If you begin with the fact that most of us have five senses and yet there is far more information available to those senses than we could possibly process – or would want to – then you have the key.

Given that our senses pick up more information than we can actually use, a **filtering** process must be going on in order to feed our conscious awareness with a manageable amount of data. Therefore each of us is aware of only a tiny proportion of what is going on at any one time. In effect, we all create our own highly subjective 'map of the world' inside our own minds. Small wonder then, that two people can emerge from an hour-long meeting with totally different views about what has been agreed or decided!

Neuro-linguistic programming (NLP) is built upon a systematic approach to understanding this filtering process, the nature of the filters – which may include beliefs, values, past experiences and languages – and the extent to which the resulting map of the world is effective.

An effective map of the world is one that supports the achievement of your goals. An ineffective part of the map is one that gets in the way of the achievement of the same goals.

NLP is also concerned with how an ineffective part of your map of the world can be adjusted to become effective. Hence NLP has generated many techniques for systematically changing behaviour, beliefs, habits, negative emotions and so on. It has also given us many equally useful techniques for eliciting information about maps of the world and the ways in which they operate, effectively or ineffectively. And ultimately, all maps of the world are effective at producing results – it's just a question of whether or not they were the results you wanted!

NLP is mostly concerned with **structure** rather than **content**. That means we're interested in the *way* that people think and act rather than *what* they're thinking or doing. This is important because there are observable patterns in the way that people think and behave. When we become familiar with the patterns we can plan our approach to take account of them.

The 'official' Society of NLP definition of NLP is that it is 'the study of the structure of subjective experience'.

The origins of NLP

NLP was developed in the 1970s by Richard Bandler and John Grinder at the University of Santa Cruz in California. Initially, Bandler and Grinder collaborated on a project to identify the structure of influential language used by some of the great psychotherapists of the day. That study yielded not only some groundbreaking insights into the way that language can change perceptions, but also a new method-ology – **modelling** – that could be used to distil the essence of the skills of any person. (Modelling is described in more detail in chapter 9.)

There are plenty of books available that describe the early stages of the development of NLP. My purpose here is to give you an experience of the practical uses of NLP in a 21st-century workplace, so rather than a history lesson, let me give you some food for thought.

THINK ABOUT IT If you were able to figure out the patterns in the way that the people around you behave or respond, and then accurately predict the best way to influence each person, what would that make possible for you?

And if you knew how to create the conditions so that you could work effectively and easily every day, what would that make possible for you?

Is it worth a few hours of your time to read this book and find out?

What's in a name?

With a name like neuro-linguistic programming, it's not surprising that most people prefer to use the abbreviation NLP. However, the full name gives us clues to what this subject is about:

Neuro: concerning the brain and the nervous system

Linguistic: concerning language

Programming: mmm, this is where a lot of people get a bit uncomfortable. When you see 'brain' and 'programming' in the same sentence, what do you think about? Brain-washing? Mind control? I think I'd better explain.

When we talk about programming in NLP, it refers to programmes of behaviour. Habits.

 What did you do between the time when your alarm clock went off this morning and leaving the house to go to work? The same as every other morning after the alarm clock goes off?

The sequence of activities that you go through every morning in getting ready to go to work can be thought of as a programme. Unless you have small children at home (in which case, anything might happen!) then it's likely that you do the same things in the same order every morning. It's a

4

programme that gets you from lying in bed to standing at the front door, bag in hand, ready to go to work. And like anything you can do well, you do it without thinking about it very much.

But think about it now. How good is that programme? Does it result in you standing at the front door, suitably dressed, having eaten a nutritious breakfast, well rested from a good night's sleep and feeling upbeat, positive and ready for your day at work? Or not?

If you're at the front door, still half asleep, not having had any breakfast, badly dressed and feeling stressed, then I suggest that this programme could be improved. Wouldn't you agree?

And even if you're facing the day in the best possible frame of mind but it has taken four hours to get ready, I might still suggest that the programme could be improved.

So a programme is a habit. A sequence of actions that we can do so well we don't have to think about it to do it. Consider some of the things you do well; is it true that you do them completely instinctively, without any conscious thought?

Anything you can do really well, you can do without thinking about.

Without NLP, changing habits is a laborious business. Remembering to do something different, something that doesn't really come naturally, is hard. Finding the motivation to keep doing it until it becomes instinctive is even harder. So if I tell you that NLP gives us the possibility to 'reprogramme' our behaviour with a one-off intervention, would you be interested to know more?

Or would you be a bit sceptical? It's good to be sceptical. I hope that you won't take my word about the information and techniques in this book. I hope you'll experiment with them and find out for yourself. I want you to make your own mind up about how useful NLP can be for you at work.

NLP for work

NLP has applications in lots of fields. In the working environment, I would list four main areas where NLP is useful, although, of course, this is not exhaustive. Once you start to use NLP, you can discover even more ways to apply it to your own work.

Self-management: As organizations get 'flatter', that is, they have fewer levels of management in the hierarchical structure, more managers have more direct reports and hence less time for each one. As organizations grow, more people work from home or on a different site from colleagues, their manager or their team members and so the amount of input from managers reduces even more. To be effective, everyone must be self-managing to some extent.

NLP techniques and principles can support activities such as goal-setting, self-motivation, overcoming nervousness before an important event, conquering mental blocks, improving decision-making techniques and managing self-development.

Communication: This is probably the biggest challenge in any organization, and the size of the challenge increases the larger the organization is. In the face of increasingly 'flat' company structures, greater reliance on technology and the growing support for diversity in the workforce, effective communication is getting harder, and yet is also becoming more important than ever.

NLP can be applied to work out effective communication strategies for different individuals and groups. By using NLP models and questioning systems we can find out a lot about how others think and how best to structure communications to achieve the desired goal.

Learning and developing new skills: The pace of life and business is increasing. In the race for market share, most companies have to be highly flexible and adaptable in order to succeed. This means that the workforce must be highly flexible and adaptable too. People need to be able to learn new skills efficiently, manage change enthusiastically and constantly seek out new sources of competitive advantage.

NLP can be used effectively by organizations to 'model' the key skills demonstrated by the organization's top performers and then teach those skills to other workers. Modelling a skill means finding out not just *what* those top performers do, but also the *way* they do it.

Similarly, for individuals, NLP can help you to formulate a reliable strategy for your own development and learn how to model skills from colleagues, specialists or even public figures.

Dealing with 'emotional baggage': There are an increasing number of people in the workforce who have experienced redundancy, a takeover, relocation, a merger or some kind of violence or harassment at work. Even the best organizations do not always succeed in helping people come through these kinds of experiences with a positive attitude. At worst, a whole organization may end up demoralized and unproductive through a badly managed merger or change programme. Reluctant though we may be to admit it, many people carry these bad experiences with them and this can hinder them from achieving their full potential.

NLP offers some of the best and quickest techniques for acknowledging the personal significance of these experiences and shaking off the negative consequences such as mistrust of employers, anger and distress, low morale, lack of motivation and loss of self-worth. Having moved through the negative effects of the events, the individual is then free to consider the value of what they have learned and apply it constructively in the future.

Overall, NLP offers a structured, systematic approach and reliable, effective techniques for dealing with the most challenging aspects of managing people – and 'people' includes yourself.

1. The NLP language and communication model

I want to begin by looking at a diagram.

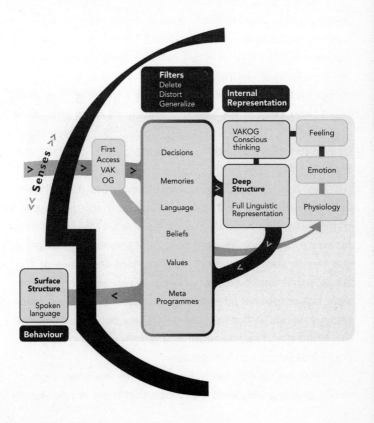

This diagram shows the 'NLP language and communication model'. This is a representation of how we process information via our senses and then respond to what we perceive.

Let's start in the top left of the diagram with information coming in from the outside world and into your senses. On the diagram it looks as if it's coming in at eye level but it is intended to represent all of your senses. The function of your senses is to translate external information into neurological impulses so that your brain can make sense of them. So, for example, your eyes transform different wavelengths of light into different kinds of neural signals so that your brain then creates a pattern of information on the visual cortex at the back of your brain. Each of our senses translates external information into neurological impulses and that's the first level of transformation that happens.

The result of this is the first level of representation, what John Grinder calls 'first access'. You'll see on the diagram that it's also labelled with the initials V A K O G. This stands for visual, auditory, kinaesthetic, olfactory and gustatory – our five senses. One thing it's important to realize at this stage is that the kinaesthetic here is purely sensory information, not emotional information. We don't detect our emotional feelings in the outside world, we only detect things like texture and temperature and weight, so it's purely sensory kinaesthetics at first access.

What we've got here is a first-level representation of reality that is purely sensory. Notice that there are no words at first access. This is the level of perception that a very small child would have before they learn language. But, of course, what makes us human, what makes us different from other species, is that we do have language, and our ability to 'make sense' of things using language is really what sets us apart.

Deletion, distortion and generalization

The second stage of transformation is when that sensory information is labelled with words and it becomes our internal reality. Referring back to the diagram of the NLP language and communication model, you will see the second phase where the sensory information goes through the linguistic filters. Below the 'Filters' heading is a short list of what the filters *do*: they **delete**, **distort** and **generalize**. Below that is the list of what the filters *are*. There are lots of different kinds of filters and the list on the diagram is a representative one: it's not completely exhaustive but it will cover most of the things that we need to talk about. So I'm going to come back and deal with that in a bit more detail, but first let's talk about the idea of deletion, distortion and generalization, because this is what language does.

 When we talk about **deletion**, it's not like you would delete a file from your PC and then it's gone. When we refer to deletion in terms of language it's more accurate to think about it as what we are not paying attention to.

13

Deletion can also happen at sensory level. For example, if you live near a train station or an airport, you probably find that after a while, you no longer notice the sounds coming from the trains or the aeroplanes, but if someone comes to visit they really notice it. 'How do you live with the noise?' they cry and you say, 'What noise?' because it's just disappeared from your conscious awareness. In the same way, we delete things from language that we think we don't need to talk about. Sometimes that's useful, sometimes it can lead to misunderstanding.

The same thing is true of **distortions**. Again, distortions can happen at a sensory level – things like optical illusions – but also distortions can happen in language because sometimes we have a tendency to want to make things fit with our reality. So we might slightly distort the way something is to make it fit in with our preconceived ideas. Then, when we talk about it, we talk about it as if it is the way we'd like it to be rather than acknowledging that in some ways it's slightly different. That's a distortion of the information we're getting from the outside world.

Generalization is the third thing that the filters do. As it sounds, that means making a principle or taking a general idea on the basis of a small amount of information.

When we generalize, we have one or two experiences, we make sense of those, and on that basis, we say, 'This must be true,' in a whole variety of different situations. We're taking information from one context and assuming that it would be true in a lot more. To do this is necessary because if you couldn't generalize, every time you changed your car you'd have to learn how to drive all over again. Every time you went to a different office, you'd have to learn how to open the door! However, generalization is also at the heart of all bias and prejudice, so it's not always a useful process.

So deletion, distortion and generalization have their uses and clearly that's why they have evolved as part of the way we interact with the world, but they also can cause problems if we're not aware of what we're doing.

When the information has come in from the outside world, it goes through two stages of transformation: the first one is at a sensory level and the second level is at a linguistic level where we label our experience, put words to it and literally make sense out of it. The end result of this is what we call our internal representation of reality.

Internal representation, conscious and unconscious

Your internal representation of the world has two elements to it: there's a conscious part and there's an unconscious part. Look again at the diagram on page 11 and see how this is represented. At the top, the conscious area, we've got V A K O G – visual, auditory, kinaesthetic, olfactory and gustatory – again to represent the sensory information that we're consciously aware of. We've also got an added element now, which is our conscious thought process. In other words, it's what we're saying to ourselves.

THINK ABOUT IT

Do you talk to yourself? Some people think that they don't talk to themselves and some people know that they do and are a little embarrassed to admit it. So let me tell you that if you talk to yourself, inside your own head, that's completely normal. Some people even talk to themselves out loud and that's actually not as abnormal as you might think!

Obviously it's a hard thing to measure but informal research suggests that most people talk to themselves more than

16

half the time that they're awake. In fact, the only time that we switch off that 'running commentary' inside our heads is when we're completely engrossed in doing something. That might be just watching a movie, it might be getting engrossed in a piece of work or it might be playing a sport. You've probably heard athletes talk about 'getting in the zone' which is when they stop thinking about what they're doing and just do it. So there are times when we switch off that commentary but often, when we're just going about doing our daily routines, we chat to ourselves inside.

 It can be an interesting experience to start paying attention to what you're saying to yourself because some of us are not quite as polite in talking to ourselves as we might be talking to other people!

What we say to ourselves, alongside all the sensory information, is a very important part of our conscious thinking. That conscious thinking interacts with the other part, which is the representation of reality that's outside of conscious awareness. The experts say that everything that happens to us, every thought that we have, every bit of information that we come across is recorded somewhere in the deep recesses of our brain. Some of that information we can get out again very easily and some of it is more difficult to access. But in terms of relative size, the unconscious part of your mind is very much bigger than the conscious part. You can really only do one thing at a time consciously but always in the background, unconsciously, you're doing lots of other things. That's why sometimes you might go to bed wondering about how to tackle a particular situation in your job and the next morning, thinking that you haven't really moved on very much, you suddenly realize that you've got the answer to the problem because, while you were asleep, the unconscious part of your mind was still working on the ideas.

 Before you go to sleep tonight, set the unconscious part of your mind a task to do. It might be a problem to solve, an idea to create or a decision to make. Explain the task to yourself in the same way as you would pass on a task to a colleague. Notice what has happened when you wake up tomorrow.

You have probably already realized that there's a lot going on outside of conscious awareness. The unconscious part of your mind is also the storage place for everything that you know.

 If I was to ask you for your phone number, even though you weren't thinking about it until I asked, you would be able to answer me immediately because the information comes out of your unconscious storage and into conscious awareness instantly. You can tell me what the number is, and then it will leave your conscious thoughts again.

Thinking about the relative sizes of the conscious and unconscious part so your mind, the metaphor that I like the most is this:

Imagine you are standing in the middle of a large, round theatre, in complete darkness but with a very powerful pencil-beam torch in your hand. Think about how much of the theatre you could light up. It would only be a very small amount at a time. You could light up most of the theatre … but not all at once.

That's what your conscious awareness is like in relation to your unconscious mind, because we can shine the light on a little tiny bit of information, and we can become consciously aware of a small piece in a given moment but, in order to be aware of something else, we have to let go of the first bit of information we were thinking of. There's a huge amount of information available at the unconscious level.

Thinking, feeling and physiology

We've looked at your internal representation of the world in terms of the sensory information and the conscious thought process. Let's have a look at how that interacts with the rest of your emotional experience and your body.

Once again, we need to refer back to the diagram of the NLP language and communication model on page 11. Look at the right-hand side of the diagram. You'll see that there is a connection between what you think and how you feel and then the physiological experience, lower down the diagram. You may also notice that there is a 'back door' route that goes from first access on the far side straight round to physiology. This represents reflex actions – the things that you can't do anything about, whereby as soon as you see or hear a certain thing, you react physically.

For example, imagine you're crossing the road and you suddenly notice there's a car racing towards you that you hadn't previously noticed: what are you going to do? You're going to jump out of the way. You're not going to go through some long thought process about how fast is the car going, the likelihood of it hitting you or whether you have time to move before it does. You're just going to jump out of the way. That's an immediate response: straight from the sensory information to a physical action. What will happen as a result of that? It's probably going to stir up a certain amount of adrenalin and that creates emotion. Emotion is just energy in motion around your body. Some people feel that, and some people don't. But suppose you've just jumped out of the way of a speeding car. Your heart's going to be pounding, and you might feel a bit afraid, or you might feel relieved because you got out of the way. You might also feel a bit cross with yourself for not having noticed sooner. So you're probably then going to say something to yourself. And, as I said earlier, you might say something kind and supportive to yourself, or you might say to yourself, 'Oh, you idiot!' I'm not going to ask you which!

There's a connection between what happens physically and how we feel, and what we then say to ourselves. But there's also a connection in the other direction: what we perceive in the outside world and we say to ourselves in response to that will also affect how we feel and will affect our physiology.

And that's how it is that by watching somebody's body language you can get some ideas about what's going on in their mind and about how they feel. Notice I say you can get *some ideas* because it's not an exact science. Yes, there are some generalizations we can make about what certain gestures and certain positions and types of body language might mean, but actually it's quite idiosyncratic. The people you know best – your nearest and dearest – you'll be able to tell what kind of thought is going through their mind or how they're feeling just by looking at them. The reason for that is that you have a lot of experience with those people; you've got memories of them telling you exactly how they feel that's associated with that particular expression on their face, or that tone of voice, or that gesture or that way of moving. Some people will say that they can walk into their house and look at the face of their loved ones, and know instantly what kind of a day has it been. Somebody even said to me once, 'I can tell by the sound of the footsteps approaching the front door whether or not my partner has had a good day.' We all have the ability to do that. We can all read body language but we're not always consciously aware exactly how we do that, or what it means.

THINK ABOUT IT

Let's go back to your own experience of this because you probably realize that there is a connection between what you think and how you feel and what goes on in your body, and intuitively you probably make use of it. There might be a time when you're working at your desk and your thinking grinds to a halt. You get a bit stuck and you don't know quite where to go next. What most of us do, quite instinctively without really thinking about it, is we get up and move around. Now we might rationalize that by saying, 'I'll go and get myself a glass of water', or a cup of coffee, or 'I'll go and smoke a cigarette', or 'I'll eat some chocolate', or maybe 'I'll just go and chat to somebody for five minutes'. The important thing is that we leave the desk and do something different. And then when we come back to the desk five minutes later, because the body is in a different state, the emotions are in a different state, and then the mind is in a different place, usually we can re-engage with the task and get on with it and make some progress in a way that we weren't able to before our thinking stopped. So we all instinctively know that there is a connection between what we think and how we feel and what goes on in our bodies. Perhaps we don't make use of it as much as we could?

There's also a connection here with physical health, which not everybody recognizes. You probably realize that if your body is not in a good state, it can affect your mood. So most people, if they have a bad cold, will feel a bit less enthusiastic about life than they would if they were feeling really fit and healthy. Have you thought about how that connection might work in the opposite direction? That maybe if you're feeling stressed or anxious, or a bit down about something, does that then make it more likely that you will physically succumb to some kind of problem, whether that's a slight headache, some muscle tension, or something more serious. That's a whole other branch of NLP – looking at how we can improve our health and well-being using NLP techniques. It's clear to me that the mind has something to contribute to the well-being of the body (more about this later).

Linguistic filters

So now that we've had a look at most of the areas of the NLP language and communication model, let's backtrack a little bit to the linguistic filters – that's the big chunk in the centre of the diagram (page 11). These are the filters that we use when we make sense of the world and they're basically to do with language because they're labels that we put on our experience.

Memories: Our memories are an important category of filters because they allow us to make sense of what's in front of us today, in the light of things that have gone before. This is how you can become really skilled in a particular type of work: you go into a new situation, you look at it and you remember dealing with things that are similar if not identical in the past, and that gives you confidence that you know what to do in the current situation. Memories also work on a visual level. For example, if you go somewhere where there are lots and lots of people that you've never seen before, as you look around the crowd, you will see people who remind you of people that you already know. You might think, 'Oh, that looks like Jo from next door,' or 'That person over there looks like Chris from work.' By comparing the faces in the crowd with familiar faces, we're able to make sense of the experience of the crowd more quickly.

If you got to know that person who looks like Jo from next door then they would stop looking like Jo. This is because although initially it's helpful to use memories to help us make sense of what's going on in front of us, at some point we would need to distinguish between Jo and this new person. At that point you start noticing all the ways that they're different from each other. But initially our memories help us to make sense of a current situation.

Memories are a very important category of filters and for a lot of people they're also a source of generalizations. This happens when there is a tendency to assume that what has gone before will happen again in the future. We use our memories to predict what we think will happen in the future and that's not always accurate.

Decisions: The next category of filters is decisions. Every time you make a decision it creates a new filter. You tend to ignore – you *filter out* – anything that might suggest that the decision you've made is not the best one, and you *filter in* anything that supports the decision that you've made. Now you might think that, on the face of it, that's kind of cheating, but consider the alternative. I have met people who do the opposite: they make a decision and then they notice all the reasons why it's not a good decision and they disregard anything that would support the decision they made. That is a really stressful way to live your life!

So, it's easy to see why, as human beings, we've evolved the ability to disregard things that would undermine decisions that we've made. I'm sure you can think of examples where having made a decision, afterwards you needed to justify it. This is known as post-decision rationalization and it's seen at its finest immediately after a bit of impulse shopping. That could be a gadget that just looked so shiny and interesting that you had to buy it, regardless of whether or not it was useful, or for certain sections of the population it applies to shoes. I'm sure you've got your own examples.

REMEMBER THIS!!! Our decisions act as filters because every time we make a decision we adjust reality to make sure that our decision was a good decision.

Language: The third category of filters is language itself. These are all linguistic filters but you may have noticed that people who can speak more than one language will experience more than just the words changing when they shift from one language to another. Sometimes you'll notice that when somebody shifts between one language and another that their whole personality seems to change; that maybe the gestures they use, the tone of voice they use, the level of energy can change along with the language.

Also you'll find that there are certain concepts that can be expressed in one language but can't be expressed in another. For example, we can translate the Spanish word *mañana* into English but it loses the nuance of the original and ends up with a different meaning. As a consequence, if you can't express something in words then you can't experience the idea. So that means that the cultures that define the languages very much stay separate until people start bringing new language into a culture.

In the English language we're not so aware of this because every time we come across something that we haven't got a word for, we just borrow it from somebody else's language, or we make one up. For example, in the last few years we've acquired a new verb in the English language which is 'to Google' – nobody ever heard of that twenty years ago because Google hadn't been invented but now people frequently say 'I'll Google that', or 'Have you Googled it?'

Our language is constantly evolving, but then there are other languages that are not so widely spoken that will have retained much more of their cultural integrity. And there are certain things that they can express and certain things that they just can't.

If you only speak one language, you might be thinking this has nothing to do with you but actually it's a demonstration of something that applies to all of us, which is that we choose the language we use depending on the circumstances.

THINK ABOUT IT

If someone asked you, 'How was your day?' you probably would answer differently depending on who was asking. So if your boss asked you, you might give a very different answer than if one of your friends asked you after you'd left work. And you might give a different answer again if a small child asked you the same question. So we adjust our language depending on the situation.

Beyond that, the language that you choose to describe your situation will affect how you feel about that situation. There's an old cliché: is the glass half full or is it half empty?

How you choose to describe it will affect how you feel about the situation.

 One of the things that I'd like you to notice is that there are always different ways of describing the same thing and yet we all tend to have habits in how we label our experiences. That's why we seem to keep repeating the same experiences over and over again – because we tell ourselves that it's exactly the same thing happening over and over again. But if we were to break out of that linguistically and call it something else, we might find that we break out of the experience and the emotions that go with it.

 To experience this, try writing down in no more than three sentences a description of an incident where you had an argument with someone and you were sure that you were in the right. Then rephrase the description as much as possible without losing the accuracy of the facts. Notice how this affects your feelings about what happened.

Beliefs and values: So moving down the list brings us to beliefs and values. You could put a dotted line between language and beliefs: above the line would be the filters that are easy to bring into conscious awareness and below the line would be the things that are less easily brought into conscious awareness. Most of us are not that aware of our beliefs and values, but they do drive our behaviour so they are a very powerful category of filters. Technically, the difference between values and beliefs is that your values are what's **important** to you, and your beliefs are what's **true** for you. They tend to go together. If you have a value you also will have beliefs that relate to that value and the combination of the value and the beliefs will drive your behaviour. We are motivated to undertake activities that contribute to fulfilling our values.

I'll give you an example: if you value friendship then you'll have beliefs relating to friendship. And they can vary widely. I did a survey in a group of people I was working with and I got some very different answers: one person said, 'A friend is somebody who is always there for you,' and somebody else said, 'A friend is someone who, it doesn't matter if you haven't seen them for two years, you can pick up just exactly where you left off.' These are quite different beliefs, aren't they? Another person said, 'A friend is someone who makes you feel good about yourself,' and somebody else in the same group said, 'A friend is someone who will always tell you the truth.' I'm not sure those two things are compatible either! The most memorable was the man who said, 'A real friend is someone who will drive all night through the pouring rain with a pocket full of cash and not ask any questions.' I said to him, 'There's a story behind that, isn't there?' and he said, 'Yes, there is, but I'm not telling you what it is.'

What do *you* believe makes a good friend?

We all have our own beliefs about friendship: what does it mean, what makes a good friend, how do friends treat each other and so on. It's the combination of those things that will drive behaviour, so if you believe that a friend is someone who always tells you the truth, then you will tell the truth to your friends. Ultimately that creates the kind of friendships that are important to you. Now, if you didn't have the value of friendship to start with, you wouldn't have the beliefs, you wouldn't behave that way and then you wouldn't have any friends. And that would be okay, because if you didn't value friendship, you wouldn't want any friends!

I'm sure you can see how the combination of the value, beliefs and behaviour gets you what you want in life. This makes our values and beliefs very powerful filters – especially considering most of us are not fully aware of what they are.

One way that you can start to get some ideas about what values you hold is to notice your emotions. Our emotional responses are a reflection of our values: when we fulfil our values, when we get what's important, we feel good. We get all the range of positive range of emotions: we feel happy, we feel satisfied, we feel excited, enthusiastic and so on.

When our values are not being fulfilled, that's when we get negative emotions. In fact I'd go further, it's when our values are being violated that we get negative emotions. So we get irritated, we get angry, we get upset, and whatever else comes to you when something's not going your way – whether you throw a tantrum or whether you just sulk or get depressed, those are all the result of your values being violated. And it could be you that's violating your values or it could be somebody else.

By monitoring your emotions you can start to get some ideas about what's really important to you; what matters sufficiently that it stirs up an emotional response. The situations where you don't feel very much – maybe you feel a bit bored, or apathetic, with no motivation – what that means is that there's nothing in that situation that is obviously connected to anything that you value.

 If there is a situation in which you need to get involved but you're currently not very interested, looking for a connection with something that matters to you is a good way to generate some motivation.

Back to beliefs and values as filters: the way that our beliefs work as filters is that what we believe will very definitely shape what we perceive. When people say 'I'll believe it when I see it,' that isn't really true because if somebody presents you with information that contradicts your own beliefs, you're more likely to reject the information than you are to reject your belief.

Let me give you an example: I was running a training programme a couple of years ago with a lot of people who were IT professionals. They were mostly project managers and there were a couple of more senior people – programme managers – within the group. As I was talking to them about subjective maps of the world and different realities, one of the more senior people said to me, 'Oh yes, I know exactly what you're talking about because we've got a poltergeist in our house and it affects people in really different ways.' He'd hardly finished speaking when I became aware of a ripple of reaction going round the room. It was almost as if people were recalibrating what they thought of this person. They were all very logical people; they worked in IT and were very good at process and very 'down to earth' for the most part. So now I could almost hear them thinking, 'Well, I thought this guy was okay really, but there must be something a bit strange about him!'

The information is coming in from the outside and if it hits a belief, in this case 'there's no such thing as a poltergeist', then rather than saying, 'Oh that belief must be wrong,' people judge that the information coming in from the outside world must be wrong.

That's quite an extreme example, but it demonstrates what happens with all of our beliefs that we're really committed to. When that senior person said, 'We've got a poltergeist in our house,' all the people around him were re-evaluating him because he believed something different from them.

Let me give you another example: think of a couple of people that you know; one who has a very strong personal faith and another who is a complete atheist. Imagine them having a discussion together about whether or not there is a God. Now that's probably fairly easy to imagine, isn't it? But can you imagine that discussion coming to a point where one of them said to the other, 'Actually, you know what, you're right, you've convinced me!' It's really hard to imagine, isn't it?

When it comes to matters of belief, people don't change their minds easily. Everything that you believe acts as a filter and that old saying of 'I'll believe it when I see it' really and truly works the other way round: generally, you see what you believe.

Values are even more deeply buried in our unconscious minds and are therefore even harder to bring into conscious awareness. Often we have values that have been with us since we were small children and that drive our behaviour, without us realizing that we have them.

The first time I went to work with my friend in Singapore he phoned me up beforehand and told me, 'Bring all your lightest clothing because its 36°C here and it's really humid.'

I was happy about that because I like warm weather and it was December in England. I couldn't wait to get out of the cold. So I did as he suggested, took all my lightweight clothing with me and when I arrived in Singapore, sure enough it was 36°C and really steamy.

The first day we were in his office and it was hot. I was grateful that I'd brought very lightweight clothing. The second day, we moved to a hotel conference suite to run our training programme and by about 10 o'clock in the morning I was really cold. I checked the air conditioning unit in the tea break and it was set to 18°C. My first reaction was, 'That's crazy – 36°C of sunshine out there and I'm freezing cold in here!'

Now I don't know about you but in the winter in England I have my central heating set to 21–22°C, and I don't wear really lightweight clothing! So it was three or four degrees colder than I'm used to and I was wearing much lighter clothing. It's not surprising that I was cold, is it?

The reaction 'that's crazy' is the sort of reaction you get when you come up against different values from your own. You get an emotional reaction to other people's behaviour when their behaviour is being driven by values that you don't share. So I thought to myself, 'Ah, this is a values clash, and I'm a trainer of NLP so I can figure this out.' Of course, we were running a training programme so I didn't have a lot of time to think about it immediately but I kept coming back to it over the days that I was there, and I kept thinking, 'What is it here that is so different? What's the values clash? Why am I continually being subjected to these arctic conditions when actually I'd like to be warm because it's sunny out there?'

It took me about ten days and when I think back now, it surprises me that it took me such a long time to figure it out, because it seems so obvious now that I know. It's a good demonstration of how hard it is to get outside of your own values and beliefs and really fully understand somebody else's reality. When the penny finally dropped, I realized that since I grew up in the north-east of England, where it's cold, I have a value that being warm is good. If you grow up near the Equator, where it's hot and steamy, you have the opposite: you have a value that cool is good, which of course is where we get that Californian, 'Oh, cool!'

So now when I go to Singapore I understand intellectually that for the locals it's wonderful to go somewhere that's *so cold* that you can wear jeans and a fleece, in the same way that for British people it's lovely to go away on holiday somewhere where it's *so warm* that you can just wear shorts and a t-shirt. The difference is that, although I get it intellectually, I can't feel it emotionally because I don't share those values.

IF YOU REMEMBER ONE THING Values are a very important category of filters. Emotions are always the clue to values. If you have an emotional response to another person's behaviour – such as feeling annoyed, amused, shocked

35

or embarrassed – it usually indicates a clash of values. Their behaviour is driven by a value that you don't share. Or sometimes you share the value but not the way that it's demonstrated.

Metaprogrammes: The last category of filters I want to look at is metaprogrammes, down at the bottom of the list. Metaprogrammes are different in that they're filters to do with the *way* that we think rather than *what* we think.

There are lots of them. Rodger Bailey and his team who did the original research in this area came up with over 70 different metaprogrammes. At Master Practitioner level we teach about 16 metaprogrammes, which account for a lot of the daily differences in the ways that people think and the way that they behave. I'm going to share with you just a couple that I think are particularly useful.

The first one has to do with motivation. A lot has been written about *what* motivates people. What's less well known is the *way* that people are motivated. It actually boils down to just one of two options: either I'll be motivated to do a task because I can see that there will be some benefit from doing it, or I'll be motivated to do the task because I can see that if I don't do it, it will cause a problem.

KEY TERMS

Towards motivation is when you're motivated to do something because you can see that if you do it there will be some benefit. The opposite is known as **away from** motivation, which is where you're motivated to do something because you can see that by doing it you'll avoid a problem.

These are two very different ways of being motivated but it's important to recognize that both get the job done. Both are effective. The difference has to do with the focus of attention. For someone who is 'towards' motivated, they'll be thinking, 'If I do this, what's the benefit?' And they'll go looking for potential benefits. They generally have quite an upbeat and positive frame of mind, although they may start projects without any consideration of what might go wrong. You really don't want someone who only uses 'towards' motivation in charge of a big project – unless they have a strong-willed risk manager as well!

Contrast that with someone who relies on 'away from' motivation: they're constantly evaluating what can go wrong. They think, 'If I don't do this, what problems will it cause?' This person will probably decide what to do from their 'to do' list by a process of elimination:

- Item one – if I don't do this today, will there be a problem? No, okay, I'll leave it till tomorrow.
- Item two – if I don't do this today will there be a problem? No, okay, we'll leave it.

And so on.

The net result of this is that someone with an 'away from' motivation pattern tends to do most of their work close to deadlines. Far out from a deadline there isn't much motivation to do anything, because nothing's going to happen if they don't do the work. But as they get closer to the deadline they can really see that it will cause a problem if they don't do the work and so they're very motivated.

THINK ABOUT IT You might think back to when you were in school and you were given homework to do. Did you do it as soon as you were given it because it would be great to get it out of the way? Or did you do it just before it had to be handed in because if you didn't then there would be a problem? That might give you a clue as to how you were motivated back then, and that may well be how you're motivated today, because this is a pattern that a lot of people carry through their lives.

Metaprogrammes can change from context to context so it's possible that the way you operate in your working life might be different from the way that you operate when you're at home. But in general most of us will have a kind of default, or a preference – the one that we do best – and then we'll use others where they are particularly useful to us, if we have a specific reason for doing so.

Therefore, in general, if you can understand how a colleague gets motivated at work, then they're probably going to use that way of getting motivated all of the time. The trick then is when you talk to them to use the same kind of process that they would use when they talk to themselves.

So, for example, if you want to get somebody to do a task for you and you tell them all the reasons why it would be really good for them to do the task, that's going to work if they're somebody who is 'towards' motivated. But if they're 'away from' motivated and you tell them all the great benefits of doing the task, it probably isn't going to make any difference. To that person you need to tell them what problems it solves.

The same message could be given in different ways – it all comes down to language. For example, I could say to you, 'There's a job I want you to do and really it needs to be done by Friday, because if it's done by Friday then first of all, you can probably leave early and relax for the weekend but also it will be really great because it will give you a flying start for Monday morning, and it's going to make you look good in the eyes of some of our customers who really aren't expecting this until next week. I think it's also going to take the pressure off some of the other people in the team so you get to be a bit of a hero in the team.' That's all the 'towards' motivation stuff.

Now if I'm talking to somebody who's 'away from' motivated I can tell them exactly the same thing but using different language. I might say to them, 'I've got this job I want you to do and it really needs to be done by Friday, because if it's not done by Friday then you might end up worrying about it all weekend, and then you're going to be under pressure on Monday morning because there's all the more work to do, and if you haven't got this one done then it's going to set you back a bit. There's also the danger that other people are going to feel let down if you don't complete the work as soon as you could and it might mean there's more pressure on the rest of the team if this particular job isn't done by Friday.'

You can see how I'm basically giving the same message but I'm using different language. And of course, if you're talking to a team where you've got both 'towards' motivated and 'away from' motivated people, then it's a good idea to do some of each. You might feel as if you're repeating yourself but for the people listening, they probably won't notice, they'll just pay attention to the bit that works for them.

 Next time you ask someone to do something for you, use 'towards' language first and notice if they seem motivated. If not, tell them the same thing using 'away from' language and see if it gets them more motivated.

(If neither motivates them, it is probably the case that you haven't touched their values.)

So, that's one example of a metaprogramme. The other one that I think is particularly useful and relevant for most of us is to look at the difference between people with a 'procedures' preference and an 'options' preference. This relates to how you go about doing a job. We've looked at the motivation to do it, now this is *how* you do it.

 Someone with an **options** preference likes to experiment with different ways of doing a job. They won't always do it exactly the same way; they'll vary things to see if they can get different results, to see what works best and so on. Someone with this preference is likely to find it quite hard to follow an exact process that someone else has specified.

By contrast, someone with a **procedures** preference works on the principle that there is a best way or a right way to do something. They want to know what the best way is and then they will always do it that way. I'm sure you can imagine that people with those opposite preferences can drive each other crazy!

It's also sometimes a source of tension in a relationship between a manager and members of their team. When you give a task to someone with an 'options' preference they usually respond best if they're told, 'This is the end result: you work out how to make it happen.' That's great if you've got an 'options' preference because you can experiment a bit, but for somebody with a 'procedures' preference it might feel as if they're not being given the whole story. They might really want to know exactly the best way to do the job, so they can do it that way.

 I had an example of an 'options' boss who had a 'procedures' member of staff and the boss kept saying to me, 'It really irritates me because every other member of the team is quite happy when I tell them the end result I want and they just go away and work out and make it happen. But this one person keeps coming and asking me, "How do you want me to do it?"' and she said, 'I'm beginning to think that maybe this person isn't up to the job.' But then, when we looked at the metaprogramme differences it became apparent that it wasn't that the person wasn't up to the job, the real difference was just that the 'procedures' person had an assumption that the boss knew the best way to do the task and just wasn't sharing it.

Of course, which of these is the more suitable preference will vary from role to role. I'm sure you can imagine that in some jobs having a preference for 'procedures' is really helpful, especially where there are legal procedures that have to be undertaken and certain things have to be done in a particular way every time. Somebody with an 'options' preference might find that overly restrictive and might get rather bored. However, if you are looking for continuous improvement, somebody with an 'options' preference, who is willing to experiment a bit and look for ways to improve things, albeit in small ways, would be a really good person to have. So again, both of these preferences have their place, they're both useful in different circumstances, but they can also both have a downside.

The reason I think this is important is that it accounts for some of the differences in the way that people approach tasks. It also accounts for the differences in the way that people talk about what they're doing. If you asked two people, one with each of these preferences, 'How is your project going?' the 'options' person will probably just say, 'Oh, it's fine. We're on track, we're working on this at the moment and everything is going well.'

On the other hand, the person with the 'procedures' preference represents things in their mind in a way that they see the whole process. So they'll start at the beginning and they'll tell you everything that's happened up to today so that you can understand why they're saying that everything's okay today. For them, it would seem like incomplete information if they just told you the end result, so they have to give you the beginning and paint the whole picture.

Similarly, if they were on the receiving end of just, 'Yes, everything's fine,' the person with the 'procedures' preference could get quite frustrated because they might feel as if you're not telling them everything that they need to know. The next time somebody starts right back at the beginning of the story and tells you everything that they think you need to know, just bear with them because it isn't that they're doing it to bore you, it's just that for their process inside their mind, they need to do that. That's how they know that they've told you everything that matters.

Metaprogrammes are a different type of filter. They filter the *way* that that we think rather than *what* we think.

(For more on metaprogrammes I recommend *Words That Change Minds* by Shelle Rose Charvet.)

Linguistic responses, cause and effect

The only part of the diagram that we haven't looked at now is what happens when we respond to information coming in from the outside. This is when we go from inside of our minds back to the surface, for example when we answer a question or we comment on something that somebody else has done.

You'll see that on the diagram we've got the labels Deep Structure and Surface Structure. This comes from the work of Noam Chomsky. The deep structure refers to the full linguistic description of everything that goes on inside your head. All of your memories, as well as having pictures, sounds and so on associated with them, also have a linguistic description associated with them.

Notice that when you say something, the information on its way back out again is also passing through the linguistic filters. So that means it gets deleted, distorted and generalized all over again. That's why, sometimes when you try to explain an idea you had, you might realize that what you are saying isn't really doing justice to the idea you've got inside your mind. What we say is only ever a tiny fraction of the thought that we have inside our head. That's why we sometimes get miscommunications and misunderstandings, and sometimes it creates tension between people if they're not really grasping the ideas and understanding what somebody else wants to put across.

Overall, what we've seen is that between information coming in from the outside world and us reacting to it, there's a great deal of filtering and processing that happens. Sometimes when I look at the diagram I think it's a miracle that people ever have the illusion that they've communicated with each other at all!

THINK ABOUT IT

Before we leave this, I've got a question for you: suppose I'm in a situation that I'm not comfortable in, so in terms of our diagram, what's in the top right – what I'm thinking and feeling – would be, 'I don't think I like this, I feel uncomfortable, I want to get out of this situation.' Consider whether this experience, this discomfort in the situation, is being created to a greater extent by what's going on in the world around me, or by what I'm doing inside my own head? Clearly both are involved but which one is having the greatest effect?

Now if you think about it, I expect you'll come to the conclusion, as I did, that really the experience I have is created mostly by what I'm doing inside my head. And that's why two people can be in exactly the same experience and can react completely differently, and will take different learning from it, and will make different principles and generalizations as a result of that same experience.

I think the important thing here is to recognize that we always have a choice. If we're willing to take the responsibility for creating our own experience that means that we have the potential to create something different when we don't like what we're experiencing. Sometimes that just starts with being willing to describe it in a different way. Often we put labels on our experiences and other people's behaviour that are actually quite far removed from the reality of things that we can see and hear and directly sense.

For example, sometimes I hear people say, 'I've got a problem with a colleague. He or she just likes the sound of their own voice,' meaning that they talk too much. But even that is a judgement. Now if we go back to the sensory experience – if we go back to first access – what's really going on there? What is happening is that the other person, the one who is being labelled as liking the sound of their own voice, talks when other people think that they shouldn't.

There could be lots of reasons for that. Some people talk when they're nervous; some people just don't like silence so if you're not speaking then they'll speak to cover the silence. Some people genuinely have a lot of thoughts they want to share but, actually, very few people talk because they like the sound of their own voice (in fact most people shy away from having their own voice played back to them on a recording). The words being used here are a poor description of either the experience or the speaker's opinion of the experience. The person who talks too much doesn't literally like the sound of their voice and the person who makes the comment doesn't believe that they literally like the sound of their own voice. It's a big distortion of reality, and one that promotes a negative view of what is happening.

So, by taking a different approach to the words that we use, by describing our experience in a different way, we can begin to get a different experience. So, if I say, 'Somebody's late and they've kept me waiting and that means they don't respect me,' that's one way of describing it. But I could also say, 'Oh, this person's late and they obviously trust me to wait for them,' so maybe that's a demonstration of our friendship, rather than the opposite.

There are always different ways of describing a situation depending on what you want to achieve. Sometimes people create the same difficult situation over and over again. Maybe you know somebody who does that: you see them one day and you say, 'How are you, how's it going, how's the job?' and they say, 'Oh well, I don't like my job too much, I don't get on with my boss very well, I don't really feel like the team values me so I don't think I'm going to get on. I think maybe I'll look for another job.' Maybe you then see them six months later and you say, 'Oh hi, how are you, how's the job going?' and they say, 'Well, I changed jobs.' So you say, 'Great, how's the new job?' 'Well, I don't really get on with the boss that well and I don't feel as if I fit in with the team and I don't know, I just don't think I'm going to get on.' And you think to yourself, 'I've heard that somewhere before.'

The reason why some people keep repeating the same experience is because they're not learning from their experience. The process of learning from experience is that you add new filters on the basis of experience, so if you do a job where you don't get on with the boss then you learn something from it. Maybe you learn something about what kind of job to go for, or what questions to ask at interview or maybe just what to do in the first few days in a new job so that you do get a good relationship with the new boss. But if you haven't learnt any of those things there's the danger that you recreate the same experience over and over again. And that definitely is going on inside your head, isn't it, because if you've changed everything in the outside environment – you've gone to a new boss, a new team, a new company, maybe even a new city or country – the outside world has changed completely but somehow the inside experience is exactly the same.

IF YOU REMEMBER ONE THING We really do create our own reality and furthermore we have choices about how we do it. If we're willing to take the responsibility for it then we can truly create the kind of experience that we want in life.

2. The presuppositions of NLP

The presuppositions of NLP are some basic principles that underpin NLP thinking and mostly have been modelled from successful communicators – people who are successful in influencing and persuading others. There isn't one single, definitive version of the presuppositions. I have listed the ones that are most often quoted and used.

Linguistically, a presupposition is something that must be true in order for what is said to make sense. So the presuppositions of NLP are principles that must be true in order for NLP to make sense. In other words, they are the assumptions upon which NLP is built. You do not have to believe that the presuppositions are true in order to use them.

 You can think of the presuppositions as filters that you use to get a different view of a situation – a bit like putting on a pair of sunglasses. Like the sunglasses, you can discard them when they aren't useful. Using one of the presuppositions of NLP means acting as if it were true, and there can be some interesting results when you do that.

The map is not the territory

This is often regarded as the first presupposition of NLP. Indeed, if we did not hold this to be true then NLP would not make sense. It really is the fundamental assumption upon which most of NLP is built. But what does it actually mean?

 'The map is not the territory' is a direct quote from *Science and Sanity* by Alfred Korzybski, first published in 1933, pristine copies of which grace the bookshelves of NLP trainers all over the world. (I say 'pristine' because even if you managed to read it once, you'd be unlikely to wade through it a second time!)

The phrase can be taken to mean this: what we experience is a representation of the world, rather than the world itself. So when we say that we 'see' something, what that really means is that the sensory mechanisms of our eyes have picked up light reflected from that thing and created a representation – or map – of it inside our minds.

All of this would be trivial, were it not for the fact that the map is an incomplete map. And that every single person creates a map that is incomplete in ways unique to that person. That means that *you* don't see the world that *I* do; nor does the next person.

This is where it starts to get interesting.

The world that we live in is a very rich environment. As we have seen, there is far more information available to our five senses than our brains can process, so we have filters in place that enable us to be aware of what is most relevant and useful to us. We disregard the rest.

Of course, we can shift our awareness from moment to moment to take in a lot of information over time. But at any given instant, we are only aware of a tiny fraction of the data available to our senses.

On different occasions, and for different purposes, we might create different 'maps' of the same 'territory'. In the same way as it's possible to have a roadmap, a political map and a geological map of your home town, mentally you can also have multiple maps of the same activity or experience. This means that you can choose how to interpret events and what they mean.

That's what 'making sense' is all about. We take in the sensory data and we make meaning of it. The thing is, there isn't always a single 'correct' meaning. And the meaning I place on a particular experience is often affected by other experiences that are not related to it.

THINK ABOUT IT Can you remember a time when you met someone for the first time and, by coincidence, they had the same name as someone you know really well? Did you find yourself kindly disposed to that person if they shared a name with one of your friends? Or were you just a little bit guarded if they shared a name with someone you didn't like so much? What if you meet someone who looks like someone you know? Does that have an effect on how you behave towards them? If you're human, it does!

These are examples of how we 'make sense' of situations we find ourselves in. Because of our limited ability to process data, our brains use short-cuts, filters and general principles to infer meaning from small amounts of sensory data.

The important thing to remember is that there is not usually just one, correct interpretation. Bear in mind that when you 'make sense' of a situation there are probably lots of alternative ways of making sense of it.

 The question to ask yourself is this:

Is the way I'm interpreting this situation useful or not? Is there another way of looking at this?

In my experience, there are always multiple ways of describing and interpreting a situation. We actually have a choice about how we perceive the world around us and about how we react to it. The trick is remembering to exercise that choice.

You cannot not communicate

This presupposition is usually paired up with 'the meaning of your communication is in the response it gets' (more on which to follow).

'You cannot not communicate' is an interesting notion. It's tempting to think that if you go to a meeting and say nothing, then you have communicated nothing. But it doesn't quite work that way.

Part of what makes us human and sets us apart from other species is the ability to 'make sense' of our experience. We constantly make meaning of our observations. We interpret and analyze, sometimes without realizing that's what we're doing.

THINK ABOUT IT

This is what people will do if I go to a meeting and say nothing.

Those who notice that I've said nothing in the meeting will make meaning of it. One person may say, 'Dianne didn't say anything today, I wonder if she's feeling okay.' (Well, it would be unusual for me to be silent for a whole meeting!)

Someone else may say, 'I guess she was out of her depth in that meeting and didn't have anything to contribute.'

A third person might think, 'She must know something we don't know.'

Whatever meaning they make of it, people are making some kind of sense of my behaviour even if I say nothing and that's why we say that you cannot not communicate.

Suppose I didn't go to the meeting at all. What meaning would people make of that? That I didn't think they were important? That I was sick? That I had forgotten?

In that sense, everything I do, or don't do, has the potential to communicate something to somebody. Everything I do can be interpreted and analyzed and people can make their own meaning of it.

That, of course, is the tricky part. People make their own meaning of what you and I do. They use the filters of their own experiences, beliefs, values and prejudices to make sense of the behaviour of others. That means that very often the meaning someone makes of another's behaviour is inaccurate or misguided. No wonder there are misunderstandings between people!

So, it must be best to talk, rather than risk others getting the wrong idea by 'making sense' of observed behaviour, mustn't it? I'd like to think so, although I'll temper that opinion with the observation that verbal communication is also open to misunderstanding. But at least you can discuss it when you notice that someone has 'got the wrong end of the stick'.

Also to bear in mind, people will make meaning out of not just what you say, but also the fact that you have chosen to say it *at that time* and *to that listener*. For example, if you heard me saying to a colleague, 'Don't forget the meeting tomorrow,' what meaning would you make of that? That I think there is a danger my colleague WILL forget the meeting?

KEY TERM

This is known in NLP as the **meta-message** in what I say. It's the message I communicate by the choice to say what I say in that context.

THINK ABOUT IT

Suppose your boss took you aside before a meeting and said to you, 'There's nothing for you to worry about.' What meaning would you make of that? The meta-message would probably be that there is something going on that might worry you. After all, if there was nothing going on why would the boss tell you there was nothing to worry about?

This is one of the aspects of communication that is particularly noticeable when there are reasons for people to be anxious or insecure. The tendency to make meaning of every small thing is usually exaggerated when people are under pressure. So if you're about to announce a restructure or you're recruiting for a key position, bear in mind that everything you do is a communication. The key is to give clear and consistent communication, both verbal and non-verbal. Consider 'how it looks' before you deliver any important messages. And here too, remember that 'the map is not the territory' and sometimes you have to give the same message several different ways to achieve complete understanding.

The meaning of your communication is in the response it gets

This is a very frequently quoted presupposition of NLP, and one that puts us firmly in a position of responsibility if we choose to accept it.

The underlying principle here is 'the map is not the territory'. You'll remember that first presupposition and how we looked at the way that experiences mean different things to different people. Two people can 'make sense' of the same events in very different ways.

Similarly, words can mean different things to different people. What you thought you meant might not be what someone else would understand by what you said. Or to put it another way, the words that you choose to express your thoughts might correspond to some rather different thoughts in someone else's head.

No word has an absolute meaning. Language develops and changes and the meaning of words can shift over time. What you understand by the words 'nice', 'disinterested' and 'gay' is probably very different from how those same words were understood 200 years ago.

In just the same way, words can have different meanings to people in contemporary times and alternative understandings can be equally valid.

This can be one of the reasons why misunderstandings arise in communication. It is especially true in written communications, because we are deprived of the voice tonality, facial expressions and gestures that would serve to clarify our meaning in a face-to-face encounter.

If you're one of the people who can spend a lot of time crafting the words in your emails and reports to convey the exact nuance of meaning that you intend, I have some bad news for you. The exact nuance of meaning that you intended to convey is probably lost on the readers of your carefully composed sentences.

Now, this where our presupposition – the meaning of your communication is in the response it gets – comes into play.

Have you ever found yourself saying to someone, 'No, that's not what I meant!' and feeling quite indignant that they have missed the point of your wonderfully articulate email? You have? Well, sorry, but the presupposition says that whatever meaning the listener or reader of your words ascribes to them *is* the meaning of your words.

And the meaning of your words can most accurately be identified by observing the reaction to them, because a response in words is subject to all the same vagaries as your original message.

So the meaning of your message is what others understand by your message, not what you intended them to understand. In other words, if you want people to get a particular message, it's your responsibility to create the understanding in their minds, rather than it being their responsibility to figure out what you intended.

 The managing director of a firm I was working with was very proud of his five-year plan and the clear objectives that he'd identified for each year. As I met different people in the organization, I asked them about the five-year plan and the current priorities. None were able to tell me what they were. When I relayed this finding back to the managing director he snapped, 'Well, they should know. I've told them.'

It was clear to me that whatever he intended and thought he had communicated, he actually had communicated nothing. Nobody knew the plan, therefore he had not communicated it.

So what's the answer? Well, for a start, ask yourself what is the response you want to your communication? To convey your message accurately, it's usually more effective to give the same message several times, in more than one way. Keep monitoring the response. When you get the response you were looking for, you may be justified in considering that you've communicated what you wanted to communicate. But then again …

There is no failure, only feedback

Of all the presuppositions of NLP, this is probably the most well known. But what does it actually mean and how is it useful?

At first glance, many people think, 'That's not true, there *is* failure: I failed my driving test' or 'I failed my maths exam' or 'I failed to win a contract' or 'I failed to get the job I applied for.' They might also think, 'One of my staff failed to meet a deadline' or failed to hit a target or failed to deliver a service to agreed standards. These are all experiences that can accurately be described as failure, so where does the presupposition become useful?

 Let's start with the example of 'failing' the driving test. I took the test when I was seventeen and I didn't pass first time. The examiner gave me a clear explanation of where my driving wasn't up to standard (I seem to remember it was reversing) and I went back to my instructor for some more lessons. Some months later when I took the test again I passed.

At seventeen, I was disappointed not to pass my driving test first time. I'd failed. But that wasn't the end of the story. I took the examiner's feedback and went for more lessons. Now I was better off because I knew what I needed to work on. I got quite good at reversing and then I passed the test. So the point is that the 'failure' actually left me better off because I knew where to focus my learning. And that's the sense in which it's feedback rather than failure.

When you have a goal in mind and you start working towards it, you might only do things that contribute to the achievement of the goal and you might achieve it very quickly. But if it's something you haven't done before the chances are that you might make some false starts, you might make assumptions that turn out not to be valid or you might get some unexpected results somewhere along the way. If any of these things happen, they're part of the learning process and they help you to decide how to proceed. That's feedback.

You could call it failure when something unexpected happens. If you did, you'd probably feel bad about it and that might get in the way of further progress. If you call it feedback when something unexpected happens, then you can feel good about that and progress is not hampered.

Now, if you've done some NLP training, or even if you haven't, you might think that this is obvious and you might be wondering why I'm writing about it. You already know that 'failure' carries negative feelings for the majority of people and that re-labelling the experience to something more constructive is helpful. Well, there's more.

 This isn't just about re-labelling the experience. It's also about **feedback**. In pure systems terms, feedback is defined as 'information generated in one part of the system that is relayed to an earlier part of the system to modify the behaviour of the system.' In other words, feedback is only feedback if it changes something. If nothing changes, it's just information.

So the point here is that this presupposition is not just about taking the sting out of 'failure'. It's about paying attention to everything you can that will help you to succeed next time. It's about recognizing that this experience of 'failure' can be valuable in equipping you to achieve what you set out to achieve.

At a really obvious level, you can say, 'Well, now I know that doing that doesn't work so I won't do that again.' That's okay, but it doesn't help you decide what to do instead. To really get the benefit of failure, you would examine in detail what went wrong and how, so that you could develop a more useful approach.

Going back to my driving test, if I'd simply resolved 'not to do that again' – i.e. not to repeat the whole experience in the same way – I might not have taken a test again! Or I might not have gone to the same test centre again. Instead I listened to the feedback and adjusted the part of my behaviour that led to the 'failure'. So the information that the examiner gave me truly was feedback.

 There is no failure, only feedback – so long as you pay attention to the feedback and act on it!

You are not your behaviour

This is an interesting presupposition. Behaviour, that is, what somebody does, is often the thing that we're most aware of, and we make judgements about people on the basis of what they do and how they behave.

The thing to recognize is that there's always more to somebody than what they're doing right now.

You might dislike somebody's way of going about something but you might respect the knowledge and experience they have in a particular field. So, there may be a bigger picture where you can accept the person even if you don't like a particular aspect of their behaviour.

I think the ultimate example of this is Gandhi, who said he aimed to love his enemies while hating what they did – 'Hate the sin and not the sinner' is among his teachings. That really is making the distinction between the person and what they're doing!

You may also have noticed this principle at work in the way that people talk to small children. There might have been a time when it came naturally to say to a child, 'You're very naughty,' whereas now a lot of people have learned that it's more appropriate to say to a child, 'That's a naughty thing to do,' because phrasing it that way makes a distinction between the child and the behaviour.

The result of that is the child has some choice about whether or not they *do* the naughty thing, whereas if you told them they *are* naughty, they don't have any choice. If you tell a child often enough, 'You're naughty', it's likely that they will accept that as their role in life and keep looking for ways to be naughty.

In the work environment, lots of people learn to make this separation between the person and their behaviour as part of performance appraisal systems. Here you criticize the behaviour or the process or the end result, rather than the person: 'What you did was not helpful,' rather than, 'You're not helpful.'

Looking at the world in this way can be helpful to us because it draws attention to a bigger picture. It takes our focus away from the irritating or counterproductive behaviour of another person. By recognizing that what they are doing is not who they are, we may start to look for ways to engage the same person in different behaviour.

Remember as well that this principle applies to you. On the odd occasion when you make a mistake, do something inappropriate or say exactly the wrong thing to the wrong person, remember – you are not your behaviour!

People have all the resources they need to succeed

This is a great NLP presupposition if you work in an environment where you need to get the best out of people. It's particularly useful if, like me, you're involved in learning and development.

It's useful because the opposite is believing that some people just can't do certain things. And if you believe that somebody just can't do something, you are unlikely to be able to help them learn it.

The essence of this presupposition is that if somebody is having difficulty doing something in a given circumstance it isn't usually because they can't do it, it's usually because they haven't made the connection between skills they have in another context and the particular context in front of them.

One of the things a lot of people have struggled with at some point in their life is public speaking. The research says that it's the number one fear of mankind – most people would rather die than have to speak in public!

So does that mean that those people don't have the capability to speak in public? I don't think so! Because what do they need to be able to do? They need to be able to open their mouth and speak, string their words together into a sensible discussion or argument, or presentation, which most people probably can do in other circumstances. You get people who, sitting round the table in a restaurant with a bunch of friends, can hold forth for ten or fifteen minutes quite easily; can tell a story, can string an argument together, can make a really compelling case for their particular belief, and yet if you told them to stand up in front of a conference and do it, they'd say, 'Oh, I can't do that.'

They have all the constituent skills – they can stand up there behind the lectern, they can speak, they can string the argument together, but somehow when you ask them to do it all at once, they say, 'Oh no, I can't do that.'

They have the resources, they have those personal capabilities, the personal strength and so on to be able to do it, they just haven't brought it to bear in that particular context.

So, one of the things that we can do with NLP techniques is to make the connection between the context where you have a certain resource and the context where you need that same resource.

People say, 'Oh, I need more confidence,' and yet, even the least confident person in the world will have areas where they are totally and utterly confident. So somebody who really isn't confident in their capability at work may be totally confident in their ability to drive a car, or ride a bicycle, or play football, or whatever it is. They will have confidence in some arena of life, it's part of their repertoire. It's just about bringing it to bear in the place where you need it.

That's what this presupposition is all about: making the connections between the resources and the circumstances where you need them. There are no unresourceful people, just unresourceful states to be in.

The successful practice of NLP enables a person to manage their state so that they have all the resources they need in the situation they're in.

The circle of excellence is a very simple and effective technique for getting yourself in the right frame of mind to do whatever you need to do. It is based on the presupposition that people have all the resources they need to succeed. If there's something in your calendar that you're not looking forward to, this technique can shift your feelings so that you are able to take it in your stride and even enjoy it.

Some examples of where it can be used:

- To deal with nervousness about making a presentation
- To boost confidence before an interview
- To relax at the end of the day
- To stay calm and alert when chairing an important meeting
- To overcome exam nerves
- To stop irritation at everyday distractions.

Here's how to do it:

- **Step 1:** Identify the situation or event coming up that you are nervous or anxious about or simply not looking forward to.

- **Step 2:** Remember an occasion in the past when you faced something similar to the situation you want to work on. Imagine a circle, about 1m in diameter, on the floor in front of you. Step forward into it as you relive the past situation. Make sure you're really feeling what it was like. Take your time and remember what you saw, what you heard and the way you felt in that past event. What was missing for you? What personal resources were you not able to access in that situation? Pick three.

- **Step 3:** For each of the personal resources required, anchor it into the circle as follows: Remember a specific time in the past (in any situation) when you had this resource. Go back and relive the memory in as much detail as possible. See what you saw, hear what you heard and when you can really feel the feelings associated with it, step back into the circle. As the feeling fades away, step back out of the circle. Do this for each of the three resources separately.

- **Step 4:** After anchoring each of the required resources in the circle, take a moment to clear your mind. Doing a mental exercise such as reciting your phone number backwards can be a good way to 'break state'. Then imagine yourself in the future event and step forward into the circle. Notice the difference.

If you identify any further resources that are needed, repeat step 3.

People are doing the best they can with the resources they have available (or, present behaviour is the best choice available)

When they first encounter this presupposition a lot of people say to me, 'I don't believe people always do the best they can.' It really depends on how you think about it. The important part of this presupposition is *with the resources they have available*.

Consider this: do you always do the best job you could possibly do? And if you think about a day when you know you didn't achieve as much as you could have, what was the reason? It's probably because there were other things going on. If you hadn't slept well the night before and you

70

were feeling tired, then maybe you didn't achieve as much because you didn't have the energy that you would normally have. In terms of the resources you had available that day, there wasn't much in the energy bank. So you did the best you could, given the small amount of energy you had. That's what that presupposition means: given whatever you've got going on at that time, you will always do the best within those limitations.

For example, one day, you might be feeling really annoyed with somebody you have to work with and that's distracting you. That's what you've got available that day. And that will tend to go against you doing as much work as you might do on another day. So people are doing the best they can with what they've got *right now*.

It can be interesting to apply this presupposition to a situation where you think somebody is being obstructive or difficult. Sometimes I see this in organizations. I might go in to run some training programmes as part of a change initiative. Quite often, somebody who's trying to drive the change will say, 'This group of people (or this individual) is being obstructive, they're being difficult,' and you can take that at face value and go, 'Okay, people are being difficult.' But if you go back to this presupposition and say, 'Well people are doing the best they can with what they've got,' that will get you thinking differently. What has somebody got going on that means that this behaviour, that's being described as 'difficult', is the best they can do?

CASE STUDY I had a good example of this in a company I did some work for – a small engineering firm that provided a service to quite a wide range of customers. The operations manager wanted to change some of their working practices and he said to me, 'Well, the guys in the workshop are being difficult, they're being obstructive, they won't do the new things.'

And when I got an opportunity to talk to them and find out a bit more about it, what they told me was that the new working practices were going to get in the way of them being able to do the best job for their customers. And they wanted to be able to do a good job for their customers. They cared about the work!

So, I went back to the ops manager and said, 'You need to sit down and talk with these guys because they're telling me that if they do what you want them to do, it will result in a drop in service. That's why they don't want to do it. Now I don't know whether they're right or wrong, but that's what they think and so that explains why they're not being very enthusiastic about your new working practices.'

So he went and talked to them and it turned out that in fact there was some information that he hadn't given them and so they'd filled in the blanks and made some assumptions that weren't actually valid (which is often what happens if people get incomplete information). And so, with a bit more conversation, they were able to come to an agreement where everybody was happy and the new working practices went in.

So, how about testing out this presupposition for yourself? If somebody is behaving in a way that you think is obstructive or difficult, ask yourself, 'What else have they got in this situation that means that their current behaviour is the best they can do?' According to the presupposition, their behaviour must seem the best choice available to them – if this seems inexplicable, you need to do some more talking to find out what's going on.

Give it a try – you may be pleasantly surprised how easy it is to deal with people who appear to be 'being difficult'.

The part of any system which has the most flexibility controls the system (Ashby's law of requisite variety)

This principle comes from systems thinking and, in terms of mechanical systems, is probably fairly straightforward.

THINK ABOUT IT

Consider a central heating system: the one in my house has several radiators that just sit on walls, and yards and yards of copper piping that are fixed in place. It has a boiler that just sits there, although it goes on and off depending on what position the switch is in.

The thing that really makes the difference to what's going on is the thermostat, which has lots of different settings. It has flexibility.

So, the human equivalent of that is that the person with the most behavioural flexibility will have the most influence in a situation.

They won't necessarily always get their own way, because sometimes some of the most senior people are the least flexible and they just say, 'We'll do it my way because that's how I want it done,' and everybody else scuttles around and does it.

However, somebody who is flexible in the way they go about achieving what they want to achieve can often have a lot more influence than somebody who only has one way of doing things. If you've got more than one way of explaining your idea, then you stand a greater chance of people understanding it and coming on board than if you only have one way of describing what you want.

Note that I'm talking about flexibility in structure; flexibility in *the way you go about things* rather than in *what you do*. I remember somebody saying to me one time, 'Well, I'm very flexible, I'll fit in with anybody.' But that's being flexible in terms of content, rather than in terms of structure. So the more flexible you can be in how you go about things, then the easier it is to get your end result. The psychologist and philosopher William James (1842–1910) said that the definition of intelligence is having a fixed goal and multiple means of achieving it.

 Flexibility is not the same as compromise. When you see flexibility in content, that's compromise. However, if you're flexible in the way you go about something, you do not need to compromise your goals and indeed you will probably get your desired end result because you will be able to relate to different people, and encourage them to do things in different ways, and so on.

So true flexibility is having multiple ways of getting where you want to go, rather than compromising on where you want to go in the first place.

Every behaviour has a positive intention

At first glance you might be forgiven for thinking that this presupposition suggests that everything anyone does is intended to do good. But that isn't what it means. (And I'm sure that you can think of some behaviours that certainly don't do good to others.) Moreover, don't forget that the NLP presuppositions are filters. They're ways of looking at the world that can create more constructive results if we choose to use them. You don't have to believe that a presupposition is absolutely true in order to use it and get the benefit of it.

If you have a pet cat, you probably practise this presupposition regularly. Do you wander in to the kitchen in the morning to discover a half-eaten or half-alive mouse, bird or other small, helpless creature? And if you love your cat, do you shout at it and complain about the mess on the kitchen floor? If you're like most of the cat-lovers I know you probably don't do that. More than likely, you say something like, 'Ah look, he's brought me a present.'

If you do that, you're looking beyond the behaviour to its purpose. Excellent! That's what this presupposition is all about. Now, can you do the same when your colleague at work drops the equivalent of a dead mouse onto your desk and expects you to deal with it? Can you look beyond the irritating behaviour of people around you and focus on the purpose behind it?

I think that this presupposition is better if it's phrased 'Every behaviour is purposeful'. What people do is not random, it's usually not even aimed at annoying you, but it does have a purpose. Granted, the purpose may be of value only to the person who behaviour is in question, but it has a purpose nonetheless.

So next time someone around you does something that you consider to be inappropriate, foolish or annoying (or all three!), I challenge you to ask yourself, 'What is the purpose of this behaviour?'

By asking yourself this question you'll be achieving two things:

1. You may arrive at a better insight into the other person's motivation and thinking.
2. You'll distract yourself from being irritated and instead become curious, interested and maybe even more motivated to talk to the person about what they're doing. This can only be an improvement, can't it?

All behaviour is appropriate in some context

The underlying principle of this presupposition is that for anything a person may do, or be capable of doing, there will be some context in which it's absolutely the right thing, and others where it may be less appropriate.

Let's take an example where somebody is shouting in an office meeting, raising their voice and perhaps getting quite aggressive about it. You might think that's inappropriate behaviour.

First of all, separate the behaviour from the context. The behaviour is 'shouting' or 'raising the voice'. The context is 'during an office meeting'.

It's the context that makes the behaviour inappropriate.

There will be situations where that exact behaviour could be very appropriate. If somebody was in danger and you wanted to alert them, then shouting to get their attention could be the appropriate thing to do. So if you look purely at the behaviour – what the person is actually doing – and take it away from the context, then there will always be some context in which that's the right thing to do. And that's what that presupposition means. After all, why would a person develop a skill if there was no value in it?

I had a coaching client some years ago, who was regarded as being very inflexible and dogmatic and difficult to influence, and not very compromising or flexible with colleagues.

I discovered that he was the quality manager in his organization and that he was very definite about standards that needed to be met. In that context, it was a really useful skill to have, to say to people, 'No, we will not compromise on this.'

There were other circumstances in his working life, such as where to have a meeting, where it would have been perfectly all right for him to be a lot more flexible. But he'd got so much in the habit of being very fixed about his ideas that he was also doing it in other circumstances where it was inappropriate behaviour.

I tend to find that with a lot of organizations, whatever is the core competence of the organization tends to filter out into everything that they do, whether it's appropriate or not. It's as if there is a fundamental philosophy of the way that you do something, which is the thing that you're in business for, and everything else follows suit.

For example, I did some work for British Airways Engineering some years ago and some of the managers there said to me. 'It's very challenging managing aircraft engineers because they're very negative and they're kind of nitpicky, and we go to them with a new pay deal and they tell us all the reasons it won't work, and it just gets to be a bit frustrating.' And I remember saying to them, 'Well, what makes a good aircraft engineer?

Is a good aircraft engineer somebody who looks for problems and solves them? Do you want somebody who's going to really nitpick, to be maintaining that aircraft that's going to carry 300 people to their destination?'

And so, that's the core competence. It's that ability to spot the problems and solve them, so you can't really blame people for them doing it in relation to other things and not just their everyday normal work.

Around the same time I was also working at the BBC World Service and the managers there said, 'People act as if they don't trust us. You go to them and talk to them about changes in the working hours, and they all go, 'Yes, but what are you not telling us? What's going on behind the scenes?"

In the same way I said to them, 'Well, what makes a good journalist? It's somebody who doesn't take things at face value. So you should expect that you're going to get searching questions when you go and present information.'

After these two examples I started looking for other evidence of a 'core competence' in organizations that influenced the culture significantly. I remembered some training programmes I did for a fire service and, surprise, surprise, everything was done on a fire-fighting basis! Nothing was ever dealt with until it was really, really urgent.

I think that what this demonstrates is that we develop behaviour that is appropriate in some context, and if it works well we may continue to use it, even beyond the bounds of appropriate contexts. The challenge, therefore, is that even if our behaviour seems appropriate, in order to achieve our goals, sometimes we need to look for behaviour that's even more appropriate to the context.

The mind and the body affect each other

This presupposition of NLP has given rise to a whole area of application. There are lots of NLP practitioners who work primarily in health and well-being and whose skills stand on this most fundamental assumption. So what does it mean?

Quite simply, it means that the mind affects the body and the body affects the mind. Or if you prefer, it means that the mind and body are not separate, they are part of the same system.

For most people, it is quite obvious that the body affects the mind. If someone is feeling physically unwell, that is often accompanied by mental symptoms like reduced ability to concentrate, lack of enthusiasm for everyday activities or lower tolerance of others. Conversely, most of us feel mentally more alert, more creative and more interested when we're physically charged up, like after a long walk or run, a fast game or good work-out.

So, you've experienced how the body affects the mind and that's often a good motivation to look after your body. But what about the mind affecting the body? Not so many people take that for granted.

It's my belief and my experience that what we think affects our physical bodies. Many physical ailments have an emotional or mental aspect to them so that we may be more likely to suffer physical symptoms when we're in a particular frame of mind. The most common example of that is stress. When we're feeling overwhelmed by work pressure, that's when the headaches, backaches, upset stomachs and allergic reactions are most likely to appear.

It might be stating the obvious, but there is another assumption here that what's bad for the mind is also bad for the body. If you think gloom and doom, and see yourself as a victim of life's injustice, your body's well-being will be lessened. If see yourself in charge of your own destiny and think about what's important to you in life, then your body's well-being will be enhanced.

Neuroscience shows us that neurotransmitters – the chemicals that transmit messages from the brain through the nervous system – actually interact with every cell in the body. So it's possible that any thought you have can affect your whole body, albeit in a very small way. Deepak Chopra, one of the leading figures in mind-body medicine, says in one of his books that an average person has some 90,000 thoughts per day. He goes on to say that about 75,000 of those thoughts are the same thoughts as yesterday! So if every one of those thoughts has a miniscule effect on your body, it's easy to see how habitual thoughts might create chronic health problems, isn't it?

Now, here's the interesting bit: NLP gives us tools to get control of our thoughts and our habits. So if we change some of the 'bad' habits we have in thinking negatively, we can potentially change the way our bodies habitually respond. Or to put it another way, it's easier to recover from an illness or break out of a cycle of chronic symptoms if you change the way of thinking that contributed to the creation of the problem.

Now, I'm not saying that all illness is 'in the mind' or that 'positive thinking' is a cure for whatever ails you. What I am saying is that I believe the body is as intelligent as the mind in its own way and that physical symptoms are not random and do not spontaneously arise for no reason.

The mind and the body are one system. Physical symptoms are a way of drawing your attention to what is going on in your body so that you can do something about it.

Modern medicine has tended to foster the notion that what you do about symptoms is take a drug to relieve them. But a little bit of time spent on considering the reason for the symptoms can increase the effectiveness of the drug, reduce the likelihood of needing it again or even remove the symptoms without the use of drugs.

There is another presupposition of NLP that says 'all behaviour is purposeful'.

I believe that, in the same way, we can regard physical symptoms as 'behaviour' of the body and if we assume that that behaviour is purposeful, that can be the key to full recovery. Many people I know who are 'body workers' – massage therapists, chiropractors or reiki practitioners – confirm that the patients who make the quickest and most complete recovery are those who are also engaged in personal development – they're are working on the psychological as well as the physical.

I realize that not everyone will agree with my reasoning here. I hope I've stimulated you to think about your own attitude to your physical well-being, and the meaning of this presupposition, that the mind and the body affect each other.

All interventions should increase choice

This final presupposition becomes most relevant when you get into using some of the techniques for change. It's just recognizing that if you're going to reprogramme some of your behaviour, or you're going to help somebody else reprogramme theirs, the ideal thing is that we look for more choice in a situation.

Suppose somebody does something that they wish they didn't do, then you could say, 'Well, we'll reprogramme so that they just can't do that.' But if we believe the presupposition that *all behaviour is appropriate in some context* then there might be a situation where the person might want to behave that way. Currently they're saying, 'I want to stop doing it because it's not useful,' but there might be some circumstance in which it's absolutely the right thing to do.

So we prefer to keep that behaviour as a choice so that they could do it if the situation arose. And, of course, if we believe the presupposition that *people make the best choice on the basis of what's available* then that's going to be okay, because as soon as they have more choice they'll choose the most appropriate thing to do.

3. Outcome thinking

'Outcome' is the general term used in NLP to refer to some desired state, achievement, goal, target, wish, dream or event. 'Outcome thinking' means focusing your thoughts on what you want. It's important because it's hard to decide what to do if you're not certain about what you want to achieve.

THINK ABOUT IT At work, do you have a clear set of goals and targets? Can you put the tasks on your to-do list in the context of your overall goals? If there is a clear connection between what you're working on now and the results you want to deliver, it's usually easier to motivate yourself to work.

Some people are very good at focusing on their goals and are motivated by doing that. Other people find it more natural to focus on problems and how to solve or avoid them. Often a combination of both will be needed to move from your starting place to your desired end result.

Problem frame and outcome frame

This is a quick problem-solving technique that you can use any time. It works well on issues that are specific to you and that you can influence. It's not very good for stuff that's way beyond your control (world poverty, climate change etc.) and it might not yield anything new on a situation that you've been mulling over for weeks or months. But often it'll shift your thinking sufficiently to resolve the problem.

Identify a problem that you'd like to resolve. Then ask yourself each of the following ten questions in turn. Answer each question fully before moving on the next.

Problem frame
1. What's the problem?
2. How long have you had it?
3. Why do you have this problem?
4. Who is to blame?
5. Why haven't you solved it yet?

Outcome frame
1. In this situation, what do you want?
2. How will you know when you've got what you want?
3. What resources do you already have that you can use to solve this problem?
4. When have you succeeded in something similar?
5. What is the next step?

Simple, but powerful!

USEFUL TIPS This process is also a good one to use as part of a coaching conversation. Even if you don't fully understand the technicalities of the situation, you can use these questions to assist constructive thinking. It's a great alternative to giving advice or trying to solve the problem yourself.

Well-formed outcomes

Many people have bad habits in the way they think about what they want, and this can be a block to making any progress towards getting it. For example, some people have thought patterns that go like this:

> 'I'd really like a new car. Oh, but I can't afford a new car.'

> 'I'd really like to go out to dinner this weekend. Oh, but nobody will want to go with me.'

> 'I'd love to learn to play tennis. Oh, but I wouldn't be any good at it.'

Patterns like this prevent any kind of focused activity towards the desired state, by presenting the impossibility of having it.

KEY TERM

The meaning of a **well-formed** outcome is that it is represented in your mind in a way that makes it easy to achieve. It's the *representation* of the outcome that is 'well formed'.

An outcome is well formed when:

1. **It is expressed in the positive.** That means it's described in terms of getting what you want, rather than avoiding something you don't want.

2. **You can describe it in sensory-specific terms.** This will be a description of what you will be able to see, hear and feel when you achieve your outcome.

3. **It's under your control.** It is only well formed if you can make it happen without relying on other people.

4. **The context is clear.** You can define where and when you want it and have identified the exceptions.

5. **You can maintain the secondary gain of the current situation.** If you have been intending to make this happen for a while but not made any progress it could be because there is value for you in *not* succeeding in this. This is known as secondary gain. The key to progress is to maintain that benefit as well as moving towards your outcome.

6. **It is ecological.** There will be no unwanted consequences of you achieving the outcome.

The keys to making it work

The six criteria can be considered in the order that they are listed, but they can also be looked at in whatever order seems natural. Sometimes your thinking on one point will naturally take you to another and it makes sense to follow that flow instead of imposing a rigid sequence. It's also quite usual to consider some of the criteria more than once. If you find that your outcome is, for example, not under your own control, then you may go back to the beginning and define what you want in a different way.

Bear in mind that you are aiming for a crystal-clear description of the end result you want, not creating an action plan for how to achieve it. With a well-formed outcome in mind, you will naturally choose behaviour and activities that move you towards the desired state.

There are considerations for each criterion that will make a difference:

Outcome expressed in the positive

1. Sometimes the starting point with an outcome is what you *don't* want. To shift into the positive simply ask yourself, 'If I didn't have that, what would I have instead?'

2. Be aware that the outcome can involve specific activities, or it can simply be an end result. If the activity isn't

compelling – 'I want to go to the gym three times per week' – then it may be more useful to focus on what that will achieve. Ask yourself, 'What will that do/get for me?' The outcome may then become, 'I want to look slim and toned in my summer clothes.' For most of us, that is a more compelling idea.

3. Avoid comparisons and go for specifics. 'I want a better job' is not as well formed as, 'I want a job as a sales director that pays at least £100k.'

Sensory-specific evidence

1. Identify the moment in time when you will be able to say, 'Yes, I've done it!' What is going to be happening at that moment that will be your evidence of success?

2. The sensory description of that moment can be associated or dissociated. For example, it can be a description of what *you* will see or, alternatively, how you will look to another person.

3. Ensure that the evidence is specific. 'I'll feel better' is not as well formed as, 'I'll feel confident.'

4. If the evidence includes feelings, make sure that they are feelings that *indicate* success rather than the feelings of pleasure at having succeeded.

Under your control

Sometimes the outcome depends on the involvement of other people. This is only outside of your control if you are unable to influence or persuade someone to get involved or if it depends on one particular person. For example, if you are looking for a new job, it won't be you that decides who gets the job (unless you decide to become self-employed!). Your new employer is the person who makes that decision, but you can influence that person through the selection process and you can apply to another company if the first one doesn't take you on. So it is under your control to get a new job, but perhaps not a specific role with a specific company.

Context

As well as a clear context for the outcome, make sure you identify any exceptions or exclusions. Ask yourself, 'Where and when do I want this?' 'With whom do I want it?' and 'When do I *not* want it?'

Secondary Gain

1. The secondary gain is often key to understanding why a long-standing outcome has not been achieved. Look for benefits of not starting or not completing the activity. Also look at what is the result of current activity – what is being gained instead of the stated outcome?

2. Secondary gain isn't always logical. It can result from old beliefs and unconscious assumptions that, once you bring them into conscious awareness, cease to be a problem.

3. Remember that secondary gain means benefits of *not* achieving your outcome. Sometimes these are out of conscious awareness until you begin to ask the question.

4. If you find that the answer to the question, 'Why don't you have it already?' is something like, 'Because I'm lazy,' that indicates that there is internal conflict. One part of you wants something and another part isn't motivated by it.

5. If self-discipline or willpower seem to be a key part of achieving the outcome, dig a bit deeper. Self-discipline usually means that there is a lack of congruency. The parts that aren't committed to the outcome will eventually rebel.

Ecology

1. The key to this is to imagine the outcome achieved, associate into the future and check for any unwanted consequences of achieving your outcome. Notice any incongruence and use that to identify any areas of conflict.

2. Remember that time is an invention of the conscious mind. At the unconscious level there may be a sense of

conflict but if you introduce time, there may be a resolution. You can 'have it all' but maybe not all at once!

Think of something that you want to achieve. It could be a big goal, or it could be something as simple as the result you want from speaking to someone on the phone or sending an email.

Run through the six criteria with your outcome in mind and make it as well-formed as you can.

Does that make it clearer? Easier to achieve?

Like any skill, making your outcomes well formed will get easier with practice. It's well worth putting in some effort on this because when you have clear outcomes in mind, you will find that you work more productively and find it easier to focus on the priorities.

I recommend that you aim to develop ten to twenty well-formed outcomes per day. Not necessarily big, long-term goals, just whatever is part of your day. Before you attend a meeting, ask yourself, 'What's my outcome?' Before making a phone call ask yourself, 'What's my outcome?' Before deciding what to have for dinner ask yourself, 'What's my outcome?' and so on.

If you do this every day for two to three weeks you will install this pattern at the unconscious level and it will become your natural way of thinking about outcomes.

When you ask yourself the question, 'What's my outcome?' what comes to mind will already be well-formed.

Often the key to a well-formed outcome is in the secondary gain. Here is an example:

Stephen had been working towards a professional qualification for some time and had twice put off taking the exam. He said that he didn't feel that he was up to the standard to pass. However, when we created a well-formed outcome about taking the exam we discovered that several of his colleagues had passed the exam first time and that Stephen wanted to do the same. The secondary gain of putting off the exam was, 'If I don't take the exam, I can't fail it.' With this new awareness, he was able to convince himself that he was ready to take the exam and passed first time!

You can use the well-formed outcome pattern to create team outcomes for a meeting, project or workshop. The elicitation of individual evidence criteria can be particularly useful in understanding different viewpoints and values.

The same principle can also be applied to company goals and targets. Goals, targets and objectives can all benefit from being well formed. Change programmes are often made easier by the consideration of the secondary gains.

What do people perceive they will have to give up to make this change happen? Can it be maintained?

CASE STUDY A medium-sized company had been through a period of significant growth, with the number of staff rising from 150 to 400 in two years. The new IT director inherited a team of around 40 IT specialists and was frustrated to discover that many of them were frequently interrupted during their working day by colleagues from other departments seeking help with PC problems.

The IT director decided to implement a formal helpdesk system and tracking process. They installed a suitable programme, designated two people to be the first line of contact and then notified the rest of the organization of the new procedure. You may not be surprised to hear that, as a result, nothing changed. Everyone continued to call on their friends for assistance with PC problems instead of using the new helpdesk.

The IT director considered his options. He could insist on the use of the helpdesk and discipline his staff if they stepped outside of the system. He could refuse assistance to requests that didn't come through the proper channels. Or he could look at it another way.

He asked himself what the benefit might be of not using the helpdesk. He realized that people wanted to ask for help from someone that they knew, that they trusted and that they believed could help. This was the secondary gain.

So he asked the two people who staffed the helpdesk to take two weeks and visit every department in the company and talk to people. Their objective was to find out which applications people used, whether they had any recurrent problems, what they might need in the future and generally understand how technology was used in each department. And also to make friends with everyone.

After doing this, the helpdesk began to be used. People stopped phoning random colleagues in IT, and rang the people who really could help – the helpdesk. This was because the helpdesk staff now fitted the criteria of being someone that they knew, that they trusted and that they believed could help.

The secondary gain was maintained and the helpdesk was operational.

---

4. Rapport, pacing and leading

Rapport

The term 'rapport' is one that is in everyday use. It's used to mean a state of friendliness and goodwill between people. In that sense, it's perfectly logical to refer to having rapport with someone you haven't seen for three weeks (or more). In NLP when we talk about rapport it usually refers to the state of play between people right now. It's important because it is the foundation upon which influence is built.

Rapport is a state of attention and responsiveness between two or more people.

So it's possible to be in rapport with the person you're talking with right now, even if that person is someone you have some reason to mistrust. It's also possible to be out of rapport with your closest friend if you meet up at a time when you've had very different experiences immediately beforehand.

THINK ABOUT IT

Imagine you meet your friend for dinner immediately after you both finish work. You've had a really satisfying day at work, finishing something that you'd been working on for a while and getting recognition for a job well done. Your friend, by contrast, has had a stressful day at work because two of his colleagues have had a major disagreement and they have both been trying to enlist his support on their side of the dispute.

In the first few minutes when you meet up, are you and your friend on the same wavelength? Are you in rapport (in the NLP sense)? Probably not. But if you're good friends it won't take long before you find the common ground again and settle into enjoying the evening together.

REMEMBER THIS!!!

Never assume that you have rapport with anyone, even your nearest and dearest.

It's also important to realize that there are degrees of rapport. In other words, there are degrees of attention and response that one person may give to another. The extent of rapport you have with another person will determine the extent of influence you will have over them.

If you approached a stranger on the street, how much rapport would you need to get them to tell you the time of day? Contrast that with how much rapport you would need to persuade them to give you £10.

Calibrating rapport

You may not realize it, but you can probably determine quite accurately the degree of rapport in an interaction between people. It's possible to gauge the level of responsiveness just by watching how people behave.

Imagine you went into a crowded restaurant. It's too noisy to hear what people are saying. Looking around, could you pick out a couple who had just had an argument? A couple on a date? Of course you could! The clues are all in the body language.

You can spot the couple on a date, because they're focused entirely on each other. They smile at each other, hold hands across the table, laugh at each other's jokes and pick up their drinks at the same time.

On the other side of the restaurant, the couple who just had a row are equally obvious. They are both sitting stiffly in their seats, not speaking. Their heads are turned from each other and they frown at their own thoughts. But they are still in rapport! They are a couple and they have been here before. Maybe unconsciously, they know what happens next. They know there is a 'programme' that gets them from the argument to kissing and making up. Soon one of them will take the next step in that programme and apologize, or storm out, or get the bill. They know what happens next. If that programme didn't exist, they wouldn't be a couple.

 Wherever you happen to be, put the book down for a moment and look around you. If there are other people around watch how they interact and gauge the extent of rapport between them. (If you're at home alone reading this, then do it next time you go out.)

 When people are in rapport with each other they tend to do the same things.

Creating rapport

In normal everyday encounters you are likely to create a degree of rapport quite naturally and without conscious effort most of the time. However, it may not always be sufficient for your purpose. Negotiating a pay rise may require a lot more rapport than requesting a few days off!

Barriers to establishing rapport naturally could be:
- You are starting from very different points of view
- You are preoccupied with your own internal world and not giving sufficient attention to others
- You are stressed or anxious
- There are cultural differences.

If the rapport doesn't happen naturally, it's very useful to be able to create rapport deliberately, or to deepen the rapport when it is insufficient to achieve your desired outcome.

 The simplest way to establish rapport is by matching and mirroring non-verbal behaviour.

Matching non-verbal behaviour is the most effective way to build rapport because it's usually outside of conscious awareness and because it's what people do naturally when they like and trust someone.

Having said that, it's not always the easiest strategy.

 Make yourself really comfortable in your seat. Notice how you are sitting: how far back on the seat are you? Resting against the back of the seat? Is your weight evenly balanced or leaning to one side? Are your feet out in front or tucked under? What is the position of your arms and hands?

Now have a look around and notice someone else who is sitting on a similar seat. Shift your position to match theirs. Adopt the same posture, position of hands, feet etc. and notice how you feel. Less comfortable? Awkward? Self-conscious?

So, if you are in the middle of a business meeting and you decide to improve the level of rapport by matching another person's behaviour, you run the risk of feeling uncomfortable, awkward or self-conscious. It's hard to see how that will help the meeting, isn't it?

The key here is that although in theory we can all sit and stand and move in an almost infinite variety of different ways, in reality we all have a limited repertoire of ways that we habitually sit and stand and move. When you move outside of your normal repertoire, you can be distracted by the unfamiliarity of behaviour even if it isn't physically uncomfortable. If it is uncomfortable as well, it will decrease rapport because you'll be paying more attention to yourself than to the other person.

The only remedy for this is practice. The first goal of your practice will be to expand your repertoire. That means becoming more flexible (sometimes literally!) in how you sit, stand and move.

TRY IT NOW! Go for a walk through your nearest shopping area or park. Notice the people around you and experiment with walking the way they walk. Try sitting on a bench in the way that someone else does it. In the interest of not causing any offence, I recommend that you 'try on' the behaviour of people at some distance from you, not those in your immediate vicinity – so take your glasses if you need them to see at a distance!

If you practise in this way regularly, you will gradually increase your repertoire of ways to sit, stand and move. You should also notice a corresponding increase in the degree of rapport that 'happens naturally' in your interaction with other people.

Obviously there are some limitations on this. If you are matching the behaviour of someone who is physically much taller, shorter or bigger than you, there may be things that they can do that are impossible for you. Just do the nearest you can.

There are also some behaviours that it's not appropriate to match. For example, most women sit with their knees together. Matching the behaviour of a male colleague who sits with his knees wide apart would look odd and inappropriate. So the best plan is to match other aspects of the posture while keeping your knees together in a ladylike fashion. In fact, my experience has been that men rarely adopt such an aggressively male posture in dealing with female colleagues if they are focused on mutual benefit. It's only when there is a disagreement or power struggle that the extreme masculine behaviour comes into play.

 Practise matching behaviour in places where it doesn't matter whether or not you can carry on a conversation. To begin with you'll find that you can't concentrate on what someone is saying if you're also watching what they're doing. Obviously this is not a good strategy for important meetings. Practise at social events, at home with the family or when you're on the sidelines of a meeting.

One of my students told me that he practised by watching TV chat shows. He would sit on the sofa and match the actions of the host or the guests as they chatted. That's a very low-risk way to practise – as long as you're alone!

Matching behaviour

You can match someone's behaviour at the 'macro' level such as standing when they stand, sitting when they sit, leaning forward at the same time and so on. Overall posture is another example of matching the bigger picture. You can also match more specific aspects of behaviour such as position of feet and hands, facial expressions and details such as shoulder position, breathing rate, and gestures.

A word of advice about gestures. In normal conversation, most people use their hands to help convey the meaning of their words. Some people use big expansive gestures, others use much smaller movements. It's good to match the style of gesture, but only when you are speaking. In a normal conversation it's only the person who is speaking who you can see waving their hands around. If you match those gestures as the person is making them, you are likely to distract them and to reduce the level of rapport – because this is abnormal behaviour.

 Remember to match gestures only when *you* are speaking. If you match someone's gesture when *they* are speaking, you'll look strange and they'll probably think you're weird!

Matching voice

You can also match the way that someone speaks. This is especially useful on the telephone. The easiest things to match are speed of talking and loudness.

THINK ABOUT IT Have you ever noticed that when you speak on the phone to someone who has a very different accent from you, after a while you begin to adopt a little of their way of speaking? Some people are very self-conscious about this and consciously try to stop it. In fact, it is an indicator that there is good rapport and should be allowed to happen. Bear in mind that you will be very sensitive to any slight changes in your own voice, because it's totally familiar to you. What you may not have noticed is that the other person has also made a corresponding small shift in their own voice to bring it closer to your way of talking.

So, while I wouldn't recommend actively matching someone else's accent – because it might sound as if you're making fun of it – if it happens naturally regard it as a good sign.

 My husband can always tell if I'm talking on the phone to my parents. I grew up in the north of England and as I've lived and worked further south for many years my accent is less obvious than it was when I was growing up. Until, that is, I get on the phone to someone with a stronger northern accent. Then my accent flies north faster than I could hurtle up the motorway!

Matching words
In matching the way that someone is speaking, you can also match their choice of words. This can be helpful when building relationships by email as well as in spoken communication.

The reason why this matters is that words mean subtly different things to different people. If your colleague suggests that a piece of work is 'a priority' and you ask, 'Why is it urgent?' then you may confuse or irritate him. Asking, 'Why is it a priority?' will make complete sense to him. You're using the same linguistic label as your colleague and that creates a sense of being 'on the same wavelength'. It's a separate discussion as to whether 'priority' means exactly the same to each of you, but for now, you've deepened the rapport.

Measuring rapport

Rapport is a multi-sensory experience and so you can detect it in a variety of ways. With practice you'll be able to calibrate quite accurately the extent of rapport either between you and someone else or between two other people. With further practice you'll be able to tell what's going on in a group and who is most responsive to whom.

How rapport feels

When you are in rapport with another person you can feel it. It's very different from the feeling you get when you're *not* in rapport. Most people describe the feeling of rapport as a warm feeling. We have that in language – you might say, 'I met the new analyst today and I really warmed to her.' The warm feeling is usually in the upper body. Some people feel it in their chest, others in the stomach area.

How rapport looks

When people reach a certain level of rapport, it is significant for them. It creates a shift in the nervous system. It's as if the body is on full alert because something important is going on. You can see this happening, because the shift causes the tiny blood vessels under the skin to dilate slightly, which results in a subtle 'warming up' of the colour of your complexion. This is easier to spot in people who are fair-skinned, but it can be noticeable in those with darker skin as well. I'm not referring to the kind of bright blush that someone might get when they're embarrassed or nervous, nor the neckline flush that some people get when they are angry or stressed. This is much more subtle.

How rapport sounds

We've already established that people match voice tone, speed and volume when they are in rapport. What you might also hear are comments that indicate a significant level of rapport. Have you ever met someone for the first time and really 'clicked'? Did one of you say something like, 'I feel like I've known you for ages'? If you did, that's good indicator of rapport. It's less likely that someone would say, 'Oh, haven't we got good rapport?' so you have to listen carefully to spot this kind of clue.

If the conversation is with someone you work with and know quite well, they might say something like, 'I'm really glad you're working on this with me' or 'You and I are a good team aren't we?'

In a social situation your friend may simply say, 'We should do this more often!'

Pacing and leading

Once you are confident that you've achieved a suitable level of rapport, you can test to see if the other person is truly responsive to you by **leading**.

Leading is when one person does something and the other person does exactly the same within a few moments, without realizing that they have done it. This is important because the person who follows is much easier to influence at that point in the interaction.

Generally you will achieve deeper levels of rapport through matching behaviour. That means that you are following the lead of the other person. Leading means that instead of doing what they do, you do something slightly different. If you really have deep rapport, they will follow your lead and do the same thing. If not, just come back to doing what they do and build up the rapport even further before you test again.

Next time you're in a conversation with a friend (outside of work) have a go at leading them to do something new. For example, you could lean back in your chair or cross your legs. You could also try getting up or walking around to see if they will follow.

KEY TERMS

Pacing and leading is the process by which you can influence someone else to do something that you want them to do.

Pacing refers to any change you make in your state or behaviour, in order to establish or deepen your rapport with another person or group. It still counts as pacing whether you do it consciously and deliberately or whether you do it naturally and unconsciously.

Once you have established rapport you can **lead** the other person to different and new possibilities by subtly changing your own behaviour.

There are three main applications of this process. You can pace and lead someone to a new **state**, **behaviour** or **opinion**.

Pacing and leading states

This is a really useful thing to be able to do, especially if you work in a customer-facing environment and you have to deal with other people's problems.

State is the overall physical, mental and emotional experience of a person at a given moment. Technically, it's the sum of all the neurological activity at that time and it describes a person's current feelings. Everyday states include relaxed, irritated, concerned, confident, tired, anxious and excited. There are thousands of words for states.

Do you ever have to deal with someone who is in a state that isn't ideal for the situation? It could be someone who is overly nervous about making a presentation, or someone who seems to have no sense of urgency about a deadline, or someone who is angry because something has gone wrong. If you deal directly with customers, you'll almost certainly be familiar with the latter example.

In all of these situations, wouldn't it be great to be able to change the other person's state and make them easier to deal with?

The principle is very straightforward. First, you *pace* by matching their behaviour and matching the key aspects of the state. Then when you have sufficient rapport, you *lead* to a more appropriate state.

However, suppose you have an angry customer to deal with. She's shouting at you and is clearly very angry. Are you going to match her?

Common sense tells us that matching the anger is not going to help anyone and I agree entirely. What most people then do in that situation is the complete opposite. They speak very quietly and calmly and invite the customer to give them the facts.

This can work, but it can take a long time to calm down the customer and find out what you need to know to solve the problem. Sometimes it can make the situation even worse. Here's why:

When someone is angry, it's because one or more of their values are being violated. When you speak to the angry person in a very quiet and calm manner, there is a meta-message which says, 'This isn't worth getting excited about.' Clearly, to the person whose values are being trampled on, it *is* worth getting excited about and so your calm demeanour makes them even more annoyed.

This is the same thing that happens when you're having an argument with your partner or a family member and, just as you are working up to the thing that *really* makes you angry, the other person says, 'Calm down'. Usually that makes you even more angry than ever!

So, if you want to avoid your customer thinking that you don't really care about their problem and you don't think it's worth getting upset over, what do you do? You match.

Don't match the anger, but match the energy and emphasis in their voice and behaviour. Speak briskly and resist the urge to drop your voice. If you look the customer in the eye and say, 'Right then, let me see what I do about this' in a suitably urgent tone of voice, what will often happen is that the customer will immediately calm down. You have shown the customer that you care, and that is a huge relief to her and she will relax and let you help.

I realize that this is counterintuitive, so I recommend that you practise before trying it out on a real customer.

Practise saying something helpful in a brisk and loud voice. For example: 'Let me see what I can do to help', 'I'd like to resolve this for you' or 'Okay, tell me about the problem.'

I taught this principle to the customer services team at one of the call centres of a large IT company. Their main role was to deal with customer complaints and they had a very good track record in solving problems. The difficulty was that the average call time was around 65 minutes, meaning that sometimes there would be a queue of calls, with customers getting even more annoyed at being kept waiting. After the team started using a brisk and more energetic voice tone, the average call time dropped by half, without any change in the rate of resolving issues.

Pacing and leading behaviour

Pacing and leading behaviour is very easy to do. It may have fewer applications at work, but you can use it to test somebody's responsiveness when you want to influence them to help you, to co-operate on a project or to buy something.

The principle is again very simple. If someone is doing something and you want them to stop it, then you pace by doing the same thing, build the rapport and then lead by stopping what you were doing and doing something else.

For example, suppose you have a colleague who repeatedly clicks a pen open and closed during a meeting. You can match that behaviour and click your own pen (or tap it on the table at the same rate; that works just as well) until you have rapport and then stop. If you have enough rapport, your colleague will stop too.

To get someone to start doing something, use the same principle. Match their current activity or behaviour and gradually transition to what you want them to do.

 I was on site with a long-standing client, an IT director who had recently changed companies. I asked him to introduce me to the HR director of the company, so that I could make sure that what I was doing with the IT team wasn't at cross-purposes with anything else going on in the company. I was also aware of the potential for the HR director to offer me further business.

The IT director suggested that we all go out to dinner. I was sitting opposite the HR director and had lots of opportunity to match him and build a significant level of rapport. After we'd been at the table for a while the IT director asked me to move and allow him to go to the bar for some more drinks. I stood up to let him through and as I turned backed I found the HR director also standing up, with a slightly confused expression on his face. He'd unconsciously followed my lead (which wasn't intended to lead him) and couldn't figure out why!

Needless to say, he became a client.

Pacing and leading opinion

To pace and lead opinion takes more time and effort than pacing and leading behaviour or state. However, it's probably the kind of influencing that you'll most often want to do at work, so it's worth learning how to do it well.

Pacing opinion means expressing agreement. This might be tricky, because if you want to influence someone's opinion, that suggests that they currently don't agree with you. So the first stage is to thoroughly understand their point of view and identify points that you can agree upon. To do this might take time. You'll have to ask lots of questions, listen and clarify so that you really know where they are starting from. Look out for basic assumptions, outcomes or 'rules' that you can agree with. Tell the other person all the things you agree with and write them up on a flipchart if that's appropriate.

The next step is to ask yourself, 'What else would they need to know, so that the decision I want them to make, or opinion I want them to hold, is a logical conclusion from the information to hand?'

You see, when two people have different opinions about something, it usually means that they had different information to consult when they made up their minds. Each person had a different set of research, experiences, beliefs, values and outcomes. Their resulting point of view will make perfect sense when viewed from the standpoint of that information, but with a different set of information to consult, it may seem wrong.

If you remember the NLP presupposition that says 'people are doing the best they can with what they've got,' it's clear that a person's point of view is derived from the resources they have to hand. To influence their point of view, you have to manage the information available to them.

REMEMBER THIS!!! If you want to influence someone else's opinion, be prepared to have your own opinion influenced as well. When you start finding out about the other person's point of view, you may find out some useful information that shifts your own view of the situation. The more you share the factors that led each of you to your individual opinions, the easier it becomes to jointly decide on a course of action, plan or standpoint.

IF YOU REMEMBER ONE THING

Pace... pace... pace... and then... *lead.*

5. Rep systems

We have six representational systems. They're often referred to as rep systems:

- Visual
- Auditory
- Kinaesthetic
- Olfactory
- Gustatory
- Digital

There is a rep system relating to each one of our senses, and then the digital system, which relates to non-sensory thinking such as facts, figures, concepts and language.

KEY TERM The rep system is the internal mechanism for representing inside our minds the information relating to a particular sense. For example, the visual system is the way we see things in our mind's eye.

We all use all of our rep systems but few people use them equally. We each have habits and patterns in the ways that we use our senses and most of us tend to favour one or two rep systems over the others. Over time, the one that we use the most – our **primary rep system** – can also be seen in personality traits, behaviour and choice of language.

In working with rep systems in NLP, the olfactory and gustatory systems are often disregarded. This is because they are the least used for most people. And for most of us, they're not a significant part of the working day – my apologies to all chefs, tea tasters, sommeliers and perfumers!

I've always emphasized that sensory preference is just something people do and not who you are. I've tended to discourage comments like, 'I'm a visual'. However, I've recently read about research that suggests that there is a physiological disposition to use one rep system over the others and that this preference can be 'read' in the iris of the eye. *What the Eye Reveals* by Denny Ray Johnson or *Eye Yoga* by Jane Battenberg will give you more details.

We all use all of our rep systems. Our primary rep system is just the one most often used; it's not the *only* one used.

To find out your own preferences, you can use the following quiz.

Representational system preference quiz

For each of the following statements, place a number next to every phrase. Use the following system to indicate your preferences:

4 = Closest to describing you
3 = Next best description
2 = Next best
1 = Least descriptive of you

Statement 1
In making a decision I am likely to:
___ trust my gut feeling
___ talk it over with someone
___ look at the situation objectively
___ study the relevant information

Statement 2
During an argument, I am most likely to be influenced by:
___ the other person's tone of voice
___ whether or not I can see what other person means
___ the logic of the other person's argument
___ whether or not I can empathize with the other person's feelings

Statement 3
Learning is made easier for me if:
___ I'm shown a diagram or chart
___ I can have a go and experience something new for myself
___ theoretical models make sense of my own thoughts
___ ideas are explained to me and I can discuss with others

Statement 4
It is easiest for me to:
___ recall the sound of a person's voice
___ remember what someone said to me
___ remember someone's touch or handshake
___ see someone's face in my mind's eye

Statement 5
I get distracted:
___ by background noise
___ by inconsistent facts and data
___ if I'm physically uncomfortable
___ if I'm in a room that is untidy or painted an unattractive colour

Scoring
Copy your answers, in the same order you wrote them on the quiz, into the spaces below.

Statement 1

___ K

___ A

___ V

___ D

Statement 2

___ A

___ V

___ D

___ K

Statement 3

___ V

___ K

___ D

___ A

Statement 4

___ A

___ D

___ K

___ V

Statement 5

___ A

___ D

___ K

___ V

123

Each number now corresponds to a letter, V, A, K or D. Now look at the grid below and, for each statement, copy the numbers into the relevant columns to reflect the way they match up in the above listings.

	V	A	K	D
Statement 1				
Statement 2				
Statement 3				
Statement 4				
Statement 5				
Totals				

(Check that your totals added together = 50)

Interpreting the results

Comparing the total scores gives your *relative* preferences for each of the four major representational systems (remember V=visual, A=auditory, K=kinaesthetic and D=digital). The order of the four rep systems is more significant than the actual scores.

Unless you have a very marked preference for one particular rep system, it's likely that you will relate to some aspects of each. We will look at some of the typical behaviour relating to each preference below.

Just because you have a low score and low preference for a rep system, it doesn't necessarily follow that you are not skilled in using that rep system. It's a bit like left- or right-handedness – I'm left-handed, that's my preference, but it doesn't mean that I never use my right hand or that I can't achieve good results by using it.

Remember that it's a quiz and not a properly validated psychometric instrument. It's highly sensitive to context, mood and manipulation!

Indicators of preference

It can be very useful to be able to spot another person's sensory preferences. Often when communication is difficult or a relationship is strained, it's because of a clash of rep system preferences. Once you know somebody's preferences, you can adjust your method of communication, your style and speed of presentation and even the language you use to make it easier to get your message across.

Here are some of the obvious indicators for each preference.

Visual: If you have a significant preference for visual thinking, you'll probably relate to some of these indicators. Unless you scored 20 for visual when you did the quiz, it's unlikely that you'll relate to all of them. As you read the list, think about other people you know as well.

- Well-dressed and groomed
- Shiny shoes
- Neat hairstyle
- Upright posture

- Quick movements and speech
- Short attention span
- Finishes other people's sentences for them
- Notices how things look and comments on it
- Distracted by untidiness, decor and bright colours
- Keeps a tidy desk
- Likes diagrams, charts and pictures
- Will draw diagrams to help explain their thinking
- Prefers email to telephone, but probably likes Skype!
- Enjoys watching movies
- Uses the language of sight: 'vision', 'focus', 'perspective', 'viewpoint' etc.

Also bear in mind that a person's values will interact with rep system preferences. Someone who values tidiness may not be visually oriented, they may simply like to know where to find everything.

Auditory: There are fewer people in the general population who have auditory as their primary rep system. If this is you, it may explain why you sometimes sense that other people just aren't on your wavelength!

- Has a pleasant speaking voice
- Measured pace of speaking and activity
- Enjoys music
- Also enjoys silence
- Always knows whether they want to listen to music, what music it is and how loud

- Distracted by background noise
- Likes to wear earphones in an open-plan office
- Uses the telephone rather than email
- Likes to discuss ideas and plans
- Talks to self out loud
- Is a good mimic of accents and voices
- Enjoys listening to the radio
- Uses the language of sound: 'talk', 'tell', 'loud', 'clear' etc.

Someone with a high auditory preference is usually very aware of your emotions when you are speaking. If you don't want your auditory colleague to know that you're annoyed about something, wait until you've calmed down to call him. Even if you think you've masked the emotion in your voice, he'll be able to hear it.

Kinaesthetic: People with a high kinaesthetic preference aren't necessarily 'touchy-feely' types. Kinaesthetic includes physical movement and sensation, not always relating to emotions.

- Takes time and moves deliberately
- Dresses for comfort
- Touches people and things
- Speaks slowly
- Sits low down and leaning back
- Distracted by physical discomfort – temperature, hard chairs etc.

- Will set up an office chair or car seat to their exact needs (and be annoyed if you change it!)
- Can maintain concentration for a long time
- Gets their sentences finished by others!
- Walks around to think clearly
- Trusts their 'gut feeling'
- Prefers face-to-face interaction to email or telephone
- Likes demonstrations and interaction
- Likes live entertainment
- Uses the language of feeling: 'feel', 'move', 'warm', 'prickly', 'touch' etc.

Most people regard businesslike behaviour to be non-emotional, so some people who have a high kinaesthetic preference disguise it or detach from it at work in order to appear more professional. Therefore you might have to work harder to spot this preference at work. A lot of kinaesthetic types look more like digital at work.

Digital: This is the non-sensory preference. If it's not obvious how someone is thinking, it might be that they have a strong digital preference. This is also the conventional mode of communication in business.

- Tends to be a 'low-responder' – more interested in what you tell them than in you personally
- Low sensory awareness, finds it easy to concentrate
- Dresses for purpose and function rather than style or comfort

- Has a large vocabulary
- Chooses words carefully
- Often pauses in the middle of a sentence – to think about how to express their thoughts
- Likes facts and figures
- Gets distracted by incorrect or illogical information
- Organizes their environment to logical principles
- Rarely shows emotion
- Uses the language of logic and fact: 'think', 'know', 'calculate', 'deduce', 'infer' etc.

The most important thing for someone with a high digital preference is for things to make sense. If you have to present an idea or report to someone like this, make sure you've got all your facts straight and your numbers add up or they won't pay attention to anything else.

Language relating to sensory preferences

People tend to use language that relates to the rep system they are using as they speak. For example, someone looking at pictures in their mind's eye will use the language of seeing when they tell you their idea. A person who is thinking logically through a process is more likely to use digital language to describe their conclusions. The list below shows some common words relating to each preference, and of course, there are lots more.

VISUAL	AUDITORY	KINAESTHETIC	DIGITAL
see	hear	feel	sense
look	listen	touch	experience
view	tell	grasp	understand
appear	quiet	contact	think
show	sound	reach out	learn
focus	loud	running	process
reveal	discuss	ongoing	decide
perspective	clear	traction	perceive
picture	silence	instinct	consider

Communicating with different preferences

Once you've figured out a person's preferences, you can begin to adapt your communication so that it really works.

Why should I adapt my style to suit other people? Do I have to do all the work?

The purpose of adapting your style to suit the person you're talking to is so that you achieve your outcome. If you are conversing with no outcome in mind, it doesn't matter how you communicate. But if there's something you want to achieve, adapting to the other person's sensory preferences will make it easier to get what you want.

Below is a list of communication strategies for each preference. Some relate to your preparation before a meeting or conversation, some are tips to follow during the dialogue. I encourage you to experiment with these and notice what differences you can make to the success of your meetings.

Visual: How it *looks* is important
- Prepare notes before a meeting rather than scribbling on the board as you go along

- Maintain a clean and tidy environment

- Make sure that documents are well formatted and look professional

- Include pictures, diagrams, charts and models

- Cut to the chase, and keep the pace lively

- Give written as well as verbal feedback and recognition.

Auditory: How it *sounds* is important
- Choose meeting locations that are quiet and do not have distracting background noise

- Keep your tone friendly and pleasant

- Avoid meetings and phone calls when you are irritated or impatient – they will be able to tell

- Allow time for questions and discussion

- Give verbal as well as written feedback and recognition.

Kinaesthetic: How it *feels* is important
- Explain your plans a few days before a formal meeting and outline the involvement you want

- Take time to set the scene before turning to specific business

- Check that the environment is suitable for the purpose

- Allow time for decisions to be made – don't try to rush the process

- Do *not* finish their sentences

- Give feedback in person.

Digital: How it *makes sense* is important
- Check your facts and figures

- Check your facts and figures again

- Use an agenda that progresses logically through the business

- Keep your comments relevant

- Do *not* finish their sentences

- Give specific, factual feedback.

Speaking to a group

If you are preparing a presentation – or an email – to communicate with a group of people, it's unlikely that you'll know the sensory preferences of everyone concerned. The simplest strategy is to appeal to all four major rep systems at different times in your presentation.

This can mean preparing some specific sentences that express your key ideas in ways that appeal to all major preferences.

For example:

> "I know a lot of people have been a little anxious about the sales figures this month, but I want you to relax and let me tell you why you haven't been hearing good news so far. I want to show you the figures so you can see for yourself that we've had good reason to keep quiet until now. I'm sure you'll feel comfortable that it made sense not to shout about our success until we could demonstrate some concrete results."

Now let's look at the language used and how it might appeal to different primary rep systems (remember V=visual, A=auditory, K=kinaesthetic and D=digital):

> "I know a lot of people have been a little anxious (K) about the sales figures this month, but I want you to relax (K) and let me tell (A) you why (D) you haven't been hearing (A) good news so far. I want to show (V) you the figures (D) so you can see (V) for yourself that we've had good reason (D) to keep quiet (A) until now. I'm sure you'll feel comfortable (K) that it made sense (D) not to shout (A) about our success until we could demonstrate (V) some tangible (K) results."

I'm not suggesting that you script everything you want to say, just spend some time on key messages and make sure that you include everyone. The rest of the time, just use your normal style.

 If you regularly take time to craft sentences using language from all four major rep systems, it will become easier and easier until you can do it without thinking about it.

 To completely engage a diverse group will almost certainly mean also preparing some visual aids to *show* your ideas to the people with a visual preference, and it's going to be important to have a *logical structure* to your material if you want to keep the attention of those with a digital preference. Allow time before you speak to *connect* informally with people who have a kinaesthetic preference and include time for *questions and discussion* that will engage those with an auditory style.

---

6. Perceptual positions

The idea of perceptual positions will probably be a familiar one. It means taking different points of view on the same situation. In NLP we usually consider three different perceptual positions:

First position: Looking at the world from your own point of view, totally aware of your own feelings, needs, experience, agenda and thoughts, without taking account of anyone else's point of view – 'How is this for me?'

Second position: Imagining what it is like for another person in this situation; considering their needs, thoughts, experience, feelings and agenda – 'How is this for him or her?' (Notice that this is not the same as wondering 'What would I do in their situation?' It's more to do with wondering 'What would *they* do in their situation?' The stronger rapport you have with another person, the easier it will be for you to appreciate their reality and achieve second position.)

Third position: Seeing the world from an outside point of view, as an independent observer, someone with no personal involvement in the situation – 'How would this look to someone who is not involved?' From this objective viewpoint you can observe, evaluate and create new and useful choices.

All three positions are equally important; none is any better or worse than the others. Aim to be able to move between them freely and use whichever one suits your purpose at the time.

Many people find it quite natural to move between first and second position and are able to appreciate another person's point of view quite readily. The third position is a useful addition to that, because it is dissociated from the situation and provides a very different and more objective perspective.

Associated means totally immersed in an experience and fully aware of your feelings.

Dissociated means detached from the situation, seeing it as an outsider and removed from the feelings.

We can describe the first perceptual position as associated and the third position as dissociated. Second position is associated to another person.

Remember a time when you had an argument with someone and you *absolutely know* that you were in the right.

Take yourself back into the memory of the argument and fully associate into first position. Experience the feelings again and rehearse your arguments.

Next, take a mental step back from the memory and then imagine being the other person in the same argument. Fully associate into second position and become aware of the feelings and thoughts of the other person.

After that, take a mental step back again. Look at the argument from third position, as if you were a completely uninvolved observer. Observe these two people arguing. What do you notice that they do not?

Finally, come back to first position and fully associate into your own experience. Is it different?

This kind of mental exercise can be very helpful in understanding difficult interactions with others or long-standing tensions. It can also be very helpful in preparing for important meetings, presentations or interviews.

For an even more thorough approach to improving relationships using perceptual positions, try the technique known as the 'meta mirror'.

The meta mirror

The meta mirror is an excellent technique for addressing tension in relationships. You can use it after a disagreement, to explore a relationship that simply doesn't seem to be effective, or to prepare for an important conversation.

Unlike the mental exercise above, this one works best if you anchor the positions to the floor, walk around and literally see things from different positions.

Here are the step-by-step instructions:

1. Mark four positions on the floor in roughly the arrangement shown below.

2. Identify the person with whom you would like a better relationship.

3. Step into position 1 (first position); imagine the person standing at position 2 and fully associate into your feelings about him or her.
    Step out and break state

4. Step into position 2 (second position) and 'be' the other person. Fully associate into their experience of you.
    Step out and break state

5. Step into position 3 (third position) and become a dissociated observer. What do you notice? What insight do you have that they do not?
    Step out and break state

6. Step into position 4, from where you can see the 'you' in position 1 and the 'you' in position 3. Imagine the 'you' in position 3 moving to position 1 and replacing the 'you' in that spot.

7. Step back into position 1. How is it now?
   Step out and break state

8. Step into position 2. How is it now?
   Step out and break state

9. Finish by associating back into position 1.

Enjoy the results!

The principal key to making this work is to take your time and fully associate into each stage of the process. If you don't take the time to really experience the relationship from each of the perceptual positions, you won't get the full benefit of the process.

Along with that, it's important to break state completely as you move from one perceptual position to the next. Physically 'shaking it off' is a good 'break state', or you could use a challenging mental process such as reciting a phone number backwards or spelling a long word backwards. Experiment to find out what works for you. The 'break state' ensures that you get complete separation between the different perceptual positions and can be clear about which emotions and experiences belong in each position.

Let's look at each step individually:

Identify the person with whom you would like a better relationship.
You can put anyone into this technique – a difficult boss, troublesome co-worker, demanding customer or irritating family member. It really can make a difference to any kind of relationship issue.

Step into position 1 (first position); imagine the person standing at position 2 and fully associate into your feelings about him or her.
Visualize the other person standing about 2m away from you, facing you. Take time to imagine this fully, and to feel what it's like for you to be faced with this other person. Remember to break state.

Step into position 2 (second position) and 'be' the other person. Fully associate into their experience of you.
You may not think you know much about how the other person feels, but once you associate into this second position you might be surprised by how much you can experience as if you were the other person. Notice the view you get of yourself in position 1; how do you look from this perspective?

Step into position 3 (third position) and become a dissociated observer. What do you notice? What insight do you have that they do not?

Make sure that your third position is sufficiently far back from the first two that you can easily 'see' both of the two people without having to turn your head. Be open to whatever insights come in this position. It might be quite different from anything you expect. Now you have gathered information from all three perceptual positions.

Step into position 4, from where you can see the 'you' in position 1 and the 'you' in position 3.

Imagine the 'you' in position 3 moving to position 1 and replacing the 'you' in that spot.

The only thing you do at position 4 is to visualize the switch of places between the 'you' at position 1 and the 'you' at position 3.

Step back into position 1. How is it now?

Again, take your time and fully associate into the experience of facing the other person. My prediction is that it will have shifted in some way. Notice how you feel and remember to break state when you're ready to move on.

Step into position 2. How is it now?

Go back to 'being' the other person and experience the shift in the relationship from their perspective. Notice what it's like now to be faced with a different attitude from 'you'.

Finish by associating back into position 1.
It's always a good idea to finish up by being yourself!

Once you've been through this process, I expect that you'll feel differently about the other person to some extent. What's interesting is how this affects your next actual encounter with that person. Because you've made a shift in your perception of that person, you'll behave slightly differently; and as soon as you do something differently, you open up the possibility that they can be different too.

 Think of a person who you don't get on with as well as you would like. Run the meta mirror with that person in position 2. Notice how it affects your perception of the other person and the relationship you have with them.

---

7. Submodalities

Representational (rep) systems are sometimes referred to as modalities. *Sub*modalities are the distinctions we make within each modality.

Submodalities are aspects of the structure of internal representation and are independent of content. They are significant because the meaning of a representation is encoded in its submodalities.

Working with submodalities can be a very quick way to get some control over what goes on in your mind. There are simple techniques we can use to increase motivation, change habits and attitudes or stop something from continually haunting our thoughts. The reason why submodalities techniques are quick to use is that they intervene directly with your internal representations.

Think of something that is on your 'to-do' list. As you think about that task, notice the picture in your mind's eye (it may not be a very clear picture – that's okay).

Notice if the picture is a still picture or a movie. Notice if it's in colour or black and white. Notice how bright it is and notice how big the picture is.

Now, just for fun, make the picture bigger. Put it in really vivid colour. Make it very bright. Make sure it's moving at a lifelike speed.

What effect does that have on how keen you are to do the task?

As you can see, when you change the way something is represented in your mind, you can change your attitude towards it. The more you practise this, the more you'll understand about how things work in your own head and the easier it will be for you to have choice about the way you think.

Submodalities checklist

In the example above, we used four different submodalities, all of them relating to the visual modality (or rep system):

- Size of picture
- Brightness
- Colour or black and white
- Movie or still

There are many more submodalities that can be used, including auditory and kinaesthetic submodalities. Here is a list of the main submodalities used in NLP techniques:

VISUAL	AUDITORY	KINAESTHETIC
Location	Location	Location
Distance	Distance	Moving/still
Size	Volume	Size
Framed/panoramic	Sustained/repeated/short/intermittent	Shape
Colour/black and white		Intensity
Bright/dim	Clear/muffled	Duration
Movie/still	Fast/slow	Colour
Movie: Speed of movement	Rhythmic or not	Pressure
	Constant/changing	Weight
Focus		Temperature
Associated/dissociated		Constant/changing

When we consider location in visual submodalities, it means the location in your visual field: is the picture straight ahead, for example, or above eye level, or off to one side etc. Obviously the picture is *actually* inside your head, but what we're considering is where it appears to be when we look at it with our mind's eye. Similarly, the distance is how far away we seem to be seeing the picture from, is it close up, at arm's length or further away?

Association and dissociation in this context can be detected from the viewpoint. An associated picture will be the view through your own eyes as if you are there, reliving the memory (in first position). In a dissociated picture you will be able to see your own face and/or body in the picture (as you would from third position). In general there will be stronger feelings with an associated representation.

The meaning of the representation is encoded in the submodalities. This means that the submodalities are your brain's way of tagging thoughts and filing them.

 Pick two memories of meetings you attended recently. Choose one that was a really interesting, stimulating meeting that achieved something tangible and that you feel good about having been part of. Choose another that was dull or difficult, that didn't achieve anything and that you feel was a waste of your time.

Now, one at a time, focus on the memory and notice how the internal representation is structured. Make a note of the submodalities as they relate to the two memories and then compare them. Pay particular attention to the location in your visual field, as this is often the key to meaning.

When you focus on representations of contrasting experiences, it's usual to find that there are differences in their structures. For example, the positive memory might be large, bright and/or colourful and straight ahead whereas the other one might be smaller, dimmer and/or in black and white and lower down.

What you have discovered in the exercise above are the 'filing codes' that your brain uses to tag 'memories of good meetings' and 'memories of bad meetings'. Everything you might think about is tagged in this way through its submodalities.

Since we've already seen that it's possible to change your internal representations at will, it won't surprise you to discover that we can use submodalities to change our attitudes to tasks, people, memories or anything else, simply by changing the 'filing codes'.

Mapping across

'Mapping across' means changing the submodalities of one representation into those of another representation that has a different meaning, for the purpose of changing your experience of, or attitude to, the first representation.

This technique is worth mastering, because once you've learned to do it, you can use it to make changes in a matter of moments. Here's how to do it:

1. Identify what you want to change (e.g. 'I want to stop eating chocolate' or 'I want to be motivated to make phone calls').

2. Specify the category in your mind that currently holds the thing you want to change (e.g. 'things I like to eat' or 'things I'm not motivated to do').

3. Note down the submodalities of the thing you want to change (e.g. when you think about chocolate, or making phone calls, do you have a picture in your mind's eye?).

4. Specify the category in your mind you want to move the thing to (e.g. 'things I eat occasionally' or 'things I don't like to eat' for the chocolate; and 'things I enjoy doing' or 'things I can do easily' for the phone calls). Be mindful of ecology in making your choice.

5. Think of something that is currently in the category identified in step 4 (e.g. ice-cream or Brussels sprouts – depending on the desired outcome – in the first scenario; and 'checking my email' or 'attending meetings' in the second scenario).

6. Elicit the submodalities of the thing identified in step 5.

7. Compare the two sets of submodalities; identify the differences.

8. Change the submodalities of the thing you want to change (elicited in step 3) so that they match the submodalities elicited in step 6.

9. Test.

You can use the worksheet opposite to help you through the 'mapping across' process.

Thing I want to change my attitude to: _____

Current category in my mind: _____

Category to move to: _____

Example from desired category: _____

Comparison of submodalities:

	Thing I want to change	Example from desired category
Location		
Distance		
Size of picture		
Colour or black and white		
Movie or still		
Associated or dissociated		
Focused or defocused		
Framed or panoramic		
Bright or dim		

8. Strategies

Back in the introduction to this book, we talked about 'programmes' of behaviour that run our habits and skills. You'll remember the principle: anything you do really well, you can do without thinking about it. When we talk about strategies in NLP, we're referring to those programmes. Some strategies drive behaviour that can be observed on the outside, some strategies relate to mental processes and cannot be observed directly.

A **strategy** is a specific syntax of external and internal experience that consistently produces a specific outcome. In other words it's a process of paying attention to a sequence of things – some in current experience, some in memory or imagination. Following the process generates an end result.

Everything we do involves a strategy. Let's take an example. If I'm attending a meeting I'll have run strategies for:

- Remembering that I've agreed to the meeting
- Preparing for the meeting
- Turning up on time
- Choosing where to sit in the meeting room
- Building rapport with other people in the meeting

- Listening
- Asking questions.

... and that's before I get to the point of making any kind of suggestion or decision.

All our daily activity is generated and maintained by strategies. Whether or not we finish what we do is governed by a strategy. How successful we are at a specific task will depend on how good the strategy is. The things we're good at and can do without thinking about, they're run by very effective strategies. The things we mess up, they're being run by strategies that don't work very well.

Working with strategies can be very detailed and laborious, so I don't propose to include everything here. I just want to share with you some knowledge about one particular type of strategy, and in particular, one very useful component of it. This will be the key to getting things done with other people.

Decision-making

Your decision-making strategy is a strategy for choosing between options. It is used in a wide variety of situations, such as deciding who to employ in a job, which of several suggestions is the best, where to go on holiday or what to buy as a birthday present. This strategy is particularly easy to observe in buying situations and very useful for sales people to know about. Even if your job doesn't involve selling to customers, it probably involves 'selling' ideas and plans to other people, so you'll find this a very useful tool for influencing others.

A typical decision-making strategy has four stages:

1. Motivation
2. Choice
3. Convincer
4. Reassurance

I'll describe these stages as they relate to a buying situation; bear in mind that they will also apply whenever a choice is made.

1. Motivation: This is how a person knows it's time to buy. It could be an 'away from' strategy such as, 'I must buy a new briefcase before the old one falls apart' or it could be a 'towards' strategy such as, 'If I buy a new briefcase I'll look smarter and more professional.'

The result of this part of the strategy is that the person is ready to make a choice.

2. Choice: This is how the person chooses between the various options. This part of the strategy can vary a lot between people. Some use a set of criteria to evaluate each option, others simply go for the first one they like. Whatever the strategy, it usually has some benefits and some drawbacks. There is rarely a 'perfect' strategy. If the strategy has a visual component then the person will want to see something before they buy, even if it's just a picture of what they are getting. If the strategy has a kinaesthetic component, the person will probably want to touch or handle the product. If that's the case, they probably won't buy by mail order unless they have been able to handle the item before ordering. This can seem a little bizarre at times – why would you need to touch a DVD before buying it? The answer is just because it's part of the strategy. And the strategy remains the same no matter what the choice is.

The result of this part of the strategy is that the person knows which option they prefer.

3. Convincer: This is how the person convinces himself or herself to act on the decision. It takes them from, 'That's the briefcase for me' to actually purchasing it. Have you ever wondered what's going on when someone seems to have made a buying decision but then doesn't buy. It's their convincer pattern at work. This is such a key piece that I'm going to elaborate on convincers later in the chapter.

The result of the convincer strategy is that the person acts on the decision. They buy.

4. Reassurance: Having bought, the reassurance strategy is the process that reassures the buyer that they've made a good purchase. This might involve external validation by showing the purchase to another person, it might simply be a case of using the item as soon as is practical to experience the benefit of owning it or it could be something else entirely. Reassurance strategies vary a lot between people, but each person sticks to their own strategy.

The result of this part of the strategy is that the person is satisfied with their decision.

Can you see how useful it can be to a salesperson to know what to do between the choosing part and the actual sale? If you know how people get from the choice to the purchase, you can help them to do it their way instead if trying to do it your way. So let's look at convincers in more detail.

More on convincers

The convincer strategy is a way of processing information in order to become convinced. Its useful to know about because a person will use the same strategy regardless of the context and the importance of the thing they are to be convinced of. Have you ever considered what it takes to convince you? Some people appear to make up their minds quickly and others take a long time. If you want to convince someone to buy, to authorize, to agree or to change, wouldn't it be useful to know how that person can be convinced most easily?

One of the greatest benefits of this can be in reducing your stress. I spent some time working with the customer services team of a large organization. These were the people who took the telephone calls that no one else could resolve. The people they were speaking to were often angry, upset or rude but the team members were skilled in winning confidence and resolving problems. However, they had some questions. For example: 'I told this customer the same thing three times, but he just wasn't convinced. Then I transferred him to my boss and she told him the same thing again and he accepted it – why didn't he listen to me?' or 'I explained to the customer exactly what to do, but she kept asking if I could fax some instructions to her – does this mean I wasn't clear?'

Another company I worked with was a small exclusive bridal shop. They couldn't understand why they were able to close some sales easily and other customers came back to the shop repeatedly but didn't place their order. They were beginning to think they were missing out on something.

They were right. If you need to influence other people then it helps to understand how people become convinced. There are two elements to a convincer strategy: one relates to the way the information is presented; the other is the time factor.

The first is the **convincer representational system** or how the person has to have the information represented in order to be convinced: Do they have to see it, hear it or experience it for themselves? Think about this: suppose you have a new colleague. How would you know that the new person was good at the job? Would you have to see them do it, hear about it, or perhaps work alongside them and experience it? If you have to *see* it to be convinced that the person is good at their job, then chances are you also have to *see* it to be convinced of anything else. Doubtless, the person who coined the phrase 'I'll believe it when I see it' had a visual convincer. Someone with an auditory convincer has to *hear* it to be convinced. The person with a kinaesthetic convincer needs to experience it for themselves.

The convincer rep system accounts for the irritating phenomenon of people who receive memos or emails but don't act on them until someone calls them on the phone (auditory convincer). Or the people who agree to your proposal outlined in a meeting but do nothing until they see it confirmed in writing (visual convincer). Or the customer who has listened to your explanation but would much prefer it if you could fax something to her to look at (visual again).

However, the convincer rep system doesn't account for the difference between the snappy decision-maker and the person who prevaricates until you begin to think that there must be something wrong.

The second aspect of convincer strategies is the **convincer demonstration**. Going back to that new colleague, how often does the person have to demonstrate their competence for you to be convinced? Answers to this question will usually fit one of four categories:

Automatic: The person with an automatic convincer will assume that the new colleague is competent on the basis of a small amount of information unless the new person demonstrates otherwise. You can convince this person quite easily, but so can everyone else! They are easy to sell to and readily give their support for new ideas. They are probably the 'early adopters' of new technology. Being easily convinced, they can change their minds quickly and don't always stay committed to a decision once they have made it. Interestingly, lots of sales people have automatic convincers and find it difficult to understand why other people are not as easily convinced as they are themselves.

Number of times: This person has to have the demonstration repeated several times before they are convinced. In a sales situation they may have to run their 'choice' strategy a fixed number of times. If you're selling to someone like this, either show them the product this number of times, or show them this number of alternatives. For the customer services team I was working with, this knowledge made a big difference. Their comments changed from 'Why did I have to repeat myself FOUR times to that man – is he stupid?' to 'I've just had someone on the phone with a four-times convincer' – imagine how much this reduced their stress. As a general rule, the higher the number of times a person has to run their strategy in order to be convinced, the more committed they will be to the decision once it is made. Persuading them to change their mind could also involve the same number of repetitions to achieve the necessary conviction.

There is potentially a shortcut to this, although it will only work if you have good rapport with the person. Suppose you need to convince someone who has a five-times convincer but you don't have time to go through your proposal five times. After the second time, you say something like 'If I've explained this to you once I must have explained it five times – isn't it time you made a decision?' As I said, it only works if you have good rapport…

Period of time: This person needs a period of time to be convinced. It was probably someone with this style who invented the 'trial period'. It might be a few hours or it might be months, but this person always needs this period of time to be convinced. If you're seeking their support for your project and they say, 'I'll think about it', ask them how long they'd like before you meet again. Don't assume that this is a polite way of saying no.

 Again, there is a possibility of a shortcut. Suppose you want to convince someone with a three-month period of time convincer. You present your proposal and they tell you they need to think about it. Do you wait three months? Unless you also have a three-month convincer, probably not. So, if you contact the person again after a few weeks, you can open the discussion with a comment such as, 'I've been so busy since we last discussed this proposal, it feels like at least three months since we spoke.' Again, it only works if you have good rapport but for those of us not endowed with the patience to wait three months for an answer, it can really speed up the process!

Consistent: This person is actually never convinced. They require repeated demonstration of your competence or the quality of your idea or your product. Nothing you can say or do will convince them. These people make tough managers, as you'll only ever be as good as your last result in their eyes. Paradoxically, they can sometimes they end up appearing to be inconsistent inasmuch as they may strongly support someone they believe to be doing well, but then if that person fails in any way to meet their standards, they will cease to support them and look for a new champion. Over a period of time it can appear that different individuals are 'flavour of the month' for a time, before falling out of favour and making way for the next one.

If you want to sell to someone with a consistent convincer, acknowledge that you can't convince them. One of the ladies in the bridalwear shop had a customer with a consistent convincer. She eventually told her, 'I know that I can't convince you that this is the perfect dress for you. You'll only know for sure when you're walking down the aisle in it on your wedding day.' She made the sale *and* the customer was happy.

To make full use of convincers, it helps to know your own convincer strategy. If you have, for example, a three-times convincer and you make a sale to a person with an automatic convincer, you might not be convinced that they have really bought unless they tell you three times! Save them the effort and tell yourself three times – it works just as well.

Of course, the main piece of information you'll need to be able to make use of all of the above is the convincer strategy of the person you want to influence. Most of them won't know themselves and even if they did, in the normal course of business it wouldn't be appropriate to ask. However, most people will tell you, if you know what to listen for.

For example, the customer services team quickly found that the way a person described their problem often gave some clues as to their convincer strategy. After all, they must be convinced that they have a problem! The kind of things customers said varied from, 'It hasn't been working properly for about a month, I knew it was time I got some advice' (period of time – one month) to 'I've tried it three times and it just won't work' (number of times – three) and 'I've never had any trouble with it and then today it completely packed up' (automatic).

By listening carefully to the way a customer describes the problem, it's possible to discover their convincer strategy and then use it to convince the same person that you have a solution for them.

Managing change

From time to time, organizations engage in programmes of widespread change. For example, there might be a change in business systems, a restructure of departments or the introduction of new working practices, equipment or standards. Often the people involved in driving the change get frustrated and discouraged because of what they perceive as 'negative attitudes' from the people required to do things differently.

In general, the reason that people resist change is that they are not convinced that the change is justified, appropriate or useful. This doesn't mean they will never be convinced (unless they have a consistent pattern), it just means that they're not convinced yet.

Change programmes run more smoothly and stand a much greater chance of success when the changes are implemented through volunteers who are ready to learn new processes, use new systems or implement new working practices. I always recommend that when an organization needs to run a programme of workshops or training programmes, that people are invited to choose which workshop or training session they attend. That way, the automatic convincers and one-time convincers can be the first to attend. They are usually the 'early adopters' and will be convinced quite quickly of the merits of the change.

They will be followed by the people with two- or three-times convincers and those with a short period of time convincer.

The third wave will be the people with longer period of time convincers and convincers of more than three times. It takes longer for this group to be convinced that the change is beneficial and to be ready to act on that decision.

Finally, there will be people with a consistent convincer who might never be convinced. They might still be reluctant to attend, even when you get to the last workshop. But there's no point in forcing them to come sooner. They'll just cast an air of gloom over the event and sow doubts in the minds of others.

By allowing people to adopt the changes when they feel ready, you eliminate the power struggle that so often emerges from major change programmes. It may seem like a leap of faith when only five people volunteer for the first workshop and you need to average twelve at each one. It *is* a leap of faith, but one worth taking.

9. Modelling

Earlier in the book I highlighted modelling as one of the key aspects of NLP that are useful at work.

 Modelling means identifying the structure of a skill that you observe someone else is particularly good at. If you can model the skill and the way the person achieves results, then you can learn to do it too.

The origins of NLP are in modelling. Richard Bandler and John Grinder modelled the language patterns of some of the great psychotherapists of the day and in doing so, not only unpicked the structure of language that influences others' thinking, but also developed the methodology to do the same with other skills.

The approach that Bandler and Grinder took was purely observational. This can be a very lengthy process, so we also use methods of interviewing the expert to find out more about what's going on in his or her head as they demonstrate the skill. Robert Dilts, the eminent NLP developer, trainer and practitioner, has contributed a lot to this more cognitive style of modelling.

If you're interested in learning how to model, there are some great books and courses that will show you how to do it. I'd like to share with you the results of two model-ling projects, so you get an idea of what can be achieved with this approach, and also to give you the benefit of two essential business skills.

Creating an air of authority

Working as a trainer and consultant, I'm privileged to meet a lot of senior people in a wide variety of organizations. Some people in senior roles have an air of authority that makes it obvious that they are in charge. Others don't. I became curious about what creates that air of authority, because I thought it would be a great thing to be able to do. So I started observing. And what I noticed surprised me, because it's really very simple to create an air of authority.

If you think it would help you at work, here's what you do. People who radiate an air of authority usually do two things:

1. Take their time
2. Take up space

Time: Taking time to do something or to answer a question or to begin a presentation gives a below conscious message that what you are about to do or say is worth waiting for. People who are nervous usually rush through everything, so doing the opposite shows you as confident and calm.

Simple ways to take your time:

- Do one thing at a time.

- After someone asks you a question, pause before answering.

- Believe that what you're about to say is worth waiting for and don't rush it.

- Stop if someone talks over you or causes a distraction.

Space: Even if you're not very tall or broad you can take up space with your belongings. When you take up space it demonstrates to people that you have a right to be there. People who feel uncomfortable in a situation often shrink away from it, so when you spread out it looks as if you're comfortable and that you belong.

 Simple ways to take up space:

- Relax. This will make you more likely to spread out, whereas if you are tense or nervous you will tend to make yourself smaller.

- In a meeting room, spread your belongings about in front of you; claim some territory (but don't encroach on your boss's space unless you want to challenge his authority).

- Stand fractionally further away from people than you would naturally.

- When speaking, make bold gestures with your hands.

Remembering names

I think that remembering names is an essential skill for all of us at work. Assuming you've been introduced to a person, when you use their name it is an acknowledgment of them and helps to create rapport. If you haven't been introduced, don't use their name by reading it off a security pass – some people will be offended and others will be startled.

Lots of people have difficulty remembering names and often the reason they can't retrieve a name from memory is that they didn't store it away in the first place. You can't retrieve something that isn't there. I'm blessed with a good memory and I've always been quite good at names, but I didn't always know how I did it.

The strategy for remembering names that I'm sharing here is the one I use and which was modelled from me by Craig Cummings as part of his Master Practitioner Certification. This was done by interview as well as observation – it would have been much harder to figure this one out by observation alone. Interestingly, having conscious knowledge of the process has made it more effective for me. Here's how I do it:

The foundation of this strategy is in the belief that it's important to remember people's names. Without that, the rest wouldn't happen. Because I believe this, when I'm about to meet someone new I make a conscious decision that I want to remember their name.

Belief/Value

- It's important to remember people's names. It makes people feel special and it demonstrates your connection with them.
- When I'm about to meet someone new I make a conscious decision that I want to remember their name.

Process

V – Look at the person's face. Concentrate.

A – Listen to the sound of their name.

V – Look at their name badge if they're wearing one, if not visualize one.

A – Repeat the name aloud, by saying, 'Pleased to meet you, John' or, if this is not appropriate, repeat the name in your head.

D – Check the correct spelling of the name, if possible.

K – Test until there is a feeling of confidence.

This process works because first of all it clears your mind of all distractions and focuses on the person whose name you want to remember. Then, by paying attention to sight, sound and spelling in turn, we create a neurological connection between the sight of the person's face, the sound of their name and the way it looks written down. If you use this process you'll be able to remember the name when you see the face, remember the face when you see the name written down, and also know how to pronounce the name correctly.

The 'testing' referred to is simply checking that I have retained the name. In a group situation I mentally go around the table saying each person's name to myself to check that I know it. I usually do this three times before I'm really confident that I know the names. (Now you know what my convincer pattern is!)

 The key to remembering names is to pay attention to them. Decide before you meet someone new that you will store away their name. Then when you meet them, clear your mind of everything else and pay attention as you're introduced.

Using modelling to learn

Many of the really important skills in life you learned by modelling. How to walk, how to speak, how to eat and a host of other everyday activities. As a small child you couldn't ask, 'How do you do that?' – you just had to watch, experiment and learn.

You can still learn that way. If you notice someone who is really good at chairing a meeting, observe more closely exactly what they do. Then try it out for yourself and see what happens. You might have a colleague who's very good at dealing with upset customers. Notice what they say, their tone of voice, their facial expressions, and have a go for yourself.

There is a lot you can learn just by observing the people with the exceptional skills (if you're going to put in the effort to model someone, don't waste it modelling mediocrity!). There may also be opportunities when you can ask someone about what they do, but be prepared to be told, 'I don't know, I just do it' – remember that everything you do really well, you can do without thinking about it.

10. Language

The two biggest complaints I hear from employees in the companies I work with are 'Nobody told us' and 'Nobody asked us'. Communication is vitally important for business success and people need to feel that they are informed, involved, consulted and listened to. The larger the organization, the more difficult this is, and the more likely it is that individuals get the impression that their voice isn't being heard.

Most people think they're reasonably good at communicating and that they know how to use language. And most people are reasonably good at expressing their own thoughts in words. However, the purpose of communication is often much more than that. Especially at work, the purpose of communication is usually to influence someone.

If all you focus on is how to express your thoughts, you're probably not going to find it easy to influence others' opinions and attitudes, even if you have great rapport with them. The key to doing this is the direct connection between what you say (or write) and the internal representation that words create in the mind of your listener. Earlier on, we established that there are always multiple ways to describe the same thing. Notice the differences between:

'The project is late and overspent.'

'The project is behind schedule on delivery and ahead of schedule on spending.'

'The plan for this project was not realistic.'

'We will have to work more efficiently if we're going to meet the next project deadline and we need to review the budget.'

Each of the sentences above are describing the same thing, but do you notice that the way it's represented in your mind shifts as the words change? Imagine how you would react to each of these statements if you were the person's boss.

In choosing the 'best' way to express a thought or idea, we naturally consider who we're going to be speaking to. It's also helpful to consider your outcome.

 If you have a clear outcome you want to achieve with your words, it's much easier to decide how to structure your communication and to select the specific words to use.

Of course, it's rare that communication is a simple matter of crafting a message and delivering it. Most of the time we're involved in dialogue and group discussion. So listen to what other people say and you'll find out whether or not your words achieved their outcome. If not, it's time to have another go – rephrase your message and try again.

Most people would agree that there are two main things involved in communication: speaking and listening. However, just because these two things are going on, it does not always mean that communication occurs.

One of the reasons that communication fails is that, frequently, when we are having what passes for a conversation with someone else, we are either not fully listening or we make so many assumptions about what is being said that we do not learn anything new from what we are hearing. We simply use it as further support for our (already established) point of view.

We have already seen how we filter our experiences to support what we already believe to be true. The more deeply held a belief is, the harder it is to challenge it. So most of the time when we are engaged in conversation, we end up with an impression of what was said that is incomplete, inaccurate or both. Not all of this is a result of the listening – what we say is also filtered to make our conversation concise and easy to follow.

Therefore, there are three main skills in communication:

1. Asking questions
2. Making sense of what other people say
3. Directing other people to think in certain ways through your choice of words

(In fact, asking questions is a special case of directing other people's thoughts with your choice of language, but it's often helpful to think of it separately.)

When you use language purposefully, there are two main ways to get results: by elicitation and by installation.

Elicitation means asking questions to find out information about the structure and content of another person's map of the world. In elicitation we presuppose as little as possible and avoid making suggestions. Good, 'clean' elicitation will not change the person's map of the world.

The result of elicitation is that you find out something about the other person's thinking.

Installation means planting a thought or idea, a belief or a memory into a person's map of the world in such a way that they accept it as part of their map. Once this is done it can be very difficult to remove it and return the person's reality to the way it was before the installation. Hence it is important to realize *when* and *what* we are installing and to ensure it is in line with agreed outcomes.

The result of installation is that you change the other person's thinking.

As a general principle, find out as much as is necessary about the current attitude someone holds before you attempt to shift it.

Asking questions – the meta model

The meta model was developed by Bandler and Grinder as a result of their modelling of the great psychotherapist Virginia Satir. It is essentially a set of questions that can be used to dig a bit deeper into what people say.

When we make an internal representation of the outside world, it is composed of sensory information. The full linguistic description of our experience, outside of conscious awareness, is known as the **deep structure**. The deep structure cannot be communicated fully; it's like trying to describe a dream. The words we actually say in describing our experience are known as the **surface structure**. The deep structure is subjected to deletion, distortion and generalization to create the surface structure.

The meta model is usually divided into three parts that correspond with the three actions of the linguistic filters: deletion, distortion and generalization. The questions challenge incomplete or inaccurate statements and recover the meaning that has been lost to the filters. The result of using it is that you can help people to be more precise and specific in what they say, and sometimes help them to view their experience more constructively.

Deletion: There are several different kinds of deletion. One of the most common forms of deletion is heard in business in comments like 'Communication is terrible at present' or 'There's a complete lack of teamwork' or 'Performance is up this month.' What these statements have in common is that they have deleted information about what is actually being done and covered it up with an abstract noun. For example, the word 'communication' replaces details about is who is communicating what to whom (or not). To recover these details, simply ask, 'Who is not communicating about what?' Similarly, for the other examples you could ask, 'What work should the team be doing together?' or 'Who is performing well at what?' Simply ask. But since this is not the kind of question that people get asked regularly, you should take care in *how* you ask. It must be done with rapport; you must demonstrate that you are genuinely interested in the details, otherwise you risk sounding like the Spanish Inquisition!

Another common form of deletion is where the information about *who* is doing something is lost. For example, 'They don't listen to me' or 'She didn't invite me to the meeting' or 'They turned up late.' You may think you know who is being referred to, but sometimes it's a good idea to check. The ubiquitous 'they' is usually worth challenging, to find out whether or not the speaker actually knows whom they are referring to! In this case all you have to ask is: 'Who specifically?'

Sometimes this kind of deletion is paired up with a further type, known as an unspecified verb. This is when the details of *how* something was done are filtered off, as in 'He rejected my idea' or 'They upset us' or 'She ruined that project.' Again, we may think we know what is meant by each of these statements – and we may be wrong again! Find out more by asking, 'How specifically?' In the former case you may find that what 'he' said about the speaker's idea was he needed more time to consider it.

Of course, if you are going to ask these questions, there has to be a purpose. You will quickly lose a lot of goodwill from friends and colleagues if you start challenging every deletion you hear. It is probably most useful to use this kind of approach in interviews, coaching sessions, counselling and investigation of training and organisational development needs.

Distortion: The second area of the meta model deals with distortion. I should emphasize that this is unconscious distortion as a result of unconscious filters, not any wilful distortion of facts. One of the most common forms of distortion is 'mind-reading', where a person claims to know someone else's feelings or thoughts, as in 'You don't like me' or 'He's angry with me' or 'They won't agree.' Sometimes these judgements are made on valid information, but if you suspect that they are simply invented you can ask, 'How do you know?' Again, done with rapport and genuine interest, this can be a powerful question that could bring someone to a useful realization that they actually have no reason to assume hostility from another person (nor indeed to assume anything else).

Another form of distortion is when opinions and value judgements are expressed without being attributed to anyone. These may be heard in comments such as 'You should work hard all the time' or 'It's not a good idea to throw away those files' or 'It's best to keep an open mind.' None of these comments are presented as a subjective judgement, but rather as objective fact (all proverbs also come into this category). A statement like this may be preventing someone from thinking for himself. To challenge it, a good question to ask is 'Who says?' or 'According to whom?' There is, as with all meta-model questions, a risk of this sounding aggressive, so ensure that you are in rapport before asking.

A third kind of distortion comes when something is taken to have a meaning that may not be accurate, for example, 'I didn't get the promotion; the boss doesn't like me' or 'Sales are down; the product range is awful this season.' In neither case does the one statement necessarily imply the other, but the speaker is taking the two to be connected in this way. There are two ways that this can be challenged. First you can challenge the logic. For example, 'How does your not getting promoted mean that the boss doesn't like you?' or 'How does a drop in sales mean that there's something wrong with the product range?' The other way to challenge this would be to focus on the counter-example. For example, 'Are there other people whom the boss likes that didn't get promoted either?' or 'Have sales ever fallen when the product range was good?' Either way, to challenge this type of distortion will focus attention on faulty deductions and get back to what is actually known as fact. This can be really useful in problem solving and counselling situations where there seems to be no way forward and no choices. Challenging the distortions will usually open up some possibilities.

Generalization: The third area of the meta model deals with generalizations. Generalizations are useful because they give us the ability to spot patterns and to apply our experience in one situation to another similar one. However, they also form the basis of prejudice and narrow-mindedness, so it can also be useful to challenge them on occasion. The most common forms of generalization involve words like 'never', 'always', 'everyone', 'no one' and 'all'. For example, 'It always rains in Manchester' or 'Nobody ever listens to me' or 'All salespeople are extroverts.' Clearly these statements are untrue, but many people act as if their generalizations are fact and miss opportunities and possibilities because of it. The 'rule of thumb' here is that all generalizations are untrue – including this one! The way to challenge generalizations is simple: you echo back, 'Always?' or 'Nobody? Ever?' or 'All of them?' (with a suitable amount of incredulity). In doing this, you are again looking for the counter-example; your questions could alternatively be phrased as 'Is it ever fine in Manchester?' or 'Has anybody ever listened to you?' or 'Are there any salespeople who are introverts?'

I would urge particular care when challenging generalizations. Often when a person says something like 'Nobody ever listens to me' (especially if it's said with some feeling) it's an indicator that somebody in particular is not listening to something important right now. The person may be feeling undervalued or rejected and a smart response like 'What, nobody? Ever?' may not be the most tactful thing you can say. In that case, treat it like a deletion and ask, 'Who in particular is not listening to you?'

While there are other kinds of deletions, distortions and generalizations, the ones described above are some of the most common I have encountered in business. The overall effect of the questions I have suggested is to challenge the validity of the statement and encourage the speaker to be more precise, more specific in what they are telling you. With practice, you will be able to avoid some of the common frustrations of communications at work – such as preparing a report and being told afterwards, 'That wasn't what I wanted' or tailoring a presentation to suit what you had been told about the audience, only to discover that the information was incorrect. Using meta model questions won't entirely remove the subjectivity from a point of view, but it may bring you closer to understanding what is really being said – and what is really meant!

Presuppositions: making sense of what other people say

We've already explored some tools for making sense of what other people say. If you pay attention to the sensory language used, you can get an idea of a person's rep system preferences. If you listen for language associated with

182

metaprogrammes, that will also help to clarify the *structure* of their thinking.

If you want to understand more about *what* someone thinks, then paying attention to the presuppositions they use will help.

 Presuppositions are linguistic assumptions. We identify a presupposition in relation to what has been said. If a statement only makes sense if a second statement is true, then we can say that it presupposes the second statement.

For example, if I ask you, 'What colour is your car?' the question only makes sense if you have a car. We can therefore say that the question presupposes that you have a car. In this case the presupposition is unspoken, but nonetheless is part of the speaker's map of the world.

Sometimes the presupposition is part of what is said. For example, the observation, 'John's angry with me because I was late' presupposes that the cause of John being angry is the speaker's lateness. It also presupposes that John is angry. In conversation we may not immediately recognize them as presuppositions – especially if we share them!

REMEMBER THIS!!!

The important thing in identifying presuppositions is to focus on the actual words used, not your own internal representation of what they mean.

Identifying presuppositions

Within any statement, there are likely to be several presuppositions. Some of these will be more obvious than others and, in terms of our responses, some will be of greater interest to us.

Take the following statement: 'I didn't apply to do the MBA because I didn't want to give up my social life.'

This statement contains the following presuppositions:

1. I could have applied to do the MBA
2. I didn't apply to do the MBA
3. I have a social life
4. It's not possible to do the MBA and also have a social life.

Another way of thinking of this is that the presuppositions are statements that can be logically inferred from what is said.

In the example above, the final presupposition is probably the one that is of most interest if you're in a conversation with the speaker. You could respond directly to that presupposition and say, 'So it's not possible for you to do

184

the MBA and also have a social life?' It depends on your outcome for the conversation.

The value to you of looking at the presuppositions in what somebody says is that they give you an insight into what they're not saying but assume to be true, without you having to ask any questions.

Influencing another person's thinking using presuppositions

Not only is it useful to be able to recognize what is assumed by the speaker, it's also possible to make appropriate presuppositions in our own responses, thus creating internal representations in line with our outcomes.

When someone listens to you speaking they make internal representations based on the language you use. The presuppositions in that language can have a great impact on the internal representations they make and how they feel about what you have said. In other words, presuppositions have consequences. It is awareness of those consequences and of our own outcomes that lead to elegance and precision in communication.

The degree of influence you achieve by using language in this way will be determined partly by the degree of rapport between you and the listener. It doesn't matter how subtle the language is, if you don't have rapport you're less likely to get the outcome you want.

TRY IT NOW! In each of the following examples, consider which language is most likely to achieve the stated outcome.

Outcome: to ensure that a colleague writes a particular letter.
1. Are you going to write that letter?
2. Are you going to write that letter before the meeting or after?

Outcome: to arrange a meeting with a busy senior colleague.
1. Can I have a meeting with you sometime next week?
2. When next week would be a good time for us to meet?

Outcome: to encourage a colleague who is about to make an important presentation.
1. You know that being nervous just means that you'll do a great job.
2. Are you nervous?

Outcome: to express frustration at lack of progress on a project.
1. You have let me down by missing that deadline.
2. I'm frustrated because we now have to work twice as hard to meet the next deadline.

Outcome: to persuade someone to make a decision now.
1. What else do you need to know to be able to make a decision?
2. What would it take for you to be able to decide right now?

Outcome: to 'sell' NLP to a colleague
1. If you were to learn NLP what would be most useful to you?
2. You ought to do NLP; it would really help you.

Outcome: to help a colleague understand a complex idea.
1. Shall I explain it again?
2. What's the one question you can ask me that will make it all clear for you?

Outcome: to challenge the approach to a task or project.
1. If this were not the best way of going about the job, how would you know?
2. Are you sure this is the best way to do it?

Outcome: to give feedback that someone may not be pleased to hear.
1. I know you're not going to like this but it's better that you know.
2. I know you are going to want to know how to improve the situation.

Outcome: to encourage a demoralized team.
1. Things can only get better.
2. Things can't get any worse.

Now that you've got the idea, you can only succeed in making your own communication more precise, more elegant and more effective.

Embedded commands

Another way of influencing another person's thinking is to use embedded commands. An embedded command is an instruction to do something that is delivered as part of a longer sentence, often a question. Native speakers of UK English do this a lot. It's common to hear people say things like 'Could you possibly shut the door?', 'Would you like to give me the figures now?' and 'Could I ask you to pass me that file, please?'

This is a pattern of speaking that most people regard as more polite than simply 'Shut the door', 'Give me the figures now' or 'Pass me that file.' However, in other languages and other countries this would be perfectly acceptable.

It's also common to hear people saying things like 'Don't worry about this. It's not a big problem' or 'It's urgent, but I can't ask you stay late to finish it' or 'It shouldn't take a long time. I don't think you'll miss lunch.'

Can you hear the way that these statements plant ideas in your mind that are actually the opposite of what the words literally mean?

Right now, this minute, don't think about what you're doing this weekend.

What came to mind, did you think about what you're doing at the weekend?

This is because at the simplest level of processing, it's practically impossible to represent 'don't' so we just represent the rest of the sentence: '...think about what you're doing at the weekend.'

So, even though at a conscious level we hear the 'don't', below consciousness, we're getting the opposite message. This is confusing and dilutes the impact of what is said.

Here's a quick exercise for you to practise spotting embedded commands in everyday language. For each sentence, underline the embedded command:

- Don't worry, it's not difficult.
- Don't waste your time doing that.
- That isn't the best way to do the job.
- Don't forget to bring the files.
- Don't start without me.

- You shouldn't use the front entrance.
- Don't laugh, but...
- Don't forget the security code.
- This isn't important, don't make it a priority.
- Don't even think about it!
- Don't think you can get away with doing that.
- It doesn't work if you do it that way.
- Don't forget to fill the car up with petrol.
- Don't lose sleep over it.
- Don't drop that!

Do you notice how the embedded command conflicts with the overall message? If you can edit this kind of conflict out of your own communication it will make a difference not just to your success in getting your message across but also to the way other people perceive you.

To avoid embedding conflicting commands in your language, focus on telling people what you want and how you want it rather than discussing what you don't want. This gives a much clearer message and also makes you sound more confident and reliable.

 If you do nothing else with this insight, scan important emails and presentations for embedded commands that you may have inadvertently included and which could detract from your carefully crafted message. Rephrase them to ensure they support your message completely.

The use of language is a vast subject within NLP and there is further reading you could do if you're interested. For the purposes of this book, though, let us finish by recapping the basic principles.

 The keys to effective use of language are:

- Know your outcome, not just for the conversation as a whole, but for every question you ask and every comment you make.

- Listen with your whole mind. Build up a clear second position. This will make it easier to tailor your communication to ensure that the person you are communicating with understands what you want them to understand.

- Notice whether the question you asked elicited the information you wanted. Notice the structure of the information.

- Be prepared to ask the same question in a number of different ways until you find out what you want to know.

A final word

NLP is not a science. It's not really an art either. It's definitely not a religion, although some people are evangelical about it. It's best thought of as a tool kit.

Like all good tool kits, there will be some bits you use a lot and some that rarely come out of the box. That's okay, you'll use the tools that are relevant and leave the ones that aren't.

This book has only been a brief introduction to some of the basic NLP techniques. Hopefully, by focusing on techniques that you can easily use in everyday work situations, it has already shown you ways in which these simple principles can become powerful tools in your life. Now it's up to you to go and experiment with what you have learned; to find out what works and what really makes a difference.

Just a suggestion: experiment with *all* the tools and find out how they work for you before you decide which ones are the best. That doesn't mean you have to use them all at once. Pick one or two and experiment with them until you feel confident that you know what they can be used for that's relevant for you.

You might pick one of the presuppositions of NLP and focus on it for a day. See the world through that presupposition as a filter and notice how it impacts your thinking and your results. Pick a different one on the next day, and see what happens.

Or you might start by paying attention to body language and by matching the behaviour of other people around you. Find out what it's like to do what they do. Experience second position.

You could simply begin by practising the well-formed outcomes pattern. Try doing five to ten per day for a week or two and notice how it affects your focus, effectiveness and motivation.

Of course, there is always more to learn, and the resources section that follows will give you some pointers as to where you could take your exploration of NLP next.

Whatever you do, if you begin with the intention of finding out how NLP can work for you, you'll quickly find ways to use NLP for work.

Resources

Further reading

Introducing Neuro-Linguistic Programming, John Seymour and Joseph O'Connor
Thorsons; Reissue edition (2003)
This book was one of the first NLP books written in the UK. It is a comprehensive look at the important concepts in NLP and in my opinion is much more than an introduction. It's written in a fairly formal style with good explanations of technical terms and an NLP glossary at the back. Perhaps not the most accessible cover-to-cover read, but a good reference text used by a lot of trainers and experienced practitioners.

NLP for Dummies, Kate Burton and Romilla Ready
John Wiley & Sons; 2nd edition (2010)
What I really appreciate in this book is the 'chunking' and layout. It has strong visual appeal and is easy to dip in and out of. It combines simple explanations of key concepts with fun activities and examples. As with most other NLP books, it covers a lot of information and would be a useful reference for practitioner training and beyond.

Business NLP for Dummies, Lynne Cooper
For Dummies (2009)
It has all the features that make the 'for dummies' books popular – clear chunking, examples, exercises and high visual appeal – and it's an intelligent guide to using NLP in business.

NLP at Work, Sue Knight
Nicholas Brealey Publishing; 3rd edition (2009)
If you are particularly interested in applying NLP in the business environment, then you will probably enjoy this book. It includes lots of anecdotes and examples of everyday business occurrences that will help you relate the subject to your own working life.

Words That Change Minds, Shelle Rose Charvet
Kendall/Hunt Publishing Co. (1997)
A classic for anyone who wants to master the art of adapting their communication style to suit the processing style of others. This book is a companion to the language and behaviour (LAB) profile and a good guide to the whole idea of metaprogrammes and how to use them. It is written in an informal and accessible style and does not presuppose any knowledge of NLP.

Performance Management, Michael D. McMaster
Metamorphous Press; 2nd revised edition (1993)
This is a thoroughly practical guide to applying NLP in a management context. It addresses the all-important issues of communication related to managing people, including planning, coaching and evaluation.

Persuasion Engineering, Richard Bandler and John La Valle
Meta Publications (1996)
This has to be the best book about NLP for salespeople! It's a wonderful exploration of communication, conversational

elicitation of values and beliefs, sales techniques and so on as well as being an entertaining history of some of Bandler's own experiences.

Me, Myself, My Team, Angus McLeod
Crown House Publishing (2000)
This book pulls together lots of aspects of NLP into a comprehensive guide to becoming an effective leader and coach. It's relevant to anyone who works with a team and can be applied whether or not you are the team leader.

NLP Workbook, Joseph O'Connor
Thorsons (2001)
I recommend this as a good third or fourth book on NLP. I wouldn't suggest it as a starting place, simply because it contains so much and some of the activities are quite complex. It is well structured and chunked into manageable pieces. It is comprehensive and thought provoking. The activities encourage the reader to explore the workings of their own mind and to challenge their own assumptions.

Modelling with NLP, Robert Dilts
Meta Publications; illustrated edition (1998)
This is a great book if you want to know more about the NLP modelling process and its applications. It defines the key communication and relational skills employed by effective leaders to achieve practical results in their working reality.

Online Resources

NLP Encyclopedia

www.nlpuniversitypress.com

The NLP Encyclopedia was created by Robert Dilts and Judith Delozier. It is a comprehensive reference library on everything related to NLP and it's free to use.

Use Your NLP

www.useyournlp.com

My online self-study programme that builds mastery of NLP one technique at a time.

NLP Conference

www.nlpconference.co.uk

The NLP Conference takes place in London in November each year. The website has all the details of the sessions and the speakers.

NLP Events

www.nlpevents.co.uk

This is a comprehensive listing of NLP training programmes and events taking place in the UK and Europe. The information is contributed by the training providers

ANLP

www.anlp.org

The Association for NLP provides a wealth of information for members and non-members too. There are articles, recommended books, forums, course information and trainer information as well as professional standards, advice and networking.

Brilliant Minds
www.brilliantminds.co.uk
This is my main website, which includes articles, my blog, course information, coaching programmes, how to get me as a guest speaker and the opportunity to join my mailing list.

Success Strategies
www.successstrategies.com
I've mentioned Shelle Rose Charvet's excellent book, *Words That Change Minds*. This is her website where you can find her excellent free resource, 'Shelle's Top Tips'.

NLP University
www.nlpu.com
I've also referred to Robert Dilts several times in this book. You can find out more about his work at this site, which includes a massive archive of articles.

Index

Notes

You can use the following pages to make your own notes on any of the exercises in the book.

Notes

Notes

Notes

Notes

Notes

Notes

Notes